A Ballad of Confetti, Cake and Catastrophes

By Helen Juliet

A Ballad of Confetti, Cake and Catastrophes

DEDICATION

For Dan, who asked me to join him in our own,
catastrophe-free, wedding.

Also to his wonderful family for welcoming me to the
fold, and to my family for being with me every step of the
way.

ACKNOWLEDGEMENTS

My first and foremost thanks have to go to my brother for his brilliant content editing and never-ending encouragement, and Alyson Pearce from Between the Lines Editing for fixing all my mistakes. Also to Alyson for the multitude of transatlantic messaging at all hours of the day and for squealing at all the right parts. You guys rock.

Thank you to the dozens and dozens of people involved in making my own wedding happen. Only an idiot would try and write a book at the same time as getting married, but you all made it worthwhile. Especially my mum and new mother-in-law, who are two truly amazing ladies.

Natasha Snow of Natasha Snow Designs cannot get enough praise for how patient she was in creating this book cover. It frustrates me that there seems to be a lack of diversity in MM romance, so I was absolutely determined to show Fynn on the front of the book. It was no easy feat, but we got there in the end and I couldn't be happier to have yet another gorgeous cover.

Finally, thank you to Carol for letting me borrow so many of your catastrophes. I hope you enjoyed seeing them immortalised in fiction forevermore.

Chapter One

(7 days to go…)

Nicholas had forgotten something important.

He just didn't know it yet.

The truth was, he probably didn't know a lot of what was going on right at that very moment. The whole wedding business had been something of a whirlwind that he had tactfully stayed on the peripheral of. There had also probably been a point in the early hours of that morning where he hadn't even known his own *name*, so he figured he could forgive himself for not knowing that Busy Lizzie was in fact a flower, and not the name of some funky cocktail.

His stomach rolled at the very thought of any more alcohol, and he discreetly covered his mouth to encourage any bodily fluids to stay *within* his body.

"I think it's crucial that we're all on the same page," his older cousin Danielle announced from where she was standing. Nicholas tried not to groan audibly.

Danielle was still in her gym gear, a look he was well used to. Her blonde hair tied back in an immaculate ponytail, a strip of her flat stomach on display and the rest of her tanned skin glowing with just a hint of perspiration. "We've got a lot of work ahead of us, but if we pull together, I know we can do it!" She sloshed a squeezy drink bottle filled with something disturbingly green at those gathered around the kitchen table, thrusting her hand forward to punctuate every point she made.

Nicholas flinched, then poked at his plate. He was perched around the central island in his parents' kitchen, along with everyone else who had been summoned by Danielle. She had proudly presented them with a homemade brunch, designed to fortify them through this pre-wedding briefing. Nicholas, being so hungover there was a possibility he was still drunk, wasn't all that impressed.

Given that it was still before midday, he had foolishly hoped for a *proper* cooked breakfast. Instead he had limp kale, and pale pink salmon, and mushy eggs so bland he was seriously eyeing up the decorative bottles of chilli oil and soy sauce his mother had on display on the counter to his right.

What he wouldn't give for some fried bread and beans.

"Thanks Danielle," Peter said from across the marble island, giving her a small smile. He and Nicholas's sister Clara were holding hands, their eyes wide as they slowly sipped cups of tea. "We'd be lost without you."

There was a small snort from the seat to Nicholas's left, but no one else seemed to hear it. He was tempted to glance over, but his rolling stomach told him to stay put for the time being. He tried a bite of eggs, swallowing with determination. *You'll feel better for it*, he argued with himself. At least the orange juice was poured from a carton.

Danielle was beaming as she sifted through the half a dozen folders piled on the island table, each labelled with a name to match one of the people in front of her. "I've printed us all out itineraries to get us through the next several days," she informed them, handing the cardboard packs out. Clara leaned forward to take hers with a keen smile, but there was tension in her shoulders. "I've got a colour coded system in place." Danielle said, laughing at herself. It was a sound like gently-tinkling glass. "I know that's dreadfully pernickety, but by failing to prepare, you are preparing to fail. And that's not going to happen to us, is it?" She looked at Clara, who nodded back, then seemed to realise what her cousin had said, and hastily shook her head.

It was going to be a long week.

Another tiny huff came from Nicholas's left. Surreptitiously, he glanced over to where Peter's sister was waiting to be handed her pale pink file from the stack that was going around the table, diminishing as each person took the one inscribed with their name. Ash Cove had short, bleached blonde hair with dark roots, cut into a pixie style that suited her elfin face. She was sat with her back straight, her face alight with interest as she popped a slice of avocado into her mouth, acting as if there was nothing she would rather be doing with her Saturday morning than attending a wedding briefing, no doubt complete with a soon-to-be-shown PowerPoint presentation. Upon seeing Nicholas's glance, she winked.

He raised his eyebrows in an inquiring manner. "What?" he mouthed. He could feel himself swaying, and a cold sweat had formed on his top lip.

Ash leant over, not too obviously, but enough so when she spoke in barely more than a murmur, Nicholas caught every word. "Nothing champ," she said, a sparkle in her blue eyes. "I was just thinking how nice a maggot sandwich would go down with a glass of toilet water."

Nicholas gagged.

Danielle paused in whatever she had been saying, and looked at him in concern. "Darling, are you quite alright?"

Nicholas coughed and wiped his face. Ash gave him a smirk and another wink. "Fine, fine," he spluttered.

Ash was older than Nicholas, however so was everyone else at the table. He had assumed that might make her more mature, but apparently not. At only twenty, he was the baby of the family, but he was still determined to hold his own weight for his sister's sake. Even if his head currently felt like it was home to a particularly vindictive marching band.

After taking another grateful swig of juice, he pushed his thick, black specs up his nose and fished out the contents of his personalised folder. Ordinarily, he wore contact lenses rather than his glasses. With his small stature and unruly dark brown hair, he'd become quickly sick of the Harry Potter comments that had started in his early teen years. But as he'd dragged himself out of bed at stupid o'clock that morning, his eyes had already been burning enough from dehydration, and he hadn't been able to face the prospect of sticking lenses into them as well.

His whole family had terrible eyes. Clara was equally sat there with her glasses on, and it amused Nicholas that she'd picked a fiancé who also sported specs. Their other sister Lauren, who wouldn't be coming until later in the week, had taken the plunge and got laser-eye-surgery the year before. Nicholas shuddered, not able to stomach the thought of being awake and having surgery on his eyeballs at the best of times, let alone when he was fighting to keep down the measly mouthful of squidgy eggs he'd been able to manage so far.

Ash chuckled, very quietly. He turned and scowled at her, but she was engrossed in studying the seating plan. Apparently.

"Oh," said Clara. She sounded wary, but her face quickly brightened as she looked up at Danielle. "I didn't realise we'd invited Michelle and Tom?"

Nicholas blinked in surprise. Michelle and Tom were good friends of Danielle's mother; his and Clara's aunt. Michelle had a cigarette permanently attached to one hand, as well as a mouth quick to smirk and cold eyes hidden under layers of black liner. She'd delighted herself in unerringly referring to Clara as 'the plump one' when they were growing up, always laughing it off as a joke whenever Clara began to cry.

"I thought we didn't have any more room for day guests?" Nicholas asked. He heard the accusatory tone in his voice, so tempered it with a smile. Or, at least he hoped he did.

Danielle waved him off with a big grin full of perfect teeth. "Oh we couldn't *not* invite them," she gushed. She swigged on the green juice concoction, causing the bits of whatever to swirl in the bottle. Nicholas's stomach flipped thinking about slimy swamps. "I'm amazed they weren't on the list before, but it's all sorted now."

Clara hummed, a smile on her lips that didn't reach her eyes, and Peter rubbed her back.

"I guess they'll be happy to sit on a table with your mum and dad, won't they?" He turned his copy of the seating plan this way and that, narrowing his eyes behind his glasses. He was a tall guy with long, unruly limbs, and usually he was the most cheerful person in the room. The odd time Nicholas had seen him be grumpy was when he thought he'd lost unfairly at Christmas board games. But by the way he was raising his eyebrow at Danielle, he must have been as much of a fan of Aunt Louise and Michelle as Nicholas was.

Looking from the outside in, a person might have been forgiven for mistaking the maid of honour for the bride at this particular wedding. But Nicholas, who had grown up witnessing their cousin lording over his sister at any given opportunity, didn't find her actions all that unusual. As much as it might piss him off, he had unfortunately gotten used to it. But for non-family members, it had come as a little bit of a shock.

"Any other last minute changes we should be aware of?" Ash asked cheerfully.

She leant back in her seat, her Spiderman t-shirt pulling tightly against her pert breasts. Nicholas wondered, not for the first time, if he should find her attractive. He decided he could revisit that old issue when the room stopped spinning.

Getting home from uni wasn't all that bad a trek. The train from Bristol into London St Pancras was quite quick, and then he'd been lucky enough to catch a fast train to St Albans. However, he'd only had a little less than three hours of sleep, after two days fuelled by nothing but off-brand Red Bull and stress. That was then followed by an obscene amount of beer, vodka, and he was pretty sure at one point *absinthe*. Therefore, as he sat in his parents' kitchen, he was almost certain he was starting to see sounds. It didn't do wonders for his concentration.

Danielle's smile didn't slip a jot as she turned to answer the question. "Oh, nothing to worry about Ashley," she said breezily. Ash's eyes narrowed, just a fraction. Nicholas didn't know her all that well, having only met her the once at the engagement party over a year ago, but he'd never heard anyone else refer to her as 'Ashley' in that time. She didn't correct Danielle however, who carried on speaking jovially. "Just little tweaks, you know how these things are. Nothing we can't handle."

"It all looks wonderful," piped up Clara's childhood best friend, Kinny.

She was sat with Nicholas and Clara's mum at the end of the table, both their packs already spread out in front of them as they began eagerly attaching coloured post-it notes and scribbling annotations on the various sheets of paper. Kinny's hands fluttered in excitement as she oohed and ahhed at all the elements that had been brought together for the big day. Nicholas saw the tension in Clara's shoulders ease as she watched her friend's enthusiasm bubble up.

Nicholas jerked as he felt something touch his leg. He wasn't certain what his over-tired mind had thought it could be – a nefarious tentacle? A hand reaching from beyond the grave? He'd been home more than ten minutes, so he should have remembered that was more than enough time to be reminded *whose* home it really was.

Archibald, his mother's large Maine Coon cat, rubbed his back against Nicholas's sock-clad foot as it dangled from the stool he was perched on. Archibald's tail swished provocatively, and Nicholas held his breath, not daring to twitch a muscle. But the cat sauntered on, disappearing out of the kitchen door, with no one else at the table seeming to have noticed him passing through.

Nicholas's mum nodded in agreement with Kinny, circling several words and underlining a number of others. "You've done so much work on this," she gushed at Danielle. "Thank you love, you're such a treasure."

"Oh, it's nothing," said Danielle bashfully. Nicholas's mum shook her head in disagreement. Ash's eyebrow twitched. Just a fraction.

Out of all of Lyn Herald's children, Clara, the oldest, was most evidently her offspring. They both had puffs of strawberry blonde curls, round features, and the customary glasses as thick as the bottom of milk bottles. They were both alike in temperament too; very trusting and forgiving.

"I think everything's just about in order then?" Danielle said, posing it as a question to Clara.

Nicholas watched his sister ruffle through the various sheets of paper she'd been presented with. "Uh, yeah, I guess so?" she replied.

She considered the menu choices, the order of service and schedule for when the cars would be arriving. Nicholas zoned out while they confirmed details between them, wondering if he could escape any time soon and get himself to a McDonalds. He wasn't going to be good to anyone if he collapsed or threw up all over the paperwork before them.

He hadn't intended to get absolutely wasted the night before. But it had been a hellish couple of weeks for most people in his halls and on his course. As first year undergrads, they had thought the last term would be the toughest, as that was when most of their exams were. But Nicholas, like almost all the others, had underestimated how hard the final essays and coursework would be before the Easter break. Many frantic nights had been spent in the library and his eyes had suffered more than usual after too many hours squinting at his computer screen, rearranging words and calculations until they had made some sort of reasonable sense.

The temptation to freak out and partake in a bender had been too much. As soon as he and his friends had stumbled into their departments to sign off their submissions at precisely 14:59, they had congregated down the nearest union bar, and things had become progressively worse from there.

But now he was home. His insides may have felt like a soapy washing machine, and his head like the inside of a drum, but he'd made it. He was pretty sure once his hangover subsided, all he would have to do was just follow the itinerary, not snap at Danielle if at all possible, and he'd get through the week just fine.

However, that was before he realised his name had been called. Twice.

He snapped his head up. He'd been staring at the diagram of the table decorations, and his eyes might have been starting to drift closed. But he was awake now. Definitely. "Yep, hello," he said. He rubbed his sleeve against his mouth *just* in case there was any drool lingering.

Danielle downed the last of her swamp juice and pointed to one of the lists she had in front of her. "It's all sorted on your end?"

A cold sensation slipped down Nicholas's inside. "Uhh…?" he said, doing his finest impersonation of the village idiot.

Kinny, bless her, came to his rescue. "With the harpist," she supplied. She flipped her long black hair over her shoulder, and mimed playing the harp with her long, delicate fingers. "For the drinks reception, and the meal. You said you had that mate at uni."

"The one whose sister played professionally," Clara prompted. She smiled at Peter, who appeared to have lost the train of the conversation.

"Just so there's some music on in the background, in case people get bored."

"People aren't going to get bored," Peter assured her, tugging at one of her curls. "It's a wedding, they're going to be having fun and drinking and talking about how pretty you look."

Clara blushed. "Shut up," she said, swatting him lightly as colour rose rapidly into her cheeks. Nicholas would probably have found the scene endearing. If he hadn't been struggling not to pass out in horror.

The harp – *the fucking harp*. He had absolutely, one hundred percent promised over Christmas that he'd ask Jones about his sister and if she was available to play the wedding. He'd promised, told them it was a done deal. He had been so happy to be contributing something special to the big day, something unique that he'd arranged by himself, that he forgot to *actually arrange* it. He'd not thought about it once since that conversation.

Oh shit, oh bollocks. Everyone was looking at him. And then the hint of a frown began to form between his sister's eyes.

"Yep," he blurted, clapping his hands together and giving her a thumbs up. "All sorted, no worries."

Clara blew out a sigh of relief.

"Fabulous," said Danielle, making a note. "Can you get me their contact details? So I can add them to the log. The venue needs it for the day. That way, if there's a problem, they can ring around people instead of asking us to do it."

Nicholas swallowed. "Uh, yeah, sure," he said. "I'll have to look them up though, not sure where I wrote it down."

"Probably on the back of a Chinese take away menu," Peter teased him. Nicholas appreciated his soon-to-be brother-in-law feeling comfortable enough to rib him, but his terror meant he was only able to give him a weak smile in return.

"Yeah," Nicholas breathed out. "Don't worry though, I'll find the details. Soon."

Just as soon as I find a bloody harpist before you find out what I did. Or didn't do.

It was fine, he would just contact Jones as soon as he could leave the table, and hopefully his sister would be available. Nicholas wasn't sure where she lived, but he had it in his head it was in London, so that wouldn't be far to travel. Plus, he had permission to pay her a crazy amount, so maybe he'd add a bit extra of his own money to compensate for such short notice.

Yeah. Yeah it was going to be fine. Everything was going to be fine.

Chapter Two

Everything was, in fact, *not* going to be fine.

"Are you sure?" Nicholas tried to keep the pleading note out of his voice, but at this stage, he couldn't really help it.

"*Sorry love,*" said the voice on the other end of the phone. The girl was genuinely apologetic, but that didn't particularly help Nicholas all that much. "*Saturdays are booked up months in advance. Especially around the holidays. I hope you find someone.*"

That was looking less and less likely.

"Thanks," said Nicholas anyway.

There was no sense in taking it out on the harpist, it wasn't her fault after all. Neither had it been the past dozen musicians' fault, but that didn't stop Nicholas from wanting to scream at someone.

How could he have been so careless, so selfish? This was his sister's one and only wedding, and he'd made a *promise*. The sun was shining down on St Albans' city centre, but that had little effect on how absolutely wretched he was feeling in the light of his failure.

As soon as he'd been able, he had escaped from his parents' kitchen, grabbed his laptop, and hopped on a bus into town where he had no chance of being overheard as he frantically started making phone calls.

He had set himself up on one of the outside tables at his favourite little greasy spoon café, Simmons. It was hidden down one of the narrow, cobbled streets, just far enough away from the Saturday market so he would be able to hear himself over the stall-sellers' cries. He'd started with Jones, but his mate hadn't even needed to ring his sister; he confirmed off the bat that she had just gone on holiday for the next two weeks. That had initiated a frantic Google search, but even as he broadened the locations farther and farther afield, Nicholas was getting the same response from everyone.

A week was just not enough time to book a classical, professional harpist.

Inspiration struck as he began on his third cup of coffee and second bacon butty. They didn't *have* to be professional, did they? He could look for music schools, perhaps reach out to department heads and see if any of the students would be willing to perform. They had to be good enough if they'd got into the Royal College of Music or something, surely?

Half an hour later confirmed that all the major colleges had also broken up for Easter, just like he had, and administration staff were not willing to hand out personal details.

Nicholas got himself a slab of carrot cake.

Did it have to be a harp? What about a flute? They were pretty classy too. He amended his search parameters, and started again.

There were even fewer professional flautists than there were harpists. The first few he called were busy with general life activities like birthdays or holidays, as well as already being booked for events. He had a spark of hope as one woman confirmed she was available, but the logistics of getting her from Glasgow to St Albans quickly became too complicated, and Nicholas regretfully told her not to worry.

He wasn't sure if a string quartet would be too overwhelming, seeing as the idea was just to have someone playing unobtrusively in the background, but he tried several anyway. They were booked up even further in advance than the harpists.

Nicholas pressed the corner of his phone to his forehead, and willed himself not to cry.

He was extremely tired. Nausea swirled in his stomach along with the remnants of last night's alcohol, and guilt and shame practically seeped from his pores. However, every time he pictured his sister's crestfallen face, or Danielle's uninhibited scorn, he picked up the phone and tried another number. There had to be *someone* in the south of England that was free to play *some* kind of instrument for a few hours. There *had* to be.

For lack of something better to do after his latest failed call, he slumped down in his red plastic chair and let his gaze drift up and down the busy street, allowing the flurry of sound and movement to wash over him. Maybe a solution would appear before him, like driftwood, if only he stopped fretting uncontrollably for a few minutes.

Growing up, he hadn't realised that not all cities in the UK were like St Albans. When he'd discovered this to be the case, he had felt sorry for places like Reading and Bracknell, with their distinct lack of historical character. Sure, there were plenty of modern towns around with lovely new architecture and shopping centres made of glass, but you couldn't really beat sitting under a genuine Tudor eave, like he was just then, so bent and crooked you couldn't help but wonder if the whole building was going to cave in any day now.

Even as his panic threatened to overwhelm him, Nicholas still took a second to appreciate being home. Bristol was a beautiful city too, but there was something unique about St Albans' many church spires and black and white Tudor buildings, mingled in with ghastly sixties-era red bricks, and an overabundance of accountancy firms and, ironically, bridal shops, that instilled him with a calming sense of familiarity. There was still hope.

He allowed that statement to roll over him several times. There was still hope, there was always hope; he hadn't fucked things up entirely yet. And it wasn't like the wedding was going to fall apart if they didn't have a bloody harp. It was just...he loved his sister, and he wanted to do something special for her big day. He *would* do something special. He'd find a solution, so long as he didn't give up.

A little girl went past where he was sat at the café, swinging on her mother's hand as they walked. The mum had her mobile phone tucked into her hijab so she could keep a hold of her daughter's hand on one side, and grip their shopping bags on the other. She was chatting happily away in a language Nicholas didn't recognise, but he was more interested in the girl. She had light-up trainers and was engrossed in playing a game of hopscotch on the cobblestones, singing tunelessly to herself, at ease in her own, contained world. He smiled, and let some of her carefree spirit wash over him a little.

She stopped and gaped upwards. Her mother paused by her side, but was distracted by her phone call, so didn't look at what the girl had seen. Nicholas did.

A girl on the fruit and veg stall bellowed '*Three fer a pand!*' from the market to his left, and the café's faint Spotify playlist could be heard through the doors behind him. The traffic was also grumbling by on the road down to his right. All of which might have accounted for why he had failed to notice a busker had started to play about twenty feet away from where he was sat. He had set himself up with an acoustic guitar in the little nook where the women's fashion boutique jutted out from the sagging wall beside it, and the little girl was now staring at him open mouthed.

He finished whatever song he had been quietly playing, and gave her a small wave. She tugged her mum over to where he had dropped a flat cap on the ground for change, and said something that Nicholas couldn't catch. In response, the busker knelt down and showed the girl his guitar, letting her touch the wood with her small hand.

After being mesmerised for a moment, the girl tugged sharply at her mum's hand, finally snagging her attention, and pointed at the money hat with a cross expression. The mother took in the scene and laughed, then addressed the busker herself. After a few words, the guy stood up and started to play again. The mum let go of her daughter so she could pluck her purse out of her handbag in order to retrieve some change, which she handed to the child.

The girl cradled the money in two hands, and walked with an over-exaggerated care to the cap. She let all the coins fall in a shower of copper and silver, then brushed her small hands off. The two of them watched him play for another minute, then the mother pulled the girl away, smiling indulgently at her pout.

Nicholas sighed, lighter from watching the sweet exchange, then clicked on another website.

Maybe he could try his luck with a wind quartet? He hadn't even known that was a thing, but apparently they played weddings.

If you booked early enough.

Another fruitless couple of calls later, he stirred his plastic spoon in what was left of his last coffee. The busker had started another song and was earning plenty of smiles as people walked on by, often tossing spare change in the direction of his cap. Despite the slight chill in the air, he just wore a vest top, decorated with a swirling design Nicholas didn't recognise, if indeed it meant anything at all. In addition to that, he sported a neckerchief and several mismatched chains, jeans ripped at the knees, and big sturdy boots.

Now he was paying attention, Nicholas could hear his voice drifting through the air accompanied by the strings he was plucking to illicit soft, melodic tones. The sounds of the city tried to swallow up what he was playing, but Nicholas kept catching notes here and there. From what he could tell, the guy was really quite good. Beautiful even.

He wasn't bad to look at either, he had to appreciate. His skin was golden brown, accentuated with a couple of silver piercings and tattoos of varying designs, but all coloured in simple black ink. His hair was styled in short dreadlocks that framed his face, and when he glanced upwards, Nicholas could tell even from where he was sat that his eyes weren't dark like he would have expected.

He realised he was gawping, and tried to focus back on the issue at hand. He needed a musician and…

And he was an idiot.

He was literally *looking* at a musician.

He was probably grasping at straws (in fact, he knew he was) but if this guy was any good, would he suffice? Would an acoustic guitar have the same impact as a harp? Probably not, but he wasn't going to dismiss it until he heard what the guy could do. He might not even be up for playing a wedding, or already have plans this coming weekend, but Nicholas couldn't bear to stamp on the little flicker of hope that had burst to life within his chest.

He needed to get closer.

There was another café the other side of where the guy was stood, but Nicholas reckoned if he sat on the furthermost table (which was currently free) he'd be about ten feet closer, and therefore almost certainly able to hear the music.

As casually as he could, with the hangover making him about a subtle as a rampaging hippopotamus, he closed his laptop, picked it up with the rest of his crap, and wondered over to the other café. This one was apparently Italian, and he probably annoyed the guy behind the counter by just ordering a bottle of water. But he needed to think straight, and the coffee was giving him as bad a headache as the tequila had.

He set up his laptop again and made a show of typing some things, but the guy had just started a new song, and this time Nicholas could properly hear. So he brought up a random webpage from one of his previous searches with a good amount of text, and pretended to read while he listened.

He was right. The guy *was* good.

His voice was deep and melodic, not overly loud or intrusive, but grabbing people's attention all the same as it soared over the cobblestones. He was completely absorbed in what he was playing, his light eyes fixed on some point across the street, not focusing on anyone except when they dropped him some change, and he would nod in acknowledgement.

Nicholas got his phone out, and acted like he was sending a text. Making sure the sound was off, he took a quick video and a couple of photos. That way, he could watch them back later if necessary, however he was pretty sure he was going to remember how good the guy really was without needing any help.

It was only as he neared the end of the song did Nicholas realise with a jolt that he recognised it. Well, not precisely because the music was vastly different, however the lyrics were familiar once he concentrated on them. It was that dreadful Katy Perry one about getting shagged by an alien. But here, in the careful hands of this talented man, it had transformed into something tender and sublime.

"*There is this transcendental, on another level, boy, you're my lucky star,*" he sang, his eyes fluttering closed as he immersed himself in the song. "*I wanna walk on your wave length, and be there when you vibrate. For you I risk it all.*"

Nicholas wasn't even sure that bit was on the normal song, it was probably what she sang when Kanye normally did his rap. But he liked it, especially in the busker's style. It reminded him of when Jose Gonzalez took that elecro-pop song 'Heartbeats' by The Knife, and made it so romantic everyone used it in their TV ads non-stop for about six months. Considering the original was about slutty space sex, it was an utterly beautiful cover.

The was only the briefest pause before he went into an Ed Sheeran number, and after that came another couple of songs more suited to his elegant style of guitar playing. Ellie Goulding, Adele, that sort of thing, as well as one or two Nicholas didn't recognise. The guitarist nailed them all, his vocal range proving more impressive with every song he tackled.

No matter the genre, the way he performed them meant they all sounded like they would be perfect for playing subtly in the background of a wedding reception. Not too intrusive, but lovely all the same. *But what should I do?* Nicholas thought. He couldn't very well interrupt the fellow, and he was just going from one song to the next without pause. He figured he would just have to wait, watching as he started on another slowed-down cover, this one of Lady Gaga's 'Telephone' that became almost haunting in his capable hands. He took another video, daring to let this one record for a bit longer.

The longer he sat there, the more he liked the idea of a classical guitarist. Sure, it wasn't quite a harp, but anyone who could play any instrument was impressive as far as he was concerned. And this guy might look a bit rough and ready, but he still had something elegant about him. Nicholas thought so at least. Was that strange? To think of a guy as elegant?

He wasn't even pretending not to stare now, which was why he noticed right away when the pause between songs lasted longer than usual. The busker visibly sighed, bit the plectrum he'd been playing with between his teeth, and slipped the guitar strap over his head. Nicholas sat up in his chair and hurriedly swallowed the last mouthful of water from the bottle, a zing of panic flying through him.

He was leaving, and Nicholas hadn't thought of what on Earth he was going to say.

He scrambled to close his laptop and shove it back in his satchel, along with all his other bits and bobs. He hurtled himself across the narrow street, doing his best not to slip on the worn-down cobbles as he fumbled to a halt in front of the guy. He was crouched down, focusing on packing up his guitar, and didn't look up at Nicholas as he took a deep breath and frantically searched for a suitable conversation opener.

"I have a permit."

Nicholas snapped his mouth shut again. With a frown, he looked down at the top of the guy's head, noticing absently that there were paler, almost dark blond strands of hair running through the dark brown dreads.

"I'm sorry, what?" he stammered.

The guy stood up, and Nicholas was able to appreciate that he was a good couple of inches taller than him. "A permit," he repeated, his gaze unflinching on Nicholas's face.

Up close, he could tell that his eyes were a metallic grey, like a stormy sea. Unfortunately they were also narrowed, and Nicholas gulped. He resisted the urge to paw at his acne scars, like he was always inclined to do when he felt he was under scrutiny, and tried to understand what they guy had said.

"A permit?" he parroted, feeling stupid as soon as he said it.

"To busk here," the guy finally elaborated. His voice was a low rumble. "I know you've been eyeballing me, and if you were wondering if I was here illegally, I'm not."

Nicholas spluttered. "Wha-no," he spat. His own voice came out squeaky, as if determined to highlight the differences between them. "I – uh – you need a permit to busk?"

That wasn't the point, but those were the words that tumbled out of his mouth anyway. The guy didn't reply. He just knelt back down and tipped all the change he had accumulated into a pouch in the lining of the guitar case, before zipping it up and closing the lid, snapping the clips shut on the side.

"Huh," said Nicholas. "I mean, I guess I never thought about needing a permit, but I guess that makes sense – and that's great, that you have one I mean, but that's not – I mean – I heard you playing and – well, I guess you know that if you saw me, but, well you're great, did you know that?" The busker looked up, one eyebrow raised. "Yeah, no, I guess you do, otherwise why would you be out here playing on the street?" He laughed weakly. "But, well seeing as you *are* great, I had this thought—"

The guy straightened up, his guitar once more over his back, and slipped the cap onto his head. "Is there a danger you might be getting to a point any time soon?" There was the tiniest hint of a smile curving at one corner of his mouth, but the eyes remained cold and Nicholas floundered.

"Did you know harpists are really hard to find?"

The guy blinked.

"Okay," he said smoothly, then turned and began to walk away from the market.

Nicholas's feet spurred into action before he had a chance to reconsider. "No, wait, I'm sorry," he cried. He fell into step with the busker, despite the fact that the bustling, narrow street couldn't really accommodate two people walking side by side without pissing off the other shoppers trying to get by. Especially seeing as one of them had a guitar, and the other a laptop bag. "Can I ask you something?"

The busker gave him a side-eyed glance, that not-really-a-smile tugging at the edge of his lips again. "You may."

"Right," said Nicholas hurriedly. He cleared his throat and pushed his glasses back up his nose where they'd slipped. "Uh, well, I was wondering if you do weddings?"

They reached the end of the street, where the path mercifully opened up into a courtyard under the old clock tower, by the side of the road. They stopped walking as the busker addressed him.

"I've been known to attend a few in my time." Wow, this guy sure wasn't one for talking much.

Nicholas shook his head, sensing he was being messed with. "No," he said patiently, aware he was just about to ask this guy a massive favour. It didn't matter if Nicholas could pay him a lot, he still understood that a week was hardly any time at all to spring something like this on anyone. "Do you play them – with your guitar and your, uh, well singing. Voice. Or do you play anything else?" he asked, the thought occurring to him.

"No, I don't," the guy replied, before Nicholas could specifically ask if he played the harp. But then he realised he had asked two questions.

"Oh," he said, deflated. "You don't...play another instrument, or you don't do weddings?"

The guy stared at him a moment, then rubbed the small amount of stubble on his chin. Nicholas didn't seem to be able to grow much of a beard, even if he felt the inclination. He had a feeling it would just look a bit creepy on him, whereas this guy wore it naturally. It was probably part of what made him seem so confident, older.

"The instrument thing," he said eventually. "I know a little piano, but not well."

Nicholas rocked on his heels, anticipation bubbling up in him. "And the wedding thing?"

The guy's half smile reached something that actually resembled amusement, quirking fully into his cheek and giving him a dimple that did something strange to Nicholas's chest. Almost like it contracted. He ignored it.

"I've not done one before," the guy admitted. "What do you want exactly – something to walk the happy couple down the aisle?"

Nicholas couldn't help but let out an excited little exhale. That wasn't a 'no'.

"We've got that bit covered, actually," he explained. He'd gone through Danielle's itinerary thoroughly, so he knew exactly what to ask for when he'd called up all those other musicians before. "This is for the wedding breakfast – the dinner part," he clarified. "I thought that was so ridiculous when I first heard it – why not call it the wedding lunch, or dinner? That's the time when you have it, not the morning. It's after the ceremony, and unless you get married at the crack of dawn, then it's not really breakfast now, is it…?"

He realised the guy was staring at him, one pierced eyebrow raised.

Nicholas gave a small cough, and tried to rein his gob in.

"The idea would be for you to play as the guests move from the ceremony room into the reception room, then while we eat. So, about an hour, to an hour and a half." He gave a tentative smile and shoved his hands into his pockets. "It's paid, well paid."

The busker rubbed his lower lip with his thumb. Nicholas found that strangely intriguing, but he put the way his stomach flipped down to his hangover. Because, that would be ridiculous to find that attractive on another guy. Right?

"You don't know what I charge by the hour."

Despite what he had just told his brain, being only just out of his teenage years meant that his mind immediately went to a sordid profession that also charged by the hour, and he had to mentally chase the thought away, fast. His cheeks still blushed, he knew, and he tried to surreptitiously rub the pinkness away. Thankfully, his acne scars hadn't left much in the way of a colour blemish, but if he blushed he went horribly blotchy and he hated it.

His kind of scars were called 'boxcar' according to the internet. He'd only had bad skin for all of about six months, when he'd got really stressed doing his GCSEs a couple of years ago, but it was enough to leave him with several unsightly dents in his cheeks. He had a particular one that he found strangely comforting to worry at when he felt flustered, on the side of his right cheek, by his ear, and it was this he pawed at now.

"Uh," he said, sounding awkward to his own ears. "I don't, I mean, what do you charge?"

The guy seemed to take pity on him, and his shoulders relaxed, just a fraction. "I'm flexible," he said. "When is this wedding anyway? No sense haggling if I can't even make it."

Knowing he was at least open to the idea meant Nicholas could relax a bit as well, and he felt the heat easing from his face. But, he now had to confess to how soon the wedding actually was.

"Right," he said, nodding. He was aware of all the people going about their business around them, but at the same time it did sort of feel like it was just the two of them standing there, alone in their private conversation. "Right, so the thing is, we had a bit of a crisis, and the harpist I was supposed to book can't do it now—" He left out the part where that was entirely his fault for not booking her in the first damn place. "And I tried a lot of other people before you came along, so I totally understand if you're not free, because it is *really* soon, but if you could!" He shook his head and whistled. "Mate, you'd be saving my arse, I swear, but no pressure—"

The guy held up a hand between them. "Do you have a date?"

"Next Saturday," Nicholas blurted. He had to get it over with at some point, he figured.

The guy raised his eyebrow. "As in, a week from today?" Nicholas licked his lips, then nodded, dread sinking into his stomach. The guy frowned, then nodded back. "Yep, I'm free."

Nicholas almost choked in his haste to reply. "What? Really?" He shook his head quickly, not wanting to talk the guy out of it, but he had to ask. "Is that enough time, do you have enough songs, or whatever?"

The guy fished into his tight jeans, pulling out his wallet from his back pocket to retrieve a card. "I've got lots. I have to go now, but why don't we get together tomorrow and I can play you some stuff, see what you like?"

Nicholas turned the small rectangle that he'd been handed over in his fingers, realising it was a business card. There were several social media links as well as a mobile phone number, and, most importantly, a name.

"Fynn Dumashie," he read out loud. "Classical guitarist."

"Dumashie," the guy, Fynn, corrected, making more of an 'ahh' sound in the middle.

"Oh, sorry," Nicholas apologised. "Wow, you're such a grown up, with a business card and everything. That's pretty awesome, how old are you anyway? Twenty-one?" He kept his guess low, for some reason finding it important that he wasn't too much older than his own twenty years.

Fynn's half smile made another appearance. "I'm twenty-three," he said. That wasn't too much older. Nicholas could live with that, for whatever reason it was so vital to him that they not be that far apart in age. "Tomorrow – are you free?"

Nicholas let out a not-too-dignified "*Uuuuh*" sound as he wracked his brains for what the itinerary had told him. "Oh, no," he said in disappointment. "I've got a bunch of family stuff tomorrow – it's my sister that's getting married."

Fynn shrugged though. "Okay. Monday?"

Monday? "I think Monday's good," he said. He gave in and pulled his cardboard folder from his back to check Danielle's schedule. He was done making assumptions. From now on, he was double checking everything. "Yes! I can do about two o'clock, if that suits you?"

After establishing that they both lived locally in the city, Fynn took his card back, and scribbled with a pen he'd pulled from nowhere on the blank side.

"Here's my home address. Are you alright to come over?" Nicholas nodded. "I'll have access to my computer, so I can look up any songs you might want that I don't know. In the meantime, maybe get a list together of ideas, if you haven't already."

Nicholas read the handwritten address as he took the card back. He didn't know the road off-hand, but he was confident he could find it online fast enough. "Sure, yeah, sounds great. Um, do you want my number too?"

Fynn jerked his thumb over his shoulder. "I really have to go," he said, starting to walk even as he spoke. "Just drop me a text. And maybe tell me your name?"

"Oh, I'm Nicholas," he replied a little breathlessly. "Nicholas Herald."

Fynn waved as he turned and began walking down the hill, in the general direction of the cathedral. "See you on Monday, Nicholas Herald."

Chapter Three

(6 days to go…)

Nicholas awoke the next day with a tentative sense of hope. His hangover had finally dissipated, and he stretched happily in his bed, grinning towards the sunshine that was streaming through the edges around the curtains.

The more he thought about having Fynn play at the wedding, the more confident he became that it was going to be okay. He'd have to double check Fynn had a suit or something to wear. Even trousers and a shirt would do, and he was bound to have that, so really, that wasn't a worry at all. And he already had some ideas for songs which he had made a mental list of last night, but judging by what he'd played on the street yesterday, Nicholas was pretty confident that almost anything would be grand.

In twenty-four hours, he'd gone from panicked despair, to feeling quite proud of himself. He had, he hoped, saved the day.

Not that a harp (or a guitar) was the most important part of a wedding. Far from it – he was pretty confident a lot of people managed to get married without any live music at all. But it was the part he had *promised* to sort it out for his big sister, and he wanted to make sure he got it right.

There was still a very small bit of him that worried if a guitar really had the same impact as a girl in a ball gown, strumming on a harp. But, after hearing even just ten seconds of Fynn playing, he knew everyone else was going to be just as enthralled as him. Or at least he hoped.

He shook his head and rolled out of bed. He was being stupid. Fynn played beautifully, and Clara was going to love him. So was Peter, he was certain. So what if Danielle got a bit snooty about it, she got snooty about everything. She loved giving waiters a dressing down if her food was anything less than perfect, and lecturing checkout girls for going too slowly, and God help anyone in customer service who got in her way when she had a complaint to make. He could very well imagine her taking one look at Fynn and being less than impressed, but he would already be playing by then, so she wouldn't be able to do anything about it. It wasn't like he was going to show her a photo of him or anything.

His stomach growled. Despite eating his way through yesterday in an attempt to make himself feel better, he was ravenous again. It was probably a good time to get up and venture into the rest of the house.

As he was spending the next few weeks at home and away from uni, he had packed a massive suitcase as well as a couple of other bags full of stuff to see him through. Upon arriving yesterday, and having more pressing things on his mind, he had simply opened the case and rummaged through it all as and when he had needed to find anything. The result was that his room now looked like a bomb had gone off, with clothes and toiletries and chargers and DVDs strewn across the floor, draped over the bed posts, and hanging from his desk chair. He had never been the tidiest person, so it made him feel more at home to see the room in a state.

He'd lived in this house for most of his life. His room had been updated many times over the years, but there were still hints of his childhood lurking about, like the troll stickers on the inside of his wardrobe and the roller skates gathering dust under his bed. The walls were pretty plain and grown up. He had taken down all his film posters before he'd gone travelling on his gap year, deeming them too childish to leave in place, should he happen to meet someone special and bring them home with him. Not that that had happened, or looked like it would anytime soon. He could remain optimistic though, and if that day came, he didn't want to explain to a future girlfriend about his previous X-Men obsession.

The idea of a girlfriend always seemed so abstract. As he hauled himself out of bed, he sort of wished he'd left his room as it was, rather than concerning himself with impressing someone who didn't even exist. Maybe he could put some new posters up while he was here for Easter?

He pulled some clothes over the boxers he had slept in, and ran a brush through his hair, before chucking his glasses on. He could put in contacts after he'd had a shower; his family were used to seeing him bespectacled.

Except, he had forgotten it wasn't just his family staying with them at the moment, and as he entered the kitchen with a yawn, he was greeted by a chorus of 'hellos' and 'good mornings'. A quick glance told him it was almost the same group as yesterday morning, except his dad had now joined them. He was sat with Clara, sharing sheets of the Sunday paper like they'd done for years.

"Ah, there's my boy," he cried jovially, pushing over the entertainment section. "We saved you your favourite bit. Coffee? Kinny's very kindly making us breakfast."

Robert Herald was in his late fifties, and peered at his only son over gold rimmed spectacles. He smiled as he passed the coffee pot from where Peter had been hording it, and Nicholas gratefully sunk into one of the chairs around the island. As usual, no matter what the weather was, his dad was wearing his standard casualwear of polo shirt, shorts and flip-flops. It could be the dead of winter, and Mr Herald would insist on cranking the heating up rather than wearing full length trousers outside of the office.

"No golf today, Dad?" Nicholas asked as he poured himself a mug. It smelled like one of the Colombian brews he loved, but only his mum seemed to know where to buy, and he inhaled the aroma deeply before adding sugar and milk.

"Nope," his dad said proudly, wrapping his arm around a pyjama-clad Clara. She blushed. "There are more important things going on."

"There certainly are," chirped Danielle. She looked up from behind her laptop like a meerkat standing on its hind legs. Of course she was already dressed with a full face of makeup. "I hope you're ready for a busy day Nicky?"

Nicholas thought about correcting her, but it hadn't worked in twenty years, so why bother now? "Sure," he said neutrally instead. "Wow, Kinny," he carried on, turning to where his sister's best friend was working by the hob. "That smells fantastic."

Kinny and Ash were both in pyjamas too, attending to a couple of pans on the cooker. "Oh, thank you darling," said Kinny with a sunny smile over the shoulder.

There were already a number of plates and bowls on the table, holding olives, sticks of cucumber, a white, crumbly cheese, and sesame seed-topped bagels. Ash had been put in charge of some spicy smelling sausages, and Kinny was fussing of a large frying pan of something interesting looking. It was a tomato based sauce, with four eggs cracked into evenly spaced pockets, cooking merrily away. Nicholas could detect garlic and cumin in amongst all the other scents, and his mouth watered.

It wasn't a fry up, but it still looked absolutely delicious, and he was anticipating it infinitely more than yesterday's sludgy kale.

"I had to improvise a bit," Kinny explained as she beat what looked like a glass jug filled with yogurt. "Sainsbury's doesn't carry everything my mum uses," she added with a laugh. Her faded t-shirt and bottoms were covered with Care Bears, and her long, thick hair was being held up with a shiny purple scrunchie. "Danielle was so thoughtful looking after everyone yesterday, I thought I'd take a turn."

"I'm helping," Ash announced.

She held up a spatula to prove her point, then poked one of the eggs as if it might explode. She was only wearing a pair of Soffe shorts and a vest top, but she didn't seem to care that she was half naked. Neither did Nicholas, he realised, and he sighed inwardly. Surely he should find that at least a little bit hot? What was wrong with him? She was pretty and sporty and kind of odd in an interesting way. Why didn't that give him even a small flutter in his groin?

He had wondered many a time before now if there was something wrong with him, especially during his later school years, when all of his mates were losing their minds over as many pictures and videos of naked women they could get their hands on. He just didn't seem to care the way they had.

Bradley Cooper with his shirt off however…

Nope. He was *not* thinking about that now. Not when there was food to be had and weddings to be planned and whatever else he could think of to distract him from that line of thought.

Because, really, he couldn't be *gay*. That seemed like the sort of thing that happened to other people, not someone so wholly ordinary as he was. He was of average height, average intelligence, average looks; even his sports abilities, his hobbies and interests, and his family's socio-economic status were all painfully run of the mill. There was nothing remarkable about him at all.

He wasn't particularly troubled by this, but being gay seemed rather sensational in comparison. That would make him Different, Unusual, Strange. If it were true.

Nicholas really didn't need an existential crisis on top of the week ahead, but it appeared the universe was not feeling particularly sympathetic towards him in this instance. Looking at the curve where Ash's leg met the first hint of her bum was not doing anything for him. However, those pictures of Fynn he'd taken yesterday…Well, he'd looked at those for quite a while before he'd finally got to sleep last night.

So what though? The guy was attractive. That didn't mean anything. Nicholas was probably just grateful towards him for coming to the rescue. He refused to give it any more thought, deciding instead to think with his stomach and not his head.

"Thanks ladies," he told Kinny and Ash. "Is it nearly ready? Can I do anything to help – maybe make some more bagels?"

His mum raised her hand. "All under control," she said solemnly. She was leaning against the counter, engrossed in texting someone, no doubt to do with the wedding. And yes, she did indeed have a stack of more bagels on a plate by her hip, waiting to go into the toaster.

Nicholas's stomach gurgled though in anticipation, and he was too restless to sit and wait. So he got up and began laying the table around the sheets of newspaper.

"Oh, not for me thanks," Danielle said as he went to put a placemat in front of her. She picked up her drink bottle, once again full of something green, and sloshed it at him. "I'm on liquids only until Saturday. Got that dress to get into, after all!"

Clara looked up at that, worry clear on her face. "Oh," she said, pushing her glasses up and staring at Danielle's drink. "Maybe I should—"

"There you go," Ash said loudly, sliding a plate full to the brim of Kinny's Finest Breakfast in front of her. "Bride gets first dibs. Do you want butter to go with your bagel-thingies?"

Clara glanced anxiously at Danielle's green drink again as she chugged it down. She was doing a good job of not grimacing, Nicholas had to give her that.

"I'll be having butter," he said loudly, heading to the fridge. "So I'll just set it on the table."

"There's cream cheese as well," said Kimmy, plonking the jug of garlic-yogurt on the table. "Make sure you get a good dollop of that with your peppers and eggs," she informed everyone proudly.

Nicholas jabbed at his steaming plate, inhaling eagerly. There were indeed peppers mixed in with the red sauce, and he quickly leant over to get some yogurt to mix in with it.

"Thanks sis," Peter said to Ash, as she brought a plate over for him. That didn't stop him though from leaning over and stealing a bit of sausage off of Clara's plate with a wink.

"Oi!" she cried. She picked up her knife and fork to wave him off. "Don't make me go bridezilla on you!"

Danielle narrowed her eyes as Clara tucked into her food, but thankfully remained silent. At least, on the subject of Clara's diet. "Oh Ekin," she gasped. Kinny looked over at her, startled, fork halfway to her mouth to take her first bite. "I don't think those sausages are Halal," Danielle continued, all of a fluster. "So you probably shouldn't have any."

A scowl flashed across Kinny's features. Nicholas wasn't sure he'd ever seen her with a scowl in his entire life, but she quickly went back to her usual happy self. "Oh no," she said with a dismissive wave of her hand. "I don't do Halal. I think it's cruel. This stuff's organic and they let the pigs wander around a farm or something." She picked up the discarded packet from the counter and gave it a quick scan, before holding it up for Danielle to see. "I'm fine with that."

If Danielle was irritated not to have stopped not one but two people eating, she didn't show it. Instead she started rattling off the plan for the day as everyone found a seat. There were just enough chairs that they could all squeeze around the island table together, and aside from Danielle, the chit-chat faded rapidly to a minimum as people dug in.

"I think we should set up stations in the den," she said thoughtfully. "I have jobs for everyone, so I'm sure we'll be done in no time! I hope you're all feeling creative?"

Nicholas's mum and dad made encouraging noises, as of course did Kinny, but Nicholas felt it best to concentrate on his toast. He wasn't particularly talented when it came to crafty things, but he'd be good and attempt whatever was asked of him. Hopefully Danielle knew him well enough not to task him with anything too complicated.

As he thought about other things going on during the rest of the week ahead, his mind naturally drifted to Fynn and their meeting tomorrow. As he'd been falling asleep last night, he'd thought of a couple of songs to suggest, so pulled his phone out to do that as he ate.

'Hey! It's Nicholas Herald, from yesterday,' he tapped out, so Fynn didn't think he was a randomer. *'Thanks again for doing this, I really appreciate it! Okay, so, I thought of a few songs. If you don't like them or can't already play them though, don't worry. First off is Taylor Swift, because you sort of have to have Taylor Swift, don't you? Clara LOVES that 'You Belong With Me' one, but 'Style' is good too. Then there's John Legend 'All of You', that's really nice. Oh, and she loves this song called 'War of Hearts' by Ruelle – no idea if that's how you spell it? Not sure you would have heard of that one. Okay! I think that's it for now, I'll message again if I think of anymore!! Honestly though, I liked everything you played yesterday, so all of those can go on the list too :) Speak soon, Nicholas.'*

Everyone had more or less finished eating by the time he'd tapped all that out, so he hopped to his feet and diligently started to clear up, running a sink full of suds. His job was always the washing up, as he didn't particularly like cooking. Everything he tried to make generally ended up burnt, soggy or in the cat bowl. But washing up, he could do.

There were enough showers in the house they didn't need to work out much of a schedule, but Danielle attempted one anyway. "Let's meet in the den in half an hour, alright!" she called to the retreating party.

Nicholas chuckled to himself, and thought he caught his dad rolling his eyes as they left the room together. He was distracted though as his phone pinged, and he couldn't help the small thrill of anticipation that it might be Fynn.

It was, but when Nicholas opened the message, it simply said '*OK*'. He frowned, and stared at the screen for another full minute, thinking he would probably follow up with more. But he didn't.

Well, it wasn't anything bad, he figured as he traipsed back upstairs to his room. He couldn't help but be a tad disappointed at its sparseness though.

The house wasn't small, but it was full to the brim with extra guests staying over. Danielle had taken over the den – the second, more casual living room that Nicholas's parents had made when they'd built the ground floor extension a decade ago. He thought she was content being surrounded with all the paraphernalia for the wedding, like a magpie in its nest with all its shiny trinkets. She hadn't even bothered setting up the sofa bed, not wanting to disrupt all the piles of decorations and stacks of paper and baskets of confetti and ribbons.

If she wanted to kip on the couch, that was her prerogative. Peter was obviously in with Clara, and Ash and Kinny were being good sports and sharing the double bed in the loft conversion that had been Lauren's room before she'd gone off travelling a few years ago. Nicholas was lucky not to have someone occupying a blow-up mattress on his floor, but he still had to wait a fair while for his turn in one of the showers.

Being a good host, he held off until last, and suffered through lukewarm water with no more than a silent protest. It was refreshing he told himself, especially having sweated through his hangover the day before.

He was, therefore, the last to arrive in the den, but nobody seemed to mind. It seemed they were going to be stuck there for the whole day, after all. He was immediately directed towards an enormous box of pastel pink confetti petals.

"Nice and easy," Danielle announced, handing him a small metal trowel, like you'd find in a pick 'n' mix bar. "One scoopful into a mesh bag, then tie the drawstring shut."

That was actually a job he felt confident in tackling, so he settled himself down next to Clara to get to work. "Wotcha got there, Geri?" he asked, giving her a light poke with the trowel.

"I'm making the board with the lists of all the tables on it," she said proudly. She already had glitter in her hair and across her face, but he had to admit the board was looking good.

"Geri?" Ash asked from across the room.

Nicholas couldn't work out what her project was exactly, but it apparently involved reams of fishing wire, and some very sharp scissors.

"It's just a nickname," Clara said with a shrug.

Nicholas wasn't letting her get away with that.

"Holy crap," he said excitedly. "Have you not heard the Spice Girls stories?"

Kinny groaned, but her grin gave her away. She was surrounded by feathers, silver butterflies and bags of plastic diamonds, but she paused in her centrepiece creation to pretend to scowl at him. "Oh no, not this."

Clara was laughing, though, as Ash looked between them, intrigued. "We might have had a slight Spice Girls obsession."

"Slight?" spluttered Nicholas's mum.

His dad shook his head from where he was sat next to her, diligently folding orders of service. "I got talked into taking you to see them *five times*," he grumbled, but Nicholas knew he wasn't really serious. "Three times when they were still together and you girls were barely tall enough to see, and then twice again when they bloody reformed."

"It was so worth it though," Clara gushed. "And we used to have slumber parties where we'd dress up as them, and learn the dances, and perform the songs."

"I remember that part," Nicholas said, pretended to shudder. Clara flicked his nose.

"You were just mad we wouldn't let you join in," she said.

Kinny waved a feather at him. "No, but there was that time Lyndsey couldn't make it though, and we needed a Sporty—"

"Oh god yes, we put you in a wig!" Clara cackled. She turned to Ash, who didn't seem to know what to make of it all. "I was always Geri you see, being sort of ginger."

"You are *definitely* ginger!" Nicholas protested, feeling the need to fight back on behalf of his younger self, and the old humiliation of that wig. Clara swatted at him. "And Kinny was Mel B."

"Not much choice," she said with a wink at Clara. "Being the only non-white girl." Clara blew her an affectionate kiss in return. "Then who were those other girls who were Baby and Posh? Was it—"

"I was Baby," Danielle interrupted. She had a tight smile on her lips that didn't reach her eyes. She was once more behind her laptop, this time perched on the edge of the couch with it balanced on her knees. "Don't you remember?"

Kinny nodded. "Oh – yeah," she said. "But, that was just here, when you visited. We played it almost every day at school for months. We'd coordinate our lunch breaks in advance so we could—"

"Clara's had so many nicknames over the years," Danielle tittered, slapping her hand to her chest, leaning towards Ash in a conspiratorial manner before looking back at Clara. "Haven't you?"

"Yeah, but I actually liked Geri," she said with a laugh.

Danielle waved her hand. "Oh, well, we all got called 'Hark-the-Herald-Angel-Sing', even my brothers and I did at our school. Kids always think that's clever. You had more than that though, didn't you?"

Clara shrugged, going back to her glitter. "I guess."

"Peter calls her 'baby girl' on the phone," Ash piped up. She made kissy noises, then squeaked and ducked when her brother threw a ball of tissue paper at her head.

"So what if I do?" he asked. He made a point of giving Clara a big, sloppy kiss on the cheek, which made Ash pretend to gag and throw the paper right back at him. "And anyway, I like the Spice Girls too, so I'm pretty chuffed to be marrying my own Geri."

Clara smiled and gave him an affectionate hug at that.

"No," Danielle carried on with determination. "I'm talking about 'Hairy Clary', you remember that don't you?" She laughed to herself. "Kinny, you were there weren't you, in that science lesson with the plasma globe? Clara volunteered to put her hands on it, and her hair turned into a proper ginger afro, it was hilarious!"

46

Kinny smiled politely. "Oh, I don't really remember that, sorry."

"It was pretty funny," Clara said to Peter. It sounded like an apology.

Ash raised an eyebrow. "I didn't think you guys went to school together?" She clicked her wire-cutters several times in quick succession as she pointed between Danielle and Clara, like a crab snapping its claw.

"Oh we didn't," said Danielle, unperturbed. "I just heard about it afterwards. And then was 'Clara Bow'—"

"After the actress," Nicholas said quickly. "You know what, before I start with all these petals, I think I might get tea. Who wants tea?"

Predictably, that got everyone's attention. He ended up taking out his phone to write up the order, but when his mum went to get up, he insisted he could manage by himself. He wanted to get a moment's peace and quiet.

He frowned to himself as he waited out in the kitchen for the kettle to boil. Even Danielle should have known better than to bring up 'Clara Bow'. It had been one of the crueller taunts his sister had had to endure at school. Her legs weren't even really that bowed, but kids were arseholes.

He wished he hadn't brought anything up about nicknames. It was bad enough that Danielle had taken it upon herself to invite her mother's unfunny friends to the wedding. He would be *amazed* if Michelle could keep her thoughts about Clara's weight to herself for a whole day – if it was just the evening, it might have been possible to avoid the two of them coming face to face. But Michelle was almost certainly going to want to amuse herself by calling Clara 'Princess Plumpling' or something equally witty.

But now Danielle was going out of her way to be extra…he didn't even know what the word was. Was she trying to show Clara up? It was no secret, as far as Nicholas was concerned at least, that Danielle had always been a bit incredulous that her 'chubby, geeky' cousin had met a nice guy, whereas she couldn't seem to keep a man for more than a couple of months. Nicholas was convinced that no one else saw that as a failing on her part, but her behaviour at the moment was coming across a lot like jealousy.

Luckily, by the time he returned with a tray heaving with tea things, there was a lively conversation going on about the latest season of *24*. It was his dad's favourite show, and he had a lot to say about it.

"I think it's good they're shaking things up a bit," he was arguing.

"But it's just not the same anymore," Peter lamented as he wrapped up a bottle of whiskey for one of his groomsmen.

Nicholas took his time handing out the mugs of tea and coffee, then made sure everyone had a plate of biscuits within reach of where they were sat. He made himself comfy with a cushion under his bum, and finally got to work on bagging up the confetti. He couldn't rush too much with it, otherwise he'd damage the petals. It was a job that required care, but not all that much skill.

He let the conversation wash around him, smiling as Clara and Peter got all dreamy as they talked about their two-week honeymoon in Disney World in Florida.

"In our day," Nicholas's dad lectured them with a wagging finger. "We thought Tenerife was bloody exotic for a honeymoon."

Then Nicholas's mum regaled them all with some stories from her wedding with his dad involving lost trousers and a drunk uncle or two. Kinny giggled, then explained how one of her sisters had had almost seven hundred people to her wedding.

"It's not a Turkish wedding if you haven't invited your cousin's wife's goat!" she laughed.

Nicholas tried to imagine how much of a headache that must have been to organise, and repressed a shudder. Clara and Peter had less than a hundred people coming to their day, including the evening, and Nicholas was thankful for it. He dreaded to think how many more bags of confetti he'd be filling otherwise.

"Ohh, hello kitty-cat," Danielle crooned from her perch on the couch. She put down her laptop, and clicked her fingers. "Have you come to help?"

Nicholas sucked in a lungful of air, and automatically seized Clara by the elbow. Sure enough, Archibald the cat had come swanning into the den, tail swishing back and forth. Neither sibling took their eyes off of him as he wound his way around people to where their mum was sat. Kinny was telling Ash and Peter more about her sister's wedding, and they didn't seem to notice that Nicholas and Clara were on the verge of a heart attack. Nicholas looked around the room, sizing up how much trouble one cat could potentially cause.

But holding their breath and silently screaming seemed to have appeased whatever gods might have been listening. Archibald crossed the room, having thoroughly ignored poor Danielle's attempts to make friends, and was rewarded by Nicholas's mum picking him up to place him in her lap.

He began purring loudly, and Nicholas and Clara slowly deflated.

It took a while for Nicholas to calm his heart down after the near miss, but Archibald looked to be behaving himself, and he and Clara slowly got back to their jobs.

He was finding the confetti bagging quite soothing. It didn't really require much thought, and allowed him to drift off, let his mind wander and relax. This was going to be a long week if he didn't take the time to chill out when he could. But the scoop-pour-tie rhythm he had going was therapeutic, and he allowed the conversation to blur around him. He thought maybe they were talking about rugby, and he was happy to tune that out.

As was usual in the past twenty-four hours, his mind eventually dawdled its way back to Fynn. He wondered what he was doing today – who he lived with, and what he might be getting up to. Was he playing his guitar again, out on the tourist-filled city streets?

He got his phone out again, half hoping he might have texted something more, but his phone screen was blank. He didn't mind though, as he'd thought of something else to message him about anyway. Maybe this one would get a longer reply?

'*My sister and her fiancé's favourite song is a bit of a weird one, but just on the off-chance I thought I'd mention it. It's Spice Girls "Say You'll Be There". I know, right? When I heard that, I knew they were destined to be together lol :)*' It was true. It had come up over dinner a couple of years ago, and although they had both been a bit embarrassed, Nicholas thought it suited them quite well.

He pressed send and went back to his bags. However, after a couple more he got his phone back out. '*Anything by Beyoncé is probably good too, but that 'Halo' one is really romantic, isn't it?*'

50

Chapter Three

A few bags later: '*NO DIDO! I don't mind her myself, but Clara has a real thing against her. Same probably goes for Coldplay, so best avoid them as well, just in case. Sorry if you like them lol x*'

He hadn't meant to add the kiss. Not at all. In fact, he didn't even realise what he'd done until he was on the next bag, and he stilled suddenly as the horror dawned.

'*Sorry about the accidental kiss. Just habit lol. Didn't mean to freak you out or anything.*'

'*Do you do any other crazy covers? I really liked the Katy Perry one you did yesterday. Oh, and that Christine and the Queens track? I think it's called 'Tilted'? Not as a remix, just as it is.*'

'*Ooh, how about Years & Years, they're really cool!*'

'*Sorry, I'll stop texting soon. I just keep thinking of songs!*'

'*How about 'Glow' by Ella Henderson?*'

"Nicky, who *are* you talking to?"

He looked up sharply to see Danielle staring at him, a smile twitching at the corner of her mouth. "W-what?" he stammered.

She licked the end of some cotton, then focused on trying to thread it. "You're nonstop on that phone – it's a miracle you've got anything done at all."

Nicholas frowned. He thought he had a pretty decent pile of confetti bags accumulated already. "Er, it's just Trev," he lied, naming his best friend from school. He had intended to text him later, so it wasn't a complete lie. "He's back from his uni too. We were thinking about meeting up maybe."

"Not this week, surely?" Danielle said. Her tone was friendly enough, but there was a frown line between her eyebrows.

Nicholas felt a flair of irritation. If he wanted to meet with his best friend, he would ask if *his sister*

51

minded. Not her. But he remembered his promise to himself to behave, so squashed his feelings down. "Don't know," he replied truthfully.

His phone gave a tiny buzz, and he was too excited to care about the raised eyebrow that answering it got from Danielle. It was from Fynn, and this time it read *'OK ;)'* Nicholas took that as an encouraging improvement.

He made it through the next couple of dozen bags without thinking of anything else to text, and only stopped when his mum got up to do a repeat of the tea order. Nicholas stretched, not realising how much his back had needed to click. Kinny cracked her fingers, and Peter rubbed under his glasses with a yawn.

"Okay," said Danielle seriously. She flipped through one of her files, and consulted her laptop. "I'm afraid I'm going to need someone to be brave, and use the hot glue gun. Now, I know that's asking a lot—"

There was a snort from the corner of the room. Ash's flailed both arms and legs as she sat upright, and wiped her mouth as she blinked several times. "Me," she said, sticking her hand into the air, looking around the room until she found Danielle. "Me, I'll do it. What do I need to do?"

Danielle frowned. "Are you sure?"

"Oh, yes," she replied with a rapid nod. "Yep definitely, I can manage hot glue." Nicholas thought she looked a little too eager.

Luckily Kinny also piped up. "I can help," offered she with a wave. "If it's complicated." Surely Danielle would trust her?

Sure enough, she agreed to let the girls loose on the gun. Apparently, it was for some sort of photo collage that Nicholas would have thought could have been made with Prit-stick. But what did he know?

While Danielle got them set up on the dining room table, already covered with an old sheet to protect it, Nicholas fired off a quick text to Trev so he felt less guilty. It would be nice to escape for a while and meet up with him, and maybe a couple of the other guys, but only if Clara didn't mind.

"Ahh, Nicky," said Danielle as she re-entered the room. "That was what I wanted to ask you. Did you find the harpist's details yesterday? I'd really like to get them on file."

His insides turned to ice. "Uh," he said.

He should just explain now, tell them about the mix-up (he didn't have to let them know he'd just *forgotten* to book her, after all). But, he had really hoped to have his first meeting with Fynn before that, just to *definitely* make sure it was all okay. That didn't matter, he should just come clean-

"Not yet," he said cheerfully out loud. "But I remembered where I wrote it down. So once I put my room back in order, I'm sure I'll find it. It's all in hand though, I promise."

Danielle pursed her lips, but didn't say anything. No one else seemed to notice anything amiss either, as they started discussing what they were going to do for lunch. But Nicholas felt his heart rate going up. Why had he lied? Why hadn't he just been honest?

He really wasn't sure, but it sat uneasily with him for the rest of the day.

Chapter Four

(5 days to go…)

The house was quiet.

Nicholas pressed his ear to his bedroom door and listened through the wood with bated breath. Nope, not a peep.

Carefully, he eased the door open and glanced left and right across the landing. No movement, no sound, nothing.

"Oh thank Christ for that." He sagged against the doorframe, and felt his mouth curl into a shaky grin. People, at times, were completely overrated.

He stretched his arms above his head and ventured out into the corridor in his pyjamas. Being a Monday, he had hoped that most of the house would be going back to work, but after yesterday's carnage, he wasn't entirely convinced it was going to happen. Especially with Danielle. He was sure he was going to wake up and discover that she had swung last minute annual leave for the week, just so she could dedicate all her waking hours to the wedding.

But a quick glance on each of the three floors showed all the doors were open and lifeless, aside from the attic room where Ash and Kinny were no doubt also enjoying a bit of tranquillity with a well-deserved lie-in.

Yesterday hadn't been all that bad, really. Aside from the sick, nagging feeling in his stomach every time he remembered lying about Fynn not being the harpist, Nicholas had actually made it through the rest of the day without any arguments, tears, or getting burned with the glue gun. They'd gotten an Indian take away in the evening, and watched old sit-coms while Danielle listened to Clara's entrance music on a seemingly endless loop through her headphones. She had counted from one to eight in a barely-there whisper for the best part of an hour, pausing to note down times on her laptop every now and again.

In all honestly, Nicholas did genuinely think it was very sweet how much effort his cousin was putting into the big day. Although her way of going about it was sometimes clumsy and, he worried, occasionally hurtful, she was still working extremely hard to make things perfect. Despite the slightly uglier sides to their relationship, she and Clara had been friends pretty much since birth, and at the end of it all, if Clara and Peter had a lovely day, that was all that mattered.

Even if Nicholas had been ready to tear his hair out after the bazillionth hushed count of eight drifted across the room.

Now, there was no sign of life as Nicholas trotted down the stairs to the ground floor of the house. There was, however, a note left by his mum on the kitchen island, telling him and the girls to have a nice day, as well as a reminder for him to go into town and pick up the groomsmen's ties from the department store at some point before five o'clock. There was also a big, smiley face, a dozen love hearts and several flowers decorating the page, which made him snort and roll his eyes.

But it was sweet to know his mum was thinking about him.

From the pair of trainers by the back door and exercise gear chucked into the sloshing washer-dryer, Nicholas guessed that Danielle had gone for her normal run before commuting into her job in London where she was a paralegal or something equally impressive. He shuddered to think what time she'd woken up. His dad worked in the capital as well, but his mum, Clara and Peter all had jobs in St Albans, so would probably have left at a much more reasonable time. Nicholas had the opportunity to take advantage of one of the perks of student life, and would be spending most of the day in his pants, logged onto Netflix.

He poured himself a bowl of chocolatey cereal, humming 'MMMBop' as he waited for the kettle to boil. He fancied tea, and maybe some biscuits too. And then he could make toast later if he was peckish.

He gazed out the window. Rain was pelting down and the sky was iron grey. He felt a twinge of worry, but then he reminded himself they had ages until the wedding. April was notorious for showers – for all he knew it would be bright and breezy again by the afternoon.

The afternoon, when he was meeting Fynn again. A nervous flutter went through his insides at the thought of it. Then he scoffed and tipped a spoonful of sugar into his tea. He needed to get a grip on himself or he was going to look like a right prat.

He couldn't help it. Fynn was so quiet, even his texts were restricted to one bloody word at a time. Nicholas was bound to talk more to fill in the pauses, and that would no doubt lead to him saying something idiotic. Like, how talented he thought he was, or how pretty he thought his eyes were. He was starting to come to terms with the fact that he might possibly have a tiny crush on the enigmatic busker, but Fynn *really* didn't need to know that.

He blew on his tea, and watched the rain creating patterns down the window pane for a bit. A crush didn't have to be romantic, did it? Maybe he just really admired Fynn. Talent was attractive, everyone knew that. So perhaps he was just drawn to his skill as a musician.

Before going to sleep the previous night, he had indulged in looking Fynn up on Twitter, Instagram and YouTube. He had wanted to see if he could find any more of his performances, and he wasn't disappointed. He'd discovered video upon video of him sitting in what looked like his bedroom, strumming on his guitar, his deep rumbling voice adding new life to songs Nicholas hadn't always paid attention to before. He told himself this was part of his research, that he was just checking up on Fynn's quality as a performer. But he had also noticed there didn't appear to be a girlfriend in any of the photos or posts...

It didn't really matter in any case, because unless Nicholas did anything, the issue of his maybe-crush was never going to come up. Fynn was probably as straight as an arrow anyway. Nicholas poured milk on his cereal and put the bottle away, vowing to try and not think about the matter anymore. There was a slim chance of that, but he could at least try.

He heard a creak upstairs and figured Kinny or Ash might be stirring. Kinny was on Easter break like he was, but she was a primary school teacher, so would have lots of homework and planning to sort out. It wasn't like Nicholas was on holiday himself – he'd have a great deal of revision to plough through too. But he had decided to wait until after the wedding to even think about that, regardless of whether or not that was a good idea.

Ash worked shifts; Nicholas wasn't sure doing what, but she'd said yesterday that she wasn't due in until the afternoon. It was probably some sort of retail, he figured. Peter was a manager at the Games Workshop not far from where he'd met Fynn in the city centre, so he could see Ash doing something similar.

It would be nice to have it only be the three of them pottering about the house for the morning, but selfishly, Nicholas hoped they'd sleep a little longer. It would be heaven to just chill out by himself for an hour or so.

He picked up his mug and his cereal bowl, and went to go settle in the living room with some trash-telly. Ordinarily, he'd bunker down in the den, but it was so full of wedding stuff, as well as Danielle's belongings, it didn't feel right. He glanced at the open door on his way past...and froze in his tracks.

In another household, seeing the family cat leaving a room might not be cause for alarm. It might not make your heart stutter or cause you to break out in a cold sweat. But Archibald had That Walk going on, the one where you knew he'd found the cream, caught the canary and probably robbed the Bank of bloody England while he was at it.

Nicholas ran.

He sloshed tea over his wrist but he didn't care that it was hot. He all but dropped his breakfast onto the table, and wiped away the liquid on his pyjama top as he hastily scanned the room for damage. Sadly, it didn't take him long to spot.

He couldn't help but slap his hands over his mouth as he gasped.

He and Clara had *tried* to impress on Danielle yesterday that the door needed to be kept closed whenever she left. But it hadn't helped that his mum had kept cooing that 'her baby was a good boy' as she stroked his tummy. And of course, he always was good when she was in the room. He was only an absolute fucker whenever Nicholas's mum wasn't around to witness it.

"ARCHIBALD!" he roared. He dropped his hands and bunched them into fists. It wouldn't do any good now, the little shit always knew to hide when he'd done something particularly heinous. But it made Nicholas feel the tiniest bit better.

However, he was rewarded with the thumping of two pairs of bare feet running down the stairs. "Nicholas?" Kinny called out as she and Ash approached, but he couldn't seem to bring himself to turn around and look as they arrived in the room. "Are you alr—"

She cut herself off with a shriek, and mimicked Nicholas's initial reaction by covering her mouth in horror. The two girls flanked his sides, and together, they stared at the damage.

"Well...bollocks," stated Ash. She ruffled her pixie-cut, and shook her head.

"Oh no," whispered Kinny tearfully.

Danielle must have wanted to air out the bridesmaids' dresses or something. Maybe she was worried about the soft, pale pink material creasing, or making sure none of the tiny crystals fell off from the shoulder straps. Why else would she have hung all three of them from picture frames against the wall? Now, Nicholas was extremely worried about the enormous slashes in the swathes of chiffon that had reduced the bottom front half of each of the dresses to nothing but holes and tatters.

"Your cat did this?" asked Ash, walking over to inspect the damage close up.

She was in her short-shorts again, and Nicholas didn't even try to muster the energy to be disappointed in his lack of a normal, red-blooded-male reaction when she bent over and peered at the material. Instead, he scowled.

"He's not my bloody cat," he snapped. He rubbed at his face and tried to think straight. He tried not to be furious at Danielle for not listening to him and Clara, but he found he was too panicked to be angry anyway. Being mad or saying 'I told you so' wasn't going to un-fuck the dresses. "What are we going to do?" he asked. "Buy new ones?"

They hadn't bought these ones though. They had been handmade by a professional seamstress in the London, and had cost an absolute fortune. They were specifically tailored to fit each girl; Danielle had designed them herself and the subtle combinations of pinks matched the wedding colour scheme perfectly. They would never find anything similar off the rack; they were perfect. Or at least they had been. Now they hung in ruins.

"Can the woman fix them somehow?" he asked hopefully. But Ash shook her head.

"She's on location in the States until May," she explained, jolting Nicholas's memory. "That's why we had to have them finished at the start of the year."

According to Clara, she'd worked on dozens of films and theatre productions and had had an actual BAFTA stood on the desk in her workshop. That's why she was so good, and why the dresses had cost that much.

Nicholas let out a high-pitched whine. Right, they weren't totally screwed yet, they had time. "We'll just have to see if we can find someone else," he said. There had to be loads of options in London; if he'd found a replacement musician, surely they could find a replacement seamstress.

Ash turned and raised an eyebrow at him. "We'll have to come clean if we do that," she said. She stood and shook her head. "I don't know about you, but I haven't got the kind of money right now that it'll take to get these fixed."

Nicholas, looked between the two of them. It couldn't cost that much to do something, anything with what they had left of the dresses, could it? But the girls' tight, worried faces told him otherwise. "I'll call my dad," he said, glancing towards the ceiling to indicate his phone in his room. "He might have an idea."

"Hang on," said Kinny, her voice muffled behind her hands. She dropped her arms to her sides, fists clenched as she stared with determination at the dresses. Almost as if she thought if she glared hard enough, they might mend themselves back together. Like something out of *Fantasia*. "There…there might be someone I can ask."

Ash glanced at Nicholas. "Someone seamstressy?" Kinny nodded, and Ash raised her eyebrows. "Someone with the time to do it?" Kinny paused, then nodded again. "Someone who might not charge too much?" Another nod. "Well," scoffed Ash, crossing her arms. "Then, yeah, let's do that!"

Kinny chewed her lip, clearly hesitant. "I'm not sure they'll help," she said slowly. "But, it's worth asking, isn't it? This is an emergency."

"I'd say," agreed Nicholas. "But, only if you're sure?"

Kinny thought about it for a moment or two, and Nicholas held his breath. "Yeah – no, it's fine." She pulled her hair out from her scrunchie and shook it loose. "I'll just – hang on while I get my phone."

Nicholas sat heavily on the couch and picked up his tea, sipping it in the hopes it might settle his churning stomach. Of all the rotten luck... He shook his head. He couldn't hash over that now. He had to remain positive, focus on solutions. He wasn't sure who Kinny might be phoning, but there was still hope if they said yes.

Although, he wasn't sure how exactly. The dresses looked beyond saving to him. But then, he didn't know anything about sewing.

Ash began to pick up any slivers of pink material that had detached completely from the dresses and landed on the carpet, collecting them carefully in her hand.

"Do you think we can reattach those bits?" Nicholas asked her optimistically.

Ash shook her head. "Nope," she replied, popping the 'P'. "But this way we can convince Danielle we simply put the dresses away, or took them to the dry cleaners."

"Dry cleaners," confirmed Kinny, walking back into the room. She had her phone pressed to her chest. "We can say they smelt musty. That way she won't go looking for them."

Nicholas looked between them both, unsure. "You don't want to tell her about this?"

Ash rested a hand on his shoulder, and looked at him solemnly with her big, blue eyes. "Of course we'll have to tell her," she said. "But would you rather do it now, or when we've got the solution all sorted out?"

Nicholas raised his eyebrows. "Very good point," he said.

"Speaking of which," said Kinny heavily. "My mum said yes. She'll help."

Ash raised an eyebrow at Nicholas, but he just gave her a tiny shake of his head. He hadn't heard Kinny talk much about her mum before. "That's a good thing," he said instead. "Right?"

Kinny blinked, then gave him a weak smile. "Yeah, sure."

She obviously wasn't going to offer up any more information, so Nicholas decided to let it go.

Between the three of them, they managed to cajole each of the dresses back into their garment bags, being careful not to damage them any more than they already had been. But when Ash jogged upstairs to get changed, Nicholas thought he should at least double check that everything was okay.

"We don't have to go see your mum," he said quietly to Kinny as they fished two big golfing umbrellas out of the coat cupboard. "Honestly, if you don't want to, we can think of something else."

Kinny gave him a bright smile though, and touched his elbow. "I'm just being silly," she said, and shook her head. "She said she'd be happy to help."

Nicholas wasn't quite sure he believed her, but he decided to leave it at that. If she had a plan, he was glad to let her take charge. After the harp fiasco, he didn't know if he could manage another crisis.

Before he headed upstairs, Nicholas made *sure* the door to the den was shut this time, lest Archibald sneak back in to wreak more havoc, but not before he gave the floor a once over to make sure Ash had got all the scraps of material off of the carpet. She was right, Danielle and Clara didn't need to know about this until they had a solution.

Nicholas hurried back up to the bathroom and hastily had a quick wash. He wasn't sure how long this was going to take, and he wanted to at least be halfway decent if he had to go straight away to see Fynn. Having met him in his dishevelled, hungover state on Saturday, he'd hate to give him the impression he was some sort of layabout with poor hygiene standards.

He was essentially Fynn's boss, he told himself as he took too long picking out a shirt to go over one of his favourite t-shirts. He needed to be presentable and professional. And if he happened to feel he looked quite attractive while doing that, then that was just a side-effect.

"Nicholas!" Kinny called up from downstairs. He could hear the anxiety in her voice. *"Are you nearly ready?"*

He had hoped to have another couple of minutes to put his contacts in, but he guessed he'd have to stick with his glasses for the third day running.

With a sigh, he grabbed his wallet, keys and phone, and pulled his door to. "Coming!"

The girls were waiting for him downstairs, armed with the three dress bags, two still-closed umbrellas, and Kinny's car keys swinging from her hand. She had so many brightly coloured keyrings, Nicholas thought it was a wonder she was able to turn the bunch in the ignition at all.

As he reached the bottom of the stairs, he obediently held his arms out to take the dresses, leaving the girls armed with the brollies. "Ready?" Ash asked, her hand on the front door handle. Nicholas could see the rain through the windows, hurtling to the ground with what felt like furious intent.

He bit his lip. "Let's do this."

Kinny's car was hard to miss. It was a bright yellow Mini Cooper, and a plastic sunflower waved at them cheerfully from the antenna, beckoning them to brave it out of the house and down the road to where their ride awaited. With what Nicholas liked to think was a battle-cry, but which probably sounded more like a panicked shriek, he and Kinny hurled themselves out into the pouring rain, leaving Ash to lock the front door with her spare set of keys.

Together, they managed to keep themselves and the dress bags more or less under the umbrellas, and only their feet got drenched as they legged it the few dozen feet down the pavement. Nicholas clutched the dresses to his chest as carefully as he could, hoping that the garment bags were waterproof. At least enough to withstand the rain that was, despite their best efforts, creeping under the golf umbrella.

Kinny only fumbled for a moment with the right key to let them inside, then she and Ash ushered Nicholas in first, making sure the dresses stayed lying as flat as possible over his lap as he squirmed into the back seat. Soon enough, Ash had thrown herself into the passenger seat, and she and Nicholas watched as Kinny squeezed herself into the driver's seat, sliding the umbrella down by Nicholas's feet.

The car started to steam up with condensation. Nicholas listened to himself pant, while the other two followed his example and clicked their seatbelts over their bodies.

And then there they sat.

Kinny wrapped her hands around the steering wheel and stared out into the murky world beyond the rain, not, as far as Nicholas could tell, really looking at anything. After a minute, he started to get uncomfortable.

Ash broke the silence first. "Um," she uttered after another minute had gone by. "Do you want a hijab?"

Kinny blinked and turned to look at her. "What?" she said, a little dazed.

Ash indicated the scarf she had around her neck. "I just thought – if we were going to see your mum – and you were nervous – it might be because you don't normally wear a hijab, and she might expect you to?"

Kinny barked a loud laugh. Nicholas felt relieved, but he was still none the wiser.

"Oh, that's so *sweet* of you." Kinny reached over and touched Ash's arm. "But, no, it's nothing like that. My mum's been with me when I've bought *bikinis* in the past. I – erm…I guess we had a bit of a fight. A little while ago. But she said it was fine to bring her the dresses – I mean – she didn't say it was *not* fine. So, we just need to go over and stop faffing, right?"

Nicholas wasn't sure. "How long ago did you have your fight?" he asked, ignoring his better judgement.

Kinny shrugged. "A year and a half." She turned the ignition, and the engine thrummed to life. The radio also burst into sound, deafening them all with an energetic nineties number about sunshine and beaches and popping pills in 'Beefa. "Shall we get going?" Kinny practically shouted. She grinned at them, and pulled out into the street without waiting for an answer.

Nicholas opened his mouth, but he found he didn't have anything to say other that asking if they were *sure* they didn't want to try another plan. Seeing as he'd already asked that already, he decided not to rock the boat. He couldn't help but feel anxious as to what they were walking into, though.

Kinny's family lived a twenty-five-minute drive across town. Nicholas had vague memories from his childhood of waiting outside there before, probably while dropping Kinny off, or picking her up. But he couldn't say he particularly recognised the blue trampoline sat in the small front garden that the rain was currently bouncing off, or the garishly painted gnomes that were peeking out from the shrubbery at them as they pulled up outside the semi-detached house. He did remember the archway over the dark green front door. Depending on the time of year, it would be covered in trailing plants with big purple blossoms that Nicholas had mistaken for bunches of grapes in his youth, and he'd always been quite captivated by it.

Now the bare leaves of the plant flinched in the rain bucketing downwards, and the trellis shook when the door was abruptly yanked inwards.

Mrs Sadik was not a tall woman. She wrapped her cardigan tighter around her as she regarded the three of them in the car while Kinny killed the engine. She pushed her rectangular glasses higher up her nose, the legs vanishing farther into her butterfly-patterned silk hijab. The garment seemed too bright and cheerful for such a grim day and the unfortunate task ahead, not to mention the scowl that adorned the older woman's face.

She beckoned impatiently towards them to make the sprint down the neatly kept garden path and into the safety of the house. Nicholas said a silent prayer to whatever deity might be tuned into them that she could help them fix their dress disaster, and undid his seatbelt.

"Here we go," Kinny murmured. Her clear apprehension did not help with Nicholas's own worries. He was starting to wonder if she had even given her mum a call at all, or whether or not they were just turning up unannounced into a whole load of trouble.

They were there now, so the three of them scrambled back out into the rain with the umbrellas. Nicholas tripped as he tried to hurry towards the house as fast as he could, but Ash grabbed his arm in time. They made it to the door without incident.

"Hurry! Quick, quick!" Kinny's mum urged them in a thick Turkish accent, waving her hand to usher them over the threshold faster. "It's cats and dogs, you'll catch your death."

She huffed and glowered. Somehow, the fluffy slippers she was wearing and the smudge of butter on her cheek didn't render her any less intimidating as they all crowded into the small entrance hallway of the house.

The front door slammed shut, and for a moment, the only sound was the rain dripping from the hastily shut umbrellas.

Nicholas shifted on his feet. Mrs Sadik had her dark eyes fixed on Kinny, who in turn was darting her gaze between the socks drying on the radiator, the key bowl on the table by the door, and the family portrait hanging just to the right of Mrs Sadik's ear.

"Hi mum," she uttered. Mrs Sadik's scowl deepened.

Nicholas decided it was time he found his voice. "I'm Nicholas," he blurted out. He jigged the dresses so he could half stick his hand out towards Kinny's mum. "Clara's brother. Thank you so much Mrs Sadik, Kinny said you could help and I'm really hoping you can, because my mum's cat really went to town on the dresses and the wedding's on Saturday and I guess we could buy some new ones, but she spent ages working on these ones – her and Danielle I mean – that's the maid of honour – and I know they didn't work on them, the seamstress did, but there were loads of fittings. Anyway, I'd hate to have to tell her they've been totally destroyed and—"

"Now, now!" Mrs Sadik waved her hands in front of his face, then clasped them around Nicholas's. "Hush hush! Nicholas, it is nice to meet you. Clara has been good friend to Ekin for years and years. But all this worry! You are a good brother I'm sure, to worry so, but we have not even seen the problem yet!"

Nicholas hadn't realised a lump of panic had risen in his throat until he tried to swallow. "It's pretty bad," he said in a small voice. He daren't look at Kinny or Ash. If they agreed, he might just lose the composure he'd been holding onto since discovering Archibald in the den.

Kinny's mum didn't look shaken. She patted his cheek instead, and gave him a warm smile. "Not with this sad, sad voice. Come on. Let's take a look and get to work. All is not yet lost!" She jabbed her finger about her head, and turned to lead the way down the narrow corridor like she was leading troops into battle. However, Nicholas didn't miss that she purposefully avoided her daughter's gaze.

"Dude." Ash whispered from behind, presumably to Kinny. "What did you do?"

Kinny didn't answer.

There was a bicycle propped up against the wall, and dozens of pairs of shoes lined up haphazardly along the skirting board. Nicholas carefully picked his way through, mindful not to knock the garment bags on any of the picture frames hanging from the walls. Kinny had several brothers and sisters. Nicholas couldn't remember how many, but there were numerous smiling faces that beamed up at him from the photos as he passed. Kinny was somewhere near the top age-wise, he thought.

They reached the kitchen, and Nicholas was instructed to lay the dresses down on the table. The units all around them were a faded beige with chipped wooden handles, but they were meticulously clean. So many pots and pans and utensils hung from hooks in the walls that he could hardly see the colour of the wallpaper, and the fridge was so covered in magnets holding up photographs and letters and postcards that they almost camouflaged the appliance in its entirety. A stack of battered board games was piled on top of the washing machine, and a selection of small cacti ran in a line on the window sill above the sink, adding a splash of green to the room.

There were several different scents of spices in the air even though nothing was cooking at the present moment, as well as a hint of wet dog, no doubt wafting from the small basket sat in the corner of the room by the back door. Nicholas automatically looked around for the basket's owner, not adverse to having a friendly fury hug to cheer him up after such a shock. Honestly, why did his mum's cat hate the world so much? Of all the things he could have gotten his claws into, did it really have to be the unique, took-months-to-make dresses?

Kinny hung back as her mum unzipped the top garment bag and poked at the dress within. Ash joined Nicholas in peering over Mrs Sadik's shoulders.

"See," he said weakly. "It's a disaster."

Mrs Sadik made a noise a bit like blowing a raspberry. "You are too dramatic, young man," she chided. Her tone was friendly enough. "Everything is end of the world with youngsters. Let us see what we can do. Come, help me get out of the bag."

"Mum, I—" Kinny began, taking a step forwards.

Mrs Sadik threw up a hand. She did not look around. "This is not the time, Ekin. I will help your friends."

Nicholas and Ash both naturally moved away, looking between Kinny and her mum. Nicholas's heart sank as he saw the big tears pooling in Kinny's eyes. "Mum, I'm sorry." Her voice was little more than a rasp.

Mrs Sadik did whirl around at that. Kinny was tall and willowy, and had a good few inches on her mum, but she still flinched at the finger that was pointed at her nose. "*Ekin Aysu Sadik!*" she snapped, followed by several words in what Nicholas had to assume was Turkish. "We have this talk. We will not have it now. I will help Clara and her family. You are saying sorry another day." She turned back to Nicholas, who was secretly hoping the floor might have had sympathy and swallowed him up by now. "I go get sewing machine. You have tea, yes?"

Nicholas coughed. "Uh, yes. Tea, tea would be lovely – Ash you'll have tea, won't you? Shall I make it, I'm happy to make it."

"No, no," said Mrs Sadik, already moving to the kitchen door and shaking her head. "Sit, sit, Basak is making the best tea, nobody better."

With that, she was gone.

Nicholas rubbed the back of his head, and glanced at Kinny. "Are you alright?" he asked quietly.

Kinny released a sob she had obviously been trying to hold on to, and slumped into the chair nearest to her. "I'm fine," she bit out, rubbing the back of her hand over her eyes.

Ash sat down beside her and rubbed her back. Nicholas followed their example and took a seat

71

too. "Sounds like you really fucked up, mate," Ash said.

Kinny let out a laugh then frowned. "You'd think, wouldn't you? We both reckon we're in the right though, and until one of us apologises, nothing's going to change."

Nicholas almost said it was fine, so long as the dresses got mended. But he figured that would be a bit insensitive. "Sometimes," he ventured, hoping he was being tactful. "I find it helps to apologise, even if you don't really mean it."

Kinny gave him a snuffle that was close to a laugh, and gave up on wiping her eyes. "She knows I won't mean it."

"Won't mean what?" A girl of about fifteen came into the room. She was wearing a unicorn onesie and had train-track braces. She glanced up from typing on her phone to give Kinny a mischievous grin. "Hey sis."

"Hey Bas." Kinny let her sister bump into her in a sort of hug, then watched as she flicked the kettle on the counter on to boil. "Nothing new."

Bas cackled. "Oh my days, is mum still mad with you about Babaanne?" Kinny grumbled under her breath, but that just made her sister laugh harder. "I knew it! Oh my god, I told you not to do it. And now you're asking for a favour? Good luck with that."

Nicholas's stomach plummeted. "You don't think she'll help?"

"It was *my* money!" Kinny said, a defensive tone in her voice. But Bas just kept chuckling as she took out a number of brightly coloured, mismatching mugs from one of the cupboards.

"You guys want tea, yeah?" she asked Nicholas and Ash instead.

At that moment, Nicholas didn't think he could drink anything, even if he was gasping from dehydration. "The dresses," he prompted her. "You think your mum won't help?"

Kinny folded her arms across her chest and harrumphed. "She's already helping. It's whether or not she can even do anything we should be worried about."

Bas scoffed. "I wouldn't help you. You guys take milk I assume?"

"Hey," said Kinny. She flopped her hands into her lap and looked genuinely upset.

"I'll take milk," said Ash. She had a sly look on her face. "And a slice of gossip. Come on kid, spill."

Kinny spluttered, but Bas let out an "Oooh!" noise. "You don't know – how fabulous."

"It's really not that big a deal," Kinny said. "And mum said she is going to help, so there's really no point in discussing it, right?"

Ash arched an eyebrow, then looked pointedly at Bas. Nicholas was torn between wanting to be nice, and finding out the story behind the argument. As it transpired, his vote didn't matter anyway.

"Alright, look," said Kinny before Bas had a chance to speak, and held up her hands. "My grandmother gave us all some money in her will." She glanced towards the kitchen door, then to her smirking sister, then leant in towards Ash and Nicholas. "She told us to spend it however we liked," she continued in hushed tones.

Bas let out a whoop. "Yeah, right."

"Just coz you have no imagination," Kinny said. Bas shook her head, and carried on squeezing teabags. "Long story short, mum got it in her head that I should use it to pay off some student loans, or put it towards a house deposit. But it wasn't enough to even come close to covering either of those things – if I did that, it would have been like she never gave me anything at all. Babaanne wouldn't have wanted that."

"Oh, but it's okay for me to do it?" Bas scowled as she plonked tea in front of Ash and Nicholas. Kinny, Nicholas noticed, had not been made a mug.

Kinny shrugged, unfazed, and got up to make her own brew with what was left of the water in the kettle. "It's up to you – it's still up to you. You should do something memorable."

Bas snorted. "I still have to live with Mum and Dad," she said. "Unlike *some* people, I can't escape their wrath."

Kinny rolled her eyes. "I wanted to use it for an experience – and that's what I did. *And,*" she added, waving a teaspoon around. "I shared it with Clara – so I don't know why she's the golden child right now and I'm the devil's spawn!"

Something clicked in Nicholas's mind. Eighteen months ago would have been November.

"No I get that, I get that," Ash said, nodding her head. "So what did you do? Travel round India? Do some yoga and find yourselves?"

"Erm," said Kinny. She cradled her mug and returned to her seat. Bas giggled from behind, leaning against the counter with her own tea.

"I'd take a course and learn a language," Ash said to Nicholas. There was a twitch of a grin on her lips that told him that maybe she knew she was barking up the wrong tree. "Or sponsor building a well in Kenya. They have droughts, right?"

Nicholas raised his eyebrows at Kinny. He was pretty sure she and his sister hadn't helped an African village. "Uhh…" she said.

Bas was obviously enjoying Ash's little show. "She could have given it to Battersea Dog's Home," she said with an innocent bat of her eyelids.

Ash clicked her fingers in agreement. "Or one of those donkey sanctuaries."

"Guys," Nicholas said warily. He felt like maybe the teasing had gone on long enough now.

"Ooh, I love those places," said Bas. She nodded and gulped down some tea. "They have those Greyhound homes too, for when they stop racing. I bet they would have loved a couple of grand."

Ash frowned. "That's not really an experience though, is it?" She raised her eyebrows at Kinny, whose face had drawn back into a grimace. "Did you go teach English to orphans in a hut somewhere."

"That would have been cool," said Bas. She ran her tongue over her braces with practiced ease. "Proper charitable."

Ash drummed her fingers on the kitchen table. "Or—"

"*We went to Vegas!*" Kinny shouted. She dropped her head into her hands.

Yep, Nicholas had been right.

Bas snorted into her tea, and Ash blinked. "I'm sorry, but, beg your pardon?"

Kinny let out a high-pitched whine from behind her palms. "We went to Las Vegas," she continued in muffled tones. "And spent it all on strippers and slot machines."

Ash drew back in her seat. "Shut the front door." A delighted smirk crept across her face. "You wild child."

Nicholas couldn't help but laugh too, now that he remembered. He'd wondered at the time how Clara had been able to book a last-minute jaunt to the City of Sin. "That wasn't all you did," he said, trying to keep a straight face. "If I recall, you also got yourselves backstage at Ricky Martin."

"No!" Ash slapped her hands to her cheeks. "Not even Britney – *Ricky Martin?*"

Bas started to sing a rendition of 'Livin' la Vida Loca', sashaying her hips as she shimmied across the kitchen. "That's definitively what Babaanne would have wanted," she said, patting Kinny on her head as she passed.

"And I believe there were tattoos?" said Nicholas.

Kinny snatched her hands away from her face and gave him and imploring look. "No, okay – she doesn't know about the tattoos, I'll definitely *never* be forgiven if she—"

A noise from the hall made her clamp her mouth shut. Bas looked triumphant though, and leant over her shoulder to whisper in her sister's ear. "I think you're going to owe me. For, like, ever."

Kinny just gulped.

Nicholas immediately felt bad. He hadn't intended to get Kinny in any more trouble, and he definitely didn't want to piss off Mrs Sadik any more than she already was, not if there was any chance she could still help them.

"Hey, look," he said hurriedly, grabbing Kinny's hand. "Let's just forget about it, okay?" He looked over at Bas and raised his eyebrows. "Okay?" She sighed, but, with a glance out to the hallway and the voices drifting down from upstairs, she nodded. "I'll talk with your mum. She doesn't need to know about the tattoo."

Kinny sniffed and scrubbed at her face. "What if she doesn't help? She still seems so mad."

Bas landed in a chair with a huff, and glanced between them and Ash. "She's not actually spiteful. Come on, don't cry. It's no fun if you cry." She leant over and wiped one of the tears from Kinny's face, eliciting a weak laugh. "I'll smooth things over."

The voices grew louder, and the four of them looked towards the doorway in anticipation.

"Kinny!" A boy of maybe ten or eleven years came charging into the kitchen and threw his arms around his sister. Nicholas thought he was probably the youngest of the Sadik brood; he certainly displayed the exuberance he recognised from being the baby in his own family. "You're here! You're here! Mum said I can help with sewing. Did you really ruin your bridesmaid dress?"

"Enver!" Kinny said tiredly, ruffling his hair. It was as liquorice black as hers and Bas's. "No, Clara's cat did the damage." Her voice died as her mum came back into the room, struggling with a sewing machine spotted with age.

Ash jumped to her feet. "Let me help with that," she offered. She reached over and helped Mrs Sadik rest the old machine onto the kitchen table.

Kinny's brother Enver took a step back, his mouth falling comically open. Nicholas couldn't help but watch as the poor boy's eyes travelled up the length of Ash's athletic figure, only clad in leggings and a t-shirt, which didn't leave much of her body shape to the imagination. Now, wasn't that the sort of reaction he was supposed to have?

"I can help too," Enver spluttered, quickly coming to their assistance and beaming dreamily up at Ash. It was pretty cute, Nicholas had to admit.

Bas also leapt up. "I'll make you tea, Mum," she announced, not waiting for an answer before filling the kettle once more from the tap. "You want a Ribena, Squirt?"

Enver shook his head. Now the sewing machine was secure, his focus was entirely on spreading out the bridesmaid dress they had previously removed from the garment bag. Nicholas could tell it was

Danielle's, as she had extra bling on the ribbon bit under her boobs. Apparently, that would let people know that she was the maid of honour.

"Oh dear," said Enver, and Nicholas's heart dropped like a stone.

"Is there no hope?" he asked, seeing as the boy apparently had an idea of what he was doing.

Enver shared a look with his mum, who was rummaging through a box of cotton reels, searching for a shade that matched the dresses. "What do you think?" she asked him. Nicholas held his breath.

Enver bit his lip and moved the slices of chiffon this way and that. After another few moment's inspection, he nodded once. "There's hope," he announced.

Nicholas couldn't help but cry out, and Ash punched the air. "You can put them back together?" he asked.

"Oh, no," said Kinny's mum. She put down the pale pink cotton she had found, and patted him pityingly on the arm. "But we can modify it – they are all looking as bad as this, yes?"

Ash leant over and flipped the shredded bits of dress back and forth, making Enver's eyes glaze over as her leggings stretched favourably across her bum. "I think this one is the worst, actually."

Mrs Sadik clapped her hands together. "Then we have no problem."

Kinny didn't risk looking at her mum, but she did give a watery smile from behind, catching her sister's eye as she gave her a thumbs-up. Nicholas agreed. This was excellent news. "Brilliant." He reached up and clasped Mrs Sadik's hand where it still rested on his arm. "Honestly, thank you so much. Whatever it costs, I can pay—"

Mrs Sadik cut him off with another of her raspberry sounds, and began threading her needle.

Enver eased out the next dress from underneath Danielle's, and Bas clinked a teaspoon against the inside of another mug as she made her next lot of tea.

Right, then. He guessed that was that sorted. He glanced awkwardly at Ash, who shrugged, and Kinny, who offered him a small smile. There wasn't much else for him to do, other than sip at his now lukewarm tea.

Surely, after this and the harp, the universe had to be done with them. There couldn't be any more disasters between now and Saturday.

Right?

Chapter Five

Once Kinny's mum and brother began to work in earnest on the three dresses, conversation stilted awkwardly. Kinny seemed keen not to draw any additional attention to herself, lest she get into another argument with her mum, and Bas left them all to go back to her biology coursework. The fact that this was the better option was not lost on Nicholas, as he tapped his finger nervously against the side of his now empty mug. He opened his mouth several times to try and say something to Ash to lift the tension in the room, but each time he decided against it. Knowing him, he'd try and crack a joke, and that would just make things worse for Kinny, he was sure.

Rescue came however, in the form of a Jack Russell terrier called Lauda. He trotted into the kitchen like nothing at all was amiss, almost in fact like there *should* be a group of strangers there, just waiting to give him a belly rub.

Nicholas wasted no time in plonking himself on the tiles and fussing over the small dog. Tickling his tummy and telling him he was not only a good boy, but a handsome one, got more than a few smiles out of Mrs Sadik, and Kinny visibly relaxed as her mum's attention was guided elsewhere.

However, once it seemed Kinny's mum and brother were confident they could do something to make the dresses wearable again, Nicholas and the girls were keen to make their excuses and escape the strained atmosphere in the house. Ash genuinely had to get ready for work anyway, so soon enough, the three of them let themselves out the front door and back into the rain once more.

Nicholas was on a schedule too, he couldn't forget. Luckily, he'd had the forethought to put the receipt for collecting the ties in his wallet yesterday evening. Therefore, he asked Kinny to drop him in the town centre so he could pick them up from the suit shop. He waved them away from under one of the umbrellas, then began trudging down the street to his destination.

He let out a long breath as he walked. It may have been an uncomfortable experience, but it seemed like Kinny's mum had a design in mind that she and Enver could implement to save the dresses. Obviously, it would have been much better if they had never been shredded at all, but if they were wearable come Saturday, Nicholas would count his blessings.

He half thought about popping in to say hi to Peter at work, as his shop was more or less on the way to the suit place. But Nicholas didn't think he'd be able to refrain from letting something slip about the dresses. Or the harp. So he just carried on to Moss Bros, wishing his trainers were a little bit more waterproof.

After the couple of days he'd had, he half expected the shop to have lost the tie order, or at least misplaced it. He felt light with relief when it only took them a couple of minutes to locate the right parcel from out the back. They even double wrapped the bag for him to help protect the silky ties from the weather.

That left him with a couple of hours to kill before meeting up with Fynn, so he took himself off to get lunch at a pizza place. He managed to successfully distract himself for a while by messaging Trev and catching up on Facebook. It seemed his school mates were thinking about going to Havana, one of the local night clubs, the next night. But he wasn't sure he fancied that, so kept his answers deliberately vague, blaming the wedding for his lack of commitment. It was true to a certain extent; he might just listen to Danielle, and not meet up with anyone until Saturday was all over.

Eventually he had to think about Fynn, and making his way over to see him. Surely, he tried to argue with himself, all he had to do was sit and listen to the guy play for a little while? Wasn't that the point of them meeting up, to check out some songs that he could perform at the breakfast? That didn't have to be all that difficult, not unless he made it so. He just needed to take a breath before he said anything, and try and play it cool.

He still felt nervous as he paid his bill and gathered up his things, carefully making sure to double check he had the ties safely packed away. His jitters only got worse as he awkwardly followed the navigation from the map on his phone and held the umbrella over his head. He winced every time the wind changed direction and made the rain swerve against him despite his best efforts, and he hugged his package tighter to his chest.

Saying something stupid was probably inevitable. The more he thought about trying to talk to Fynn, the more nervous he got. And the more nervous he got, the more he was going to blabber. He was probably going to have to clamp his tongue between his teeth and bite it to stop him from embarrassing himself, and that didn't sound like a very pleasant prospect.

He sighed as he crossed the road. Maybe he just needed to accept the fact that he was going to come across as a bit of a prat, no matter what. That way, he could try and relax, even just a little. So what Fynn was cool and talented and really good looking? Nicholas wasn't trying to be his friend, he just wanted him to play at the wedding.

So why did it seem so important for Fynn to like him?

With a start, Nicholas realised he had reached the position on the map with the pulsing dot. He stopped walking, and looked up. He had been expecting a house, but he was now stood in front of a very nice block of flats, flanked either side by three-story town houses. The flats were gated, and he stood feeling a little foolish for a minute as he looked around for an intercom panel.

Eventually, he realised it was located in a metal box on the other side of the gate. He hoped no one had been watching him look about gormlessly for the last minute or two, and darted over to the box. He carefully extracted Fynn's business card from his pocket, and without dropping the ties or his umbrella, attempted to keep the rain from spattering it while he scanned the handwriting. When he was reasonably confident he'd deciphered the numbers correctly, he pushed his thumb against the 'twenty-three' button, then held his breath and hoped for the best.

Just as he was starting to fret that his ring had gone unheard, the intercom clicked alive.

"Hello?" a woman's voice buzzed through the speaker.

"Hi! Hi," Nicholas spluttered, slipping the business card back into his jeans pocket. "Um, I – is this where Fynn Dumashie lives? I'm, uh, Fynn, that is – I'm here to see him. This was the address he gave me. I'm Nicholas." *Nice. Very smooth.*

There was a pause, and he anxiously chewed on his lower lip. "Of course," came the woman's voice again. It was faint as it competed against the sound of the downpour. "Come on in. Second floor."

The line went dead, but Nicholas didn't mind. It seemed like he was in the right place, so he'd got over his first hurdle. He heard the tell-tale click of the gate, and hurried to push it inwards before the lock reactivated itself.

Once inside the courtyard, he felt another flutter of nerves. Which out of the two doors was he supposed to go through? Would he need buzzing in a second time? Out of the pair, he randomly chose the door on the right, only to realise that that was the side for flats thirty and above. Cursing, he splashed back through the rain to the other side, and yanked at the door. Locked.

"Urgh!" he growled.

There was another metal panel to right though, and at least now he was under a slim awning which gave him a small amount of protection from the rain. He ran his gaze down the numbers, and jabbed at twenty-three. "Hello!" he squeaked as a buzz of static told him the line was open. "Sorry, it's Nicholas again. I went to the wrong door, if you could let me in—"

The door clicked. The woman didn't speak again though, and the line went dead just like it had on the outer gate.

Brilliant. He wasn't even in the building yet, and he'd announced himself to be nothing better than the village idiot. There wasn't much he could do though aside from grit his teeth and lean into the glass door.

Inside was awfully modern compared to the red-brick exterior, suggesting it had been remodelled in the past decade or so. Everything was glass and chrome, and Nicholas felt the cool touch of climate control on his damp skin as he slid the umbrella shut and shook off the excess rain onto the bristly welcome mat that stretched across the first several feet of the corridor.

"Second floor," Nicholas muttered as a reminder of his previous instruction, and headed off at a brisk walk. Rather than risk making a further mockery of himself by chancing being unable to operate the elevator, he jogged up the stairs instead. Eventually, after what felt like half an hour since he had arrived at the destination on the map, he found himself standing outside flat twenty-three. His fist hovered an inch away from the pale wood finish of the door. "Just knock," he hissed to himself as his knuckles failed to make contact.

Before he could muster his courage though, the door swung inwards, and he jerked his arm back in surprise.

A woman a foot taller than him stood over the threshold. She had skin a shade or two darker than he remembered Fynn's being, and was dressed in a bright red shirt with flowing, cream trousers. She wore chunky gold jewellery in bold, angular shapes on her fingers, neck and lobes, and had a Bluetooth headset nestled in her left ear. Her hair was closely cropped, leaving barely a centimetre of dark curls. The lines around her eyes gave the impression she might be in her late forties, but her trim figure made Nicholas question that assumption.

"Yes," she said, and Nicholas opened his mouth to reply, guessing she was the one who had answered the intercom. "No, no, I'm not sure that's wise." She pointed to her headset, then waved her hand twice to encourage Nicholas to come inside. "Well, I don't know if there's the funding for that."

She had a well-spoken English accent that he typically associated with the home counties.

Nicholas offered her a tentative smile, then gave the brolly one last shake onto the navy blue carpet in the corridor. When she turned her back to retreat into the flat, Nicholas followed, listening to the clack-clack of her heels on the dull wooden floor as she hummed at what the person on the other end of the line had said.

Good. Hopefully, she hadn't responded to his second buzz through on the intercom because she'd been on the phone. Not because she thought he was a moron who wasn't worth wasting even a word of further dialogue on. In fact, she turned and gave him a smile and pointed down the end of the hall.

Presumably, that was where Fynn was.

The woman, who Nicholas took to be his mum, wandered back into a living room area, nodding her head and folding her arms across her chest. The place was a bit of a state if he was honest, with stacks of paper and magazines and newspaper clippings everywhere. Dirty dishes balanced on several different surfaces, and boxes, bags and even a suitcase by the window spilled their assorted contents onto the floor. Cobwebs hung from the ceiling, and Nicholas thought he might have even spied some Christmas decorations poking out from under the dining table, practically groaning from the weight of all the manila folders and loose sheets of paper that were piled up on top of it. The only things that looked clean were the two laptops open on the coffee table.

Nicholas toed off his soggy trainers, feeling it was best to leave them by the front door. The temperature in the flat was warm, which he was grateful for seeing as he was now stuck with dank jeans and half-sodden socks. But it meant his glasses had fogged up, so before he could go anywhere, he had to wipe them off.

Awkwardly, aware that the woman was still slowly pacing the living room while talking to the person – or persons – on the other end of the phone, he juggled the umbrella and ties until he could yank his specs off his face, and then hastily use a couple of fingers to pull out some material from his jumper, and clean the condensation off the lenses.

He felt it would be rude to linger any longer, so he once they were dry he jammed them back on his face and headed down the corridor the way the woman he indicated. He passed a long, narrow kitchen, which was an equal state of disarray as the living room, a bathroom, and what he thought might have been a bedroom, but the door was only open a crack. Along the wall hung various framed posters of different species of butterflies, labelled like you might expect to find in a textbook.

He reached the end of the corridor, and found himself facing a closed door. This must be where Fynn was.

He only hesitated a moment before knocking this time. "Hello?" He frowned at the way his voice wavered, cleared his throat, and tried again. "Hello? Fynn?" There was no answer after a good minute had passed, and Nicholas figured he could only knock and wait so many times. So, taking a deep breath, he placed his hand on the round handle, and gave it a slow turn.

The door wasn't locked, and it swung away from him easily to reveal a painfully neat and tidy bedroom. Nicholas didn't take much in at first glance, as his instinct was to look back over his shoulder and check he was still in the same flat. Which was stupid, of course he was, so he pushed the door open a little wider, and stepped inside the room. He realised he recognised it from the YouTube videos. It felt strange now seeing it in person.

Fynn was sat on his bed wearing a vest and three-quarter-length trousers. He was barefoot and had his head bent over a notepad as his whole body bounced subtly to the beat presumably coming through the large, wireless headphones resting completely over his ears. His bedspread was dove grey (much like his eyes, Nicholas's brain helpfully reminded him) and was made with a crisp, white sheet folded over the top lip. Most days, Nicholas was lucky if he managed to pull the duvet straight once he'd toppled out of bed, let alone manage a flat sheet as well.

The floor was clear of any debris, although there was a full looking clothes hamper by the door that meant the overall impression Nicholas got wasn't totally pristine. It was oddly reassuring. If there hadn't been any socks poking out, the room might have felt too cold and distant.

The walls did give it character though. There were several posters of musicians that were framed, and not just with the simple Perspex clip-frames you got from Ikea. They had crafted wooden edges that gave the pictures contained within them more gravitas, and Nicholas was drawn to them immediately. He didn't get a chance to inspect the artists contained with them any closer though, as Fynn glanced up from his notes, and spotted he was no longer alone.

His lips curled into the half smile Nicholas remembered from Saturday, and he couldn't deny his stomach did a little panicky flip.

"Hey," said Fynn, seemingly completely as ease. He used both hands to remove the large headphones, then tapped on the phone by his knee to stop the music. "You made it."

"Um, yeah, hi." Nicholas clutched the tie package and the still-damp umbrella to his chest, and pushed the door closed again. "I'm not early, am I?" he asked, knowing full well he was bang on time. "I could come back, if you're busy. I don't want to intrude, I mean, I did knock."

Fynn folded the headphones away into a case he fished out of a drawer by his bed and shook his head. "No, you're on time. I was actually listening to some of your suggestions, working out a few chords." He held up his notepad for Nicholas to see, but the scribbles on the page didn't mean anything to him.

"Oh, okay," he said. He then stood there, staring at the guy. The only sound was the crinkle of the plastic bag in his hands.

Fynn smiled again, slowly, like he was considering Nicholas, then used the notepad to point. "Why don't you take a seat?" he suggested. He indicated a swivel chair in front of a computer desk at the foot of the bed. "I didn't have anything particularly formal planned for today. I just figured I'd play some of the songs you wanted. Like an audition."

"Oh," said Nicholas. He shuffled over to the chair, and let himself drop into it. He kept the ties hugged to his chest, but he let the umbrella drop to the floor. This room though, he realised, was carpeted. It was a darker grey than the bed covers, but it would still soak up the rain water. So he chucked the tie package by the computer keyboard on the desk, and hastily snatched the offending brolly off the floor once more. "Sorry," he blurted. "It's tipping it down out there. I can just leave this in the hall, or—"

Fynn pointed over Nicholas's shoulder, where there was a door he'd assumed to be a closet. "Why don't you leave it in the en-suite?"

Nicholas blinked. His parents had an en-suite bathroom, and he'd always been a little jealous of it. "Oh cool," he enthused, jumping back to his feet.

He flicked the light switch on to illuminate another tidy room. The bathroom wasn't huge, but it was clean and finished in a similar chrome to what Nicholas had seen on his way up from the lobby.

"Wow, this is sweet. Do your parents have one too, or did they let you have the best bedroom?" He laughed at himself as he opened the umbrella to stand it on the tiles in order to let it dry. "My sisters would never let me take an en-suite from them if one was on offer – do you have any siblings?"

He came back into the bedroom to find Fynn just where he'd left him; cross-legged on the bed, looking at him with faint amusement. *Jesus Christ*, Nicholas berated himself. He was such a child. He needed to stop saying whatever just flitted into his brain.

He rubbed his face, and sheepishly sat back down. But Fynn surprised him by answering his rambling questions.

"It's just me and my aunt here," he said. He jutted his chin towards the door that lead back to the hallway, and Nicholas reasoned he must be talking about the woman that let him in. "My brother and sister are a lot older than me, and my parents live abroad. But, yeah, Ellen has full use of the main bathroom. She prefers it that way."

Nicholas studied the fabric of the chair cover for a moment, then looked back at Fynn. "Oh, cool. That's cool then." He wanted to ask why he was living with his aunt, but that seemed rude, so he clamped his jaw together. He didn't resort to putting his tongue between his teeth; he'd save that for if things got worse later. "So, what song were you working on?"

Fynn reached over the side of his bed. It was a motion that made his muscles shift in a favourable way, and Nicholas frowned. He'd never been all that athletic, and even though Fynn wasn't exactly buff, by the looks of it he'd have no trouble pinning Nicholas down. That particular image made him feel hot and uncomfortable. He crossed his legs and coughed, willing his cheeks not to redden before Fynn sat up again.

When he did, he had a familiar guitar case in his hands. He slung it over to land on the bedspread before him and clicked the clasps on the side open. "Actually, I quite like that Ella Henderson one," he rumbled.

Nicholas wondered idly when his voice had broken. It was so low, it must have been a shock to the other boys at his school. Nicholas's voice wasn't exactly squeaky, but it sounded like it in comparison to Fynn's.

"Uh, yeah," he said, attempting to drop the pitch of his words by a decibel or two. But he sounded ridiculous, so he gave up before Fynn noticed. "That's a great one."

Fynn laid the guitar across his lap and strummed it a few times with a plectrum he'd fished out of the case, tweaking the knobs at the top to tune up the strings. "What's the venue like?"

Nicholas wasn't sure what he meant for a moment. "Oh, for the wedding. It's the town hall, it's really cool – have you ever been there?" Fynn shook his head and glanced back down at the strings as he carried on strumming. "Well it's nice, all high ceilings and big windows and everything's white, it makes me think of ancient Greece."

"Big?" Fynn arched an eyebrow and looked up. His fingers and the pick were still wandering around the strings though in a mesmerising way.

Nicholas had to think for a second. "Oh, no, not really. There's about seventy people coming to the dinner I think."

Fynn considered his words. "I'm trying to work out if I can play acoustically, or if I'd need to use an amp or PA system."

Nicholas shifted in his seat. "Err," he uttered. "No idea. Sorry. How big would it have to be to need an amp?"

Fynn stopped playing, and drummed his fingers against the wooden body of the guitar instead. "I could go and take a look on Wednesday," he mused. "I have a day off. It would probably be useful to see for myself."

"Great," spluttered Nicholas, nodding enthusiastically. "Does that give you enough time though? If you need an amp, does that mean you'll need to play an electric guitar – are they very different, would you need time if you were going to switch over?" He jerked his head as he glanced about the room. "Do you have an electric one?"

Fynn laughed, low and assured. "This is an electro-acoustic," he said. He held it up so Nicholas could see the bottom, and sure enough, there was a plug jack for a cable to slot into. "So it won't matter. It'll just affect what equipment I bring on the day."

"Oh, cool. That's good then." Nicholas pulled at a loose thread on the chair, then realised it wasn't his chair to vandalise, and quickly sat on his hand. "Um, so, did you like the songs I sent you? I wasn't really sure."

Seeing as Fynn had barely replied with more than a word or two to any of the messages, if at all.

Honestly – was it that hard to formulate a sentence?

Fynn nodded, and began quietly noodling around a melody that Nicholas half recognised. "Yeah, there was some nice stuff there. A couple I already knew, too." He looked up, and stopped playing. "Can I make a few suggestions though?"

"Of course," said Nicholas, practically leaning forwards. Suggestions meant he was interested, that he cared.

Fynn took his time answering though, walking around the same melody a couple more times. "How about something released before 2010?"

Nicholas sat back again, and rubbed at his face. Hot shame crept into his belly at the implied criticism, and he couldn't help but rub again at his face with his thumb.

"So," he said, willing himself not to get upset or flush red. It was too much to look up, so he concentrated on the chair thread again. "You didn't actually like the songs."

From the corner of his eye, he could see Fynn frown. "Sure I did," he said. He was staring at Nicholas, so he sighed and glanced back up. Fynn rewarded him with a full smile, not just a half one, and Nicholas couldn't help but relax a little. "I just think it might be cool to play about a bit with the set – I'm guessing you'll have older guests there too? They'd probably appreciate some classics."

Nicholas bit his lip, and stopped rubbing his scar. "Okay," he conceded. "Like what? Something from the '90s?"

"Or '80s, or '70s," Fynn suggested, then laughed as Nicholas grimaced. "Not a fan?"

Nicholas shrugged. He was happy Fynn didn't want to dismiss his selection, just broaden it. But he didn't want any naff songs being played. Danielle was probably going to be miffed enough at him for swapping a harpist for a guitarist. He was sure that playing ABBA or Donny Osmund wouldn't earn him any favours either. "I don't know," he said, tugging at the thread again. "What were you thinking of?"

"Well," said Fynn. "How about this?"

He nestled his guitar further into his lap, and started plucking out some familiar chords.

"Oh," Nicholas couldn't help but utter as he sat up straight.

Fynn smiled, his eyes on his hands as he coaxed the melody out. "*Ohh ah ha haa ha,*" he sang, in barely more than a whisper. "*So true, funny how it seems. Always in time, never in line for dreams.*"

Nicholas edged the chair closer. "Spandau Ballet?" he asked, even though he knew that's who sang the original. Fynn nodded, and flashed his eyes up briefly along with a lopsided smile.

"*Why do I find it hard to write the next line? Oh, I want the truth to be said.*"

Nicholas was so mesmerised, he just stared for the first minute or so. But by the time the second chorus came around, he couldn't help himself. "*Ohh ah ha haa ha,*" he quietly joined in. "*I know this much is – truuuee.*"

Nicholas forced himself to be quiet for the rest of it, sitting on his hands and clamping his jaw together. That way, he could appreciate what Fynn was doing. After another minute or so, the song was done, and Nicholas didn't even think about whipping his hands free and applauding.

"That was lovely," he gushed. He clasped his hands into his lap to stop making any more of an idiot of himself. "Okay, yes. That kind of classic I can get behind. Any others?" Fynn laughed, and shook his head. "What?" Nicholas asked, only slightly defensively.

"Yes," said Fynn, almost entirely deadpan. "I have a few other songs from the last three decades."

Nicholas stuck his middle finger up at him, then laughed too. "Oh shut up. Well, go on then." He waved at Fynn imperiously.

He obediently launched into a very nice song which Nicholas later identified to be by Eurythmics. Then another by Michael Jackson, then one he recognised but couldn't name, then Bob Marley. Nicholas couldn't say that he felt reggae would be all that well received by the guests he knew were coming along, but he enjoyed listening to it all the same.

He didn't like a couple of sappy seventies ones, which he could tell irritated Fynn. He wasn't going to have songs played at his sister's wedding that he knew she wouldn't like. Even if it did pain him to see that frown on Fynn's face after the third rejection. So he frantically cast his thoughts open to suggest an alternative.

"What about something modern, but like—" He rubbed the back of his neck and picked the right words. "Unusual? Something most people wouldn't know?"

He was rewarded by Fynn's light eyes opening wide, and that half grin tweaking at the corner of his mouth. "Oh yeah, I've got a tonne of stuff you've probably never heard of. If you're sure?" Nicholas nodded, pleased again to have drawn out such enthusiasm.

"Go for it."

Fynn adjusted the small triangular plectrum in his fingers, then began the new song. It immediately sounded very sweet to Nicholas's ears, a clear line of melody floating above the slower chords. Fynn made some of his beautiful 'ooh' and 'ahh' noises that Nicholas was becoming accustomed to, rambling over the notes like a breeze drifting over a hill.

His voice came out in little more than a murmur. *"I was falling apart, I was lost and astray. I was a ship, drifting on the waves."* The words were wholly unfamiliar to Nicholas, but he absorbed them, finding himself nodding as Fynn carried on. *"I was looking for love, I was out in the cold. But then you came, and melted all the snow."*

Fynn leant back, pausing. He let the silence hang between them as he stared down at some point between him and the end of the bed. Then he inhaled gently.

"Like a plane, in the sky, you got me so high. Make me la la la, make me la la la." The words were a little nonsensical, but they sent a shiver down Nicholas's back nonetheless. *"In the darkest of nights, boy come be my light. Make me la la la, make me la la la."*

Not for the first time, Nicholas noticed that Fynn didn't change pronouns. Or, at least, he assumed he hadn't deviated from the original, seeing as he'd chosen to say 'boy'.

And, oh, *boy*, did that do something deep within him.

Fynn didn't play the whole song. He stopped after he finished the first chorus, and raised his eyebrows at Nicholas. "What did you think?"

It took Nicholas off guard, as he'd been expecting another couple of minutes to formulate his thoughts. "Yeah, yeah," he said gruffly. He cleared his throat and tried again. "Really pretty." Oh shit, should boys say 'pretty'? Probably not to each other. "You, know, nice, like, good for a wedding. Who sings it? The artist I mean." Who else would he mean? *Urgh.*

Fynn didn't seem too bothered though. If his smile was anything to go by, he didn't mind

Nicholas's prattling if it meant he liked his suggestion. "It's the acoustic version of a Melodifestivalen entry from a couple of years ago. The singer's called Dinah Nah. She has pink hair." Fynn ruffled his own, short dreads, and his eyes twinkled as he looked over at Nicholas.

"Oh," he said. But he could feel himself frowning. "What's Melody-thingamajig?"

Fynn shrugged, and dragged his pick down the guitar strings. "The Swedish competition for selecting their Eurovision entry. It's generally much better than the rest of Eurovision though," he added with a laugh.

"Well, yeah," scoffed Nicholas. "That's not hard, is it?"

Fynn frowned, and he realised he might have put his foot in it. Again. "Not a fan of that either, I take it?"

There was no stopping the heat rising into his cheeks this time, but he still rubbed them quickly regardless. "Erm, well, who is?" he asked meekly. "Eurovision is just so…"

"Gay?"

Nicholas spluttered. Ice flew through his body and made his fingers tingle. "No, I mean – well yeah, it's got a reputation for gay guys liking it I guess, I mean it is pretty camp. But I was, uh, I was going to say…" He trailed off. Which was more offensive? "Lame," he finally added, deciding he'd rather be a bit insulting to the show rather than come across as flat-out homophobic.

Fynn however chuckled, and shook his head. "Some of it is lame, really lame," he agreed, and the tension in Nicholas's chest eased a smidgen. "The UK is particularly bad at sending decent entries. But a lot of other countries take it very seriously, and there's a huge number of great songs that have come out of it over the past decade or so." He began playing the same tune again, this time quieter and looser around the rhythm. "Sweden is the top dog though. Maybe I could show you some of their better entries some time?"

"Oh, yeah, sure," Nicholas quickly agreed, keen to endear himself. Then he stopped to process what Fynn had actually said. 'Some time' sort of sounded like he wanted to hang out another day. Even though Fynn had just implied he might object to something – or someone – who was gay. "So, um," he began asking before his brain could catch up with his mouth. "Are you, um, you know?"

"What?" Fynn prompted patiently while Nicholas struggled to get the word out. He'd stopped playing again, and Nicholas was acutely aware of the sound of his own heartbeat in his ears.

"Gay?" As soon as he said it though, he regretted it. "Oh god, sorry. That's totally none of my business, forget I asked." He bit his lip, wondering if it was time to clamp his tongue between his teeth yet. "It's just, if you were, and I'd implied that I didn't like gay things, like Eurovision, that would be shitty. And not true!" he added, his voice almost a shout. He reached forward, his hand moving seemingly of its own accord. What did it hope to do? Grab Fynn's vest from six feet away? "I don't have a problem with you being gay, if you are. It's, like, a *not* issue. I shouldn't even ask you that though, sorry. It's not like you're asking me if I'm straight." He laughed weakly, then pressed his lips firmly shut.

Fynn was surely either going to flip out either way now. He'd properly put his foot in it. His expression was on the calmer side of neutral though, so Nicholas prayed he hadn't done irrevocable damage.

"Are you?" was all he asked.

Nicholas blinked. "Huh?"

Fynn chuckled again, lifting Nicholas's spirits somewhat. "Are you straight?"

Nicholas's mouth opened to say 'of course'. But all that came out was an "Uhhh" noise.

He had been avoiding answering that rather simple question for the past few days. Ever since he'd met Fynn in fact. But it had been on his mind for longer than that, he knew. Surely, he should just be able to dredge up a 'yes' or a 'no'. Hearing it out loud was very different to have it flit over the peripheral edge of his thoughts though.

Before the Christmas break, he and some of the girls from his hall had ventured into the Queenshilling for a drag show in town. He'd had no shortage of boys around him there who had tested his sexual uncertainty quite thoroughly. Particularly that cute Politics student, who had bought him a pint and, when they'd drunkenly stumbled into a dark corner away from his friends' prying eyes, had given him an extremely sweet kiss.

He had tried to tell himself in the few months between then and now that it was just a bit of inebriated fun. At the time, he'd just giggled shyly at the boy, and said thank you, but he was straight. But, if he was really honest, it had made him smile fondly many times when he'd been alone, and it might have also tentatively fuelled one or two of his more adventurous wank fantasies. More than a kiss with any girl had for sure.

Was he straight?

"I'm just messing with you," Fynn said once the silence had stretched on just a fraction too long. "Yes, I'm gay. So I hope that isn't a problem?"

"It's the twenty-first century," Nicholas snapped automatically, parroting his middle sister Lauren from one of her many outbursts. "Anyone who has a problem with people being gay is a moron."

That much, he was absolutely certain of. It was just whether or not he included himself in that category, he wasn't sure.

But Fynn was. He was gay and not afraid to tell someone he hardly knew. Admittedly, Nicholas probably didn't come across as much of a threat, but he wasn't stupid enough to think it was easy to announce something so personal about yourself to a near stranger.

How did he feel about that? The being gay thing? He was honest enough to admit he had become a bit infatuated with Fynn over the past couple of days. And to now know that Fynn himself was attracted to men…

Nicholas wasn't sure how to unpick that just yet, so he stowed it away for later.

Fynn raised his eyebrows again, and nodded at Nicholas's firm stance on homophobia. "Fair enough. You want to hear some more stuff?"

If he was willing to brush the whole, awkward exchange off, Nicholas was eager to jump on board. "Totally," he enthused. "Classics, or more unusual modern ones?"

Fynn gave him some samples of lesser known tracks that Nicholas was happy to approve of. He also strummed his way through a couple of '90s singer-songwriters like Tori Amos, Alanis Morissette and Sarah McLachlan, who he knew thanks to his mum's mild obsession with Lilith Fair. When he mentioned this, Fynn went on to play another few artists famous from the festival, and then a pretty awesome mash up of 'Tom's Diner' and 'Centuries'.

"Bloody hell," said Nicholas, shaking his head and rubbing the bridge of his nose under his glasses. "You know so many tracks. I didn't need to worry at all, did I?"

He gave a short laugh, and was inordinately pleased that Fynn smiled along with him. "It's important to me to get the best selection of songs though," he assured him. "It takes a while to get to know someone's tastes."

Nicholas hoped he was remembering his sister's tastes enough when making all these decisions. He wasn't half as sure about Peter's musical inclinations, but on the whole, if Clara was happy, then so was her husband-to-be.

"Hey, do you know this one?" Fynn asked.

He bent the first note, and Nicholas's heart all but leapt out of his chest.

Fynn didn't stop playing, but he watched as Nicholas's feet seemed to move of their own accord. Before he really knew what he was doing he had crawled onto the foot of the bed, and was sat cross-legged opposite Fynn, his eyes wide with astonishment.

"You know 'Boys of Summer'," he whispered.

He was graced with a full smile, rather than the usual half, as Fynn carried on playing the introduction. "We've found what you're a fan of, huh?"

Nicholas nodded, his eyes glued to the guitar strings as Fyn coaxed the melodies out. How many nights had he laid in bed, playing the song through his earbuds until he fell asleep? It was his go-to soothing track, the one that would whisk him away from whatever troubles were on his mind. He'd never heard music that sounded more like a sunset to him. It gave him hope that love was out there, that it was strong, but most of all, that it was beautiful. Just like the song was.

"*Nobody on the road,*" Fynn sang, and Nicholas couldn't stop himself joining in in a murmur. But

Fynn caught his eye, and nodded in encouragement, so he became a bit bolder. *"Nobody on the beach. I feel it in the air, the summer's out of reach."*

It was easier to watch Fynn's hands than his face, but Nicholas was happy anyway to keep his focus on those strong fingers as they worked the stings under their voices. It stirred something sensual in him, he realised with a jolt. Those hands could do anything.

"Empty lake, empty streets, the sun goes down alone. I'm driving by your house, but oh no, you're not ho-ome!"

Nicholas bounced as he belted out the chorus, his joy bubbling up from inside him.

"But I can seeee you, your brown skin shining in the sun. You got your hair pulled back, and your sunglasses on, baby. I can tellll you, my love for you will still be strong. After the boys of summer have gone."

His glasses had slid down his nose in his exuberance, and he pushed them up again as he grinned at Fynn. He was a little taken aback to realised that Fynn was just watching him as he played, his smile still firmly in place. Nicholas had been singing alone.

But Fynn nodded and raised his eyebrows. "Keep going," he rasped, repeating the intro to the next verse to give Nicholas a chance to come in on time.

"Oh," he said. He rubbed his neck and felt awkward, but Fynn was waiting, expectantly.

He knew the words off by heart, without hesitation, even though the lyrics in the chorus varied slightly every time. His skin was hot as this beautiful guy allowed him to serenade him about how he'd always love him, even after all the other boys had gone. His pulse raced, and he couldn't stop smiling.

"*Remember how you made me crazy? Remember how I made you scream?*" He had to close his eyes to get through that lyric.

He wasn't sure if he hit all the notes, but whenever he glanced up to catch Fynn's expression, he never found him wincing or scowling, so he hoped he wasn't that bad.

"You have a nice voice," he told Nicholas as he wrapped up the end of the song, negating the fade-out from Don Henley's original.

Nicholas didn't even try to quell the blush that blossomed on his face. "Nah," he mumbled. "I just love that song – oh!" He turned and looked at the bedroom door in horror. "Your aunt's on the phone, she was probably cursing my name!"

"I've been singing for over an hour," Fynn said, deadpan, and arched an eyebrow.

Nicholas shrunk back again, his hands in his lap. "Yeah," he mumbled. "But you're really good."

"I liked it." Fynn's tone was dismissive as he looked at the time on his phone, and Nicholas guessed he'd irritated him. God, what had he been thinking, jumping in like that? He'd probably majorly embarrassed himself.

"Sorry," he muttered. But Fynn wasn't listening.

"Shit, is that the time?" Nicholas glanced over at the screen. It had been more like two hours they'd been playing for. "Sorry mate, I've got to get to work."

He hauled up the guitar case between them and Nicholas flinched at the thump it made on the bed. "Oh, sorry, right," he said. He hopped off the bed and rubbed his arms. "I guess, um, do you need me to go then?"

"Unfortunately, yeah," said Fynn, shrugging and not looking up. He carefully placed the guitar in the soft velvet sheathing, and closed the case once more. "My shift starts in forty-five minutes, and I need to take a shower."

"No, no worries," Nicholas assured him. He watched as Fynn darted past him into the en-suite. He snapped the now-dry umbrella down, and handed it back out to Nicholas without looking at him. "I think I heard enough, you know?" Nicholas babbled as Fynn got the water running. "Why don't you send me a final set list, if you want?"

"Sure, whatever," said Fynn absently. He started peeling his t-shirt off, and Nicholas very much took that as his cue to leave.

"Right, well, uh," he said, backing away towards the door. "I'll uh, talk to you later, maybe. And I'll definitely see you at the wedding, so, um, yeah thanks. Text me if you have any questions."

"Will do," Fynn told him. He hung onto the door frame, but Nicholas could still see the corner of his naked chest. And then he winked. "See ya."

He shut the door with a bang, and Nicholas spun on his heels, back out into the flat. He was down the corridor in no time, and jammed his feet back into his still soggy trainers, making his socks damp again. He opened the front door without even checking to see where Fynn's aunt was, or thinking about saying goodbye.

He raced down the stairs and back out into the rain, as fast as his feet would carry him.

Chapter Six

(4 days to go…)

It was precisely 02:17 when Nicholas sat bolt upright in bed, his forehead prickled with cold sweat.

He fumbled for the phone that was plugged in and charging on his bedside table. He yanked it free of the cord so he could frantically unlock the security screen. He wasn't sure if he'd dreamed up the realisation, or if reality had summoned something unholy to poke him in the soles of his feet to wake him up.

'*OMG!!! I LEFT THE TIES FOR MY SISTER'S WEDDING IN YOUR ROOM!!!*' He took a moment to inhale deeply, and not freak out completely. '*At least I think I did??? PLEASE LET ME KNOW IF I DID?!? If so, can I please come and get them back off you tomorrow. Or, sometime before Friday. Anytime. I'm in sooooo much trouble if my family find out. If they're not there, I need to go back to several places in town, I just can't remember – no, I'm sure I had them at yours. Gah, sorry, your probably asleep, so just text me in the am. THANK YOU!!*'

He smacked the send button, then read the long message back.

'**You're, not your. Urgh! Sorry. Sleep well x*'

He pressed send too quickly, again, and just stared at the kiss in dismay he'd added automatically in his sleepy state. Well, things could hardly get any worse. If Fynn hadn't taken offense by now, a little kiss was hardly going to upset him. Unless it was the final straw, and he never wanted to speak to Nicholas again.

He was being overly dramatic. Or, at least, he hoped he was. He'd done a pretty good job of embarrassing himself the day before, after all. He'd been too eager, blathering on like usual and then singing all over that song. He winced at the memory, and draped his arm over his forehead. The streetlight slipping between the slim gap in his curtains just about made the objects in his room visible despite the fact his glasses were on the table next to where the phone had been lying. He stared despondently at the ceiling as he tried to calm his heart rate back down.

The ties were bound to be in Fynn's room, he was almost certain of it. He remembered bringing them in with the umbrella, making sure they stayed dry. Had he left them on the bed or the desk? It had to be one of the two.

He squeezed the locked phone in his fist. Why did he have to be such a disaster? He'd never stood a chance of impressing somebody as talented and cool as Fynn. He just seemed so *together*. Nicholas was just an idiot who he was probably looking forward to getting rid of.

What did Nicholas expect, really? That they could ever be friends? That was laughable, they didn't have anything in common, except that maybe they were both guys.

Could they ever be boyfriends, then? a voice in the back of his head whispered.

So, Fynn was gay. The thought kept sneaking up on him, no matter how hard he tried to dispel the notion that it might be of some significance to him. Somehow knowing that was the case made a difference. Nicholas kept thinking that if he maybe *did* want to kiss Fynn, there was now a possibility Fynn might want to kiss him back.

"Urgh," he said to himself. That was ridiculous, Fynn would never be interested in someone like him. Just because they both might be that way inclined.

But was he? Was Nicholas gay? Or maybe bi? Two-thirty on a Tuesday morning seemed about as good as any time to finally think about it.

When boys at school had gone mental over Gigi Hadid, Emma Stone and Ariana Grande, he'd always just assumed he was picky. Or that he needed to meet the right girl, in person, before he could really feel that spark.

But he needed to be honest with himself. Thinking about that kiss in the Queenshilling, and especially the way Fynn was occupying his thoughts; maybe he just needed to meet the right *boy*. When his mates had been gushing about how much they wanked over that dragon chick from *Game of Thrones*, he agreed as much just to fit in. But how did that compare to the flair of excitement he'd always felt at seeing Hunter Ford saunter into a classroom?

He'd been another one too cool for school, though not a quarter as talented as Fynn. He'd come from America and exuded a fuck-you sort of attitude, but also while managing to keep himself in the top sets of almost all the classes. He'd gone through half the girls in their year, the year below and even some from the year above. Nicholas was embarrassed to remember how many daydreams he'd had imagining Hunter finally noticing him, maybe inviting him to hang out with his mates after school, doing whatever it was the cool kids did.

Nicholas had always just thought he was desperate to be friends because then that would make him cool too. But 'friends', to his mind, had meant Hunter talking with him, sharing private jokes at the back of the classroom like he did with his other cronies. Nicholas hadn't seen him since they'd both gone to different colleges to do their A-Levels at the age of sixteen. Now, with a few years gone by, he was pretty sure that Hunter was a wanker and bully, and would probably have been a lousy friend. But it hadn't stopped Nicholas imagining just the two of them, hanging out in his room…

What if he was there in his room right *then*. He bit his lip, and considered it, picturing Hunter and his mop of light brown hair and perfect smile, the way his jeans always clung to his hipbones like they might slip at any moment. How would it feel if Nicholas was to roll over on his side, and have him there beside him?

For a split second, as he turned his head and looked at the other pillow in the gloom, he imagined it to be Fynn. But that was way too close to home right then. No, if he was experimenting, Hunter seemed like a safer option.

He had his phone still gripped in his left hand, and he didn't want to move too much least he break the cloud of lust that had settled over his skin. He just closed his eyes, and let his right hand slip under the covers, trailing down the t-shirt he was wearing over his chest. He imagined Hunter would be the kind to smile a lot when he was making out. He'd laugh softly and sweetly as Nicholas's breath hitched, giving him little fluttery kisses like he used to do to the girls that sat on his lap in the common room.

Nicholas let his fingers tease the edge of the elasticated waistband of his boxers. Just to test, he tried imagining it was Ash's hand, that she'd crept down from that attic room to see him. But even picturing it made him grimace, dampening the fizz in his abdomen. Maybe Ash wasn't the right girl; and he briefly thought about the lovely Gigi in her leather outfit from the 'Bad Blood' video. Nothing really tingled for him, so he went back to Hunter.

Hunter had had beautiful hands. He didn't do anything particularly useful with them, like play sports or make art, or even write much down. But they'd been big with long sturdy fingers. Nicholas let himself squirm a little, envisaging his hand dipping below Nicholas's boxers, stroking over the tight curls that crept up from between his legs, reaching down until-

Nicholas jerked so hard he was in danger of falling out of the bed. His phone had pinged, vibrating in his hand to alert him of a text message.

He sucked in a lungful of air and shook his head, irrational guilt flaring in his chest. He was allowed to wank in his own bed for crying out loud. But when he saw Fynn's name on the screen, he felt a flurry of a whole bunch of emotions on top of the guilt. There was excitement at seeing his name, bewilderment that he'd be awake as well at this time of night, and then another fresh wave of guilt. Except, he couldn't work out if it was guilt over almost touching himself while thinking about him…or that in the end he'd been thinking of someone else.

That was beyond ridiculous. He wasn't – what? Cheating? That was an utterly stupid notion.

Still, he righted his boxers and smoothed down his t-shirt before opening the message.

'Hey, yeah, no sweat, they're here. Wanna swing by tomorrow and get them? Any time before 4pm. We can jam again if you like :)'

Nicholas blinked to make sure he was reading it right, then leant over to get his glasses just in case. Not only had Fynn replied, promptly, in the middle of the night, but he'd used more than one or two words. In fact, he'd used over two dozen (not that Nicholas counted). And a smiley face.

Nicholas's chest thumped a bit louder than normal as he started tapping a reply. He was glad no one else was there to see his ridiculous grin. *'OMG thank you! I'm so relieved :) I'm such a fucking moron, I'll come over as soon as I can. Thanks again :)'*

He breathed out in relief as he sent the message off. It was okay, he hadn't fucked something else up.

The text alert made him lift his phone up from where he'd rested it on his chest. *'You're not a fucking moron. I kicked you out. My fault.'*

Nicholas read the words several times. They were short, but there was something sort of sweet about them too. *'Lol, thanks, but I'd firmware my head if it wasn't screwed on, I swear. So how come you're up so late?'*

He really needed to start reading his messages before he sent them.

'Forget!! Not firmware, jeeze auto correct, how'd you work that one out?'

He stared at the screen, until the little dots started bouncing up and down, indicating that Fynn was replying. *'Haha. Got in from work, then started watching Netflix. Always dangerous.'*

'Oh yeah, but I love it!' Nicholas quickly typed back. *'Watching anything good?'*

'Daredevil.'

'*OMG, I LOVE DAREDEVIL! Which season? I love the fight scenes, so well choreographed, and the writing and acting and directing is all so good.*'

He began to glare at his screen as the response was not forthcoming. But after a few minutes spent with his heart slowly creeping into his mouth, he exhaled as the dots started dancing again.

'*Very good. Just finished an episode. Gonna head to sleep if you're gonna be around. Text when you're on your way.*'

Nicholas smiled. Fynn wanted him to come over, and he was going to sleep so he'd be refreshed so they could play again. That didn't sound like he was terribly pissed off with him. Kind of the opposite.

'*Yeah, good idea. I think I'll do the same now I know I don't have to trawl through all of St Albans tomorrow lol. Thanks again, sorry for being a bother. See you tomorrow.*'

'*You're not a bother ;)*'

That had come so fast, Nicholas almost missed it as he went to lock his phone and go back to sleep. He let the words soak over him. *You're not a bother.* But he was; he was a pain in the arse who'd forgotten to book a harpist and left half a dozen silk ties lying around like old rubbish. What did he say to that? How did he translate the warmth that had settled on his chest like a purring cat? (Not a cat like Archibald, obviously. A nice one. A kitten even.)

In the end, he just went with a simple smiley. '*:) Night night x*' He chose to put the kiss on, and held his breath.

'*Night night x*'

Nicholas's jaw dropped open. He held the screen right in front of his nose, and peered through the curved lenses of his glasses. What did that mean? Had Fynn sent him a kiss, too, on purpose? Goose bumps flurried over his skin as he finally let the screen go blank, and he rested the phone once more on his bedside table, along with his glasses.

What if he'd done it on purpose?

It took a long time for Nicholas to fall asleep again, what with all the thoughts chasing around his head. But eventually, he figured it was okay if, just in the privacy of his own head, he pretended that Fynn really had sent him a kiss, and meant it.

***

Thanks to his late night, Nicholas slept through everyone leaving for work again. He was grateful for the rest though as he stretched and rolled out of bed to relieve himself in the bathroom.

When he got down to the kitchen, he was met with the site of Kinny washing up in the same colourful pyjamas she had worn the last couple of days. She was bouncing along to the radio, and even from behind Nicholas could see how that made her boobs jiggle nicely without a bra.

He glanced inwardly at himself, probing for any kind of excitement. *Nope. Nothing.* Like it or not, he was pretty sure the crisis he'd been going through the past few years had finally come to a head. *I'm gay.* Wow. That wasn't the kind of realisation you faced up to every day. He had to admit there was something freeing about admitting it to himself.

Ash was at the table in her usual tiny PJs, her knees drawn up to her chest as she watched Kinny dance to Rhianna, a faint smile on her face, her fingers wrapped around a cup of tea.

"Morning," said Nicholas cheerfully, going to the fridge.

Ash jumped so badly she sloshed her tea all over the table, and she leapt from the chair so as to avoid it running into her lap.

Kinny turned around and laughed kindly. "Oh dear," she tittered, then bent over to wipe the tea off with the washing up sponge. "Morning Nicholas, you sleep alright?"

She seemed totally oblivious to the beetroot shade Ash was turning, and Nicholas frowned at her in confusion. What on Earth had that been about. "Yeah, great," he said. Which, apart from the fright he'd given himself, was the truth. He was still buzzing from his chat with Fynn, and couldn't wait to see him later on.

He felt like he had permission to be excited now. Even if it was solely kept private for the time being, it was scintillating to allow himself a little hope of something more with Fynn.

"I need to get to work," Ash announced, loudly. She stood with her hands in fists by her legs, stiff as a board as Nicholas and Kinny turned to look at her. She looked between Nicholas and the fridge. "Don't go in the bottom drawer. I had to bring some work home with me. Some of it's not stable." Then she spun on her heels and all but sprinted out of the kitchen.

Nicholas blinked. Surely she was joking? But he opened up the fridge door, and found the vegetable drawer on the right had been emptied. It was now filled with several neatly stacked petri dishes. His eyes widened. That really couldn't be okay. Also, his theory about Ash working in retail was obviously way off the mark.

He looked back at Kinny to see if she found this as bizarre as he did, but she was preoccupied with the suds in the sink. "That's um, a bit odd, right?" He nodded into the fridge.

Kinny just chuckled though, and didn't look up from the washing up. "You must have really scared her," she said. She must have though he meant the way she'd jumped and sloshed her tea. Which had been a bit off as well.

Nicholas shrugged, not quite sure what to make of it. "You know we have a dishwasher?" he said, changing the subject.

"Nah," Kinny said. She shook her head and glanced over her shoulder at him. "When it's only a couple of things, you might as well get them sorted right away."

Nicholas couldn't say he agreed. He felt dishwashers were there for exactly that reason – to be loaded up with as much as possible, until nothing more could physically fit, then all you had to do with shove in a tablet and press a button. Easy.

It was sweet that Kinny was such a conscious houseguest, so he didn't say anything. No way his mates Trev or Jones would be that thoughtful, he knew.

"Everyone leave okay?" he asked as he fished out the milk bottle and closed the fridge door.

It turned out there had been no drama that morning, but there was still a bit of tension left over from the night before. Although Kinny said it nicer than that. "Danielle was still worrying a bit," she admitted.

Danielle had lost the plot just a tad last night when she had realised the bridesmaid dresses were missing. Nicholas and the girls had been fully intending to tell her, and everyone else, about what had happened with Archibald. But at Danielle's near-immediate hysterics, the three of them had unanimously bottled it. Kinny had done a great job smiling it off, saying they were at the dry cleaners, but Danielle couldn't seem to get over the fact that they had made a wedding decision without consulting her.

"I just don't know *what* you were thinking?" she kept saying all evening.

She laughed every time she said it, but it was too high pitched for Nicholas to trust that she was really joking. Peter did his best, plying her with several glasses of wine and praising her on the excellent job she'd done on finalising the table plan display board for the guests when they walked into the room. He was going to be a good brother-in-law, Nicholas could tell.

Thankfully, that little to-do had the unexpected benefit of making everyone too distracted to notice the ties were also missing. If he had any luck, Nicholas would be able to get back from Fynn's house before anyone thought to ask, and he could just claim they had been kept safely in his room the whole time.

Once he'd had a simple bowl of cereal for breakfast and finished chatting with Kinny, he took himself off to have a proper shower, complete with a thorough shave. Fynn might have been able to get away with stylish stubble, but it just made him look scruffy.

He picked out another favourite t-shirt to pair with a chequered shirt he had got for his birthday a few months ago. He even dug through his drawers to get out an old necklace he'd picked up on holiday last year. It was just an adjustable leather thong with a silver pendent in the shape of a symbol that apparently meant 'truth'. Although Nicholas was aware that could have been the locals having a tourist on, and it probably meant 'canoe' or 'dog'. But it was kind of cool, and he thought maybe Fynn might like it.

He finally got to put his contacts back in. After several days without them, his eyeballs had been grateful for the respite, but his nose was getting that mark over the bridge that he didn't like. He fussed over his hair, and even put on some aftershave he'd left behind when he'd moved out into uni halls in September.

"This isn't a date," he muttered to his reflection as he put bio oil on his scars. But he smirked back at himself. Maybe not, but it wasn't really professional either. It definitely felt like they were meeting up as friends.

He snatched up his phone from his bedside table and unlocked it to send a message to Fynn letting him know he was on his way. He already had a text waiting for him though, and for a second he hoped it was Fynn. But it was Trev, also back home from uni, wondering if he was going to join them going out in the evening.

Nicholas dithered in deliberation for a while wondering how best to reply. One the one hand, he'd quite like to see his school friends, it had been a while. On the other hand, going to a club wasn't really what he fancied at the moment, he'd much rather go down the pub for a chat rather than thrust himself into a packed, sweaty crowd and attempt to dance. Plus, with the wedding coming up, it didn't really feel right to go out and party.

In the end, he mostly told the truth. '*Would be great to see you, but wedding stuff is hectic. I'll let you know :)*'

Then he tapped out a quick note to let Fynn know he was leaving, and would probably get there in about half an hour.

Unfortunately, it was still pouring with rain from an iron-grey sky. Nicholas stared forlornly up at it from the threshold of the front door, and sighed heavily. The best he could do was put a more waterproof pair of boots on, and walk quickly.

He'd already explained to Kinny that he was going out for a while to see a friend. It was their last day before everyone else's annual leave kicked in and the place became a madhouse again, so she was happy to be left alone to get her marking and planning done, encouraging Nicholas to go have fun. Nicholas said he'd try, a shiver of anticipation flurrying over his skin.

With a yell goodbye, he slammed the door and trudged out into the rain. At least he had his music on his phone to keep him company, and he put the whole lot of random so it could surprise him as he made the journey across town.

He could get a bus for part of the way, but the rest of the route was a bit convoluted, and left him sloshing through the deluge. *This better bloody clear up by Saturday*, he challenged the universe as he shivered outside Fynn's apartment complex once more.

He answered the intercom himself this time, after only a few seconds. *"Come on in,"* came his low voice over the speaker. He also let him promptly through the second door, and was waiting by the flat's front door with a lazy half smile. "You lose your glasses?"

Nicholas paused in front of him, and then realised Fynn had only ever seen him in his specs until now. "Oh, no," he said, a little breathlessly touching his face. He wasn't sure if it was more from the run up the stairs, or the fact the Fynn had noticed a change in his appearance immediately. "I've got my lenses in today – it's easier with the rain."

Fynn nodded in understanding. "Still tipping it down then?" he asked, indicating the dripping umbrella that Nicholas trailed behind him as he entered the flat.

"Yeah, sorry," said Nicholas. He handed it over when Fynn offered wordlessly to take it, and quickly unzipped his boots in the hallway where he'd left his trainers the day before.

Fynn chuckled. "You apologise a lot, did you know that?" Nicholas blinked at him. "It's not your fault it's raining, is it?"

"Yeah," replied Nicholas with a frown. "But, I am dripping all over your aunt's floors again, aren't I?"

Fynn propped the umbrella up in the corner of the untidy kitchen. "Sure, okay. Cup of tea?"

"Uh, yeah, thanks," said Nicholas with a shrug, and followed him in. There didn't appear to be anyone in the living room. "Is your aunt home?"

"Why, do you want to apologise to her too?" Before Nicholas could feel the sting of the barb though, Fynn glanced over his shoulder and winked. "She's teaching today."

"Oh," said Nicholas, uncertainly. "But it Easter's holiday?"

The kettle boiled and Fynn concentrated on making to mugs for a moment. "Milk? Sugar?"

"One sugar, lots of milk."

Fynn nodded, making one mug to Nicholas's specification, and the other the colour of mud with only the barest hint of milk. "Ellen's a lecturer, at one of the London unis. I think she has a guest conference in this week, visiting from far and wide." He smiled as he handed Nicholas his weak tea. "So we have the place to ourselves."

That sent a hot flush through Nicholas's innards, and he focused very hard on taking his tea in both hands. "What does she teach?"

Fynn tapped a fingernail on his mug, and stared out into the hallway in concentration. "It's something to do with human geography, socio-economic patterns. I think," he added with a huffed laugh.

"Oh," Nicholas perked up. "I study economics. And maths, so not really the same thing, but yeah. Over in Bristol. It's nice there, have you ever been?" Fynn took a sip of tea, and shook his head. "Oh, well, yeah, I'm enjoying it. Still in my first year, but it's got off to a good start. Are you at uni?" he asked Fynn. "Or, I mean, did you go? You'd have graduated now, unless you took a few gap years..." He trailed off. Not even five minutes and he was already unable to control his mouth. Fynn was going to regret inviting him back, that was for sure.

He picked up the wet umbrella though and inclined his head towards the door, indicating to Nicholas that they should head into the hall. "I went to performing arts college," he said as they walked back down to his bedroom. Once again, it was neat and tidy with the bed pristinely made. "Graduated a couple of years ago."

"Oh, wow, that's cool," Nicholas said. He plonked himself down on the desk chair again, and watched Fynn put the umbrella once more in the en-suite. He was trying not to be a dork, but he really was impressed. "That's awesome, honestly. I've never been good on stage, I always freeze up." He laughed. "So, do you dance and act and all that as well?"

That got a laugh from Fynn too. "Occasionally I was made to act, but it was never really my thing. I like dancing, but it was always about the music for me."

"Oh my god." Nicholas put his mug down of the desk (by the tie package, he noticed) and clasped his hands under his chin. "Is there footage of you somewhere doing musical theatre?" Fynn cocked an eyebrow at him, and slurped

119

meaningfully from his tea as he perched on the bed. "There is, there so is!" Nicholas crowed in delight. "Oh go on, what did they make you do? *Little Shop of Horrors? Les Mis?* Oh, oh! *West Side Story?*"

Fynn growled. It was a rather delicious sound. "It was *Fame*," he said reluctantly. "Of course, I had to be Tyrone, the troubled black kid." He grimaced. "And they made me kiss a girl."

Nicholas was surprised at how genuine and relaxed his laughter was at that. Bringing up both the gay thing and the race thing in one breath could have been awkward, but Fynn wasn't treating it as such, so neither did Nicholas.

"So, the West End wasn't for you then?"

Fynn rolled his eyes. "Hardly anyone makes it there, you know. It's pretty depressing. But, no. I always knew I wanted to make music." At that, he got his guitar back out again. He leant back against the pillows of his bed, and stretched his legs out as he gave the strings a quick tune up.

Nicholas pulled at his trusty thread on the chair again. "So, you write you own music too?" Fynn nodded, and began to tease a melody out of the instrument quietly. He was so in sync with it, Nicholas found it hard to picture him ever being without it in his hands. "Can, I mean…" He bit his lip. "Would you play me something of yours?"

Fynn gave him a tight smile. "Maybe. One day." That was a no then. "I have a demo out with several producers right now. I'm waiting to hear back, see if they think it's worth investing in."

"Jesus, fuck," Nicholas spluttered. "That's so epic, have you really? How many tracks? Like, a whole album?"

To his delight, Fynn looked pleased with his enthusiasm. "There's eleven songs at the moment, all original. But you never know with these things.

Nicholas realised his mouth was open, so he picked up his tea again for something to do with it. "So, you're going to be a recording artist?"

Fynn smiled warmly at him, both corners tugging up in that way Nicholas was starting to treasure. "I'd love to record one real album," Fynn said. He watched his fingers work the strings and the plectrum for a while, then looked back up at Nicholas. "I love performing other people's songs too, so I was already looking to get into function stuff when you approached me. And I've done session work. It keeps me busy."

Nicholas felt proud of himself for no good reason whatsoever. All he'd done was fail to book any other musician, and asked Fynn as a last resort. But, still. It felt nice that Fynn had been wanting to do weddings and stuff, and the universe had put them together at just the right time. Sort of like serendipity.

"So, is that your evening job then?" Nicholas guessed, aware he was asking a lot of questions. But Fynn didn't seem to mind. "Session work?"

Fynn chuckled ruefully, and rolled his eyes. "I wish. I wait tables at one of the Italian places in town."

"Oh," said Nicholas, unsure of how else to respond. He knew he was lucky; he and his sisters had never had to work while they were studying. Their parents insisted they focused all their time on their education. "Is it one of the good ones?" he asked instead.

"You'll have to pop by some time," Fynn said, "and find out."

That was the second time in this visit alone he'd alluded to seeing each other again. If he wasn't careful, Nicholas was going to get his hopes up.

"How about you?" Fynn asked, moving the conversation forward and sparing Nicholas the trouble of having to work out how to answer his downright flirty proposition. Because that couldn't be right – someone like Fynn would never flirt with someone like Nicholas. Even if they were both that way inclined. "You know what you want to do after uni?"

Nicholas finished his tea and shrugged, listening to the rain tapping against the window over Fynn's gentle strumming. "Not really, I still have a while to figure it out. And I might do a masters too, to get the extra qualifications." He wound the thread from the chair around his finger, making the tip go pink, then white. "Maybe some sort of analyst? I'm really good at seeing patterns in things."

"I can tell," Fynn told him, nodding. But that made Nicholas frown.

"How?" he asked, genuinely bemused. They'd never even mentioned maths until today.

Fynn jutted the guitar neck towards him. "You've got a good musical ear. And rhythm. Being good at maths isn't that different."

Nicholas scoffed. "Yeah, right," he said, rubbing bashfully at his face. "I'm tone deaf."

Fynn arched an eyebrow at him. "No, you're not." He stopped playing and patted the bed duvet by his knees, indicating the end of the bed. "Why don't you sing again, I'm sure we can find something else you know they words to."

Nicholas stared at the spot he'd indicated with his hand. Fynn was inviting him to sit with him again. Bloody hell. "I thought the point was for me to listen to you sing?" he asked weakly.

Fynn didn't seem perturbed. "We can both sing. Do you know 'Wild Horses'?"

As a matter of fact, Nicholas's dad was a pretty big Stones fan. Nicholas didn't know the words off by heart, but he knew the tune, so figured he could get the lyrics up on his phone. "It's a bit depressing for a wedding though, isn't it?"

Fynn grinned. "Which is why I didn't play it yesterday. But it's one of my favourites to sing. We can just muck about a bit, for the fun of it. You gonna join me?"

It seemed like an awfully big distance between the desk chair and the bed, but as apprehensive as Nicholas was, he wasn't about to annoy Fynn, or pass up on an opportunity to get closer to him. So he rallied his courage, and nipped across the gap.

'Wild Horses' was one of those songs that a lot of people had a crack at, but Nicholas did genuinely think it was so beautiful it was pretty hard to ruin. His mum had a version by Charlotte Martin that she and his dad played when they were being sappy, and as much as Nicholas and his sisters would protest, he did think it was really sweet.

With the lyrics up on his phone screen, he was able to keep up with Fynn as he made his way through the first few lines. Nicholas kept his voice quiet, following Fynn's lead as he wandered around some of the melodies, but after a while he began to relax.

"*I know I've dreamed you a sin and a lie, I have my freedom but I don't have much time,*" they sang. It was Nicholas's favourite bit. "*Faith has been broken, and tears must be cried. So let's do some living after we die. And wi-ld horses couldn't drag me away. No, wi-ld horses couldn't drag me away. Couldn't drag me away.*"

"It is sad, isn't it," Nicholas commented once they were done. "I mean, it's beautiful but I kind of feel like their love is over, and he – she – whoever can't let it go."

Fynn nodded. "I get it, though," he said, starting up another tune that Nicholas didn't know. "You can't rely on people, they'll just let you down. But, if you can make something so timeless out of it – that pain – then I think it's worth it."

Nicholas sat back, and gave a nervous laugh as he considered him. "Wow," he said. "Bleak, bitter millennial, much?" he teased, but he did sort of mean it.

"Not bitter," said Fynn, unfazed. "Practical."

"That you can't rely on people – anyone? Ever?"

Fynn shrugged. "Not completely, no. Art lasts. People don't." Before Nicholas could respond to that particularly pessimistic statement, he flashed him a grin. "Hey, do you know this one?"

Nicholas let the comment drop, but it niggled away at the back of his mind as they worked their way through a few more songs. Did Fynn really believe people were just destined to let him down? That didn't sound very promising.

Nicholas wondered again where his parents were.

Fynn distracted him though by launching into a favourite Killers track of his, and by the time Nicholas was done belting his way through 'Mr Brightside', jumping around the room like a deranged lunatic, he'd forgotten all about the bleakness of their last conversation.

Chapter Seven

Sadly, after a couple of hours, Nicholas had to call it a day. "There's something complicated going on with fairy lights this evening," he admitted to Fynn as he triple-checked he had the package of ties in his hands. He couldn't forget them again, because then Fynn would think he was doing it on purpose to make an excuse to see him, and that would be pure mortification. "The whole family has to be there, and my job is to unbox everything before they arrive."

"Hey, no worries man," said Fynn. He clapped him on the back as they both stood, and Nicholas froze. He was pretty sure that was the first time they'd touched. They might have shaken hands, but to feel his solid presence on his back...

He got a hold of himself. "It's been fun."

Fynn retrieved his now-dry umbrella for him. "Yeah," he agreed. "Well, I'm checking out the town hall tomorrow. You're welcome to join me, if you're not buried under a mountain of confetti."

Nicholas laughed, but it was a serious concern. "Sure, uh. Sounds great." He really didn't have much of a clue why Fynn was keen to keep hanging out with him, but he couldn't bring himself to question it too much. He just wanted to enjoy it while it lasted.

Nicholas did an awkward thing where he paused at the front door too long, then stepped back with a nervous laugh. "Right, see you later," he said, then turned to head for the stairwell without looking back. He didn't hear the door close, but Fynn probably just did it quietly.

The walk back seemed quicker than before, despite the fact Nicholas decided not to wait for a bus as the traffic was bad. He hummed along with the music blaring from his earbuds, the ties clutched protectively to his chest.

When he got home, it was just Kinny still, and although she said hello and had a quick chat with him about the weather (with them both determined not to start panicking just yet) he could tell she was still busy with her work. Instead, he headed upstairs with a beer, put on one of his latest playlists on his laptop, and tried on his entire wedding outfit.

The ushers were all hiring matching suits to complement the groom, but Nicholas hadn't wanted to intrude on Peter and his friends. He got on well with the guy, but he hadn't been upset not to have been included in the wedding party. He and his mates had been close since school, where they'd run the role-playing society for three or four years. Sometimes their Warhammer matches and Dungeons & Dragons games lasted for hours (or years if you counted whole campaigns) and they had all these old in jokes that were sometimes hard to follow.

It had been enough for Nicholas to go on the stag do, which had involved LARPing in the woods. They'd been completely smashed, so the whole thing had been pretty hilarious. He was glad to leave them to it for the wedding preparations, and anyway, on the day, he would definitely want to help look after Clara, who was bound to be nervous.

So that meant he'd been free to sort out his own suit, and he had to say, thanks to a little help from a rather fabulous shop assistant, he thought he'd done a bang-up job. He'd decided to go for an inversion of the colour scheme, so while all the groomsmen would be sporting black suits, silver waistcoats, white shirts and pink cravats, he'd gone the other way. His suit was silvery grey, and was tailored perfectly to his slim frame. He had a black shirt, white pearl cufflinks, and a beautiful pink bowtie. The bowtie had only just been delivered over the weekend, as had his black and white spats shoes, so this was his first time trying on the whole ensemble.

He felt really cool and stylish as he twirled around admiring his reflection in the mirror, and maybe just a little bit cute. He hoped Fynn would like it, and blushed at his silent optimism. Tomorrow he should ask Fynn what he was planning on wearing; not that he was worried he'd make a faux pas, more so he could picture it in his head before the big day.

By the time he'd carefully packed everything away again, he'd finished his beer. So he went downstairs to fetch himself another, then opened the door to the den to face the fairy lights. He noticed Archibald had made himself pretty scarce since the dress incident, and Nicholas suspected the cat knew that this time, he had really fucked up.

He sat himself on the floor and carefully unwound the first lot of the boxes of lights like he'd been told, then began slowly wrapping them around some wicker wreaths his mum had bought from a craft wholesaler. He heard voices as people started to arrive back home, but nobody came in to bother him until Danielle came home.

"Oh, there you are," she sighed by way of a greeting. As if he wasn't doing exactly what she'd asked him too. "There's been a disaster, you better come into the kitchen."

Nicholas's heart plummeted. Had she found out about the dresses? Or the harp? Not knowing what to expect, he made sure to lay the lights down where they wouldn't get tangled, and closed the door behind himself as he headed to the kitchen.

The island was covered in pizza boxes, and he sighed happily as the smell of hot cheese and meat hit his nose. His dad handed him another beer. "You had a good day mate?" he asked as they both cracked their bottle tops off.

"Yeah, sure," he said, eyeing up everyone as they scrambled to get into the pizza boxes. Well, everyone except Danielle, who was stubbornly blending another green something-or-other. He waited until she was finished and the noise had diminished. "So, what's the big emergency?"

"Oh, it's not that bad," his mum assured him as she handed out plates to people.

Danielle huffed, and Clara swallowed her bite of chicken wing. "Aunt Sally has food poisoning," she said gravely.

Nicholas frowned. That was it? Sally and her family were coming down from Scotland, but they weren't flying until Friday evening. That gave her three whole days to recover. Four until the actual wedding.

"Umm," he said. That was nothing compared to the bridesmaid dresses, which, admittedly not everyone knew about, but still, he wasn't sure he was seeing the catastrophe. "That's a shame," he offered.

Danielle huffed. "If she can't come, it's a disaster."

"Well, yeah, it'll be a shame," Peter agreed. He still had his Games Workshop polo shirt on, which was unfortunate as a big dollop of barbecue sauce dripped down his front. "Ahh shit – oh, sorry." He looked guiltily around at Nicholas's parents, but they didn't care about things like a spot of bad language.

"Oh don't worry love," Nicholas's mum said, proving him right. She handed him a sheet of kitchen roll to wipe it off. "I'll just pop it in the wash later. Robert, is your sister really not well?"

Nicholas's dad sighed, and swallowed a mouthful of pizza. "She had to go to hospital today."

"Oh no," Kinny gasped. "That sounds serious." Nicholas had to agree, and paused with his slice halfway to his mouth.

His dad shook his head. "She's already been discharged, but yes. They treated her for dehydration and a pre-existing stomach ulcer, so it's a little more serious than just a bit of throwing up."

"Poor Sally," bemoaned Clara. She was nibbling as a slice of pizza, anxiously glancing at Danielle's smoothie again.

"So she might not be able to come?" Nicholas asked. "That's really sad." He liked Aunt Sally a lot; she and her four sons, Nicholas's cousins, had a serious Pokémon obsession and were always good fun to be around.

"No, it's not sad," Danielle interjected, then rolled her eyes. "I mean, of course it's sad, but if five whole people drop out now, that puts our entire seating plan into serious jeopardy. That's half of a whole table gone. Not to mention we've already printed everything up, it's too late to change it now."

Nicholas had to say, he was a trifle more concerned with his aunt's health than he was some poster, but he didn't feel like incurring Danielle's wrath just then. "Can't we just have a table of five people?"

"The minimum is eight," Clara told him.

"Alright," his mum said cheerfully. "Well, what are they going to do if people just don't show up on the day? That's not our fault."

"It'll look uneven," griped Danielle.

Nicholas got himself another slice of pizza and tried not to lose his patience. "So – we move some people from another table."

"All the tables are composed of different friendship groups, and organised by both sides of the family," Danielle said irritably. "We can't just pluck a couple from here, and a couple from there. We spent weeks balancing everyone out!" She sloshed her green juice around in its bottle, and Kinny winced.

"Fine," Nicholas shot back, not sure why he was the one that had been targeted for this rant. "Is there anyone we can bump up from the evening guest list, to fill the space?"

"Ooh, that's a good idea," Peter chimed in.

Danielle did her fake laugh that really grated on Nicholas's nerves. "And who do we pick that won't upset other people? It's all politics; everything has a knock-on effect. If we ask one friend to the day and not another, there'll be anarchy."

Nicholas opened his mouth to tell her that if she didn't want solutions, she bloody well shouldn't have asked them in the first place. And also, that she should probably check the dictionary for a definition of the word 'anarchy'. But his dad spoke over him. Loudly.

"Well, we'll just have to hope for the best, and with any luck Sally and the boys will fly down as scheduled."

Clara swallowed her pizza and nodded emphatically. "I'm sure it'll all be fine Danielle," she assured their cousin. "Please don't worry."

Danielle tsked, and Clara's hurt expression pissed Nicholas off even further. He shoved a whole stuffed pizza crust into his mouth to stop him from retaliating. That wasn't a plan, and that wouldn't solve the problem if they were five people short come Saturday. But he still maintained that wasn't the end of the world anyway. If Danielle wanted to stress for the sake of stressing, he said let her.

A purring reminiscent of a lawnmower caught his attention, and he froze as a familiar heap of fluff wound its way around the legs of the kitchen chairs, on the hunt for Nicholas's mum. *Don't you dare, you fucker.* Nicholas wasn't sure exactly what he was forbidding Archibald from doing, but it seemed best to cover all the bases by suggesting 'anything at all bad'. He didn't have much hope, but maybe the universe would take pity on him.

Archibald glared up and him, and Nicholas scowled back. He was determined not to back down, even if it was to a mean-spirited cat. Thankfully, after a minute, he slunk off out the cat flap into the rain.

After that, conversation was mainly carried out by Kinny and Nicholas's mum, with Clara chipping in every now and again. They were talking mostly about her wedding dress, which thankfully was being kept at the shop until Thursday, where it was much less likely to come afoul of Archibald's claws. Nicholas excused himself as soon as he could, feeling the need to go and play some sort of video game which involved blowing stuff up. Fortunately, he had a vast supply of those. He didn't feel bad leaving the others to finish the fairy lights, as he'd already worked for an hour on them already.

He couldn't help but feel that even though he'd won with Archibald, he'd lost to Danielle, which irritated him more than it probably should have. She always had to be right, had to have the last word and be the smartest person in the room. It had shaken off his good mood from earlier, which made him even grumpier. She shouldn't be able to take that away from him.

But now he was feeling like he couldn't do anything right, especially as he kept blowing himself up rather than the enemy planes, and he was getting ready to throw the controller across the room. Fuck, he was such a waste of space. He talked too much even though no one wanted to hear what he had to say, and he would never be good enough for the likes of Fynn. He took another swig of beer, and scowled at his computer monitor.

A knock on his door took him by surprise. He paused the game (not that it mattered if he died again, anyway) and turned on his chair. "Come in," he called, expecting his mum.

He was greeted by Ash sticking her head around the door. She must have just come home from her mysterious job with the petri dishes, but she wasn't wearing any kind of uniform that would help him identify where it was. Just a strappy top and some jeans.

"Hey dude," she said, leaning on the doorframe and giving him a small wave.

"Oh hey," he said. She had an infectious calmness about her that he was growing to like.

"There's pizza if you're hungry. And beer." He waved his bottle in her direction.

She nodded. "Had a slice, thanks." She slipped her hands into her back pockets and rocked on her heels. "It was more the booze thing I was wondering about actually. You don't, like, fancy getting out of here for a few hours, do you?"

Nicholas blinked. "What, like, go into town?"

"Yeah," she replied, nodding and looking around his room. "Uh, just had a sort of full-on day and, kind of just need to blow off some steam. Thought you might know somewhere good?"

Nicholas laughed. "Well, I don't know about 'good', but some of my school mates are going clubbing. An average sort of place, but Tuesdays are cheese nights, so it could be fun?"

Ash's face broke into a smile. "Like '90s cheese?"

"They always, without fail, play the *Baywatch* theme," he informed her solemnly, conveying just how cheesy this place was prepared to go.

"Give me five minutes."

Before he could say anything else, she sprinted upstairs. *Well*, Nicholas thought. *I guess I'm going out after all.*

Now he was already on his third beer, he was more up for hitting a club. So he quickly opened his wardrobe and flung on a fresh t-shirt and gave himself another squirt of aftershave. He texted Trev to let him know he'd be coming after all.

And then his thumb hovered over Fynn's name.

Oh, why the hell not? Life was too short.

'Hey dude. So, you're probably working, but if you fancied it, I'm meeting some mates at Havana – the club near the station. It'd be nice to buy you a drink for all your hard work!'

He sent the message before he could change his mind, then smiled at the dozen or so varied happy faces he'd received in reply from Trev at the news he was coming out with them.

Ash hadn't changed her clothes, she'd just thrown on some eyeliner and made her hair more pointy. She still looked awesome though, with the cotton and denim clinging to her petite frame. Nicholas told her she looked hot, then immediately worried if that was skeezy. But she took it in the spirit it was intended, and told him likewise. There was never any drama around Ash, which he was definitely starting to appreciate.

It was already nine o'clock, and they were both keen not to waste any time. She called them a cab to ferry them across town, giving them ten minutes to get out the door.

Nicholas went around the house, and in turn invited Peter and Clara, Kinny, and as a show of good sportsmanship, even Danielle. However, nobody else fancied coming out. Danielle even managed to only tut very quietly at the notion of going drinking when there was wedding stuff to be done, but Nicholas was feeling generous having reclaimed his good mood, so chose to ignore her.

Once they heard the honk of the horn, it was just him and Ash that ran out into the rain and threw themselves into the back of the taxi. The cabbie laughed at them as they shook themselves off.

"Sorry," Nicholas said, then thought of Fynn. But it was polite to apologise when you were making someone's car wet.

"No room for an umbrella then?" he asked as he pulled off down the street.

Ash grinned. "Not in these jeans, mate." Nicholas snorted.

He checked his phone, but there was no reply from Fynn. Still, he kept the phone in his hand the whole drive there, just in case. He was probably still at work – chances were, he couldn't check his messages if he was in the middle of waiting tables, so Nicholas kept a little flicker of hope alive that he might still decide to come out later.

He'd been thinking about Fynn dancing. He bet he was really good. He was so in sync with his music, he would naturally have a good sense of rhythm, Nicholas was certain. But then again, he was also inclined to run hot and cold. Perhaps dancing was beneath him? He seemed to flirt, and then he shut down. One minute he was ignoring texts, the next he was sending him kisses.

Nicholas was glad the taxi was dark, as he was sure he blushed at just thinking about that. For the love of god, he needed to get a grip on this going red all the time business, or he was going to really embarrass himself very soon.

But it was difficult. Now he was almost certain he was gay himself, getting a kiss in the middle of the night from another, rather gorgeous, gay guy was bound to leave him feeling flustered. Even if he was convinced it couldn't really mean anything. There was no way Fynn would be flirting with someone like him, but it was quite nice to imagine he could be flirting, just for a moment.

Luckily, the queue outside the club was low, otherwise they would have gotten drenched. Within a minute or two, they were inside paying at the booth to get into the club proper. Nicholas had thought that it might be a bit dead on the floor thanks to the lack of a line, but that was probably more due to the fact that it was reasonably late in the evening for a Tuesday, and most people were already inside. The club was plenty busy.

That was good. At least if he was going to be forced into dancing, the crowd would be so dense that people wouldn't really pay attention to him.

Havana looked like an old school from the outside, or maybe even a church. It was all brown brickwork and cream arches and even a round, stained glass window at the very top. Inside, though, it was extremely purple thanks to the backlighting at the bar and around the walls. At two stories high, the bottom floor contained the main dance area, lowered into a well. That way, people in the booths and table areas could watch the dancers, and so could those from the second-floor balcony that ran all around in a circle. Everything was designed for you to be seen, for people to meet and make a connection, or just show off if you were that way inclined.

Nicholas still hoped he wouldn't draw any attention despite all that. He wasn't there to pull, he was there to see his mates, and maybe help Ash shake off her stressful day.

"Shall we go to the bar?" he shouted in her ear as they pressed their way into the throng. "Then we can look for my friends – Trev said they were in the back on the right."

Ash gave him two thumbs-up, then entwined their hands so she could tug him through the people in their way. People in the dance area were thrashing around to some classic RnB which Nicholas recognised, but didn't know the name of. There seemed to be a lot of grinding going on though, with pelvises thrusting and hands wandering over hips and bums. Nicholas definitely needed another drink if he was going to get anywhere near that.

Ash slipped past through people easily, with a big smile and the occasional bounce of her boobs. People like her knew how to use flirting like a currency, without actually committing to anything. Nicholas had no idea how that worked. She also used her charms to get them served extra fast by the girl behind the bar, who may have been covered in glitter and smiling, but her eyes showed how tired she really was. Ash managed to make her laugh though, which, considering how loud the music was, was no easy feat.

"How do you do that?" Nicholas asked as they moved back out into the crowd, plastic beer bottles clutched in their hands.

Ash winked at him. "It's easier when you don't know them," she assured him. He wasn't sure he believed that, but he was happy to have his drink so fast, so didn't question it.

They found Trev and another half a dozen other guys from school holed up in the corner behind some large, fake potted plants where they'd managed to grab a table. There were drapes everywhere stretched across the lower ceiling under the second floor, and pulled down to the floor. It gave the impression of a sort of Moroccan marquee, although the four-tier chandelier hanging over the centre of the dance floor didn't really fit with that aesthetic. It still looked pretty.

The guys moved up to make room for them in the booth, though Nicholas made sure to perch on the edge. He was feeling a little antsy and didn't fancy being penned in. Ash squirmed right on in and began holding court immediately, although she was too far away for Nicholas to really catch what she was saying. The guys around her were enraptured pretty quickly. Nicholas shook his head. He wasn't sure he was up to having one of his friends come back to his house and shagging his soon-to-be sister-in-law, not that there was the room to get up to anything like that. He'd have to keep an eye on things though, and see if Ash needed rescuing from any of them at any point.

At the moment she looked perfectly happy, making the guys either side of her laugh with some story she was telling. So he turned his attention to Trev.

"What's up, mate? How you doing?" he asked. They clinked bottles, but as they were plastic, it was more of a feeble tap. The sentiment was still genuine.

"Good, yeah, really good!" he shouted back. Trev was an overweight guy with an insane talent for art. For some reason (Nicholas suspected his pushy mum) he'd gone off to do a business degree, and would probably end up stuck in his dad's office for the next forty years if he wasn't careful. But for now, Nicholas still had time to try and corrupt him.

"How's *The Night Shift* going?"

Trev had been illustrating his own comic book for a couple of years now. He'd met a writer online called Pembroke, and the two of them had started publishing their detective stories via various websites to increasing success. Sure enough, his eyes lit up at the mention of his pet project.

"Holy shit, dude – didn't you see on Facebook?" Nicholas shook his head. He was always missing things. "We got a place at a MCM in London – to exhibit! We're going in May – Pem is actually flying over, we're finally going to meet in real life!"

Nicholas could help but goggle at him for a second. "You're going to be at a convention?" he asked, not quite believing it. "As a guest – people are going to come over to you?"

"Yeah!" Trev cried, bouncing up and down. "My parents don't know, obviously, but my five thousand followers do. We've already got pre-bookings!"

"Mate," Nicholas said sincerely. "I'm so happy for you." And he meant it. But, it was also hard not to feel just the smallest bit put out. "Fuck," he laughed as they tapped bottles again. "You're off signing comics, and Fynn's recording an album, and here I am just impressed that I can keep on top of my laundry and get my essays in on time." He shook his head.

"Who's Fynn?"

"Hm?"

Trev poked his arm. "You said 'Fynn's recording an album' – who's that? Sounds cool!"

"Oh."

He had said that, hadn't he? That was the first time he'd spoken to another person about Fynn, he'd used his name and everything. He hadn't dare slip up at home, otherwise it might lead to some questions about a certain lack of harp players. But he hadn't even realised he'd done it with Trev. He must have been bursting to get it off his chest. Shit, that was embarrassing.

"Um, just a friend. He sings and plays guitar, he's amazing. He's uh, actually playing at my sister's wedding for her. He's going to be fantastic. Honestly—" He sat up and turned his body towards Trev. "He can take a song and completely change it. Like, a terrible pop song, and make it really romantic. He totally deserves to get a record deal."

Trev was looking at him with a slightly funny expression.

"What?" Nicholas asked, feeling that prickling over his skin that suggested he was probably going to blush. Again. For fuck's sake.

"Nothing," Trevor assured him quickly. "You've just, uh, never mentioned him before. He sounds very cool, no wonder you're proud of him."

Nicholas scoffed, and decided to move the conversation in a safer direction. "Not as much as you, you smug prick. Go on, show me your latest pages. What are you bringing out for the convention?"

Trev got out his phone, and bashfully talked Nicholas through his recent work. Nicholas honestly could have burst with pride. If Trev could gain success with his art before he even graduated, then maybe his parents wouldn't force him into a job he was going to hate.

Nicholas was lucky with his family, he did know that. It was probably why he tried his best to remain patient with Danielle. Her parents were awful, and he was certain they only stayed married because they thought getting divorced was too scandalous. Even though they did nothing but argue and try and get one up on each other. What a terrible way to live.

Nicholas's parents were still so happy after more than two decades together, and they supported and loved all their children no matter what. When his sister Lauren had decided to take her savings and go travel Europe instead of going to university, his mum and dad had encouraged her. They had even helped her buy a house when she settled down with her boyfriend and their daughter in Italy. Nothing was too much to ask when it came to Clara's wedding, and they hadn't batted an eyelid at the fact Peter 'only worked in a shop'. They were so happy together, and he treated Clara like a princess, so that was all that mattered to the Heralds.

How would they react then, if their only son was to come out as gay?

Nicholas sipped on his beer and let his friends' conversations drift over him, mixing in with the pounding music as he watched the dancers flinging their bodies about on the central floor.

He'd never thought that would be him; having to sit down and officially tell his family he liked men instead of women. That he was Different. But it seemed like he was, so he guessed – maybe after the wedding – that was something he should think about tackling before he went back to uni. Now he knew, he didn't feel like he wanted to hide it, even if it meant he faced some tricky times ahead. He hoped it wouldn't be too awkward or anything.

His sister Lauren would be absolutely fine with it – that he knew a hundred percent. She'd always been a human rights crusader and a stickler for political correctness. But she was all the way over in Italy, so if he was going to rely on her, he'd only have the days before and after the wedding to bring it up. Would that be fair? He didn't want to take the limelight away from Clara in any way.

How had it been for Fynn? Had he come out to his parents? Or, had it been his aunt? How long had he been living with her? Perhaps just she knew, or perhaps none of them did?

He checked his phone again, however there weren't any new text messages from him. But Nicholas suddenly burned to know if it had been hard for him, if he'd had any friends to go through it with him or if he'd felt alone. He probably shouldn't ask – he'd already put his foot in it just by asking about him being gay, but Nicholas didn't want Fynn to feel like he was alone.

Christ, he was definitely getting drunk. Fynn probably had loads of friends. A good-looking guy like that wouldn't be lonely; the world bent over backwards for people like him. He had almost certainly been fine – was fine now. Nicholas should be worrying about himself. He didn't know if he had the strength to be gay, to exist in life being that fundamentally different from everyone around him.

Except, he didn't feel that different. He still liked the same things, still enjoyed his old friends' company – if only he could only pay a bit more attention to them. He shook himself, and focused on Reg talking about a documentary he'd watched on volcanoes a little while ago. Once he got his head around how to tell them, he hoped none of these guys would treat him any differently. Was that too much to ask?

After a while, Nate and Billy convinced Ash to go dance. During the shuffle around, seeing as he was now standing up anyway, Nicholas thought it would probably be a good idea to nip to the loo. He'd not been since before he'd had pizza, and his bladder suddenly needed fairly urgent attention.

"I'll be back in a bit," he shouted at Trev and the other couple of guys who were happy to remain at their table and guard it from anyone looking to pinch their empty seats.

As soon as he started making his way through the crowd, Nicholas realised he was a bit drunker than he'd previously thought. He was fine to walk, he wasn't going to pass out or be sick or anything, but he was certainly a bit wobblier than he would have imagined himself to be. He supposed he had had four beers now, and only a couple of slices of pizza for dinner. He decided once he'd gone for a piss, he'd nip to the bar to get him and Ash another round, and maybe include some water as well as the beers.

There was some sort of kerfuffle going on in the downstairs loos, so Nicholas was forced to go upstairs and avoid the ruckus. At this end of the club, the stairs were through a set of doors that, while still inside, took customers around the back. Nicholas had generally avoided the back stairs in the past, as they felt secluded and just a little dangerous. He was probably being stupid, as there were bound to be cameras all over the place. Plus, he really needed a piss now.

Sure enough, his trip up the measly two flights was completely uneventful, and he sighed as he unzipped and relieved himself in the urinal. The music was reduced to a faint thud of the bassline through the walls, and he felt himself sober up a little. After he washed his hands he didn't even try to stop himself checking his phone again. He was disappointed not to have heard from Fynn still, even though the little ticks showed him he'd read the message. But they weren't really friends, he *had* to remember that, and Fynn didn't owe him anything. A reply to say he was too busy or too tired would have been nice though, even if it was a white lie.

Nicholas shook himself and ventured back into the corridor, where the music throbbed a bit louder again. He could either turn left and go to the balcony level, or go right and head back to his friends. He hesitated for a moment, filled with the mad urge to go and look around the top floor, just in case there was someone, no one in particular, up there that he recognised. A minute or so wouldn't hurt he decided, so that's what he did.

Of course he didn't see Fynn. He spotted a gaggle of girls he thought might have been a couple of years below him at school; they were probably there taking a break from their A-Level revision. Bloody hell, that seemed like a lifetime ago, especially as he'd taken a gap year as well.

He shook his head, acknowledging he'd been stupid to come and mope around hoping to catch a glimpse of Fynn, and went back through the doors to head downstairs and back to his friends.

As he pushed through the doors, he collided straight into another person. It was Hunter Ford.

Nicholas staggered back, and took a moment to realise what he was seeing. Hunter was just as stunning as ever, with his all-year tan and

American-perfect teeth. He also had James Wash and Jamal Asfour by his sides, just like back when they were at school. Like the good bodyguards they always had been, they looked set to jump Nicholas for even daring to breathe the same air as their unofficial leader.

But Hunter barked out a laugh as soon as he righted himself, and pointed at Nicholas with his almost empty beer bottle in delight. "Sticky Nicky!" he cried with his Californian lilt. "No way! Dude, how are you?"

Nicholas winced at the reminder of his old nick-name. Hunter didn't sound like he was using it with malicious intent, but nobody wanted to be reminded of the time when their face looked like a puss-filled nightmare.

"Hey," he managed to reply with a convincing amount of enthusiasm. After all, Hunter was still talking to him – he remembered his name, even if it was a less than favourable version of it. "Fancy seeing you here."

"We're back for Easter break," Hunter explained proudly, sloshing his bottle towards his two friends. He was swaying a little more than was normal, and Nicholas prayed to God that he wasn't planning on driving home.

Thankfully, his flunkies had backed down at Hunter's excited response to getting slammed into by an old schoolmate. People were pushing past them as they moved up and down between levels, but Hunter didn't even seem to notice getting buffeted every thirty seconds or so. Nicholas supposed the stairs could be busier; they actually felt like they had a modicum of privacy.

"How about you?"

"Oh," Nicholas replied. "Same."

"I thought you didn't get into uni?" James asked. The bluntness made it clear he was saying it as a slur, but Nicholas shrugged it off.

"I just took a gap year," he told them, which was true. "Went to South America to 'find myself'." He added air quotes and rolled his eyes to acknowledge how clichéd that sounded, and hoped they wouldn't take the piss.

Thankfully, Hunter laughed. "Oh, I wish I'd done that. The old man wouldn't hear of it though. Maybe after I'm done with school? Hey!" His glazed eyes widened, and he punched Nicholas's arm a little harder than was probably necessary. "Maybe you could tell me some cool places to check out, hey? Nicky? We're friends on Facebook, right?"

"Uh, yeah," Nicholas agreed.

It wasn't like he'd drunkenly stalked his old-school crush on several occasions. Oh lord, how could he have not realised it was a crush? Why was he just working out now, today, that he was gay? Of all the times to run into Hunter Ford.

It was fine. Hunter was smashed, and if he just kept it cool he probably wouldn't even remember running into spotty, specky Sticky Nicky at Havana.

"Sure," he responded, keeping his eyes on Hunter and avoiding catching the gaze of the other two. "I know lots of cool places. I'll drop you a message, you'll find yourself in no time."

Hunter laughed, but Jamal sneered. "I would have thought you'd just need to look in the back of the closet to find yourself." That got a hoot from James, but Nicholas's insides turned to ice.

"W-what?"

Hunter was clicking his fingers though. "Oh yeah!" he said. "We had a pool going on whether or not you were gonna turn out queer – how'd that work out for you?" He waved his beer around again, then drained it as his mates smirked. "Did you find a little Latino boy to pop your cherry?"

Nicholas's heart rate had rocketed. His eyes darted to his right, but he couldn't quite see the doors leading into the club. Suddenly, the corridor felt completely deserted. "I don't—" he said. "I, no." He laughed. "No, no boys."

"You're telling us you're not a poof?" James asked, his lip curled.

"Oi, oi." Hunter frowned and poked James with his finger. "The correct political term," he slurred, concentrating on his words. "Is LB – LGBT, right Nicky?" He raised an eyebrow at him. "It's cool if Nicky's a gay, we like the gays, yeah?"

Jamal scoffed and James huffed, but they didn't disagree.

Nicholas shook his head though. "I'm not gay," he lied. The first people he was going to come out to was *not* going to be these pricks.

Hunter flopped over onto Nicholas's shoulders, his breath laced with beer and Sambuca. "Hey man, it's *cool*," he said. He then leant in closer, speaking into Nicholas's ear where the other two definitely couldn't hear him. "Hey, hey, why don't you come into the bathroom with me? You can suck my cock, I bet you'd like that?"

Nicholas jerked in surprise, but Hunter had a hold of his shoulders. "I, uh—" He fumbled for a response. "No, that's—"

"Shh, hey," Hunter said. He dug his fingers into Nicholas's arm. "It's cool, it's cool. I saw the way you used to stare at me." He laughed at himself. "Can't blame you man, I am pretty fucking hot. Wouldn't you like a little piece of this, for the road?"

Nicholas tried to push him gently off. If he shoved, Hunter could get angry, and his mates didn't need any excuse to go for him. Bile was rising in his throat. If he rejected him, what would they do? Would Hunter laugh it off, and save face?

Or would they decided the little fag needed a beating, and take him somewhere to kick the shit out of him?

He was preoccupied scrambling for an answer as Hunter leered at him, so he didn't entirely register the burst of sound as the doors into the club opened behind him, allowing someone to walk through.

"Hey, Nicholas. Is that you?"

Nicholas didn't know if he wanted to cry in relief or mortification. The question made Hunter look up, and Nicholas used the excuse to spin around and step away. "Fynn," he squeaked. "You're here?"

Fynn smiled, ignoring Nicholas's schoolmates, and handed out one of two beers he was holding. "Yeah, just arrived. Was at the bar back there and spotted you looking around, so got you a drink."

Oh thank god, thought Nicholas. His silly little look around had actually paid off.

"Hey man," said Hunter loudly. He stuck his hand out around Nicholas. "You a friend of Nicky's?"

Fynn eyed the proffered hand, then shook it once. Nicholas took the opportunity to step away and stand beside Fynn. Fuck, his whole body was shaking. He couldn't tell if it was visible or not.

"You his boyfriend?" James asked slyly, and Jamal guffawed.

Fynn didn't flinch. He just graced them with a lazy half-smile. Nicholas thought there was something sharp in his eyes though. "We're friends, yeah. You guys know each other too?"

"We went to school together," Hunter said. His gaze was flitting between Fynn and Nicholas, and

Nicholas prayed silently that this wasn't going to get any uglier than it already had.

"Well, it was nice to meet you," said Fynn. He nodded at the guys, then placed his hand on the small of Nicholas's back to steer him firmly towards the club entrance behind them.

Nicholas was trembling so badly he couldn't help but sag into Fynn's side as they moved back into the busy balcony area. Fynn didn't stop until they found a clear patch beyond the bar he must have been standing at when Nicholas made his sweep of the room. Nicholas gratefully leant his whole weight against the wall.

"Thanks," he whispered, but Fynn seemed to lip read him alright over the din.

"Did they hurt you?" he demanded. His hand was clasped protectively on Nicholas's arm, and his eyes flickered back and forth as they searched Nicholas's expression.

Fuck, he felt like such a baby, but he couldn't stop the sob escaping from his throat. "I'm fine," he said.

"You don't look fine," Fynn argued.

Nicholas wanted to refute it, to say he was. But had he almost just been attacked? Had he almost just been…

He couldn't bring himself to even think the word. Surely Hunter wouldn't have forced him to do anything. Would he?

Nicholas sobbed again, and scrubbed angrily at the tears that started to fall. He tried to turn away from Fynn to preserve what little dignity he might have left. But that was difficult when Fynn grabbed him and pulled him into a tight hug.

"You're okay now," he said, just audible over the hammering beat of the music. "I'll fucking kill them if they come near you again."

Nicholas managed a small laugh. "Honestly," he said. "It was nothing, really. Sorry, I'm just making a fuss." Fynn released him, and Nicholas missed the contact immediately.

Fynn stared down at him. "No, you're not allowed to apologise. I saw the way he was all over you. You were clearly trying to get away from him, and those bastards were just laughing."

He glared back towards the door twenty feet behind them. But Nicholas didn't want him doing anything stupid. "Hey," he said. He was feeling a bit calmer, at least he thought he was. "Everything's fine now, thanks to you." He waited until Fynn turned back to look at him, then he gave him a small smile. "It wasn't nice, and yeah…maybe it might have got worse. But they didn't hurt me. I promise."

Fynn rubbed at his short beard. He looked stunning as usual. How did he get away with making just a vest top and jeans look so hot? "I'm glad I came out," he said eventually.

Nicholas nodded. "Me too." Exhaustion hit him like a bus out of the blue, and it must have shown on his face.

"Do you want to go sit down?" Fynn asked, concern drawing lines on his brow. "Are your friends still here?"

"Uh, yeah," said Nicholas. Nausea swept over him, and he swallowed a mouthful of beer to try and temper it. It was a bad idea though. He needed water. And sleep. "Actually, I think I want to go home."

"Sure," said Fynn quickly, but that just made Nicholas feel bad.

"Oh, but," he shook his head. "You just got here."

Fynn scoffed. "Don't worry about me. Let's get you home – I could take you?"

Even in his bleary, distressed state, Nicholas still registered the spark of interested that flared in his abdomen at the idea of going home with Fynn. But that wasn't an option, and he wasn't sure he could have coped with the possibility right then even if he had come alone.

"I'm with my sister-in-law," he said. He hugged himself, feeling like he couldn't stop trembling. "Thank you so much, that's so kind, really. But, I think maybe I should go find her."

Fynn didn't give any hint of protest. He just nodded, and put his hand at the base of Nicholas's spine again. "Do you know where she is?"

"She was dancing," Nicholas told him.

They used the balcony to its advantage, and peered over at all the dancers in the central well. Sure enough, after a few minutes of feeling like he was searching a Where's Wally book, Nicholas pointed down at Ash's blonde pixie hair.

There was no sign of Hunter or his two friends thankfully, and Fynn kept it that way by guiding them down the interior stairs on the other side of the club. Nicholas was fretting about how he was going to get Ash's attention, as he really didn't think he could push his way over to where she was dancing. But as luck would have it, as he and Fynn reached the edge of the well, she looked over in their direction.

Nicholas tried to smile, but before he'd even managed to wave, Ash's face dropped into a concerned expression. She began making her way through the throng, with Nate and Billy quickly following behind. Nicholas sighed. He looked that bad, huh?

They didn't have to wait long before she climbed up the few steps to meet them on the threshold. She glanced once at Fynn, then focused on Nicholas.

"Hey bro," she said. She'd never called him that before, and Nicholas felt so touched it was all he could do to swallow around the lump that rose in his throat

"I uh," he began. But the tears threatened him again. Fucking hell, how was he going to explain this? *Nothing had happened.* Except, he couldn't quite believe it was entirely nothing.

"Nicholas needs to go home," said Fynn. "Are you his sister-in-law?"

"Will be come Saturday," Ash corrected him. But her tone wasn't hostile, just determined. "I'm Ash."

"I'm Fynn," he told her. "Do you need to get anything, or can you leave now?" He didn't even check if she wanted to leave. Maybe he assumed that if she didn't, then he would just escort Nicholas home instead. The directness was oddly comforting.

"I can leave now," said Ash. Nicholas wanted to hug her.

She turned around and told Nate and Billy that the two of them had to go, and asked them to let Nicholas's other friends know. Fynn plucked Nicholas's beer bottle from his hand. He hadn't even realised he was still holding it.

"Come on," he said into his ear as he placed both bottles on a nearby table, and Ash fell into step beside them.

"Are you coming too?" she asked without a hint of judgement.

Fynn shook his head. "I'd just like to make sure you get into a taxi, if that's okay?"

Ash stared at Nicholas for a moment, before nodding back at Fynn. "Of course, lead the way."

Nicholas felt stupid. He felt bad for leaving without saying goodbye to Trev. But he wanted to be somewhere quiet so badly, and it felt so nice to just do what Fynn was telling him to. Fynn left the club with them and didn't bother to get a re-entry stamp. He never took his hand off of Nicholas's back.

It was still raining, but it wasn't quite so bad as before, and the taxi rank was just down the road at the station. The lights shone through the dampness of the evening like a welcoming beacon, and Nicholas felt a surge of relief as the first driver in the rank rolled down his window. Ash leant in and gave him the rough area to drive to.

"What about you?" Nicholas asked as Fynn helped him open the door.

"I'll get my own one," Fynn promised him. Nicholas started to protest that that would be expensive, but Fynn waved him off. "I saved money hardly buying any drinks, remember?" He smiled, and leant in to block out some of the rain and look down at Nicholas where he sat. "Can you – uh." He rubbed the back of his neck. "Can you text me when you get home, okay?"

Nicholas may have been cold from the rain, and from the shock he'd just had. But that simple question made his insides feel like they were glowing with warmth. "Sure."

All too quickly, the door was shut and Nicholas and Ash were on their way. Nicholas couldn't stop shivering, and the taxi driver had to ask twice for the address they were headed to before Ash finally stepped in and answered him.

"Sorry," Nicholas rasped.

What had just happened?

Hunter thought he could do that, because he'd somehow worked out that Nicholas was gay, years before he had. They'd had a bet on it. It had been funny. And because he was gay, Hunter and his friends thought it was okay to threaten him. To try and force him to do something he didn't want to do, to degrade him. If he wasn't gay, they wouldn't have done that. He wouldn't have almost got hurt. What the fuck, how – what –

Before his thoughts could swallow him whole, he felt a cold hand slip into his own. He glanced over, and saw Ash looking at him, their hands linked in the space between their seats in the back of the cab. She gave him a small, tight smile, then lifted his hand to lightly peck a kiss on the back of his knuckles. Then she stared out into the rain as the taxi swiftly took them home.

Chapter Eight

(3 days to go…)

Nicholas sat on his bed for quite some time. He managed to pull his jeans off, but figured he'd just sleep in the t-shirt and boxers he had on, even though the shirt was technically one he kept for best.

He kept telling himself he was okay, but he felt violated. He'd allowed Hunter to talk to him like that, to degrade him. Why the hell hadn't he told him to fuck off?

Because he'd been scared for his safety, that's why. The realisation made him feel powerless.

He was surprised by the knock at the door, but like earlier in the day, it was Ash. She only poked her head in the crack, and gave him a small smile. "Can I come in?"

"Sure," he said. He pulled the covers up, hugging them to his chest.

She bumped the door all the way open with her hip. She was wearing her short PJ shorts with a different t-shirt. Nicholas recognised it as a Sarah Anderson comic design, though not one he'd seen before. Appropriately for the evening Ash had just had, it depicted a two-part design that showed a 'What I think I look like when I dance' image next to a 'What I actually look like'. It was funny in an innocent sort of way, and it made Nicholas smile.

Ash had two large mugs in her hands, and she carefully walked over with one held out in Nicholas's direction. "Hot chocolate," she said by way of an explanation.

Nicholas felt that lump rise in his throat again, but he shoved it back down. "Thanks," he croaked, and took it from her.

She'd sprinkled mini marshmallows over the top of a squirt of whipped cream, and Nicholas wondered if he'd ever smelt anything so divine. He took a sip, and the cold that had seeped all the way to his bones from the rain crept up a few degrees.

Ash perched on the edge of his bed with her feet tucked under her bum. She sat up straight and blew on her own chocolate as they sat in a silence that was surprisingly comfortable. Nicholas glanced at his phone, but he could see it wasn't blinking, indicating he had no new messages. He'd text Fynn as soon as he'd got into his room, but so far, there was no response.

"I think something happened to you tonight." Ash was staring right at him as he raised his gaze to meet hers. "And if you don't want to talk about it, that's fine. That's why hot chocolate exists. But if you do, you can. To me or someone else, but you can. Because you're important, and you should look after yourself." She gulped down two mouthfuls of chocolate, then wiped the back of her hand over her mouth, not taking her wide, blue eyes off him.

"Um," said Nicholas, squirming a fraction under her scrutiny. He'd told himself he'd just forget about what had happened, that he really didn't want to hash over it. But Ash had asked him directly. It wasn't surprising she'd guessed something was amiss after he'd made he leave so suddenly. He probably did owe her an explanation, even if it made him uncomfortable to discuss.

Plus, she was still staring.

"I guess," he began, his words stilted. "Uh, someone said something kind of shitty to me, and uh. They sort of put their hands on me a bit. But that was it. I think I'm more freaked out by what could have happened, but, I guess, I mean… It sort of still feels like a violation. But it's fine, I'll be fine. Because the bad thing – or things—" He shivered, then took a moment to recollect his thoughts. "It didn't happen. So I probably just need to get some sleep and I'll be fine. Because I have hot chocolate." He raised his mug to her. "And you guys got me out of there, and I'm home, and I think I might be gay." He closed his eyes and took a big mouthful of hot chocolate, his whole body vibrating and prickling with heat. But then he let out a long breath, and smiled shakily before opening his eyes. "I'm, uh, gay."

Ash's face broke into a huge smile. She grabbed his ankle through the duvet and gave it a hard squeeze. "Yes," she said. He waited for more, but she just kept grinning.

He found he didn't need her to say more. He could feel tension ebbing out of his body. "I'm gay." He said it again, just for good measure.

"I wondered." Ash nodded and poked at one of her marshmallows with her finger. "I try not to assume things like that, but, yeah. It crossed my mind. I'm happy you felt like you could tell me."

Nicholas smiled, tears of gratitude pricking at his eyes. "Thank you. I've not actually told anyone before." He patted her knee. "You're pretty easy to talk to."

"No problem," she told him sincerely.

He laughed, feeling a bit surreal. He'd done it.

"Seriously, if you ever want to come out, I'd be happy to return the favour."

Ash blinked owlishly at him, her expression wholly serious. "Really?"

Nicholas hadn't been expecting that. He had meant what he'd said though. "Absolutely," he told her, nodding fervently.

Ash chewed her lip for a little while. Nicholas began to think she'd changed her mind, but he went against his nature and didn't ask her anymore questions. She would talk when she was ready.

Sure enough, after a few minutes and a few more mouthfuls of chocolate, she took in a deep breath.

"I don't always feel like a girl," she said.

He'd guessed that she was going to confess that she *liked* girls. Not that she wasn't one. He wasn't sure how to respond for a second. "Oh. Okay."

"Sometimes," said Ash, not moving her eyes a millimetre from the rim of her mug. "I feel like a boy. I am a boy."

Nicholas took a sip of his chocolate to quickly gather his thoughts. What would Lauren say? She was always good with this sort of thing. "Well," he said, picking his words with care in light of such an unusual revelation. "You can be a boy if you want."

She shook her head. "Only sometimes." Her gaze met his, but only for a flash and then she was back to her hot chocolate.

Nicholas tried to remember the name of that actress from *Orange is the New Black*. He'd read an interview with her a while back, and she'd said something very similar. "So, you switch back and forth between them?"

Ash nodded, then took a careful gulp of her drink, licking cream off her top lip. "Some days…"

she continued. A nervous laugh bubbled up, and she covered her mouth. But she nodded, and inhaled slowly. "Sometimes I'm neither. I just feel like a 'they'."

Nicholas was glad his last beer had already been starting to wear off. He really didn't want to say the wrong thing. "As long as you're *you*," he said, "does it really matter what gender you are? I mean," he added hastily. "It matters if you tell people you want them to, uh, use different pronouns." *Was that how Lauren would say it?* "But, as long as you're happy, I'm sure people won't mind."

"Like Peter?" She looked hopefully at him.

"You haven't mentioned this to him?" he asked. She shook her head. Both hands were firmly cradling her mug, and she looked back down as she swirled the drink inside. "Well, no, I don't think he'd mind at all. I know I don't." He hoped that counted for something.

Judging by the shine on her eyes when she looked back up, and the grin that split across her face, it did. "Good," she whispered, nodding into her chocolate. She blinked a few times. "Good. Good."

Wow. So, he was gay, and Ash was...whatever the right word was. Gender fluid? He hadn't seen that coming a week ago. It felt oddly freeing, knowing they'd both got something so big off their chests.

They sat for a little while longer, not saying anything. Just grinning to themselves and finishing off their hot chocolates. Eventually, Nicholas yawned twice in a row, and his eyelids started to droop. Ash stood, taking his now empty mug wordlessly, and headed towards the door.

"Who was the guy who walked us out?" she asked. She paused halfway out the door, one foot in the dark corridor outside.

Nicholas licked his lips, tasting the residual chocolate. *The guitarist for the wedding*, his brain shouted at him. *The guitarist for the wedding!*

"Just a friend."

She nodded. "I think he seemed like a good friend." With that, she took herself out, and closed the door behind her.

***

Fynn still hadn't texted back by the time Nicholas woke up in the morning, which kind of hurt, because he could see from the ticks that he had read it. He'd seemed so concerned last night, and that had made Nicholas feel so much better. But now he couldn't even be bothered to reply to the message he'd asked Nicholas to write?

It was still chucking it down, which Nicholas couldn't quite believe. He laid in bed for a while, listening to it spatter against his bedroom window beyond the closed curtains.

As much as the weather was cause for concern, and Fynn's lack of response irked him, Nicholas kept coming back to one irrevocable fact.

He'd come out.

Sure, it was just to Ash. She was just one person, and he was going to have to do it over and over again until everyone knew. And probably to an unknowable number of people he'd yet to meet in his future. But he'd done it. He'd said the words out loud.

"I'm gay," he said to himself. It made a warmth fizzle through him. "I'm gay," he repeated with more determination.

And Ash had shared her secret with him too. He wasn't really sure he understood what she meant – how could she feel like a boy, if she was a girl?

Sure, her hair was short, but she didn't have a cock between her legs. And her boobs weren't massive, but for her frame they were still pretty hard to miss. She didn't have boy biology either – there wasn't an overabundance of testosterone swimming about her system.

But, it seemed like none of that really mattered to her. It didn't really matter to Nicholas, he supposed. He didn't have to understand it. He just knew he really liked Ash, and if she said she was a boy from time to time, what difference did that really make?

He thought about their evening last night – before and after the incident with that prick, Hunter. They'd gone out just the two of them and held hands and she'd even kissed him. Not on the lips, but still. However, until that moment, lying there, it didn't strike him that any of the could have been romantic. All Fynn had to do was look at him, and he felt like his knees had turned to water. But with Ash, it just felt cosy. Right.

Bloody hell; she did feel the same, didn't she? She hadn't been coming on to him this whole time had she? Nicholas chewed on his lip. He didn't think so, but, he might be completely oblivious. He'd never thought of himself as a particularly sexual person before, but he'd been dealing with misinformation. He might not know when a girl was flirting with him, because he'd always been too hung up on someone like Hunter paying attention to him to notice.

He scoffed and rubbed at his face. He was a maths dork who'd had terrible acne. He doubted he'd missed any flirting, and he was almost certain that wasn't the vibe Ash had been giving him all this time.

In fact, he had a sneaking suspicion that she'd only told him about her boy-girl thing so that he'd come out to her. He couldn't say for sure, but if so – if she suspected he was gay already – then it would be a bit weird if she was secretly nursing a crush.

As it was now Wednesday, that officially marked the start of everyone's annual leave. Beyond his door, Nicholas could tell people were already waking up and getting geared up for the day. He sighed and tried to steel his nerves to go out and begin the activities lined up for them all. Without reminding himself of the official schedule, he already knew there was something going on with the speeches. Danielle had probably set aside time to coach his dad and Peter through every word of theirs. The name-place card thingies that they'd ordered weeks ago for the dinner were also due for delivery sometime in the afternoon. There was probably more arts and crafts to be done, seeing as the photo collage board wasn't yet done and there were still last minute details to be added to the table centrepieces, and Nicholas vowed he would do whatever he was told.

He hoped for Ash's sake there might be an opportunity to play with the hot glue gun again. It seemed to be the only job that had managed to keep her awake the other day. He wondered if she hated arts and crafts as much as he did. Playing with something dangerous had obviously piqued her interest.

He negotiated his way through the bathroom between his mum and Clara, forgiving the tepid water in the shower, figuring it was better than it being freezing cold. He dressed quick enough and sorted his hair, then took extra care rubbing in the bio-oil to his scars, as he'd neglected to do it before he'd gone to bed. As he massaged his cheeks, his eyes wandered over to his phone.

He'd still heard nothing from Fynn, although he'd swapped a number of texts with Trev, who'd been pretty upset that Nicholas had had to go early. Nicholas thought Trev maybe assumed he'd not been feeling well, and he didn't bother to correct him. It was nice enough that he'd messaged several times to make sure he'd gotten home and was feeling alright this morning. But Fynn, who had walked him out to the car and specifically told Nicholas to text him once he'd made it back safely, remained silent.

He made a snap decision, and once he'd wiped the oil from his fingers, he snatched his phone up and unlocked the screen.

'Hey, sorry about last night. It couldn't have been too much fun for you. I'm feeling okay though today.'

"Thanks for asking," Nicholas snorted out loud to himself.

'If you'd rather go check out the town hall by yourself, I understand. Nx'

The kiss was almost a test, he realised. He hoped it might push Fynn to letting on how he was feeling. Even just a little bit.

He kept his phone out where he could see it during a help-yourself breakfast of cereals and fruit, and in front of him as he sat and cut out paper love hearts for a variety of things Danielle apparently had in mind.

Eventually, he got bored of unlocking the screen every few minutes to see if the ticks had changed to show Fynn had read the message. After an hour, he still hadn't looked at what Nicholas had written, and seeing the same grey ticks over and over was making him irritable

So he made himself stop, and after a while, he forgot about it, getting involved in discussions about car timetables between the house and the venue, and organising the fresh flowers that would be delivered on Saturday morning. He even left his phone on the sofa when he popped to the loo after a simple lunch of sandwiches, and didn't think to check on it until after he'd finished chewing his way through a Snickers bar.

He was so used to the blank screen, he had to do a double take a the message sat there waiting for him.

'*Of course not. I'm just on my way to the cathedral. Meet me there? x*'

Nicholas realised how fickle he was, but all his ire vanished in the face of finally getting a response. He couldn't help but grin, so he extracted himself from the room as unobtrusively as possible. He didn't forgive the fact that Fynn had failed to text him until now, but he couldn't help but feel a bit giddy. He still wanted to meet up, and he'd added another kiss.

'*Yeah sure! What time?*'

'*ASAP?*'

Nicholas chewed on his lip. Could he really head off into town, while his family were all busy working? This was *technically* wedding prep, he argued to himself. Surely they could spare him for a little bit.

"I need to pop to the venue," he said from the door. He addressed his mum, since she seemed the least scariest. "To show the musician around. They want to check out the acoustics. For the reception." He smiled and attempted not to fidget on his toes. "Is that alright?"

Danielle scowled, but Ash chimed in before anyone else could speak. "I think we've got this for now," she announced with a dismissive wave of her hand.

"You've done quite a bit already while we've been at work," his mum also said. He felt like that wasn't strictly true, but he wasn't going to argue with her. "Just be back for dinner."

"Will do," he assured her. He tried his best not to sprint from the room. But as far as he could tell, no one had picked up on the fact he'd said 'musician', and not 'harpist'.

***

St Albans was known for its cathedral almost as much as Winchester. It was a mighty structure, perched on the edge of town at the top of a hill that rolled downwards with long stretches of grass and the occasional looming, centuries-old tree. When Nicholas had read Harry Potter when he'd been younger, he'd pictured the cathedral as Hogwarts. Until the novelty had worn off, he'd imagined himself to be the eponymous hero, coming with friends or his sisters to play Quidditch in the grounds at the weekends.

Nicholas wasn't sure why Fynn wanted to meet here, but his last text had said he was inside. So Nicholas joined the soggy tourists who were bumbling through the massive front doors into the coolness of the cathedral's belly. Even for someone not even remotely religious, he couldn't deny its grandeur. Half a dozen enormous archways lined the aisle down to the alter, and the numerous stained glass windows loomed from up above.

The enormous organ was on the second-floor balcony overlooking the whole interior, and someone unseen was quietly playing typical sounding 'church music' as Nicholas thought of it. As it was the Easter holidays, plenty of people were milling around, but it wasn't hard to spot Fynn's short dreadlocks as he scanned the room.

He was sat by himself in the middle of a row, so Nicholas had to awkwardly scoot down to reach him. There was no chance Fynn was ever going to mistake him for being cool at this juncture, however, so he tried not to let it bother him.

"Hi," he whispered. He propped the dripping umbrella against the bench by his knee, and hoped the rain water would stop spattering on the stone slabs sooner rather than later.

Fynn turned to greet him with his silvery grey eyes. "Hey," he said. He seemed to consider his words, then turned to face the front of the cathedral once more. "Glad you came."

"Sure," said Nicholas.

He interlaced his hands and let them drop between his knees. As beautiful as this place was, churches gave him the heebie-jeebies. He hated the idea some celestial being was glowering down at him in judgement, especially now his circumstances had changed.

"So, um," he started, not sure if he was supposed to talk if he wasn't talking to God. "Are you praying, or just here for the scenery?"

Fynn smiled and let out what might have been an indulgent sigh. "Neither."

Nicholas licked his lips. "Are you religious?"

"Yes," Fynn answered with a nod.

"This religion?" Nicholas's theology may have been patchy at best, but he did know from growing up in the city that this was a Church of England cathedral, and that there were other kinds of variations of Christianity out there.

Fynn raised his pierced eyebrow at him, but Nicholas couldn't tell what it meant. "Not technically, no," he agreed.

"So that's why you're not praying?" On his walk over, Nicholas had promised himself he'd try and keep a tighter rein on his motor mouth, but apparently his gob hadn't got the memo.

Fynn turned and angled his body a little more towards Nicholas. "I don't really feel it works like that," he said. He wasn't cross, he sounded patient. "I like to come here to feel closer to God. Sometimes I talk to Him, sometimes I don't. It's not really about that."

"Oh," said Nicholas. He wasn't sure he followed – wasn't that why people had different religions and churches? So they could have their own ways of doing things? But, he knew his mum liked coming here to chill out from time to time, and she was atheist. So, maybe it was maybe just a therapeutic place. "Um, so it's okay for you – in your religion, to uh, be like you are?"

There was that eyebrow again. "You mean gay?" Fynn asked.

Nicholas's cheeks burned. He shouldn't have asked that. He was just trying to juggle his own, many thoughts on the matter. "Yeah," he mumbled, and rubbed at his face in an attempt to dispel the redness.

He was shocked as Fynn's fingers gently circled his wrist, and urged his hand away. "You do that a lot," he said. "Did you know?"

"Do what?"

"Pull and rub at your face," he replied, frowning.

Nicholas stared at where his fingers were resting lightly on his pulse point. "Uh, yeah," he said. "Old habit. Acne scars."

Fynn let him go, but his shoulders were still turned towards him. "It looks like poking it hurts."

"Not really," Nicholas told him with a shrug. "It's ugly scar tissue." That wasn't strictly true; sometimes the point was to make it hurt. He hated how disfigured his face was, and making it sore somehow made him feel better about it.

Fynn scowled at him. "They're not ugly."

Nicholas scoffed, then clapped his hand over his mouth as the laugh echoed around the room.

"Says you," he said, making sure to be quiet. He rolled his eyes. "You don't have potholes all over your face."

Fynn was still scowling. "They're just a part of you." Then he gave a smug, lopsided grin. "They give you texture."

Nicholas did a better job of containing his laughter that time, but he still shook his head. "Shut up," he said. Still, it was probably the nicest thing anyone had said about his face. Mostly people just ignored it as best they could.

"God is love," said Fynn after a minute's contemplation.

Nicholas didn't quite follow. "Uh, cool," he said.

Fynn held his palm up. "You asked what God thinks of me, being gay. How that works with my religion. And, I know not everyone agrees by a long shot, but I know that God is love. And love comes in all kinds of shapes and sizes."

Nicholas thought about that for a moment. "Really?"

Fynn nodded.

"We love our families, we love our friends, we love our passions. Some people even love their pets," he added with mirth. Nicholas nodded, although he couldn't say he had all that much love for Archibald. "And there's romantic love. Not everybody gets it, or wants it, but those of us who find it shouldn't be judged if two people are happy."

Nicholas considered what he was saying. "My mum has a friend who's married to a man who is, like, twenty years older than her. She's always been a bit...judgy about it," he admitted. "Maybe because he left his first wife for her. And I always thought she was right. But, if they're happy, isn't that what really matters?"

Fynn smiled wryly. "I don't know if the first wife would agree," he said with a chuckle. "But, yeah. In principle, I think if they're happy, that's what really matters. Whether people are from different races, or are a generation apart, or are the same gender. I think God is totally fine with that. In fact, I feel that's the point of life, right? To be happy?"

Nicholas had to agree. "I'd hope so."

"And if you find someone to share that with, isn't that pretty great?"

"I think so," said Nicholas quietly. He looked up at the massive stained glass window above the organ.

Despite his own atheist nature, Nicholas found that sort of comforting to hear. If perhaps there was a grand old deity out there, he'd really like to think they wouldn't smite someone like him once he reached whatever afterlife might be waiting for him on the other side.

"Shall we make a move?" Fynn asked after they'd spent several minutes looking up at the altar. "I guess it's too much to hope the rain has stopped?"

Nicholas scoffed. "Not as far as I can tell." Bloody weather.

He picked up the still-damp umbrella, and they both stood. It was awkward to shuffle out from between the pews, though Fynn looked less like he was going to topple into the next row at any given moment compared to Nicholas.

It was only a about a seven-minute walk along the crooked streets with their overhanging and lopsided Tudor houses. As it was still bucketing down, they both huddled under Nicholas's umbrella together, their shoulders rubbing together in the most agreeable way as they walked slowly towards the town hall. Their route would take them down the lane where the two of them had first met on Saturday.

"I'm sorry about last night," Nicholas said after a few minutes gnawing over his thoughts. He didn't want to have a go at Fynn for neglecting him, so apologising for his own behaviour seemed like a good tactic to open up the conversation.

Fynn tutted. "Why would you apologise? You didn't do anything wrong." His voice had taken on a hard edge.

But Nicholas felt a surge of hurt. As nice as it was that Fynn had texted in the end, his lack of communication was really starting to rankle. "Well, what am I supposed to think?" he said. He awkwardly pulled his arm free to put a bit of space between them. "You told me to text you, then didn't text back. I assumed it was because I'd pissed you off by inviting you out, then bailing the moment you arrived."

Fynn stopped walking on the street corner opposite the large furniture store, forcing Nicholas to do the same so they both remained under the umbrella. "Why would you think that?"

As much as he liked Fynn, Nicholas had had enough of the radio silences. He wanted to try and make him understand why he was upset. "What else was I supposed to think? A normal person would say thanks for doing what they'd asked, or at least follow up this morning to make sure I wasn't freaking out or something. So, I figured you were just being responsible asking *me* to text *you*, then just carried on being pissed off about having to leave the club early."

Fynn opened his mouth, then closed it again. He rubbed the back of his neck. "You really thought I was mad at you, for forcing me to go home?"

Nicholas hadn't heard his voice sound that small before, and despite his best efforts, he softened a modicum. "It was one of my theories," he said. "Yeah."

"But…" He frowned. "I didn't want to stay if you weren't there."

Nicholas shrugged. "How do I know you didn't really want to dance until three in the morning. Or get trashed on Blue WKD? You acted like you cared, and then…you didn't. I guess, I'm just confused." Nicholas needed to stop talking. He was getting dangerously close to sounding like he wanted to know if Fyn really *did* care about him.

Fynn dropped his hand from his neck. "Oh." He stared down the street, watching the cars slowly chugging by for a few moments. "I didn't mean any of that. It didn't even occur to me that you might think of it like that. I—" He looked sheepish and rubbed his hands together. "I was really happy when you texted. I just…went to sleep. I had no idea you'd be expecting a response."

Nicholas was tempted to excuse his behaviour by saying he was overly needy, or a drama queen. But that wasn't right. So he was simply honest. "I like a response. Otherwise I worry."

Fynn seemed to think about that carefully. "I'm sorry."

"That's okay," Nicholas told him.

But Fynn shook his head. "I just wanted to know you were okay, I thought that was obvious? I was…I was glad to hear you got home in one piece."

"And you're not grumpy that I wasted your evening?" Nicholas didn't want to fish, but he needed to hear Fynn say it.

The clock tower chimed two o'clock overhead, and they both took a moment to glance up at it. "You didn't waste my evening," Fynn said once they both looked back down. "You're right, I'm pissed off. But it's because I keep thinking about what might have happened if I hadn't been there."

"Look," said Nicholas with a sigh. "Don't get me wrong, I'm glad you were there, and I'm not going to say it was fine what happened. Or that it didn't shake me. But, it really could have been much worse, and I'm okay now." He smiled and touched Fynn's arm through his jacket, offering a little truce. "I was kind of more upset about the lack of text today."

Fynn looked pained. "Oh fuck, I'm sorry," he said heavily. "I was at the gym, and my phone was just sat in my locker for ages. I swear I texted you as soon as I saw it."

He slipped his hands into his jeans pockets, and looked kind of whipped. Nicholas felt the last of his anger melt away. "Okay," he said kindly. "But, just don't do it again."

"Not text you back?"

"Yeah." Nicholas grinned. "Even if it's just a 'yes' or a 'no' or a 'thanks'. It'll make me happy."

Fynn stepped closer to him again, and they linked arms under the umbrella once more. "Then that's what I'll do."

They began walking towards the town hall together again in amicable silence. The idea that Fynn would keep texting Nicholas at all made his heart flutter. He couldn't know what would happen once the wedding was done, but it was hard not to hope that whatever it was between them might carry on.

They wandered into the entrance of the town hall and spoke to a very helpful middle-aged lady on reception called Rebecca. She wasn't really supposed to let them through, but seeing as there weren't any events taking place at that very moment, she agreed to quickly escort them through to the main room where both the ceremony and the reception would take place.

"Only because that Danielle is the most organised bride I've ever had the pleasure of dealing with," she informed them as they followed her waddling down the main corridor. She wagged her finger at them with one hand, and unlocked the door with the other. "Everything on time or early, she's been such a pleasure."

Nicholas decided not to mention the fact that Danielle wasn't in fact the bride. They'd got what they'd wanted, and Fynn only needed a minute or two, apparently, to assess the acoustics of the room. He nodded to himself as he stood in the middle and took in the space. It just looked like an empty hall at the moment, but Nicholas had seen it all decked up when they'd visited for the wedding fair and knew it would look impressive as anything once all the chairs were in and Danielle had worked her magic with all their decorations.

His phone sounded off in his pocket, so he quickly fished it out to answer the call. He knew from the Spice Girls ringtone it was Clara without looking at the screen. "Hey sis," he said, with just a touch of guilt. He really should have been at home, helping with whatever last minute things needed doing.

He held his hand up to Fynn to get his attention, then walked back out the room so he could speak without interrupting Fynn's artistic assessment.

"*Oh Nicholas,*" Clara's voice came through the phone. She wasn't crying, but she wasn't throwing a parade either.

"Clara? What's wrong?" He stood in the empty reception where no one was around for him to bother.

"*We've have a bit of a hiccup,*" she said. In the quiet of the entranceway, Nicholas could just about pick up the sound of his cousin screeching in the background.

"Is that Danielle yelling?" he asked. Familiar dread was swirling in his guts again. He wondered if it was a new crisis, or if they'd finally found out about the bridesmaid dresses. Or the harp.

As it turned out, it was a fun, new mishap. "*She's talking to the company that made the place cards. We got sent the wrong ones by mistake.*"

Nicholas sagged against the reception desk. "You're kidding," he cried. How much bad luck could one wedding have? "Where are our place cards?"

There was a pause. "*Sydney.*"

Nicholas couldn't help the shriek-like bark that escaped his throat. "Sydney, *Australia?*" Well, there was no getting those back then. "What are the other place cards like?" he asked. After so many disasters, he was getting that much quicker at slipping into problem-solving mode. "If there are enough, can we bastardise them and put our guests' names on them instead?"

"There are probably enough," Clara admitted. "But they're all emblazoned with the Sydney FC logo."

Nicholas blinked. "As in...the football team?"

To her credit, Clara laughed. "*Yeah. Not exactly compatible with our romantic spring love theme.*"

Nicholas scoffed and rubbed his eyes under his glasses. "I don't think that's compatible with anyone's idea of romance. That poor bride."

"*Or groom,*" said Clara.

Nicholas's expression was impressed, but of course Clara couldn't see that.

173

"Or groom." He laughed. "Urgh, okay. What can we do?"

Clara sighed on the other end of the line. *"Danielle is determined to get our money back, but as for replacements, I guess we'll be doing some more arts and crafts."*

Nicholas grimaced, and reminded himself that he loved his sister, and would do anything for her special day. "Yes, it's going to be fine," he said firmly. "Look, I'm in town right now. If you want me to pick anything up, just let me know, alright?"

Clara promised she would, and without much more to say, they closed the call.

Fuck. Just what else could go wrong? Nicholas wasn't one to believe in signs, but it was sure looking bad from where he was standing.

"I think acoustic will be fine," Fynn's voice floated up from behind him.

Nicholas spun on his heels, clenching his fists and trying not to whimper. "This wedding is *cursed.*"

The receptionist eyed him suspiciously as she took her seat again. Fynn however just stepped closer and rested his hand on Nicholas's shoulder. "It's not cursed."

"It bloody is," said Nicholas. Sadly, that just made Fynn smile sympathetically.

"Come on." He put his hand on the small of his back again, gently urging him towards the door. "Do you fancy coming back to mine for a cup of tea? Or do you have to rush off?"

Nicholas was immediately torn. He felt he should head home, or stick around in town if Clara or Danielle wanted him to pick anything up for them. But a quick glance at his phone told him they hadn't messaged him yet.

There was no point in hanging around on the off chance they wanted him to buy card or stickers or whatever they might want for the new name places. And he didn't fancy being around Danielle's wrath if he could help it. If they contacted him later and asked for something, he could swing by and pick it up on the way home from Fynn's.

"Sure," he said gratefully. He picked up the wet umbrella from where he'd stashed it by the door. "A cup of tea would be lovely."

Fynn insisted they get another taxi. Nicholas made a feeble protest at the cost, but the weather truly was miserable. "Plus," Fynn told him, a sparkle in his eye. "I just got paid for this wedding gig I'm doing at the weekend. I'm minted."

Nicholas toyed with his phone throughout the short journey, half listening as the Uber driver ranted good-naturedly about politics. Fynn did a good job keeping up with him, but Nicholas couldn't really tell who or what he was for or against, but he did know that 'they' couldn't get away with it 'for much longer'.

Fynn had an account already set up on the app, but he did accept Nicholas giving him a few quid once the guy stopped outside his apartment building. "Cheers mate," he said, showing the driver the five-star rating he'd given him on his phone screen. He then followed Nicholas and his umbrella out into the rain.

Clara still hadn't texted him asking for him to buy anything, so Nicholas pocketed his phone and concentrated on making the now-familiar journey across the courtyard and into Fynn's building.

"Is your aunt back today?" he asked as they stepped inside. His glasses fogged up as usual under the might of the climate control, but Fynn was ready and waiting to take the umbrella off his hands so he could wipe the lenses off on his t-shirt.

Fynn shook his head. "Her conference is a three day one, so she's in London until Friday. I mean, she's back in the evenings, but I basically have the place to myself right now."

That sent a thrill down Nicholas's spine, he couldn't deny. They would be alone again. And with his new-found acceptance of his feelings and who he was, he couldn't help but find the prospect just a little bit enticing.

"Have you lived with your aunt long?"

Nicholas had been wanting to ask about Fynn's circumstances since Monday, but he'd not had the opportunity to do it without sounding like he was being completely nosy. He was curious, obviously, but it was because he wanted to get to know Fynn better, to understand why he didn't live with his parents and if he was okay with that. Not because he wanted gossip.

Fynn took his time fishing his keys out of his jacket. "A few years now," he said. He jammed the right one into the lock and let them inside. "My parents always wanted to live in France. They have a *chateau* in Dordogne, but they had to wait until I went off to college to move there permanently. They'd packed up and gone by the time I finished my first term, but my aunt already agreed to take me in, so I had somewhere to go outside of school."

He propped the umbrella up in the same corner as before, and flicked the kettle on as if nothing was amiss. But Nicholas was a bit stunned.

"They just…left?" he asked as he wriggled out of his shoes and coat.

Fynn's focus was on his tea making. "I wasn't planned," he said. He threw a smile over his shoulder at Nicholas. He was obviously aiming for flippant, but there was definitely something sad in his grey eyes. "My brother and sister are over a decade older than me. My mum and dad had already had to put off their retirement for several years because of me, so I can't say I blame them."

"For literally fleeing the country the first opportunity they got?" asked Nicholas. He stomped into the kitchen and stood in front of Fynn where he couldn't miss him. He crossed his arms and raised his eyebrows. "They ditched you!"

"Don't be daft. I still Skype them most weekends," Fynn insisted with a frown. "And my dad's on Facebook *a lot*. They're just living their lives, and I'm living mine."

Nicholas felt hurt on his behalf. What a way to tell a kid he wasn't wanted. Even if they had to hang on before they got to go have their fancy retirement, why would you tell your child that? Had Fynn always known he wasn't wanted? That he was an accident? Nicholas remembered what he'd said before: '*Art lasts. People don't.*' He had a better idea of where that little mantra had probably come from now.

"Well I'm glad you were born," he said quietly, his gaze on the linoleum floor.

He realised that sounded a little intense, but rose his head to find Fynn looking fondly at him. "Is that so?"

Nicholas cleared his throat. "Yeah. I mean, who else would save my sister's wedding?"

"Literally any other musician," Fynn said. He looked pleased, and made Nicholas's tea the way he liked it without having to ask for a reminder. "So, how exactly is this wedding cursed?"

Nicholas groaned. "Urgh! You don't even know. Everything's going wrong, and I'm pretty sure it's my fault."

Fynn lead the way with the soaked umbrella, just like the day before, and opened it up in his en-suite to dry. He closed the door to his room, even though they were alone, and for a moment Nicholas forgot what he was saying.

"How is it *your* fault?"

"Well, first it was the harp," he said.

He realised he'd sat on the end of the bed before he knew what he'd done. It would seem weird if he moved now, so he got comfy despite worrying it was too intimate. He held his fingers up, and started ticking off the catastrophes.

"Then the cat shredded the bridesmaids' dresses. We'll be lucky if we can save them, and if we can't, the girls will probably end up in Primark's finest. Then my aunt from Scotland got food poisoning, so we're not sure if her or her boys will make their flight now, and if they don't come that apparently destroys the table plan in its entirety. And don't even get me started on how our name cards got sent to the other side of the world, and the ones we have now are bright blue and orange, and I actually *care!* I care that these little bits of cardboard aren't right, and that the seats may be all wrong if we can't rearrange things. When I thought I lost the ties?" He pointed at Fynn, hoping to convey the gravitas of his woe. "I sat bolt upright in bed in the middle of the night, clutching my heart like Frankenstein's monster coming to terrible, terrible life, and thought the world was ending. Because of some ties!" He sucked in a deep breath, then caught sight of the umbrella sitting innocuously in the en suite. "Oh! Oh! And this bloody rain won't *stop!* Honestly, I'm just waiting for the groom to get struck by lightning, or for a plague of locusts to descend. It's probably only a matter of time!"

Fynn was gazing at him over the top of his mug with amusement in his eyes. He'd settled against his pillows, and the déjà vu from yesterday was getting a little strange. Except Nicholas liked it. It felt easy, like they already had a routine that was theirs alone. "And *how* is that your fault?"

Nicholas huffed. "Well I started it, didn't I? If I'd just remembered to book my mate's sister to play, perhaps the universe wouldn't be smiting me now."

But then, he would never have met Fynn. He squirmed. He was so tempted to say that out loud, but he didn't want to sound obsessive.

He sighed instead and smiled at Fynn, who was still watching him from behind his tea. "Hopefully it'll all work out for the best," he said. "I mean, you're probably better than some stuffy harpist, right?"

"Damn right," agreed Fynn with a positively sinful grin. "Hey, I thought of another song to play. I think you'll really like it."

He swapped his tea for his guitar and only needed to give it a quick adjustment before it was all tuned again.

"Is it one I'll know?" asked Nicholas, grateful for the distraction. If he was honest, he was even more pleased with the idea that Fynn had been thinking about songs Nicholas would like. He was warmed with the notion of being in his thoughts.

Fynn nodded, strumming the first chord. "Should do." He played another couple of simple chords. "This is my girl Hannah Trigwell – her version I mean."

Nicholas nodded back to show he was listening, eager to see what song Fynn had thought he'd appreciate.

"*We're no strangers to love,*" Fynn began slowly. He raised his eyes, watching Nicholas for his reaction, but he didn't recognise the song yet. "*You know the rules, and so do I.*" The guitar part was really stripped back, just one clean chord after another. But the vocal was gorgeous, and Nicholas already liked it very much. "*A full commitment's what I'm thinking of. I wouldn't give it to any other guy.*"

"It's beautiful," Nicholas murmured in encouragement. Fynn added a few extra notes to the melody, picking up and down the cords with the plectrum.

"Yeah?" he asked, grinning. Nicholas didn't quite get why that was funny.

"Sure. I think it'd be a great to play at the wedding."

Fynn licked his lips, and played the twiddly part for a bit longer. "*I just want to tell you how I'm feeling. Gotta make you understand.*"

Something twigged in Nicholas's brain. "Wait…"

"*I'm never gonna give you up—*"

"No!" Nicholas shouted. He almost lunged forwards, but his tea sloshed in his mug, and he quickly righted himself.

"*Let you down, run around, desert you.*" Fynn was cackling. He hopped of the bed as Nicholas tried to grab at his guitar again. "What's the matter, I thought you liked it?"

"You fucker!" Nicholas howled. He scrambled off the bed and slammed his mug down. "You are not Rick-Rolling my sister's god damn wedding!"

"*Never gonna make you cry, say goodbye,*" Fynn continued skipping across his room as Nicholas chased after him.

"Stop it!" giggled Nicholas, swiping at Fynn. But he was bigger and quicker, and he swung out of his reach.

"But I thought you liked it?" Fynn pretended to pout. "*Tell a lie or huuurt you.* It's *beauuutiful*, remember?"

Nicholas darted left and right, trying to get his hands on Fynn. They were both laughing like loons now. "It's Rick fucking Astley is what it is!" he cried, cornering Fynn by his wardrobes.

"Is it?" he asked innocently. "*I'm never gonna give you up…*"

He nipped past Nicholas's reach, turning them around and forcing Nicholas to stand against the wall. "Bastard!" he stammered through his laugh.

"*Let you down, run around, or—*"

And without warning, that was when Fynn leant in, and kissed Nicholas softly on the lips.

Chapter Nine

It was over before Nicholas even really knew it had begun.

Fynn pulled back, their lips separating, and the guitar's last note diminished between them. "You kissed me," said Nicholas. It seemed the obvious thing to point out.

Fynn was very still, his hands gripping his instrument tightly at both ends. "Yeah." His eyes didn't blink, or move even in the slightest. "I'm sorry."

Nicholas was all breath and no real voice. "Now who's apologising?"

"I should have asked."

He seemed absolutely torn up, which Nicholas couldn't understand at all. His heart was dancing on cloud nine. "So ask."

Fynn looked at him, the guitar hanging between them like a chastity belt. "May I kiss you? Again," he tacked on with a twitch of a smile.

"Oh god yes," rasped Nicholas, lunging for him.

Fynn grabbed the back of his head as Nicholas seized two handfuls of his t-shirt. This wasn't a kiss, it was a collision. There were more teeth than Nicholas had ever experienced before, but there was more tongue too, and Fynn's hands were yanking and pulling, and they couldn't see to get close enough.

Fynn ripped away, but before Nicholas could protest, he saw it was just so Fynn could hoist the guitar over his head, and set it carefully against his chest of drawers. And then his hands were slipping around Nicholas's waist and behind his neck, pulling their bodies together.

Nicholas felt his legs give way, but Fynn had him. His own hands moved from Fynn's shirt and wrapped around his back, feeling the muscles move as he sank into the kiss. Fynn cradled him upright, and then took a few steps backwards.

Towards the bed.

Nicholas followed.

His skin was alight with want; he'd never felt so heady. He allowed himself to be gently pulled downwards.

"Oh fuck," Fynn breathed into his mouth. It was all Nicholas could do was whine in response.

Fynn hit the mattress and broke contact to back himself up against the pillows, where he'd been perched for the last couple of days, and yet, Nicholas knew there and then he was in a whole new territory now.

He crawled up after him and was soon swallowed again in his embrace. He realised his glasses were in the way, so he took them off and twisted to try and put them somewhere where they wouldn't get broken. But Fynn plucked them from his fingers, and placed them on the bedside table for him, taking care to sit them the right way up. And then they were cuddled up once more.

Fynn's lips were thick and plush and needy. They moved against Nicholas's over and over, giving and begging in equal measures. Nicholas snuggled into the pillows, and let himself be claimed.

He had noted over the past few days that Fynn's hands were large. But he hadn't really appreciated how much so until they were roaming up and down his back, gripping his hip, slipping up his arm, combing his scalp. He moaned. It was highly embarrassing.

Fynn, however, responded with shifting his body a few inches, and with that he was hovering over Nicholas, kissing him with an intoxicating desperation. Nicholas reached up and dug his fingers into those gorgeous dreads. They were a little scratchy under his fingers, but he loved it, because they were Fynn's and they were amazing.

"Fynn," he whimpered, not really sure what he was doing. Just that saying his name, like this, pinned under him, it was unfathomable and yet all-consuming.

Fynn cradled his face with both his hands as he kissed him. His short beard was soft, but Nicholas's sensitive skin was unaccustomed to the sensation, and he winced.

"Are you okay?" Fynn asked, pulling back.

Nicholas felt like yanking him back down again, but he did need to catch his breath, so he settled for resting his hands on his chest instead. "Yeah," he rasped. "Yeah, I think so. This is brilliant. I, um, I'm really enjoying it."

Fynn smiled, and started lacing delicate kisses down his jaw on onto his neck. It made him shiver from head to toe. "I was kind of hoping," he admitted.

"Um." Nicholas tried to control his mouth, he really did. But seeing as it was no longer otherwise engaged, he couldn't seem to stop it. "Not that this isn't incredible, but, um…"

That did get Fynn's attention. He paused his ministrations and looked down. One hand held the back of Nicholas's head, and the other moved down to rest on his waist. "Is this okay?" he asked. There was a hint of strain around his eyes which portrayed his concern.

"Yeah, it's definitely okay," Nicholas was quick to assure him. "I just, I guess," he laughed nervously. Fynn's eyes looked so big when they were that close to him. "I'm a bit surprised."

The apprehension in Fynn's eyes melted away. "Why?" he asked. He wasn't helping Nicholas's concentration though, as the fingers around his waist were rubbing in little circles, and he dipped down to nuzzle his nose against his neck and clavicle.

Nicholas moaned, his eyes fluttering closed. "Well," he whispered, breathlessly. "You're you. You're gorgeous, and talented, and cool. And I'm just this dork—"

The bite on his shoulder was wholly unexpected, and made him break off his words in an undignified yelp. "We're going to have to work on your self-esteem," Fynn growled. He kissed and sucked at the spot at which he'd nipped, and Nicholas squirmed. "Do you want to see how much I like you?"

Spots danced in front of Nicholas's closed eyes, and he gasped for air. "Uh," he uttered. "Yeah, but, I – I've not done, um, anything…"

Oh fuck. Was there anything more mortifying than admitting to someone as hot as Fynn that he was a virgin? He'd barely ever made out with anyone; he'd never been interested before. When he had, at the odd birthday party or school disco, it had always been burdened with a sense of obligation. That he *should* have been enjoying himself, rather than actually deriving any pleasure from it.

Now he was drowning in pleasure, and he was about to blow it with his honesty.

But Fynn would very quickly work out he was totally inexperienced if they were going to carry on like this, and it was probably best to let him down now.

"If you're looking to just mess around," he blurted quickly before he could change his mind, "you might want to find someone better."

Fynn kissed his way up Nicholas's throat. "You're an idiot."

Nicholas huffed. "That's sort of my point. Why would you want to—*ngh*." He lost all coherency as Fynn took his earlobe between his lips and sucked. Who on Earth would have guessed that that felt so toe-curlingly sublime? "I don't know what I'm doing," he managed to bite out.

Fynn released his ear and gave him another tender kiss on the lips. "We can go slow," he promised.

But Nicholas shook his head. "Why would you want to go at all?" His voice sounded pathetic, but he couldn't help it. "Why would you be interested in me?"

Fynn frowned. It wasn't very attractive, Nicholas realised, whining and fretting. He couldn't help how he felt. "Because I am," said Fynn simply. "I like you. You're funny and thoughtful and seriously cute."

Nicholas blushed, obviously. "Yeah?"

"Yeah." Fynn took his time kissing him.

"I like you too," Nicholas managed to mumble as their lips parted briefly for air. Fynn grinned.

"Well, that's nice to know," he teased. "Can we carry on making out now?"

Nicholas rolled his eyes and acted annoyed, but it couldn't have been very convincing. "Oh, alright." He leant up to capture Fynn's mouth once again.

He realised he was being rather passive in this whole affair. He remembered his hands, which he'd just left pressed against Fynn's chest, and moved them along his body to hold his back and his neck. His skin was so warm under Nicholas's palms, and he wondered how good it would feel without clothes in the way.

Fynn shifted again so their bodies were closer together, and it became evident to Nicholas that his jeans were getting uncomfortable in the crotch area. He was hard as a rock, and his dick was definitely looking for some friction to give it some release. Fynn must have felt him fidgeting, and responded by rolling his body along Nicholas's. There were so many solid muscles moving over him, and Nicholas rubbed shamelessly back against them, like a cat seeking more petting.

"Oh my god," he mumbled into Fynn's mouth, his fingers digging into his back as he pulled him down closer. He finally got what his friends were going on about when they'd felt the need to share every gory detail after they'd snogged or groped a girl. This was incredible, it was like flying and getting high and being on fire all at once.

He and Fynn were undulating against one another now. Fynn, of course, had steady rhythm, so Nicholas used all his concentration to try and keep in time with him. He just wanted more. He felt like climbing on top of him, or wriggling completely underneath so he was squished; whichever felt better. He was insatiable.

But Fynn chose that moment though to reel in is efforts, leaning back and teasing Nicholas with little kisses, looking at him between each one with a lopsided smirk.

Nicholas whimpered and pouted, which seemed to be what Fynn wanted, as he grinned even broader. "You like that?"

"I like the proper kissing better," he grumbled.

"But you're adorable, I can't help it." However, he did relent and reward Nicholas with a languorous kiss. Meanwhile, he trailed his right hand down Nicholas's stomach, making his muscles contract at the ticklish sensation. But then he froze as Fynn's hand dipped lower, dragging over the denim of his jeans, heading between his legs. Nicholas twitched involuntarily as his hand cupped his groin, breaking the kiss. "Is this okay?" Fynn asked, his voice a low rumble.

Nicholas nodded. It was definitely okay. "Don't stop," he begged.

Fynn was nothing if not obliging. He rubbed his hand firmly but slowly over Nicholas's cock as he kissed him again. Nicholas wasn't sure what to do with his hands – should he be doing the same? It was all he could do to cling onto his shirt, he couldn't think about tackling Fynn's hard-on yet. He'd not honestly thought about touching another guy like that. His tentative fantasises had revolved around him getting touched. He'd have to gear himself up if he was going to look someone else's cock square in the eye.

But he got the impression it was something he'd get into pretty quickly. Having Fynn palm him was crazy hot, and he pushed wantonly against his hand. Their kisses were messy and aggressive, tongues thrusting against one another and teeth bashing against lips. The only sounds were their ragged breaths, and the moans escaping from Nicholas's throat.

How could he have ever thought he didn't want this? How could he have seen Fynn standing on that street, playing his guitar, and not yearned to feel his hands all over him, to taste him on his lips? He was completely lost in sensation, adrift in a sea of lust.

So when Fynn's fingers graced over his zip, he didn't hesitate arching his pelvis up to encourage him. "Please." Whatever Fynn had in mind, he wanted it.

Fynn seamlessly moved his kisses to the edge of Nicholas's jaw, just by his ear. "If you're not sure, we can stop at any time."

"If you stop now," Nicholas said, running his hand through his hair again. "I just might kill you."

He knew by now he liked making Fynn laugh, but feeling it rumble through his throat while his fingers deftly flicked open the button on his jeans was about a thousand times better. Nicholas turned his head into Fynn, rubbing his cheek against Fynn's stubble before he buried his face into his neck. He couldn't cope with anything else, other than the feel of Fynn's warm palm as he fished Nicholas's erection out from his boxers.

Nicholas had first discovered wanking at the age of fourteen. He knew guys that had been into it before then, but Nicholas wasn't all that fussed until he found his first porn. Having a computer in his bedroom meant he'd had the time and privacy to find some pretty decent stuff without having to pay for it. He was fussy, he knew, but now he appreciated it was because he'd more than likely been overly interested in what the guy looked like, rather than the girl. But he had certainly had his fair share of wanks since then.

But there wasn't really much to prepare him for the feeling of someone else's hand stroking down his length. It was impossibly erotic, and he even in his far-gone state, he was exceedingly glad that Fynn's aunt wasn't home. He was making all sorts of ridiculous noises, and he wasn't being quiet about it.

Fynn was cradling him to his chest, his breath hot as it ghosted over Nicholas's ear. He sped up his hand, tugging without lubrication against Nicholas's skin, making him snag his breaths in.

"Going to…" he uttered.

"It's okay," Fynn urged him. "It's okay."

It was an embarrassingly short time in which to come, but there was no way Nicholas could stop himself. He arched his body as his orgasm hit him like a train. Lights genuinely exploded behind his eyelids and he cried out, clutching at Fynn as the force of it swept over him. And then he flopped back on the bed, completely spent.

He heard Fynn chuckle, and he smiled as he felt him gently kiss his cheek. "Do you want to get cleaned up?" he asked after a few moments.

Begrudgingly, Nicholas peeled one eye open, then another. Fynn was still holding him, but he blinked as he realised he was lying there with goo all over his t-shirt and jeans, and his now soft cock was flopped on his belly like a dead fish. "Oh, yeah, sorry," he muttered in embarrassment, trying to cover himself as he made to move.

But Fynn grabbed his shoulder, and planted a firm kiss on his lips. "Nothing to apologise for," he told him, a steely glint in his eye. Nicholas gave him a tentative smile, then nodded.

"Okay," he said.

He slipped off the bed and hurried into the en-suite. He manoeuvred around his still drying umbrella, and, with the door pulled to, hastily mopped up his mess, wiped himself clean and did his jeans up again.

He could feel the panic rising in his chest. What had he just done? Was Fynn going to be weird with him now? He'd acted like a total hussy, a *selfish* hussy. Weren't both people supposed to come when you had sex? Was that sex? Did that count?

Was his still a virgin, or did the fact that someone else had made him come dissolve that now?

Oh fuck. How was he going to go back out there? Fynn was waiting. It was highly possible he was waiting because Nicholas needed to fulfil his half of the exchange. Was he ready for that, could he touch Fynn like he had him? He would almost definitely fuck that up. Fynn was so confident, Nicholas would probably take one look at his cock and choke, or faint, or start jabbering absolute nonsense.

And what if—

A soft knock came at the door. Nicholas hadn't even realised he'd been holding the sides of the sink so hard his knuckles had turned white, and he struggled to lessen his grip as he glanced over his shoulder. Fynn was stood leaning against the doorframe, his hands in his pockets as he regarded Nicholas.

"Hey," he said.

"Hey," Nicholas croaked back. His vision was a little blurry without his glasses, but at this distance, he could still make out the soft expression on Fynn's face.

He reached his hand out wordlessly, and curled his fingers a couple of times towards Nicholas. "Come here," he requested. With a little bit of effort, Nicholas managed to release the sink. His heart was in his throat as he stepped around the umbrella, and let Fynn take him by the hand. He pulled him into an embrace, and rested his chin on top of Nicholas's head. "Are you alright?"

"Um…"

Once again, Fynn walked them to the bed, but this time he did so with care, guiding Nicholas slowly until they were both lying down, facing each other. Nicholas's head settled comfortably on Fynn's shoulder, and he felt content with his hands wrapped loosely around his waist. Nicholas clasped his own hands together between their chests. "Do you, uh," he began. He swallowed thickly, and tried again. "Are you, should I…?"

"No," Fynn said, cutting off his awkward stammering.

"No?"

"No." Fynn tucked a lock of hair behind Nicholas's ear. It was an extremely sweet gesture. "I'm fine, don't worry about me."

"But you didn't—"

Fynn chuckled. "I'm fine, I promise. I liked seeing you happy."

Nicholas was pretty sure he turned the colour of beetroot. "Was I really loud?" he whispered, not sure he really wanted to know the answer.

But Fynn smirked. "Yes," he confirmed, and Nicholas groaned and smacked his chest. "It was brilliant."

"Shut up," Nicholas mumbled.

"I'll have to see if we can't get louder next time." Fynn wiggled his eyebrows. Nicholas just looked at him dumbly. Next time, as in, he wanted to do that again? His thoughts must have showed on his face, and Fynn gave him a small squeeze with his hands to get his attention. "If you want there to be a next time?" he asked.

The question was perfectly neutral. There was nothing in his voice to suggest he wanted that as much as Nicholas did, but neither was there anything that indicated he was eager to get Nicholas out of his room as soon as possible. "If that's what you want?" he whispered, almost too afraid to look at him.

But Fynn responded with a slow kiss and a full smile. "I'm pretty sure this is what I've wanted since Sunday," he said.

Nicholas's heart did a swan dive.

"Sunday?" he squeaked. "But I didn't even come over until Monday?"

Fynn licked his lips. If it were possible, they looked even more bee stung from all the kissing they'd been doing. *I did that*, thought Nicholas.

"Your texts were very sweet," said Fynn. "Every one of them made me smile a bit more."

Nicholas snorted and poked his chest lightly. "You didn't reply to hardly any of them." His tone was playful however, and he was pleased with the bashful grin it earned him.

"Yeah, yeah," Fynn grumbled. "Lesson learned, mister. I'll be better."

"You promise?" Nicholas said. How did he explain how much he wanted this? Whatever 'this' was. He wanted all of it, everything he could get. Fynn texting him and Fynn touching him and him being important and special to *Fynn*.

Fynn nodded. "So," he said slyly. "Are you telling me you *didn't* want to snog me since Sunday?"

Nicholas cringed, but it was an agreeable sort of sensation. "You made me realise I was *gay*," he said, not quite able to meet Fynn's eye. "Surely that counts for something?"

"It sure does," Fynn agreed.

Nicholas wasn't sure how long they lay there kissing. It wasn't the same as before, there wasn't that desperate urgency, although it was still invigorating in its own way. Surprisingly Nicholas didn't get another stiffy. There was definitely interest down there, of course, but it stayed as an enjoyable hum rather than something explosive.

He ran his hands all over Fynn's front and back and arms and hair. He found a little trio of moles on his neck that he had fun sucking on. He suspected his hickey wasn't going to be as good as the one Fynn had given him; he was lucky it was low down by his collarbone, or that might have caused some interesting questions at the wedding. But he still wanted to mark Fynn too, to show the world that he was now his. Even if no one else saw them, it thrilled him to know they were there, like a matching set.

It was getting late, and Nicholas knew he *really* needed to check his phone to see if Clara or Danielle had messaged him. Some of the shops closed at five o'clock, and he didn't want to miss being able to get any supplies just because he was getting lucky.

Really lucky.

But he was scared that if he moved, if he left this little bubble they'd created, the spell would break. Fynn had said about them doing this again, that he'd wanted to kiss Nicholas since Sunday. (Which was insane, by the way. Nicholas wasn't getting his head around that any time soon.) But did he really mean it?

Fynn touched his chin with his thumb. "Penny for them?"

Nicholas blinked, until he realised he meant his thoughts. "Um," he said, then changed his mind. "No, nothing," he said. He didn't want to come off clingy. That was a major turn off. Even as inexperienced as he was, he knew that. He tried to lean in for another kiss, but Fynn pulled away, keeping a few inches between them. "What?" Nicholas demanded.

Fynn arched an eyebrow. "You tell me."

Nicholas scowled. "It's nothing," he insisted, but Fynn scowled right back. "I just," he said. He didn't want to come across needy, but he felt it couldn't hurt to get a *little* reassurance. "Uh, well, I wasn't sure, I mean…" He took a breath and made himself chill out. "What happens now?"

"Between us?" Fynn asked, and Nicholas nodded. "Whatever you like."

That put the ball uncomfortably in Nicholas's corner. He wanted Fynn to take charge. He tried not squirm or get embarrassed, but for some ungodly reason he could feel tears pricking at the back of his eyes. What the hell was that about?

"Um, well, maybe…more?" he said gruffly. He blinked his eyes several times, and willed the moisture to go away.

Fynn chuckled. "Sorry, I guess I assumed that much."

"I've not done this before," Nicholas said in a rush. "Not dated anyone I mean – not that I'm saying—!" He clamped his mouth down, trapping the rest of the sentence. Once it was safely swallowed, he carried on. "I don't know what you might want to…do. Erm…" Oh Christ he was cocking this up. Well, in for a penny, in for a pound. "Have you ever dated anyone before?"

Fynn stroked the side of his face, his expression pensive. "I had a boyfriend at collage," he admitted. Nicholas's heart sank, immediately picturing some dancer hunk, sweeping Fynn off his feet. "For about nine months. And I dated a few guys since, but no one stuck." Was that what Nicholas was? Just 'the next one'? His insides went cold. But Fynn rubbed his thumb against his cheek, urging him to pay attention. "I'm not seeing anyone else right now though, and I plan on keeping it that way," he said.

"Oh." Nicholas didn't trust himself to say much more than that. But he did allow himself a little hopeful smile.

Fynn licked his lips and rubbed their noses together. "Other than you, I mean."

Nicholas's heart sped up. Was Fynn really asking him…something? "Me?"

"If you want?"

That was a dumb question, but Nicholas loved that he asked it all the same. "Yeah, yes, I mean… I'd like that a lot."

"Me too," Fynn said. He cuddled him close again, and gave his earlobe a quick tug with his teeth. He must see what that did to Nicholas's senses, the bastard. "Are you free tomorrow?"

Without looking at the itinerary, Nicholas wasn't sure what wedding shenanigans might be planned for then, especially with the crises piling up. But if Fynn wanted to see him, he was determined to find a way. "I'd love that," he admitted. "If I can."

"No pressure," said Fynn. He gave him a little kiss on his tip of his nose. Nicholas was so used to his skin being a problem, to it being something repulsive, the simple action made him shiver. Fynn liked him. He even liked his pockmarked face. If that wasn't remarkable, he didn't know what was.

***

Nicholas listened to 'Walking on Sunshine'. On repeat. The whole way home.

It was hard to concentrate on anything at all. He almost walked out in front of two different cars, stepped in several ankle-deep puddles, and if it hadn't been for his umbrella he would have smacked straight into a lamppost. It didn't matter, though, he just laughed every mishap off.

He'd just been kissed. By Fynn. Fynn fancied him. Fynn wanted to carry on seeing each other, regardless of the wedding. Fynn wanted to kiss him more. Fynn wanted to do…other things too.

That sent an apprehensive, but also sort of delicious shiver down his spine.

Guys could obviously give blow jobs to one another. Nicholas had always watched those online with a mildly grossed-out fascination. Was it really as great as everyone made out? The idea of having someone's – Fynn's – mouth sucking on his cock seemed sort of disgusting. Maybe if you'd just had a shower it would be okay, but otherwise it had to taste kind of awful, right? But if the hand job was anything to go by, then maybe he could be convinced otherwise?

And then sex. He sort of knew that gay guys took it up the arse, but that had always seemed so abstract – a punchline to a joke. His mates would wind each other up about giving one another a good bumming all the time. But, again, if people really did it, then maybe it was actually kind of enjoyable?

Nicholas shook his head as he crossed the road, careful to avoid being splashed by the vehicles tearing through the puddles. That was definitely too advanced for him. He was still a newbie gay. For now, he turned his thoughts around to just how it would feel to *see* Fynn naked, let alone touch him.

He'd gotten a fair enough impression of his manhood through his jeans earlier, enough at least to know it was a decent size. Would it be darker than the rest of his skin? Nicholas's went pretty red when it was all excited. It looked kind of angry, if he was honest. Still, it seemed Fynn had been more than keen to get his hands on it. He had no reason to feel proud, but he did anyway. It was just the cock he'd always had, that he'd been born with, but it was one of the most intimate parts of his body, and Fynn had liked it.

He amused himself mulling that over the rest of the way home. They'd left it that Nicholas would assess the situation once he got back and do his best to make time to see Fynn the next day at some point, even if they only met up in town for a coffee.

Although, Nicholas knew he'd much rather meet at his flat again. In his room. With the door locked.

He hadn't received a text from his sister or cousin, but Nicholas was still feeling a twinge of guilt at being out for ages. But he was also more than a little relieved that he hadn't had to put himself in the middle of another crisis either, especially an arts and crafts one. The idea of having to sit and glue fiddly bit of lace together or do anything with glitter made him want to bang his head against the wall.

But now he was back, he'd do it if they asked. He'd had one of the best afternoons of his entire life. The least he could do was spend the evening folding name cards.

He was surprised as he rounded his parent's driveway to find Peter outside, lurking away from the rain under the protection of the carport. Nicholas didn't miss as his soon-to-be brother-in-law looked up and realised he was no longer alone, so immediately dropped the half-finished cigarette from his mouth and crushed it with his trainer.

"Hey," he called out sheepishly as Nicholas approached.

"I thought you'd quit?" Nicholas asked. He didn't put any judgement into his words, although he knew how much Clara had hated it before.

Peter rubbed the bridge of his nose and pushed his glasses back up. He was a gangly sort of fellow; all limbs and heavy feet, like a puppy. He was taller than Nicholas, but then most guys were. He was about as skinny, though. Clara joked that both of their big appetites would catch up to their waistlines one day, but so far, their metabolisms remained on their sides.

"Emergency," said Peter glumly. "I haven't had one for months, I swear."

Nicholas shook his head. "Hey man, your secret's safe with me." He fished into his pocket and pulled out the packet of gum he'd just bought. He wasn't sure if kissing gave you bad breath, but it had seemed like a sensible precaution. "Did the girls sort out the name cards."

Peter took a couple of pieces gratefully and popped them in his mouth, then shoved his hands in his pockets. He was only wearing a light shirt over his t-shirt, but he didn't seem to be shivering. "Yeah, they've got some plan. Kinny was printing things off the computer when I came out. It's not that."

Nicholas was almost too afraid to ask. "Then, what?"

Peter shook his head and looked out into the rain. "It's this whole wedding, it's such a circus. Why does one day require so much fucking faff?"

Nicholas laughed nervously. "It's just the nature of it, I guess," he told him. "But, it'll be worth it, right? Clara's worth it?"

Peter seemed to take a moment to process what he'd said. "Oh god no," he cried, then yanked his hands from his pockets to wave them at Nicholas. "I mean, yes, of course she is! No, no, no, this isn't cold feet!"

Nicholas let out the breath he'd been holding. "Okay," he said, grateful Peter had picked up on his fear immediately. "Sorry, you had me worried for a second there."

He and Peter hadn't really hung out much over the years, but Nicholas did like him very much. He knew Danielle looked down her nose at the fact he was 'only' a manager at a roleplaying games shop, but he truly loved what he did. Nicholas had popped in once or twice on a Saturday in the past, and he'd seen him running Warhammer battles for eager pre-teens. He liked advising people on the perfect way to mix their paints for the models and he knew which books were just for right for their Dungeons & Dragons campaigns, because he'd read them all. Nicholas got the feeling he'd be an amazing dad one day.

Maybe his cousin's snooty attitude was finally becoming clear after a week spent in each other's company. The last thing Nicholas wanted was for Peter to feel unwelcome in the family.

"I supposed Danielle is making a big deal out of a lot of things, isn't she? Other people's weddings probably aren't run like a dictatorship."

Peter snorted, then immediately looked guilty. "No, no," he said quickly around his gum. "She's fine – great! And I knew she was highly strung, but this has really brought out her, um, enthusiastic side."

Nicholas was impressed at his tact. "You can say she's being a controlling bitch, you know," he told him, grinning.

Peter looked shocked. "No," he said hastily. "I didn't mean it like that."

But Nicholas clapped him on the shoulder and winked. "Of course you didn't. Look at it this way, it's only for a could more days. Then you'll be on holiday – and married! That's pretty awesome, right?"

Peter did give him a smile at that. "Definitely awesome," he agreed. "It just feels like there's a mountain to climb between now and then."

"Urgh, tell me about it."

"Well," said Peter slowly. *Oh dear lord,* Nicholas thought as his heart dropped. What now? "The photographer is double booked."

For a moment, Nicholas just stared. "What?"

"He double booked himself." Peter sighed and bit his lip. "If I'd made the booking sooner, we would have got in first. But as we were second, he has to honour the first couple."

"That's not your fault!" Nicholas yelled. He didn't want the neighbours to hear, so he got a hold of himself. But he was so angry at the universe he could honestly have screamed. "How can a professional double book himself like that? That's outrageous!"

"To be fair," said Peter, "he was totally ashamed."

Nicholas scoffed. "That doesn't bloody fix the problem, does it?"

Peter bobbed his head. "He did say he had some people he knows that might be able to step in," he said. "Other photographers."

"They better bloody give you a discount now," said Nicholas.

Peter raised his eyebrows. "Really?"

"Hell yeah. That's the least they can do!"

Peter mulled it over for a moment. "Well, that would be pretty cool if they did."

Nicholas was tempted to ask for the numbers himself and do the chasing, but if the photographer was truly keen on redeeming himself, he'd probably do a better and quicker job of ringing around his contacts. He didn't want to undermine Peter either; he was a grown man, he could manage one disaster. There were plenty to go around, after all.

"Does Clara know?"

Peter looked at his watch. "No, I was hoping the photographer and I could get a replacement before anyone else found out," he admitted. He shrugged and rubbed at his mouth, obviously feeling guilty, but if there was anyone else who could sympathise with his plight, it was Nicholas.

"You've still got time. Besides," he added. "I'm going to let you in on a little secret." It was a gamble telling him, but he hoped it would make him feel better until he heard back from the photographers. "The bridesmaids' dresses aren't really at the dry-cleaners. They're at Kinny's mum's, getting altered after the cat ripped the fronts of all three of them."

Now it was Peter's turn to ogle. "Oh shit." He laughed unsurely. "Who else knows about that?"

"Just Kinny and Ash," Nicholas said with a sigh. "It's probably dangerous to surprise Danielle with them, but none of us could face her stressing until we had a solution to give her."

Peter clasped his shoulder. "You're a brave man," he told him.

Nicholas was going to reply that he was actually a total coward, but the back door burst open before he could speak.

"Oh," cried Danielle in surprise. "Nicholas, you're back. Good. Everything alright with the harpist?"

It's a guitarist. IT'S A GUITARIST. "Yep, fine."

Oh yeah. *Total* coward.

"I must say, that's very diligent of her to assess the venue beforehand." Danielle nodded. Despite being in the middle of a frenzied crisis, she still had perfect hair and makeup, and a nice top on with her jeans. Nicholas wasn't sure how she did it. "Okay, well if you boys could come back in, we're ready to get the production line going." She clenched her fist and gazed into the middle distance. "We'll get these cards finished tonight even if it kills us."

Nicholas suspected it just might.

Chapter Ten

(2 days to go…)

Come Thursday, Nicholas tentatively began to hope they were on their way out of the woods. Not there completely, but tiptoeing along the path with the sunshine peeking enticingly through the trees, spurring them on.

Figuratively, of course. It hadn't stopped bloody raining.

But one of Clara's good friends from uni had thoughtfully suggested Clara get a wedding umbrella, just in case. It wouldn't have even occurred to Nicholas that such a thing existed, but the night before, his mum had gone online and found a lovely white brolly with a frilly edge, like a petticoat, complete with sparkly handle. She'd paid a fortune for next day delivery, but it gave them all the peace of mind that even if the weather continued to spite them, they had a backup plan.

At the breakfast table that morning, Peter had caught Nicholas's eye, then waited until no one else was particularly paying attention before he gave him two excited thumbs up from under the counter. That could only mean the photographer had come through with a replacement, and Nicholas felt his whole body sag with relief.

Then, Kinny had pulled him to one side, and showed him pictures of two of the three finished bridesmaid dresses. Her mum and her brother (who'd text her the photos) had done a beautiful job of transforming the ruined skirts into a 'layered dip-hem' as Kinny called it, and even added extra clear sequins to the new edge to give them extra sparkle. Apparently, the last one would be finished by tomorrow morning. It was all going to be fine.

Which is probably why, when they were loading up the car to take everything to the venue in advance of Saturday, Nicholas only felt a tiny bit bad lying his arse off.

"Trev's had a bit of an emergency," he said to his mum in a moment when he got her alone. "His parents are trying to stop him going to this convention for his comic book, and he needs some moral support. Are you alright if I don't come with you?"

He definitely felt bad at the outpouring of concern his mum unleashed in support of Trev. "Oh that woman," she fumed, referring to Trev's mum. "I'd like to give her a piece of my mind!" She ruffled her hair and searched angrily through her handbag for her lipstick. She always reapplied her lippy when she was feeling agitated. "Yes, of course love. We've got more than enough pairs of hands to tackle loading and unloading – there's only so much space in the cars as it is. We'll see you this evening, yeah?"

Nicholas told himself he'd done enough fretting in secret, so it was okay to tell a bit of a white lie. Besides, he was too excited about seeing Fynn again to dwell on it for long.

Between so many of them, they had indeed managed to get the new name cards made before midnight the previous night. Which had given Nicholas plenty of opportunity to lock himself away in his room, then start delving through the internet as he launched into his new and exciting phase of sex education.

He'd started on a couple of his usual porn sites, this time venturing into the men on men sections. It wasn't like he'd never drifted that way before, but this was the first time he was looking with intent. He made sure to angle himself so he could see his door, just in case he was disturbed, kept only one headphone in, and then he began.

There seemed to be a lot of really macho stuff that tried to convince you that the beefed-up actors were really straight. He thought that was a little odd, but he'd long ago decided that he firmly believed in 'each to their own' when it came to porn. One of his and Trev's mates from school was obsessed with Asian girls who looked barely legal, and a guy he knew from uni halls had a strange fixation with sheep, neither of which he could say he was all that comfortable with. So, if certain gay guys got off thinking about turning straight ones with their wicked ways, that seemed sort of tame in comparison.

Nicholas was drawn in by descriptions that included the words 'Twink' and 'Fem'. Not because they looked like Fynn – none of the guys really looked like Fynn – but they did look kind of like him. Slim and more effeminate. There were some movies that paired them with bigger guys, but he found himself getting lost for over an hour watching a few of the prettier guys who had been paired together. He had lapped up their adventurous session all over a rather fancy hotel room, as they went at it again and again.

He'd been left with a raging hard-on that hadn't taken long to sort out, but also a slightly clearer understanding of the mechanics of how certain things worked. He still wasn't sure about giving head, or receiving it, but the boys' faces in the films had looked like they'd loved every second of it. He was, therefore, determined to keep an open mind.

A big difference between a man with a woman and a man with a man seemed to come down to stretching. He supposed it made sense that lady parts were naturally good to go, whereas if you were coming from around the back, you needed to take a bit more time and effort.

Again, Nicholas had reassured himself that the actors had really seemed to be having fun as they'd shagged on the bed…and the sofa…and the fluffy rug by the fireplace…and against the wall. But that was their job. They were paid to put on a show. Nicholas wasn't sure he really fancied the idea of something being pushed inside him over and over again. He was too timid to even experiment with it himself, once he'd slipped into bed and turned the lights out. But at least he didn't feel so completely clueless that morning as he waved the others off.

He went back inside to collect his things and texted Fynn that he was on his way. He was working his usual shift at the Italian restaurant, so that gave them a few hours to spend together.

His aunt would still be at her conference, so they'd be alone again. Nicholas's mind drifted back to the videos he'd watched the night before, and he felt a flutter of nerves. Fynn would probably want to do that. He'd had other boyfriends before, so Nicholas would have to catch up fast, otherwise he could lose his interest. He had an irrational flare of disappointment at himself that he couldn't have worked out his preferences sooner. Maybe then he could have messed around with a boy or two as well, and not be such an embarrassing newb now for Fynn.

He was lost in thought as he picked up his keys and slipped on a jacket. When the paw came out from under his bed and several claws sliced at his ankle, the shock got him almost as much as the pain. *"Archibald!"* he screamed, clutching at his ankle. *"Get out!"*

The cat shot out into the hallway. He then turned on the spot and sat looking at him, his eyes narrowing in satisfaction as his tail swished back and forth. As if he hadn't caused enough damaged already, he had to go and draw blood. Nicholas muttered under his breath as he grabbed the last of his things and slammed his door behind him. That finally made the feline scarper.

The scratches stung a little as he pulled his shoes and socks on, but once Nicholas started walking, he calmed himself down, and managed to forget about the pain.

He was getting himself worked up over nothing. Fynn had panicked about kissing him yesterday, and stopped to check Nicholas was happy every step of the way before he'd jerked him off. He wasn't going to get pissy if Nicholas said he wasn't ready for anal. Surely?

There was no need to over-think things. They were just going to hang out, like they had been the last couple of days. Except this time, with maybe a bit more kissing. Kissing Nicholas could definitely get on board with.

The bus was nowhere to be seen, but Nicholas felt like walking anyway despite the rain. It would only take him half of the route anyway. A bit of exercise would dispel some of the nervous energy that had built up despite his best efforts to stay chilled. By the time Fynn let him into the apartment building, he was a mixture of excitement and dread, and he kept swaying between the two.

He half-imagined that Fynn might jump him as soon as he reached the apartment door. However, all he got was a soft kiss on the cheek as Fynn greeted him, before leading him straight to his bedroom. Nicholas struggled with a flurry of conflicting emotions as he followed him down the corridor. Had Fynn changed his mind? Was he only bringing him in to dump him? Or was he going to swing the other way, and ravage Nicholas on the bed. Images of the movie he'd watched the night before rushed through his mind, and he couldn't work out which made him more nervous.

Instead, Fynn just opened up his umbrella in the en-suite like he had the day before, and then sat at his computer desk. "I thought we could watch a film," he said, getting Netflix up on his screen.

"Oh," said Nicholas, stepping closer.

A film was safe. Nicholas was at war with himself again though, struggling between relief and disappointment they weren't just going to jump straight to the sex. He wasn't sure how he really felt. As soon as he was close enough, Fynn pulled him over to sit on his lap, cradling him with one arm. The height difference meant that Nicholas tucked into his side nicely, and that felt all kinds of nice. He finally stopped fretting, and resolved himself to just enjoy being with Fynn.

"What do you fancy?"

"Um," said Nicholas shyly. "I don't mind. What were you thinking?"

Fynn beamed down at him, and nuzzled his nose through his hair. "Have you seen Ghost in the Shell?"

It turned out, Fynn had quite a thing about anime, and the original Japanese version of the film was one of his all-time favourites. Nicholas happily agreed, jumping at the chance to get to know him and his interests a little bit better.

Before they started watching, Fynn tugged his hand and lead him into the kitchen. "I hope you're hungry?" he asked. He proudly showed him how the night before, at the end of his shift, he'd got the chef to make him two portions of the restaurant's renowned tagliatelle carbonara to take away, and he quickly heated them up in the microwave. "I also got us some Krispy Kremes," he informed Nicholas between kisses, as they hugged by the kitchen counter. The sink was still full of dirty dishes, and there were crumbs and food packets everywhere, but in that moment it all seemed extremely romantic to Nicholas.

"Oh," he exclaimed with a laugh. "My sister and her husband *met* at a Krispy Kreme. It wasn't their first date exactly; their World of Warcraft team had a meet up in real life, and they just happened to pick there to get everyone together. They'd got on online before, but it's a bit hard to flirt while you're raiding mythical forests apparently. As they soon as they met in person she said she just *knew*. Isn't that romantic?"

Danielle liked to tell people that Peter and Clara had 'met online', and definitely mislead them to think she meant on match.com or something. But Nicholas remembered that back then, dating websites were seen as being pretty lame, so he didn't really understand how that made it any cooler. Besides, wasn't it better that they'd met doing something they both loved?

"Very romantic," agreed Fynn, giving him another kiss.

But Nicholas realised he might have put his foot in it and felt the familiar hint of embarrassment flush up his neck. "Oh, uh," he spluttered, not quite able to meet Fynn's eye. "Not that I meant that *this* was a date…"

"It isn't?" Nicholas peeked up between his lashes at him. Fynn looked amused, and he rubbed his hand up and down Nicholas's back.

"Erm," he ventured, attempting to be brave. "Can it be?"

Fynn grinned and gave him a long kiss. "I promise, once the wedding is over and we get some sunshine, I'll swap some shifts around and take you out to dinner, okay? But, yeah, I think this counts as a first date."

The thought made Nicholas dizzy.

He didn't know where this was going, or what 'this' even was yet. But if he got to have one date with Fynn today, and they were already talking about the next one, that seemed incredibly exciting to him.

Nicholas's mum had a thing against having hot food in the bedrooms, or anything that would get bits in the covers, so he wasn't accustomed to having much more than cups of tea in bed. But Fynn's room was more like his own little apartment, especially with the independence of the en-suite. So it didn't seem so strange to have a pair of bean-bag trays propped on their laps, with glasses of juice and the doughnut box waiting for them on the bedside cabinets. They snuggled close together, and Fynn used his phone to start the film.

Nicholas quickly realised he wasn't a big fan of anime. Or at least, this particular kind of anime; he'd most certainly gone through a Pokémon phase in his youth. This was beautiful, for sure, and he could appreciate the depth and complexity of the plot. But he couldn't seem to keep his full attention on it. He guessed he preferred his action and sci-fi with a bit more humour.

Still, he absolutely loved being cuddled up with Fynn; they were actually under the covers. He didn't care they both still had their jeans on, the concept was definitely heady. The pasta was creamy and tangy, with tender lumps of bacon lurking in the sauce, and Nicholas was more than occupied for some time in cleaning his plate. That and the Krispy Kremes got him over halfway through the film, and then Fynn encouraged him to lay against his side, his head resting on the dip between his shoulder and his chest.

Nicholas was still most definitely praying for the rain to pack up by Saturday. But in that moment, it made him feel so cosy, being all wrapped up with a gorgeous guy, hidden away from the gloom in their little bubble of contentment. Ordinarily, if he was bored during a film, he'd start chatting, asking questions, or purposefully trying to distract his companions by whatever means possible. But seeing Fynn so wrapped up in the action was its own reward, and he allowed himself to flit his eyes between the screen and his date, letting his mind wander.

He couldn't believe it had only been five days since misfortune had thrown them together. He could never have predicted that this was how events would turn out; that he'd realise his own sexuality in such a sudden manner, and then that this gorgeous boy would be the one to make the first move on *him*. Him. Little Nicholas Herald, who wasn't particularly special or good at anything, had caught the eye of such a stunning, talented hottie. He felt like he was in a fairy-tale.

"What?"

Nicholas hadn't realised he had been staring. But Fynn was now looking down him with mischief. "What?" Nicholas repeated back.

Fynn bit his lip and arched the pierced eyebrow. Nicholas quite liked when he did that. "You're missing the end of the film," he chastised, but Nicholas was pretty sure he didn't really mind.

"Oh, sorry," he said anyway. He made a show of readjusting himself and concentrating on the screen.

After a few minutes, he could feel a hole being burned into the top of his head. "What?" he demanded, glancing upwards. He had a feeling though that the smirk on his face gave him away.

"Nothing," said Fynn devilishly.

It was a good job they'd already moved the trays and plates away to the floor, because it meant there was nothing to hinder Fynn as he shimmied down under the covers, coming face to face with Nicholas.

"Hi," said Nicholas nervously.

Both their heads were comfortably on the pillows now, and Fynn pulled their bodies closer together, his arms and legs all wrapped around Nicholas. He felt deliciously trapped.

"Hello," replied Fynn. There was a teasing note to his voice, and Nicholas might have thought before that Fynn was mocking him. But now, after a few days spent getting to know him, it just sent a shiver down his spine.

The kissing started off slowly. Fynn's hands drifted along Nicholas's arms and down his back. But then the top hand slipped under his t-shirt, skimming across his hip, and the temperature under the duvet shot up several degrees in an instant.

Nicholas moaned and chased the touch, making Fynn laugh into his mouth. Nicholas growled. It probably sounded like a puppy, but he tried to make it commanding, and without thinking, made the bold move of capturing Fynn's lower lip between his teeth.

He was still vaguely aware of the film still playing in the background as Fynn suddenly shifted so he was straddling Nicholas, looming over him with the covers pooled around his waist. He licked the lip Nicholas had just nipped. And then he took his t-shirt off.

It was one fluid motion. He just reached over his back, seized the material, and with one tug it whipped past his head, banished to the floor. Nicholas gulped. He had no finesse whatsoever, and fumbled even the basic task of trying to remove his glasses. But then Fynn's fingers were brushing his temples, and he gently pulled them from Nicholas's face, taking care as he laid them by the empty box of doughnuts.

He stared at Fynn's chest, running his hands over his pecs and shoulders. The few tattoos he'd already glimpsed along his arms were joined by another couple down his ribs and by his hip. They were all black ink, but other than that, Nicholas wasn't sure what they had in common. Some were just tribal looking swirls, others were stars and animals, one looked like a quote and there was definitely some sort of magical-looking pirate scene going on over his left shoulder and down to his bicep. Nicholas would have to ask him about them one day.

Fynn wasn't overly muscly, but he had good definition. Nicholas had never had any interest in going to the gym, he was just naturally slim and wiry. But right then, he wished he'd made a bit of effort. He definitely didn't want to take his own top off.

But Fynn didn't seem to have the same hesitations in the slightest. After allowing Nicholas to have a bit of a perv and a grope, he slipped both his hands under Nicholas's shirt and ran them upwards, dragging the material with him. Nicholas flinched. He hadn't meant to, but he'd reacted before he could think.

Fynn froze immediately, and he felt a surge of guilt. He didn't want them to stop, or for Fynn to feel bad. But he couldn't help his hesitations.

"Too much?" Fynn asked, because even though he was shit at texting, he was apparently pretty good at communicating in bed.

"No, no," Nicholas quickly insisted. "I just...well I don't look like you."

"What?" Fynn cocked his head. "Black?"

Nicholas's laughter rang obtrusively through the quiet room. But the tension left him right away, and he slapped Fynn's arm good-naturedly. "No, smart arse. Buff. You're, um, you know? Pretty hot. And I'm all skinny and stuff."

He wasn't surprised by the flush that blazed across his cheeks, but he was surprised by Fynn's predatory smile. "You don't think you're hot?" he asked, leaning in closer.

Nicholas scoffed. "Of course not, shut up."

Fynn didn't seem convinced, judging by the way he started lacing open-mouthed kisses up Nicholas's neck. "You don't think you're pretty?"

That made Nicholas squirm. "Boys aren't supposed to be pretty," he said.

Fynn came up and rubbed their noses together. Fuck, he was good at this. Nicholas felt just as clumsy and inexperienced as he had yesterday, despite his little research venture the night before.

"Says who?"

"Like, the whole of Western society," said Nicholas.

"Well *I* like pretty boys," said Fynn. "But I won't call you that if you don't like it."

Now Nicholas felt like he'd made a fuss. "Um, maybe I could get used to it?"

Fynn kissed him on the mouth, and rolled his body down over Nicholas's. "How about *gorgeous?*" he suggested. "Cute? Hella fine?"

Nicholas squeaked out a laugh and shoved him spiritedly. "Shut up," he said. But he didn't really mean it.

Fynn took his time, distracting Nicholas with kisses and stroking his large hands over his ribs and stomach. His fingertips found Nicholas's nipples, and he was shocked at how good it felt to have someone pay attention to them. He got that boobs were important; everyone involved always seemed to enjoy those being played with. But he hadn't appreciated it could feel good for a guy as well, and he groaned helplessly.

This time when Fynn moved to take his t-shirt off, Nicholas helped him.

He gasped as Fynn covered his body with his own. The sensation of so much skin on skin was incredible, and he shuddered all over. Fynn trailed his kisses away from Nicholas's mouth, along his throat, and then down his chest, until he wrapped his lips around one of Nicholas's nipples.

He choked out a cry, slapping his hand over his mouth and screwing his eyes shut. The boys in the porno hadn't done this, but they bloody should have. It was like a magic button of tingly deliciousness. He tried not to writhe, but it wasn't easy.

He felt the hum of Fynn's laugh vibrate through his skin, and he wriggled and gasped in appreciation. Fynn was sucking and licking, making the soft flesh hard and sensitive. "Oh my god," he whispered.

Fynn didn't stop there. He'd well and truly disappeared under the covers now, and Nicholas panted as he felt his kisses marking a path down his belly, and his fingers working on his zip, the same as yesterday. Except, this time Fynn didn't seem intent on using his hands.

Nicholas whimpered, and, not sure what else to do, reached up and gripped at the pillow under his head. His breathing was ragged as he felt his jeans and boxers being shifted down and the light touches of Fynn's kisses through his thick thatch of hair. *Oh fuck, he wasn't prepared for this!* Shouldn't he have trimmed, or shaved, or *washed?* He'd walked here for fuck's sake! It was probably horrible and nasty down there, and just as he'd made up his mind to lift the covers and shriek at Fynn to stop, his brain ground to a halt.

Fynn slid his tongue over the sensitive tip and then followed it with his plush lips, giving a gentle suckle. Nicholas twitched from his head to his toes, then his whole body went slack. "Oh, oh, oh." He couldn't manage anything much more coherent than that. All his previous inhibitions regarding blow jobs were flying out the window into the rain.

He bucked his hips, wanting more, but Fynn gave a muffled grunt and pushed him against the bed with both hands. Not so it hurt, but enough to make it clear he didn't want Nicholas to fidget around too much. Nicholas cringed; he'd already fucked up.

"Sorry," he gasped. But he wasn't sure Fynn heard him. He wasn't sure he was actually annoyed either, as he hadn't faltered in what he was doing, and Nicholas tried to relax again. Despite his squeamishness still telling him this was way out of his comfort zone, if he closed his eyes and focused on the way it felt, he could really start to enjoy it.

Fynn had circled the fingers of one of his hands around the base of his cock and gave it a firm squeeze. It didn't hurt like he thought it would, but it did feel a bit strange, and it was definitely doing something to stave off his building climax. Tentatively, Nicholas craned his head up, wondering if it might be good to see what Fynn was doing to him. He'd liked watching the porno after all. But the only view he got was the covers bobbing over his head, so he saved his energy and dropped his head back onto the pillows with a thump.

He had absolutely no control over the sounds coming out of his mouth. But Fynn was *sucking* and it was more overwhelming than anything he'd ever experienced before. He was almost relieved when it stopped, despite not reaching his climax yet, as it gave him a chance to catch his breath.

When Fynn re-emerged, he was grinning like the Cheshire cat. His dreads were stuck out at odd angles and his lips were glistening. "I'm guessing that was okay?"

Nicholas very nearly blurted that was his first ever blow job, and he was lucky he hadn't come within the first five seconds. But he did have a filter sometimes, and he really didn't want to come across any more hopeless with Fynn than he already had. So instead, he grabbed the back of his neck and kissed him sloppily.

He tasted a little bitter and salty, and Nicholas realised he was in fact sampling his own intimate flavour. It wasn't gross or repellent. It was, in all honestly, extremely hot. "Yeah," he breathed between kisses. "It was brilliant, I loved it."

He was sort of hinting that he'd like Fynn to go back and carry on, but then something better happened. Fynn rolled off him, and made short work of kicking his own jeans and underwear off.

He managed to do this while still under the covers, so Nicholas didn't quite realise that was what was happening until he rolled back on top of him, and lined their bodies up together.

Fynn's cock was throbbing with heat, and it felt so good pressed up against Nicholas's own member. His jeans were only pushed down as far as his thighs and they were getting in the way. So he tried to shove them down…and bashed his head against Fynn's.

He yelped out in pain as Fynn jerked back and grabbed his forehead. "Oh fuck," Nicholas gasped. He desperately blinked away the stars and pawed at Fynn's chest. "I'm so sorry, oh shit!"

But Fynn was chuckling, and once he let go of his face, he planted a big kiss on Nicholas's lips. "Don't worry," he said. "Let's get you out of those jeans, shall we?"

The two of them shoved to get the denim down over his legs, and Nicholas did the last few kicks to flick them out on the floor, along with his socks and pants. And that was it. He and Fynn were totally naked together.

He'd caught a glimpse or two of the rest of Fynn's body, but then he was lying on top of him again, the duvet draped over his back. He lined up their bodies so their groins were perfectly placed to rub against one another. Then, he lifted his hips and wrapped his big hand around both their cocks, forming a warm, slick tunnel for them to thrust into. If Nicholas had struggled with his timings yesterday, this threatened to undo him completely. But he held onto Fynn's shoulders, his face screwed up in part due to the effort of concentration, but also the unparalleled sensation of feeling his dick sliding against the smooth, hard flesh of fingers and another cock.

One of them was obviously leaking pre-cum, or maybe both of them, as the motion became more like gliding, and Nicholas knew he wasn't going to last long. "I'm going to come," he said between kisses and gasps for air.

"Me too," Fynn grunted. It only took a few more thrusts, and Nicholas could do no more to hold off his climax, firing his hot load between them with a shout. He arched his back and dug his fingers into the skin on Fynn's back, just as Fynn buried his face against Nicholas's neck and howled.

For several moments, Fynn lay on Nicholas as they both panted and aftershocks rippled over their bodies. Then, with a groan, Fynn rolled to the side, and Nicholas automatically scooted over to press himself next to him.

Nicholas hadn't made a complete twat of himself, he supposed, but he hadn't exactly been suave. At least this time they'd both come. What if Fynn had wanted to more, and he'd not felt Nicholas was up to it? That would suck if he gave up on him before even asking. But he hadn't really felt up to it, so maybe he should feel relieved?

He was over-thinking things. He really liked what they'd just done, and he hoped maybe Fynn had as well. If the stickiness between them was anything to go by, he had, and that cheered him up and distracted him from his worries. The covers had slipped down more towards their hips, and he let out a small giggle as he poked at the mess they'd made.

"Eww," he said. He turned to grin at Fynn.

Fynn responded by smothering him in a cuddle, squidging the goo even further between them. "Yum," he countered, smacking noisy kisses over Nicholas's chest, neck and cheeks. He laughed even harder at that.

He'd always imaged sex would be this great big dramatic thing, undertaken with utmost respect and sincerity. He never thought it could be so *fun*. He reckoned he preferred it this way.

Fynn kissed his lips softly and sweetly, but it soon became apparent that they were both getting cold and uncomfortable from all the bodily fluids drying on their skin. "You want to use the shower?" he asked, brushing some of Nicholas's hair back where it had stuck to his damp forehead.

Despite being a total newb, Nicholas did know a thing or two. Did Fynn mean he could use his shower...or did he want to shower *together*? "Um," he said.

He desperately didn't want to panic now, he'd done so well with the whole getting naked part of the afternoon. But it had been easier when he'd been caught up in the throes of passion. Now he was clear headed, the idea of standing in a shower with Fynn seemed far too exposed, he cringed at just the thought of it.

Before he could get too worked up, Fynn tapped his nose lightly with his index finger. "If you take mine, I'll brave my aunt's bathroom. There should be everything you need in there."

Nicholas felt an enormous rush of gratitude. "Okay," he agreed. Whether Fynn had anticipated his nervousness, or read his apprehension at taking that step forward on his face, he really didn't mind. Either option left him feeling cared for.

He tried not to gawp as Fynn strode out of bed, but his backside was gorgeous, mouth-watering even. Fynn either didn't notice or didn't mind that Nicholas watched him walk out, as he didn't falter in his step. But then he was gone, out the door and down the corridor, and Nicholas was by himself.

Irrationally fearful that Fynn would change his mind and come back, he bolted out of bed and spun like a tornado as he snatched up all his clothes that he'd been divested of during their tryst. He closed the now-dry umbrella and propped it against the computer desk, then securely locked the door to the en-suite behind him.

His clothes in an untidy pile, he spent a minute working out how the shower operated, then got it to a good temperature. It was probably a good idea to let it run for a little while, in case it was one of those ones that took a while to regulate itself. As he waited, he stood and took in his reflection in the mirror, turning this way and that.

The way he looked wasn't so bad; he didn't *dislike* it. But he couldn't really agree with Fynn that he'd ever qualify as 'hot'. The skin over his small frame was pale, and he had a hefty dusting of brown hairs along his arms and legs, a distinctive trail running down from his navel into the forest around his now-limp cock. Fynn didn't really look like he had much hair on his legs, and he definitely didn't on his arms. Nicholas wondered if he minded the difference. Maybe he'd want Nicholas to shave, or wax? He wasn't sure he would be up for that.

It probably wouldn't hurt to tidy up a little for him though; trim around his groin. It was so bizarre, having to think about another person seeing under his boxers, about trying to make it appealing. He sighed and figured he probably still had a lot to learn about being with somebody else.

Stepping under the hot water, he relished it hitting his skin. As much as he liked having proof that what had happened between him and Fynn *had* really just happened, he felt gross with so much cum smeared all over his skin. He'd probably get used to it; in fact, he vowed to put up with it as much as possible if it meant he could keep doing this with Fynn. But it was still nice to scrub his whole body and freshen up. Besides, he still had his hickey from yesterday, just by the edge of his shoulder on the fleshy part above his collarbone. He ran his fingers over the mark as he lathered soap over himself, and smiled.

Getting naked with someone else was causing him to feel raw and exposed in a way he'd never experienced before. Afterwards, it was easy to fret that he wasn't doing it right, that he was making a fool of himself. But during the act itself, he needed to remember that he genuinely loved it. Having the hickey was a good way to do that. It was a little bit of Fynn, etched onto his skin.

Thankfully there was an extractor fan in the bathroom, so he could keep the door closed while he dried off and got re-dressed. He wanted to allow Fynn some privacy to put his clothes back on as well. He tried to ignore the voice in his head that said he might have been eking out the time he had to hide. Instead, he insisted to himself that he was just regrouping. It was a big deal, what he'd just been through, and he was allowed time to process.

He was definitely less scared compared to yesterday when he cracked open the door and peeked out. Fynn was waiting for him on the bed, clothed and showered, and once again with his guitar out. Nicholas was immediately comforted by the sight. Today was the longest he'd gone without playing it, and it didn't quite seem natural for him to be parted from it like that.

"Hey," he said with a bright smile. "Find everything you needed?"

Nicholas nodded and came to sit back on the bed. However, this time, unlike the last two times he'd sat and listened to him play, he scuttled up beside him, resting his back against the pillows. "Good water pressure," he complimented. He never thought he'd care about something so mundane, but after two terms with the dribble he had to wash with at uni, he'd come to appreciate a good, hard shower.

Fynn stopped fiddling with his strings and leant across to give Nicholas a little kiss. He didn't ask him outright this time if he was okay with what they'd just done, but he felt the action was seeking the same answer. Nicholas grinned unabashedly back at him, and bumped their shoulders together. *I'm great*, he hoped that conveyed. More than great really.

"What are you playing?" he asked.

Fynn licked his lips and noodled around a bit more. "Want to hear?" Nicholas nodded. There might come a day when he got bored of listening to Fynn play, but he suspected that day was very far off indeed.

He restarted the song, chugging out several jaunty chords that immediately made Nicholas smile. Fynn's knee bounced as he strummed, a glint in his eye.

"*It's on the wind*," he sang brightly. "*It's on the sea. It's in the air, across the land, it's calling me. Take your troubles out to fly, give me a wink as I pass by. And never let the sun stop shining on you.*"

He looked so happy, Nicholas couldn't help but grin at the side of his head. He didn't recognise the song, but there had been plenty of ones that Fynn had played him over the last couple of days that he'd only known the chorus of, or not at all if they were more obscure.

Fynn was humming something that Nicholas thought might have been a hint of another instrument, although bass, piano or kazoo he couldn't say. Whatever the song was, Nicholas was liking it already. It made him feel warm and joyous.

"*Oh my love*," Fynn bellowed, drawing out the 'o' in love spectacularly. "*Look how you soar. Come lift me away, and we'll fly away, from it all. Oh my love. Don't let me fall. Come lift me away, and we'll fly away, from it all.*"

Fynn struck the last chord then slapped the strings to cut them off, leaving the last notes hanging in the air like a puff of smoke from a suddenly extinguished fire. He turned to Nicholas and bit his lip. "What did you think?"

Nicholas felt that was a bit odd. Before, Fynn had certainly been keen for him to like certain song suggestions more than others, but he wasn't so insecure to be bothered if something wasn't particularly Nicholas's cup of tea. This wasn't even one for the wedding as far as he knew, just something Fynn was fooling around with.

"I loved it," said Nicholas truthfully. "It had a great beat, and I could tell there was more going on with other parts, even though it was just you playing. The lyrics were nice too, really fun. What's it called?"

Fynn rubbed the plectrum between his fingers, averting his eyes. "It doesn't have a title yet," he said, somewhat more subdued.

It took Nicholas a second to work out what he meant. "Oh shit," he cried, lurching forwards on the bed to face Fynn. "Oh shit, that was one of yours, wasn't it? Oh my god, that was amazing!" He grabbed Fynn's feet and waggled them in glee. "Holy crap, is there any more? Can you play me more?"

Fynn laughed at him and shook his head. "That's all there is for now. You sort of inspired me."

Nicholas blinked and looked down at the guitar. "I – that was…Did you write me into a song?"

He was surprised to see Fynn look mildly abashed. He didn't think he was capable of being shaken. "Little bit," he said. "Do you mind?"

"Mind?" Nicholas let out a snort. "That's brilliant, how many people can say they've had a song written about them?"

Fynn grinned, back to his usual demeanour. "Pretty much every song out there was written about *somebody*."

Nicholas slapped his leg and crawled back up to sit beside him. "Well no one *I* know has been immortalised in lyrical form," he said. "I'm determined to feel special."

"That's because you *are* special," Fynn said. He leant over and gave him a sloppy kiss, causing Nicholas to squeal in protest. He was making a spectacle of himself again, but he was caring less and less.

He sat for a little longer, listening to Fynn play some songs again that he was planning on putting in the wedding set. He was trying out some more complicated bits in and around the more basic chords, and Nicholas was happy to sit and let the music wash over him.

His mind wandered back to Fynn playing 'Wild Horses' the other day. Nicholas had been so caught up in concern for the person lamenting their lost love. But he now remembered how Fynn had thought it was incredible that the love – even if it had turned to pain – had created an irreplaceable piece of art.

Was that what Nicholas was now? No matter what happened between them, would his song get pressed onto a CD and listened to by countless strangers who had no idea he'd had his heart broken by his first ever boyfriend?

He gave himself a mental slap. There were so many ridiculous things about that statement he didn't even know where to start. For one, Fynn wasn't his boyfriend. He *wasn't*. They were just hanging out, and it was fantastic. He didn't need to spoil anything by going nuts with labels. Then there was the fact that the song wasn't even finished. Fynn didn't have a record contract, and as long as he kept his head on his shoulders there was no cause to get his heart broken.

He needed to get a grip on this over-analysing. Couldn't he just bask in the fact that he'd known Fynn less than a week and they'd already hooked up twice, and he'd started writing a bloody song about him. As flings went, he was pretty confident that this was off to a great start.

***

By the time Nicholas got back, it was kind of late. He'd had plenty of time on the journey home to work up a healthy amount of guilt at being out almost all day, so close to his sister's wedding. But every time he came close to feeling bad, he remembered how it had felt to come hard and fast as he and Fynn had rubbed their cocks together, and he got over himself pretty quickly.

He was bobbing around in a daydream as he entered the house and shook his now-trusty umbrella off in the porch. His parents were in the living room watching the news on TV. "Where's everyone else?" he asked after saying hello.

It turned out Danielle was in the den rehearsing a flash mob dance she'd secretly organised and choreographed for Clara's friends to perform during the reception. Nicholas knew Clara's friends, and he reckoned he could accurately predict how much enthusiasm they probably had for the notion of public dancing. He also knew they'd all probably fumble their way through it regardless, bless them.

Kinny and Ash had apparently retreated to their attic room and were watching a film with a bottle of wine. Nicholas thought that sounded like great fun and was half tempted to join them depending on the film they'd picked. But then he asked if Clara was with them, and his mum had said she was in her room, staring dreamily at her dress.

He kicked himself. It was Thursday, which meant they'd been to the wedding dress shop, done the final fitting, and brought the damn thing home. He'd completely forgotten in his own lust-haze, and his negligence made him feel guilty where most other things that day had failed.

Without a second thought, he bid his parents a good night, and jogged up the stairs, keen to give Clara his full attention and gush over the most beautiful (and expensive) dress she would probably ever own. He knocked, but he and Clara had always been close, so as usual it was only a formality before he pushed his way through.

"Hey sis!" he said as he opened the door. "I heard you said yes to the—"

He stopped dead in his tracks.

Clara was sobbing uncontrollably on her bed, the white wedding dress looming before her from the wardrobe door like a spectre risen from the grave.

Nicholas was assaulted by several thoughts at once. First, he slammed the door shut behind him so no one else would hear. Second, he scrambled around his brain to locate where Peter might be, but Danielle's itinerary had told him earlier that the groom was scheduled to be taken out by his dad and uncles down a local pub for a few pints.

At least that's what he assumed. Peter had *said* he was unequivocally not suffering from cold feet yesterday, but…

"Clara. *Clara!*" he cried. He ran over to her bed, threw himself down, and grabbed her shoulders. "What's wrong, what's happened?"

She sniffed and hiccupped a couple of times, her whole chest jumping. "N-nothing," she said. Her face crumbled and she snatched up another tissue from the box by her bed, so Nicholas didn't feel bad about calling Liar, Liar, Pants on Fire.

"Has Peter," he said. He didn't want to put his foot in it, but he had to ask. "Um, he hasn't, uh…"

That seemed to clear Clara's head. "Oh *no*," she all but shrieked, her fluffy curls bouncing and she waved her hands. "No, no, nothing like that, he's great, everything's fine." She swallowed another sob, and Nicholas arched an eyebrow in defiance.

"So, you're just crying your eyes out because…?"

Clara scrubbed at her face under her glasses and blew her nose. Her chest shuddered a couple more times, and she turned her big, watery eyes on him.

It was astonishing in many ways how much the three Herald siblings didn't look alike. Clara, the eldest, was a dead spit for their mum. She had always had curves, from chubby baby fat into awkward pre-teen boobs and hips, and now what Nicholas considered to be a voluptuous woman. He teased her about being ginger, but honestly, he didn't get why that was such a thing. Her shade of strawberry blond hair was objectively beautiful.

He and their middle sister Lauren definitely took after their dad. Although she was tall and broad-shouldered, and he was obviously not, they both had his dark hair and slim frame.

But even strangers noted when they were seen in a threesome how much their mannerisms reflected one another's. There was a connection between them, especially with him and Clara, that bordered on telepathy. So he couldn't unravel how, but when Clara turned her trembling lip and reddened eyes his way, he instinctively glared at the wedding dress.

"What's wrong with it?" he asked. Because he was pretty sure he'd reached Commander level of some shit when it came to dealing with wedding catastrophes, and if that dress wasn't spot on, he was going to march right back into town tomorrow morning and cause all levels of unprecedented hell.

She sniffed and managed a sheepish smile. "Nothing," she said between hiccups. "It's perfect."

Nicholas shifted on his side of the double bed. He loved that Clara hadn't changed her childhood room much at all since she had moved out, so it was pretty much still decked head to toe with anything she had got her teenage hands on connected to *Buffy the Vampire Slayer*. She'd had a particular obsession with all the spin-off stories about the slayers who had come before Buffy, so there were all manner of comics and drawings and sketches of badass ladies throughout the ages looking down at them from the walls. Nicholas mentally saluted them, and tried to pick out the best way to rescue his big sis in that moment.

"Who do I need to garrotte?

Clara laughed, more tears spilling from her eyes, but it was a laugh all the same. "No one." She wiped her eyes and took a long, deep breath. "I'm just being stupid."

Nicholas scoffed. "Try me." He'd been more than happy to commit a murder over a harp on

Saturday. He was willing to place money on Clara's issue not being stupid.

Clara tried to speak once, twice, and then several more times. But every time it looked like words were in danger of leaping from her mouth, she buckled down and refused to let them go. So Nicholas went against his own nature for the second time that day, and simply draped his arm over her shoulders and squeezed.

"Brides aren't…" she eventually hissed. Nicholas clamped his teeth around his tongue. "Brides aren't…they aren't…" She made an angry noise in the back of her throat, and snatched in a breath. *"Brides aren't supposed to be fat,"* she spat out, then pulled away from Nicholas's hug.

He was so flummoxed, he let her go. "What?" he managed to force out.

Clara bit down on her knuckle as she cried. "That dress would look so pretty on a thin girl," she cried, her tone harrowing to Nicholas's ears.

A flame of pure rage flared though Nicholas's insides. He threw both his arms around his sister, and pulled her into a full body hug. "Bull-fucking-*shit,*" he said. "That dress is gorgeous on *you. You're* pretty. And if anyone's told you otherwise, I will…I will beat them up. *Capisce?"*

That had the desired effect of making her laugh at least. No one could ever imagine Nicholas beating anyone up, but he liked to think, for the people he loved, he'd try. "No one had to say anything," Clara said, her tears falling thick on his sleeve. "I just, don't look right in it."

"Oi, oi," Nicholas said, getting cross. "Do you think that's what Peter's going to say, when he turns around and sees you walking down the aisle?" He huffed. "I'm not quite sure you're thinking with your sane brain here, babe."

Thankfully, Clara chuckled again. "Um…"

Nicholas decided to lay it on thick. "Do you think he's going to take one look at you, and run screaming." He knew he'd made a mistake immediately.

"Maybe?" Clara whined, thick sobs rattling her chest again.

"No," said Nicholas firmly, and he gave her a shake. "Look, when was the last time he told you you were beautiful?"

Clara took a moment to blow her nose on the damp tissue she still had clamped in her hand. "This afternoon," she said. "Before he went out."

"And what were you wearing?"

That got another little chuckle. "Mostly dust, sweat and confetti," she said.

Nicholas noogied her head. "Right. He loves you inside and out. So, he's probably going to come in his pants when he sees that dress and all the hair and makeup and other sparkly things you and Danielle no doubt have in mind."

"*Eeww!*" She gave him a shove. But he felt like he was getting through. "I guess he won't be mean or anything," she said.

Nicholas rocked her back and forth a couple of times. "Tenner says he cries," he said.

Clara scoffed, but then she seemed to realise he was serious. "Deal," she told him, some of her old confidence sneaking back in as they shook on the bet.

Nicholas knew he'd been selfish spending time with Fynn all day. But now, he felt he had the chance to make that up a little bit; because when it came down to it, the one and only thing he cared about come Saturday was that Clara was happy.

"Hey, do you want some ice cream?"

For a second, he feared he'd horribly misjudged the moment, but with one final rub around her eyes, Clara levelled her stare at Nicholas. "There better be some Chocolate Fudge Brownie left."

Nicholas swatted the side of her head. "Alright bridezilla. If there isn't, I promise to go out and get some. And I'm buggered if that doesn't qualify me for the best brother ever."

"You're my *only* brother." But after she'd given him a wobbly smile, she threw her arms around him. "Promise me we're going to *nail* this wedding, okay?"

Despite all the problems they'd faced so far, and despite the niggling voice in his head that warned him to be cautious, Nicholas nodded furiously and without hesitation. "We're going to *nail* it," he assured her.

After all, they only had one day to go.

Chapter Eleven

(1 day to go...)

It started at four-thirty in the morning.

Nicholas was in such a deep sleep, he couldn't quite work out what the noise was going off by his head was until it started up a second time. His phone was ringing. Why would his phone be ringing in the middle of the night?

"Hello?" he said into the receiver, rubbing the sleep out of his eyes.

"*Hello? Hello, Nicholas?*"

The panic in his sister's voice woke him up much faster than any coffee had. "Lauren?" He sat up in bed and snatched up his glasses to slide onto his face. Whatever was going on, he felt he was better prepared if he were able to see. "What's the matter? What time is it there, what's happening?"

"*Oh Nick,*" she cried, her voice thick. "*I tried Mum and Dad but you know they turn their bloody phones off at night and I didn't want to worry Clara but—*" She broke off into an angry burst of Italian, and Nicholas jerked the phone away from his ear. "*Sorry, sorry, are you still there?*"

Nicholas nodded, then felt immediately stupid. "Yes, still here. What on Earth is going on? Aren't you supposed to be getting on a plane?"

Lauren wailed. "*That's just it!*" she said from the other end of the phone. "*Franko was supposed to check Milly's passport and he thought he did but it's run out and now we have to get to the passport office and see if we can get it fast-tracked or apply for an emergency one—*"

"Whoa, whoa," said Nicholas. "Slow down. Did you say Milly's passport is out of date?"

"*Yes,*" said Lauren with a sniff.

"So…" Nicholas pinched the bridge of his nose and willed this not to be happening. "You're going to miss your flight."

Lauren was audibly crying on the other end of the line. "*We have to get to the passport office. It doesn't open until nine. We'll fix this, I promise, tell Clara I promise, okay?*"

"Hey, calm down," Nicholas said a little firmer. "Yes, it's going to be fine. You can get another flight tonight, yeah?"

He heard Lauren blowing her nose. "*They go all the time to London,*" she said. "*But someone needs to pick us up. What if it gets late? It's the night before the wedding and we can't make Dad come all the way out to Heathrow or something.*"

"Then you get a taxi," Nicholas insisted. Even though Heathrow, Gatwick and City were all so much father out that Stansted airport, they'd all be preferable to Lauren not making it at all. "No matter the cost, we'll all chip in if we have to. This isn't the end of the world, alright?"

Lauren inhaled shakily, then sniffed once more. "*Okay, yeah. You're right. Okay, we're going to make our way into the city now. Milly's so tired and cranky, poor thing, but now she's had some food she's calmed down.*"

"That's because she takes after her uncle," Nicholas said with a touch of humour. It had the desired effect, and Lauren's breathing evened out on the other end of the phone as she got her wits back together.

"*You're the best, Nick,*" she said. She was the only one who ever really called him that, and it made a rush of affection swell over his chest.

"No problem," he assured her. "Although I didn't really do anything."

Lauren chuckled. "*Will you let Mum and Dad know?*"

Nicholas sighed. Yes, he'd be delighted to be the bearer of yet more bad news. But honestly, this was just a mistake. These things happened. Poor Franko was probably feeling wretched enough without anyone having a go at him. Although, knowing Lauren, she had probably lost her temper quite spectacularly when she'd first found out.

"Of course," he reassured her. "Don't you worry about us, everything's fine here. Just focus on getting little Milly sorted. We can't wait to see you all, no matter what time it is, alright?"

With a few more reassurances, they closed the call. Nicholas sat in the dark for a while, with the corner of his phone pressed against his forehead.

He believed what he'd told her, he genuinely thought it would all be fine. It would have just been nice if this hadn't happened on top of everything else.

It was impossible to get back to sleep, he was too agitated, so the best he managed was to doze on and off until other people started getting up. His stomach fluttered with nerves as he hid under the duvet for as long as possible, wanting to delay the inevitable. But he knew his dad would be preparing to drive out to Stansted soon, and he needed to get a hold of himself and relay the bad news.

He brushed his teeth and sprayed some deodorant on, however he didn't have the energy for anything else, so just pulled some jeans on trudged downstairs. The only people missing from the kitchen were Kinny and Ash; everyone else was bustling about making tea and eggs and bowls of cereal. Clara was sat at the island looking tired and a little puffy from the night before, but Peter had his arm around her and was mumbling something into her ear that was at least eliciting a twitch of a smile every now and again. Nicholas hoped their chat in her room had helped, as he was just about to drop another stinker into her lap.

"Oh, good morning sweetheart," his mum cooed when she spotted him. "Look, the sun is shining!"

He hadn't even noticed. Having been obsessed with the weather for the past several days, he couldn't believe he'd missed the bright blue skies that were currently hanging outside the kitchen window. Well, that was something at least.

He didn't want to drag this out any more than he had to, so he just cut to the chase. "I've got some bad news," he said, bracing himself. "But before anyone panics, we're sure it's all going to be fine, there's just a bit of a delay."

"A delay to what?" asked Danielle.

"Who's we?" chimed in Clara.

Nicholas took a deep breath. "Lauren missed her flight. Milly's passport ran out, and they didn't realise."

He was assaulted with a cacophony of sound, but eventually he was able to explain that they would already be at the passport office by now. They'd most likely pay a fortune to get her a new one printed the same day, but it would be worth it.

"They'll be on a plane by tonight, and I said if we had to, we'd all chip in for an Uber, yeah?"

In the middle of hashing back and forth exactly what was going on, Nicholas heard the front door open and close. But he was too busy texting with Lauren to pay much attention. She assured him that they were in the queue and would be seen shortly, which Nicholas was trying to explain to everyone was a good thing. However, his mum was too busy being miffed that her daughter hadn't called her, even though Nicholas explained again and again that her phone had been switched off. Danielle was flicking through incoming flights from Rome on her phone, trying to anticipate which one Lauren and her family might get. Clara was looking close to tears, and the only thing Nicholas's dad seemed capable of doing was making excess cups of strong tea, plonking them in front of people with a sturdy "There, there, it'll sort."

Somebody cleared their throat.

As Nicholas was still standing with his back to the archway into the kitchen, he didn't quite understand why everyone suddenly was staring at him, their eyes widening. It took him a second to realise they were in fact staring *behind* him, and he spun around to see why.

He couldn't help but gasp.

Kinny and Ash were both wearing their newly-altered bridesmaids' dresses, and Nicholas almost wept they looked so good. The pastel pink fabric flowed to just above their knees, where it then cascaded down at the back to float just behind their matching white, sparkly high heels. The clear sequins Mrs Sadik had added around the new hem complimented the bling on the shoulder straps, and all in all Nicholas thought they made a breathtaking sight.

Ash did look obviously uncomfortable in her dress, hugging herself and rubbing her arms as she hunched in on herself slightly. Like she was trying her best not to be seen. But Kinny was by her side, resembling some sort of glorious Disney princess, even though she wasn't wearing any makeup and her thick, dark hair was simply piled on top of her head. She had a protective hand placed on the small of Ash's back, and Nicholas didn't hesitate to rush to their side.

"Oh my god," he gasped. "They look amazing, you look amazing! Kinny, your mum did a fantastic job!"

Kinny gave him a look of relief, but before she could reply, Danielle's voice cut across the room. "What have you *done?*" she demanded, a horrified tremble in her words.

Nicholas wrapped his arm around Ash's waist, and the three of them faced the room together. "Please don't freak out," he suggested. But they were a bit too late.

"Freak out," said Danielle. "*Freak out!* You've changed the fucking dresses, the day before the wedding!"

Nicholas winced. She never swore. "Danielle," he began.

"Are they all like that – is *mine* like that?"

"Why did you change them?" asked Clara.

Nicholas's mum tried to intervene by waving her hands about. "Everybody please calm down. Nicholas, what's going on here?"

"We didn't have a choice," he said.

But Danielle was pacing up and down the side of the breakfast bar, her hands tangled in her hair. "What could have possessed you to do such a thing?" she shouted. "They were fine as they were, why would you do this? Kinny, why did you let your mum muck about with them, she's hacked them in *half!*"

"Because," said Ash, standing a little taller. "You left the door open to the den, and the cat used the dresses as scratching poles. Kinny *fixed* your mistake, so don't you *dare* shout at her!"

She'd gone bright red, and her eyes pooled with tears. But before anyone could say or do anything else, she spun on her high heels and stormed out of sight.

For a moment, Peter's head swung comically back and forth between his sister and his fiancée. But Clara nudged him, and as soon as she gave him a nod, he bolted on after Ash.

Nicholas's mum laughed nervously. "Surely Archie wouldn't have done that, would he?" She was met with an awkward silence. "Oh, but he's such a good boy!" she cried. "Aren't you, pumpkin?"

Nicholas hadn't realised the demon cat had snuck in through the flap in the back door, and with a strangled cry he leapt between him and Kinny in her dress. "Oh no you don't!" he hissed, jabbing his fingers at the nefarious feline. His ankle was still a little sore from the assault he'd received yesterday.

"Nicholas, you're being ridiculous," his mum scolded him. She bent down and scooped Archibald up. He immediately began purring like a lawnmower, and glared daggers at Nicholas from her lap. Nicholas glared back. "Did a little scratch really warrant changing the whole dress designs?"

"It, um, wasn't a little scratch," Kinny said. Her hands were clasped in front of her, but her shoulders were still set. "Ash was right, they really were ripped to shreds. And rather than worry everyone, we wanted to try and fix it ourselves. But, maybe we made a mistake?"

She glanced behind her to where Ash had run off. Nicholas reached out and took her hand.

"We thought it was better to shoulder the burden ourselves," he told them. "And obviously since then, we've had a few more hiccups." Half of which, most people didn't even know about. "So we kept it to ourselves. But Kinny's right, maybe springing it on you now wasn't the best idea."

Nicholas's dad shrugged. "I think you look lovely Kinny, dear," he said, dunking a custard cream into his tea. "It was one less thing for poor Clara to think about. Danielle, I bet yours looks just as nice."

Danielle seemed to have been struck dumb. She was just gawping at Kinny with her hand over her mouth.

"Do you really hate it that much?" Kinny asked in a small voice.

"It was the best we could do," Nicholas jumped in defiantly. He glowered at Archibald, and the cat stared right back, challenging him from his mum's lap. "Kinny's mum salvaged three whole dresses in four days, and I think she's done a magnificent job."

"Lovely," agreed his dad.

His mum was chewing her thumb anxiously. "They are nice," she said. "Just, a bit different I guess. A bit of a shock."

Clara looked between her and the dress, but otherwise hadn't show much of a reaction.

Everyone else went quiet as they anticipated Danielle's response. She continued to stare for a few more moments, before finally dropping her hand. "Archibald really wrecked them?"

"Completely," Nicholas affirmed. "There wasn't much left at the front other than ribbons."

"Oh dear," said Nicholas's mum guiltily. She addressed the fur ball in her lap. "Archibald, how could you?"

Danielle shook her head. "You did tell me. You both did." She turned and faced Clara, who was still sat chewing her lip at the kitchen table. Danielle took a deep breath in. "Do *you* like them?" she asked.

Clara took a moment to realise she'd been addressed. Indeed, Nicholas stuck his finger in his ear to give it a quick clean, just in case he'd misheard. Was Danielle actually defaulting to Clara?

"Oh," said his sister. She glanced at Danielle, as if wary to believe she'd genuinely asked for her opinion, then scooted off her chair to come inspect the dress closer. She and Kinny exchanged a warm smile, then Clara touched the edge of the material carefully, like it might still fall apart. "Well, like you said Mum. It's not what we designed. But...I like them. I really do." She turned back to Danielle, and raised her eyebrows questioningly.

Danielle swallowed, and nodded. "Then I had better go and try my one on then," she said graciously. "Hadn't I?"

Nicholas felt a wave of relief wash over him. "I'm sorry," he said again to everyone. "That must have been a bit of a nasty shock. But trust me when I say it was more of a shock to *find* the dresses. They look a million times better than they did on Monday." That, thankfully, got the laugh he was angling for.

Kinny took Danielle and Clara to see the final dress, so that Danielle could try it on. Nicholas was aware that Peter had gone to see if his sister was okay and didn't want to intrude, but she had looked after him on Tuesday night, and he felt he owed it to her to go deliver the good news that people had calmed down about the dresses.

After a few more words with his parents, he passed Danielle and the others in the den, and made his way up the stairs. He didn't go in Lauren's attic room very often any more. Being the middle child, it wasn't all that surprising that she'd been a little different to him and Clara. A staunch vegetarian, she always had some humanitarian cause she was championing, and wanderlust had taken her off around the world the moment she'd left school at eighteen. She'd insisted to their mum she could redecorate however she liked, so the small room now had more of Mrs Herald's personality about it that it did Lauren's.

Ash and Peter were perched on the end of the cream-coloured bedding, and although Ash wasn't crying, she didn't look all that happy. She'd already changed out of her dress; it was back on a hanger dangling from the top lip of the wardrobe, and she was once again decked in jeans and a t-shirt with a rainbow on it. She gave Nicholas a little wave as he came through the door.

"Hey," he said. He went and sat on the cream stool by the white dressing table. His mum had made the furnishings as neutral as possible, which although a little boring, gave the room a fresh, calming feeling. "It's okay," he explained hastily. "Danielle came around. She's trying on her dress now. I think she and my mum feel pretty awful that Archibald caused us such a headache."

That got a small smile.

"See," said Peter, rubbing her back. "Everything's fine."

Ash sighed. "It's not really that," she said, glancing back towards the dress. "I just feel so uncomfortable in it. It's going to be hard to wear it all day."

Nicholas frowned. "Could Kinny's mum let it out a bit if it's that bad?"

Surprisingly, she laughed at him, loudly. "You're so sweet," she said with genuine affection.

"But I didn't mean that sort of uncomfortable. It's just *so* girly. It's pink and frilly and sparkly, and now everyone can see my legs too." She grimaced.

"I thought you liked them," said Peter. Nicholas thought he had every right to be annoyed – it was sort of late in the day to be objecting to the bridesmaids' dresses. But his tone was sympathetic. "You said they were pretty."

Ash bit her lip and stared at the offending garment. "It's pretty on *Kinny*," she said quietly. "Really pretty. I'm just not that girly."

Peter laughed. "Well, we all know that," he agreed. He gave her a hug around her waist.

But Nicholas caught Ash's gaze, and he raised an eyebrow. He wanted to ask if this was linked to her not always feeling like a girl, but he didn't dare risk it in case that put her in a situation with Peter that she couldn't backtrack out of.

She seemed to catch his meaning though, as she responded with the tiniest of nods. "Um," she said, pulling at the hem of her t-shirt. "Peter?"

At her tone, he sobered up. "Yeah?" he prompted.

Nicholas gave her a nod, then headed out of the room. He felt this was a private moment between siblings, and he didn't want to intrude.

Danielle was by herself in the hallway when Nicholas came back down the stairs, studying her reflection in the mirror by the front door. She had her hand on her stomach and was staring intently at herself as she turned this way and that in her newly altered bridesmaid dress. If he was honest, Nicholas felt it was hanging off her a bit where she'd lost so much weight, but she was still a very beautiful girl. "Do you like it?"

She turned and watched him descend the final couple of steps. "Yes," she said firmly. "It's a little different to what we planned, obviously. But now

I'm getting used to it, I do like it." She gave him a tight smile.

He felt like she worried about so many things at once on an average day, she must have really struggled in the run up to the wedding. Relatively speaking, he was impressed that she'd coped with this last-minute change as well as she had.

"You look amazing," he told her sincerely.

The doorbell went and Nicholas said he'd get it, as he correctly predicted that Danielle wouldn't want anyone to see her in her dress before the big day, even if it was just the postman. So once she'd scuttled off, he undid the locks from the night before and welcomed the person on the other side.

It turned out it was the delivery of the wedding cake, and he couldn't help the small scream he let out at seeing it. They'd got an independent cake-maker to create the three-tied masterpiece, rather than a bakery, and she was struggling under the weight of the confectionary in her arms. Goodness only knew how she'd rung the doorbell. "Come in, come in," urged Nicholas with a wave.

"Oh bless you, love," said the woman.

She looked to be in her late fifties and had a bird like frame. Her wispy dyed-brown hair was pushed back with a head scarf, and she wore a Barbour jacket and hunter boots that put her very much on trend with most of the middle-class ladies in and around St Albans. He believed her name was Peggy, although he could have totally made that up. Between the lady who was providing the chair covers, and the one who was doing hair and makeup, and the one from the council who'd sorted out the registrar, he'd lost track of all the different names Clara and Danielle had mentioned.

"Where do you want this?" she asked.

Nicholas showed her through to the kitchen where she placed it on the counter. It was absolutely gorgeous. Clara's theme (under Danielle's direction) was springtime romance, and the cake was adorned with all manner of flowers and birds and love hearts. It was all very Danielle, but that didn't mean it wasn't beautiful. "Are we paying you today?" Nicholas asked. He worked out by now that a lot of wedding businesses operated via cash-in-hand, especially if they were little one-man-bands like Peggy.

"Yes please, my love," she said with a wink.

Nicholas directed her to the den, where he assumed his parents had gone, and explained that his dad would take care of it. "Would you like a cup of tea while you're here?"

"Oh that would be darling, yes it would," she said, patting his shoulder. "Two sugars, lots of milk."

Nicholas busied himself at the kettle, getting her a mug sorted. They were so nearly there. The dresses had been a bit of a shock, but ultimately, they'd gone down well. The cake was here, the weather had cleared up and, according to his dad, their Aunt Sally was feeling well enough to traveling that evening. So long as Lauren could sort out her daughter's passport and get the three of them on a plane by tonight, there was a chance this wedding might actually happen tomorrow the way it was supposed to.

He tapped the teaspoon on the side of the mug, set it against the edge of the sink, turned around. And froze.

Archibald had jumped up on the kitchen island where he wasn't allowed at the best of times, but especially not when there was an enormous wedding cake sitting their vulnerably. It hadn't seemed that close to the edge before, but now

Archibald was standing next to it, staring at like he did when he stalked fish in the garden pond, it suddenly felt like it was balancing like that van at the end on *The Italian Job*.

Nicholas squeezed the mug handle so tightly he thought it might seriously shatter. "*No!*" he hissed. "No, you fucking don't. Scat – SCAT!"

Archibald turned his large head towards Nicholas, and glared with his massive golden eyes. Then, without looking away, he reached a paw out and touched the edge of the cake plate.

"No!" Nicholas's heart rate rocket. "No, no you fucking bastard. *Get away!*"

He took a step forward, but the arsehole jabbed at the lower tier again, going so far as to get a smear of icing on his paw. Nicholas instinctively stopped moving and sloshed hot tea over his hand. He winced, but the pain was nothing compared to the panic swelling in his chest.

"Please," he begged. "Please don't do this to me. I'm sorry I said you were a devil cat. I'm sure those dresses deserved to get slashed – they look better now anyway! Just leave the cake alone. For the love of Beelzebub, I swear, I'll do whatever you want. You can destroy my room; the posters, the bed, everything. I'll buy you that catnip you like, the one that makes you proper mental. I'll never put you on the travel carry case again. Just – *don't fuck with that cake!*"

Archibald tilted his head, and let out a meow that sounded more like a banshee's screech. Nicholas knew all was lost.

He lurched forwards, ignoring the tea as it splashed up and over the rim of mug. But it didn't matter, because he was never going to be able to move fast enough. Archibald hissed at him, displaying his pointed teeth, and leapt into the air towards the counter on the other side of the kitchen aisle. Unfortunately, he used the rim of the cake plate as his launch pad.

Nicholas felt like time ground to a halt in front of his eyes. The cake slid just enough to the left that gravity was allowed to do its work. All he could do was scream, begging the universe to intervene on his behalf as ten pounds of sponge, cream and butter icing plummeted in a graceful arch to the kitchen tiles below.

Time eventually caught up. The cat landed, the cake exploded, and Nicholas dropped the mug of tea so it shattered all around his feet.

The silence was deafening.

For a moment, he just stared. Archibald was licking the remnants of icing off his paw, as if nothing had happened. There were splatters of cake up the cabinets and against the walls, and even across the bottom of Nicholas's jeans. Tea dripped from what remained of the mug handle, and Nicholas realised his socks were getting wet from the slowly expanding puddle on the tiles.

He still didn't seem to be able to move though. It was like he'd just watched six hundred quid blow out the window on a capricious summer breeze.

Eventually, he became aware of footsteps and someone calling his name. But he didn't look away from the carnage until a shadow darkened the entrance arch to the kitchen, accompanied by a shrill scream.

"What the—!"

His mum was joined by his dad, Clara, Kinny and Danielle, who were still in their bridesmaids' dresses, and finally Peggy, the cake lady. There was a good deal of yelps, wails, and profound abuse of the English language.

"What happened?" Clara asked tearfully. She was staring at the jagged shards of cake plate sticking out from the mess like ghoulish tombstones.

Wordlessly, Nicholas pointed at Archibald. He was sat on the worktop, swishing his tail in a manner that Nicholas couldn't help but interpret as being extremely proud of himself.

"ARCHIE!" bellowed Clara. Danielle looked like she was trying not to cry, and Nicholas's mum's face turned thunderous. But bizarrely, she didn't yell at her cat.

"Nicholas," she snapped. "Why did you let him up on the counter? You know he's not allowed!"

The injustice of the unfair accusation stung. "I tried to get him away!" he fired back. After all he'd done that week for this bloody wedding, he was not going to be blamed for this. "He's a menace!"

Peggy was looking between the Herald family members with increasingly widening eyes, her wodge of cash for the payment clutched tightly to her breast. "Well, um. I'll just leave you all to it, shall I?" For a lady of more senior years, she did a good job of bolting for the front door before anyone could stop her. Nicholas couldn't fault her for it really. He'd escape if he could too.

"Okay, everyone calm down," said Danielle with a sniff. She delicately wiped under her eyes with her fingertips, managing not to smudge her makeup. "We're just going to have to come up with a solution. It's hardly Nicholas's fault, it was just an accident."

Nicholas couldn't quite believe his ears. But coming from family favourite Danielle, his mum was more likely to listen and calm down. He was still pissed off with her for turning on him, but emotions were running high and people were bound to say things they didn't mean. At least, that's what he hoped.

He gave his cousin an appreciative smile, and she responded with a fraction of a nod.

"Fuck me sideways." Ash and Peter had obviously heard the commotion, and come down from upstairs. Ash had her hands in her pixie hair, her mouth hanging open. Peter looked like he was desperately trying not laugh. *Well*, thought Nicholas, *it was pretty ridiculous.* "What happened?" asked Ash.

"It seems Archibald is feeling like he's not getting enough attention," said Nicholas's dad sagely. Archibald flicked his tail as people looked over to him. "Okay, let's leave this be for now. Nicholas, come on through, try not to step on anything. We'll go back to the den."

Everyone else had found a place to sit or stand by the time Nicholas made it to the front of the house, and they were all looking to his dad for answers. Peter was hugging Clara, and Kinny was pulling off her high heels and rubbing her feet.

"So," said Nicholas, signalling his entrance. "We just pop into town and buy another cake, right?"

"We won't get a wedding cake at such short notice," Clara said thickly. She rubbed her nose and hiccupped. "I didn't even get to *see* it," she added in a tiny voice.

"No," said Nicholas firmly, looking to his dad and Danielle for backup. "It's just a cake, right? People do all kinds of wacky things nowadays, it could look like anything."

"I went to a wedding where it was a cupcake station," piped up Kinny. She leaned over a squeezed Clara's knee. "There were all different flavours cakes, even gluten free ones, and you added whatever toppings you wanted."

Nicholas's dad's eyes lit up. "I like the sound of that."

"Or something even simpler," suggested Danielle. "We have so much to do before tomorrow, let's not go for something overly complicated now."

"Who are you?" asked Ash dryly. "And what have you done with Danielle?"

Thankfully, that got a laugh out of people, and the tension lifted a little in the room. "She's right," said Nicholas. "Simple is good, although I do like the cupcake idea. You can get those stands, can't you? We could make a big cupcake mountain. That way it would look like the same sort of shape as a wedding cake."

"That could work," said Clara with a nod. She rubbed her forehead and let out a sigh. "It's such a waste of money though."

Their mum threw her arm around her. "Oh don't you worry about that, love," she said. "What matters is that you like it. We could go get any kind of cake, but it would be nice if it matched the theme, if it was personal to you two."

"Oh!" said Nicholas. Everyone turned to look at him. He quickly evaluated the idea that had just popped into his head, and decided that it wasn't totally preposterous. "I, um, have a suggestion."

"I'm open to anything right now," Danielle assured him.

"Well," said Nicholas. He pushed his glasses up his nose, just to give him another second to think. "You guys met at Krispy Kreme, right?" Danielle opened her mouth, probably to try and remind him that they met 'online'. But Clara and Peter nodded, so Nicholas ploughed on. "Right, so, what if instead of a cupcake tower...we made a doughnut tower?"

He was met with blank stares. That was, until Peter clapped his hands. "I love it, I bloody love it."

He jabbed a finger at Nicholas and clapped his hands again. "Genius."

"But, for a wedding?" Nicholas's mum asked dubiously. "It's, um. Well it's not exactly classy, is it?" Nicholas was tempted to tell her she should have trained her menace of a cat to behave better, then they wouldn't be in this mess in the first place. But he held his tongue. Because Clara was smiling.

"It *is* where we met," she said, looking between Peter and Nicholas.

Ash stuck her hand in the air, then pointed at her brother. "Just FYI. Peter absolutely hates cake. So, there's that too."

Danielle's head swung around to stare at the groom. "How can you hate cake?" she demanded, horrified.

He grinned sheepishly. "I don't hate it, exactly," he said, rubbing the back of his neck. "I just wasn't going to eat any. Doughnuts though? I love doughnuts."

"They come in all the pretty coloured glazings, don't they?" added Kinny. "We could get a mad selection. I have loads of tiered cupcake holders, pretty china ones, I bet they'd look lovely."

"We could decorate them with sugar flowers too," suggested Clara, tapping her fingers on her cheek as she thought. "And little hearts. It could look very nice."

"And it's personal to you," said Nicholas's dad, saluting the couple with his tea. "I think it's a fab idea mate," he added towards Nicholas.

Danielle bit her lip, then glanced at Nicholas's mum. They were both obviously not quite convinced, but eventually, Danielle nodded. "Let's go now, so we can clean out the store. We're going to need about a hundred doughnuts, so maybe we should ring them beforehand."

"And we can also go to the big Sainsbury's," said Clara excitedly. "They've got a whole baking aisle, we can get pretty little decorations."

"I'll go to my flat and get the stands," said Kinny.

Nicholas didn't want to jinx anything, but he felt like they had a plan.

Luckily, between everyone running around to get ready to leave the house, he thought to check his phone. Surprisingly, a text was waiting for him from Fynn, and he was glad he was alone in his room because he broke into the goofiest grin.

'Hey Nicholas. Any chance we can meet up today?'

Nicholas crossed over to his bedroom door and pushed it to. Then he bunched up his fists, closed his eyes, and let out a high-pitched whine of jubilation. Fynn wanted to see him again already. Whatever else this nightmare of a week had laid at his feet, he would be forever grateful that it had brought the two of them together.

Sadly, a bootie call was not on the cards for today though. *'Ahh, I'm so sorry, it's manic here! Believe it or not we've just had another catastrophe, but we're all pulling together to fix it. I don't think I'll be able to slip away :(I'll see you tomorrow though! Xxxx'*

He was surprised when he got a reply right away. *'Could we meet halfway in town? I need to talk to you.'*

Nicholas's happy spirits immediately dropped like a stone in water. That sounded horribly ominous. He read it again and again, trying to put a positive spin on it, but all he could think was that he was about to get dumped. He wasn't even sure if they'd been in a relationship yet. He was probably just being silly.

'*Is everything okay?*' he hastily typed. '*I'm actually just heading into town, so we could meet if you needed to have a chat. But you can tell me over text if something's wrong. I hope you're alright xxx*'

He was aware of everyone bustling outside his door, but he stared at his screen until the little dots started dancing to indicate that Fynn was typing. '*Where in town?*'

That was it. But Nicholas physically shook himself. There was no reason to jump to pessimistic conclusions. What if Fynn wanted to ask how they were going to present themselves tomorrow – maybe he wanted to officiate things between them and be there *as a couple*. Perhaps he felt that was too important a conversation to have via text. Nicholas made up his mind that Fynn wanted to hold his hand when he asked him to be his boyfriend, and that's why he was being particular.

Almost entirely convinced by his theory, he made himself smile, and started typing a response back. '*I'm going to Krispy Kreme,*' he explained. They'd decided he and his dad would go, so his dad could pay, and Nicholas could help with the carrying. '*If you get there within the hour, I might treat you to a doughnut ;)*'

He chewed his lip, waiting for the response. But it was worth it when it came. '*See you there gorgeous xxx*'

Ha! Nicholas had been right. He'd wound himself up over nothing. Fynn just wanted to see him, because he liked him. And who knew? Maybe his boyfriend theory was right? He tapped out a few kisses and sent them back, then headed out the door.

He was sure it was going to be fine.

Chapter Twelve

As it transpired, the manager at Krispy Kreme St Albans was both very helpful and, Nicholas suspected, a little bit bored. Once she'd spoken to Danielle over the phone and understood what they'd wanted, she'd become energetic to say the least, nattering on about how romantic it was, and how she never dreamed she'd be able to make someone's wedding cake for them. Danielle had been able to place an order for an assortment of doughnuts with pink and white toppings, and some even in the shape of love hearts.

While Kinny went back to her place to get her cupcake stands, Clara and their mum went off to Sainsbury's to get the sugar flowers as well as any other decorations they could lay their hands on. Peter and Ash stayed home to clean the kitchen, and to wait on any news from Lauren. That way, they could jump in Peter's car to go collect them if they suddenly got on a flight. Plus, Nicholas was sure that everyone felt better leaving someone behind to guard the rest of the wedding paraphernalia from Archibald while they all went out.

Nicholas's dad had a sporty Mercedes Benz that he only really got to play with on weekends, so he was more than happy to drive into town with Nicholas. Traffic was a nightmare, so once they got close enough, Nicholas suggested that he hop out and go on ahead to Krispy Kreme. It probably wouldn't have made a difference if the store manager had had to wait another twenty minutes or half an hour for them both to arrive together, but the way his week had gone, Nicholas didn't want to risk anything to chance. He'd rather sit and wait, and pick up the order as soon as it was finished.

Sandra, the manager, came bustling out from behind the counter as soon as she realised Nicholas was there. She pulled him into her ample bosom, clapped him on the back, and assured him in her strong Jamaican accent that the order would be ready soon. She was apparently putting the final touches onto the glazing herself. In the meantime, she fussed around and got him a table in the reasonably crowded diner, then sat him down with a complimentary coffee and doughnut.

Nicholas sipped the coffee, and saved the doughnut for Fynn.

He wasn't sure what he'd do if his dad arrived before he did. But just as he was mulling the possibilities over, the chime on the door sounded and Fynn walked in from the sunny street.

He was dressed in a pair of cargo pants with a white vest top and a lightweight stone-coloured jacket. Like on the first day they'd met, he was also sporting a neckerchief and several chains, and a big pair of combat boots. The only thing missing really was his guitar.

Nicholas felt like he lit up at the sight of him, and tried not to wave him over too enthusiastically. Fynn gave him a small half-smile and walked over with his hands in his jacket pockets, which wasn't the most exuberant response. But before he sat down, he leant over, and grazed the softest kiss on Nicholas's cheek.

Nicholas's whole body rushed with hot pride and a flicker of embarrassment that someone might object. But a quick glance around the diner showed that no one seemed to have noticed a thing, and were all going about their own business as before.

"Hi," said Fynn in his low, rumbling voice. He took the seat opposite Nicholas on their little, round table. They were in the corner, and Nicholas felt like that afforded them a bit of privacy.

"Hey," he replied shyly. He slid the napkin with the regular glazed ring doughnut over. "Um, that's for you."

Fynn smiled down at the offering, but he didn't pick it up. He just toyed with the corner of the napkin. "So, you had another mishap?" he prompted.

Nicholas snorted and readjusted his glasses. "The cake lasted about thirty seconds before the cat pushed it on the floor. Like I said, this wedding is cursed."

Fynn smiled again, but he didn't laugh. Then he looked around at where they were sitting. "Ahh, because of their first date," he correctly deduced, whirling his finger around to encompass the whole store.

"Yeah," said Nicholas. He was quietly thrilled that Fynn had remembered the story he'd told him. "I'm waiting on nine dozen doughnuts that we're going to pile up into some sort of replacement cake. But, it should hopefully all be fine. What about you? You said you wanted to talk to me about something."

He was aware of the anxious strain that crept into his words, but he didn't seem to be able to do anything to stop it. Fynn reached over with one of his hands to grasp Nicholas's briefly, then he dropped them both into his lap. "I got an email from Storm Sailor's people," he said without preamble.

Nicholas blinked. "Um, who's that?"

Fynn chuckled. He was rubbing his thumbs together between his knees. "He's one of my favourite Swedish music producers."

Nicholas took a second to realise what that meant. "Oh shit!" He banged his leg against the table in his excitement and almost upset his coffee. He slapped his hand over his mouth and threw an apologetic glance to the young mum sat on the table next to them with her kids. "*Sorry*," he mouthed over to her, then turned back to Fynn. "That's incredible!" he said at a more reasonable volume. "Right? I mean, what did he say? Did he like your demo?"

Fynn sat forwards, his clasped hands resting on the table edge. "It was his PA who emailed, but, yeah." He allowed himself a little smile. "He liked my stuff. He wants to meet."

Nicholas bit on his knuckles to stifle his scream. "Fynn, that's beyond amazing," he cried. "Why aren't you more excited?" There was definitely something Nicholas was missing. Fynn swallowed, and his gaze was fixed on the table top.

"He's only in London for the weekend, and his schedule is really packed."

"Okay," said Nicholas, still not quite getting it. "But he can squeeze you in, ri-*oh!*" The penny dropped. As did Nicholas's heart. "The weekend. As in…this weekend?"

Fynn didn't move for the longest time. "I'm so sorry Nicholas, I don't want to do this to you."

Nicholas waved his hands. "Stop, wait," he said, refusing to panic just yet. "What time is your appointment, interview, audition – and how long is it? Maybe there's a way to make this work – you can't pass up this opportunity."

"No," said Fynn, still not looking up. He was fiddling with the napkin again, and he licked his lips. "I can't."

"So, I'm sure there's a way to do both, right?"

Fynn finally raised his grey eyes, and shook his head. "The appointment is at three o'clock on Saturday. In central London."

So, basically, exactly when he was supposed to be playing at the wedding. A knot was tightening up in Nicholas's chest. "Okay, well, can you ask if he can fit you in in the morning, or on Sunday?"

Irritation flashed across Fynn's features. "It doesn't work like that," he said. Then he scrubbed his face with his hand, and his tone became softer. "Look, I feel awful, but this is my career. It's a once in a lifetime opportunity. I can't pass this up."

Nicholas swallowed around the lump in his throat. "And I'm not asking you to," he said carefully. He'd gone from ecstatic to fighting off tears in a matter of thirty seconds. "I'm just saying – asking – can't we at least *explore* some possible ways we could make this work?"

Fynn drummed his fingers on the table. "I know you paid me already, I can give that back—"

"That's not what I'm talking about," Nicholas spluttered. The idea that this came down to money made him feel sick. He now wished he hadn't had that coffee before; it was just churning in his stomach. "All I'm saying is it can't hurt to ask. If they know you have a wedding, they might be sympathetic."

"Nicholas," he said with an air of barely-contained patience that irked Nicholas no end. "I feel awful, okay. I got the email last night, and I've been torn up trying to work a way around this. But I'm literally *nobody*. If I go back to someone like Storm Sailor demanding a different time, I could get branded as being difficult, a diva. It might get my name blacklisted with other producers as well. I just can't *risk* that."

Out of the corner of his rapidly watering eyes, Nicholas spied the young mum hastily scooping up her toddler and pushing her baby away from her table and out the door. Nicholas didn't blame her. He was swiftly yearning for an out from this conversation himself.

"You're not *nobody* to me," he whispered. He lost his battle with his tears, and he angrily wiped the back of his sleeve over both sides of his face.

Part of him sparked with hope as Fynn's face dropped with sympathy, and he reached out with both his hands to scoop up Nicholas's. He squeezed them tight. "Please don't cry."

Nicholas screwed up his mouth. Sure, it wasn't like having live music was essential. But it was the *only* thing he'd been asked to contribute to the wedding, and now he was going to be left with a whole load of nothing. "You won't even try to ask if they'll change it?" he asked. "You're just going to chuck me under the bus and assume you're not worth even asking for some consideration."

"Darling," Fynn said softly. The term of endearment hurt. "I can't see any other way."

Nicholas pulled his hands back towards his chest. "No," he said flatly. "You just don't want to try. I mean, I'm just some weirdo you met this week, you don't owe me anything—"

"Nicholas," Fynn tried to cut in, but he didn't want to hear it.

"I get it," he bit out. "You barely know me. You have to do what's best for you. And I want that." He made himself look at Fynn, even though he felt about an inch tall. "I want you to get a contract. You're so talented, you deserve it. What's a silly wedding compared to that?" *What am I compared to that?*

Clara's wedding wasn't silly, but Fynn hadn't even committed to it this time last week. It was *Nicholas's* fault he'd forgotten to book Jones's sister to play harp back at the start of term. And now, thanks to that selfish oversight, he'd set off a chain of events that had just spiralled out of control.

What did he want? He wanted Fynn to *try*. He didn't want him to abandon his shot at a big break, but he wanted him to at least make Nicholas feel like he was worth pushing the envelope, worth trying to find a solution to work around the problem.

But he wasn't, was he? He was just some weedy, specky little virgin with a scarred face. What did he ever expect to get back from a cool, up and up, on the rise, gorgeous talent like Fynn? He needed to just escape with what dignity he had left.

"I appreciate what you've done," he said. He was glancing back and forth to the counter, praying his sister's order would be ready soon. "But you're right, your career has to come first."

"Hey, no, Nicholas," said Fynn. He didn't like the way he kept using his name. It made him feel like he was being backed into a corner. "Please don't make me feel like the bad guy here. I don't want to hurt you, I just don't see a way to make both things happen. I can't."

"Nicholas?" Sandra called out. She must have heard his silent, begging, prayer. He was almost relieved.

He gave Fynn a pinched smile. "It's been fun, but don't feel bad, alright? Go live your dreams, I'll be fine."

He stood up and marched over to the counter. He could feel Fynn rise up behind him; heard the scrape of his chair, saw his reflection in the glass divider in front of the doughnuts on display. But he didn't have much more he could say. He'd been a dalliance, a bit of fun. Who was he to kick up a fuss over some covers played over dinner when Fynn had the chance to make his mark on the music industry for real?

Take your troubles out to fly, give me a wink as I pass by.

It had been a really nice wink.

Fuck, he was glad they hadn't gone all the way and had actual sex. Nicholas felt ridiculous enough now, without offering that up to the first guy that had really turned his head. Next time, he'd need to be a little bit more aware.

"Thank you," he said to Sandra as she placed the last of the boxes on the counter.

She was beaming, but then her smile faltered, no doubt as she took in his blotchy, tear stained face. She looked between him and Fynn, who he could tell from the glass reflection had moved up to stand next to him. Jesus Christ, he hoped people in the diner weren't listening in. It had been bad enough that they'd scared off that mum and her kids. "Don't worry about the money," he said quietly over his shoulder. His throat was so thick, he was amazed he squeezed the words out. "I wish you the best, we'll work something out for tomorrow."

Fynn wouldn't leave tough. He reached out, and wrapped his fingers around Nicholas's wrist. "I'm sorry," he said again. "I wish... Can I call you? Later?"

Nicholas smiled and shook his head, his eyes itchy and hot. "What's the point? I think we both knew you'd be heading places. I'm going back to uni in Bristol anyway. So, if you can't play the wedding, what's the point?"

His last few words took on a savage tone, but he didn't know how else to protect himself. He should have known the second something between them got difficult, someone like Fynn wouldn't – shouldn't – be expected to stick his neck out. He had his own life to think about.

"Art lasts," he said, turning to face him with the best smile he could muster. "People don't. Remember? I'll be fine, don't worry. Go make some art. Sing me a song."

Fynn gnashed his teeth, and shoved his hands into his pockets. "I don't want this to be the end," he growled.

But they'd never really had a beginning, had they? If he wasn't playing for the wedding, what did they really have in common? What did Nicholas have to offer him?

"I'll maybe text you next week, or something, yeah?" he said dismissively. He really just wanted him to leave now. He was done being humiliated.

He'd let himself be stripped down, exposed. He should have known that Fynn wasn't really here to stay. He had always been bigger than little Sticky Nicky.

"Okay," Fynn uttered, stepping away. "I'll wait to hear from you. I – I really am sorry."

So was Nicholas.

He listened to the bell chime, and watched in the reflection as Fynn walked quickly out of sight, hunched down in his jacket despite the glorious sunshine. Once Nicholas had received the last of the boxes from a more subdued Sandra, he gave her a nod, carefully picked them up to cart back over to his little round table, then sat silently as he waited for his dad to come in and pick him up.

Chapter Thirteen

(The Wedding)

Robert Herald was a man of few words. He generally approached any given situation with the attitude of 'it'll sort', and left the fretting to his wife. Nicholas was in no doubt he got his motor mouth from her, but he had to say there were many times when he appreciated his dad's quiet nature more than he could say.

So when Mr Herald had walked into the Kristy Kreme diner and seen his son struggling to fight back tears, he'd not said a word. He'd squeezed Nicholas's shoulder, then gone up to the counter with big smile to thank Sandra numerous times for her speedy work, compliment her on doing such a great job, and pay her with gratitude. All it had taken to get them going back to the car was him picking up half the boxes and a nod towards Nicholas to do the same.

"Everything okay mate?" he'd asked as they'd walked.

Nicholas had answered with a nod and a sniff. "I'll be fine."

The journey back in the car was just as quiet between them. Nicholas had let the rock music from Absolute Radio drift over him, the well-known classics and the newer popular tracks washing over him as he attempted not to think of anything at all.

The house had spent most of the afternoon in chaos, but his dad had told everyone that Nicholas had a terrible headache and was going to rest up for the big day ahead. And therefore, he'd been allowed to spend the rest of the day and night curled up in his bed, trying his best to forget about the world.

It didn't realty work, but he tried.

At some time around one o'clock, he had the vague memory of turning over and seeing the sweep of headlights in the driveway below. The front door had opened and closed quietly, footsteps had creaked up the stairs, and Nicholas guessed his dad had come back from the airport. Thank goodness. At least everyone was in the country now.

Lauren and her family had agreed to stay two nights in the hotel they would all be staying at after the reception. Her old room already had Kinny and Ash camped out in it, and it would be less disruptive for little Milly to stay in the same place for the whole weekend. Selfishly, Nicholas was also quite glad that that would limit the hours a screaming three-year-old would be running amuck in the house. He loved his niece dearly, but tomorrow was going to be undoubtedly stressful, and Nicholas felt like he was hanging on by a thread as it was.

There was the small matter of there being no musician for the wedding breakfast. But that was a problem for the morning. As Nicholas tossed and turned he only had one thing on his mind: Fynn.

He felt empty, and numb, but at the same time, like he had too many thoughts battling for his attention. When he wasn't sobbing into his pillow, he was staring into the darkness with barely a blink.

He tried to be angry with Fynn, but all he could muster was a disappointment that he hadn't been willing to at least *try* and move the audition around. But even then, Nicholas kept coming back to the knowledge that he wasn't worth his time, and he'd be foolish to expect Fynn to go out on a limb for him when they'd only know each other a few days.

That was his train of thought when he was feeling like a husk. A tired-out thing. But then the floodgates would open when he thought of never getting to be near Fynn again. He had wrestled with the fact that Fynn had asked to call him, but he was convinced it was just because he was feeling guilty about bailing on the wedding. Fynn wasn't his to keep, he'd move on quick enough, and he'd soon forget about that odd guy barely out of his teens who had had his first gay fool-around with him.

That was when his crying got really gut-wrenching; when he pictured Fynn moving on with someone else. He'd meet all kinds of interesting and talented people in the music industry, and they'd be more experience and more confident than Nicholas probably ever had a hope to be. He would meet someone who was his equal.

No wonder Fynn didn't want to bother with him; he shouldn't have created such a fuss about the wedding. He should have been more supportive of Fynn's amazing opportunity. If he hadn't been such a cry-baby and taken it so personally, Fynn might have been more inclined to come back and give him another chance.

Nicholas tortured himself into the small hours of the morning agonising over whether Fynn might have been genuine about his offer to call, and then picturing his imaginary future lovers. Fuck, he'd let Fynn get him off – *twice*. He shouldn't have been so selfish that first time, and insisted on reciprocating the hand job. Why would Fynn want to stay with someone so useless in bed?

Really, he'd been lucky to get even a few days with someone so incredible.

He managed to doze off into some semblance of R.E.M. at about four in the morning, but then the house started going crazy at not long after six, and he knew he'd be fighting a losing battle to try and get any more sleep. This day, he figured, would have to be sponsored by coffee. Lots of coffee.

After sourcing some toast to go with his caffeine, Nicholas quickly sussed that the best plan would be to stay out of everyone's way. The hairdresser arrived at half past seven and set up in the living room, and the photographer not long after that. Nicholas took it upon himself to make sure that they had a never-ending stream of tea. The rest of the time he curled up on the couch to close his eyes for a few minutes at a time, until he could seize his opportunity to nip into the shower when it was free for a few minutes.

Ash didn't need her hair styled, as it was so short there was very little you could do to it outside of her normal daily routine. But she did obediently sit and allow several tiny flower gems to be clipped in atop her head. As soon as the last one was in place, she thanked the lady, then unceremoniously grabbed Nicholas by the hand and hauled him out into the garden.

The sun was still shining, although the mud beneath the extremely green grass was still quite squishy. So they stood on the patio, Ash with her arms folded, Nicholas shading his eyes so he could see her without squinting too badly.

"Um," he said nervously, having been dragged the length of the house in silence. "What's up?" The question came out as a squeak.

"That's what I was going to ask you," she countered. "You look like your dog just died. What the hell?"

Nicholas winced. "Is it that obvious?"

Ash shrugged. "I think other people are doing their best to ignore it, or pretend that you've still got that headache." She scoffed to indicate how much she'd believed that excuse yesterday. "But you're sad. And today's a day you should definitely be happy. So. What's up?"

Nicholas rubbed his eyes under his glasses. He was so tired, he'd decided to wait until later to put his contacts in. He was dreading it, but he didn't have a choice.

He sighed, and figured, finally, it was time to come clean. "I fucked up," he blurted unceremoniously. He threw his hands up, and slapped them on his thighs. "I had one job for today – *one*. I was supposed to book my friend's sister to play her harp at the breakfast. But I completely forgot, and instead of coming clean, I *lied.* But then it was all okay, because I couldn't get a harpist, but I found this—" his voice caught, but he powered on through "—*incredible* guitarist, honestly, his voice is so beautiful. And then he cancelled on me yesterday afternoon. So…that's it. No one to play the wedding."

"Right," said Ash after a moment. She raised an eyebrow, then reached into her back pocket for her phone. "First off, no one's going to notice the music at the reception – I promise. A harp was a great idea, and I'm sure the guitar would have been great, but everyone will have had too much booze by then. They'll just be fighting over the bread basket and placing bets on how long the best man speech goes on for. Look." She held up her screen. It was a Spotify playlist, titled 'Wedding Classics.' "There. Sorted. You don't need to worry about it a second more. Any music will do. And as for this guy letting you down *yesterday*," she spat out as she put her phone away again. "What a prick. Not your fault."

Nicholas was still reeling from the fact he'd never once thought about saving his skin with a pre-made playlist. It wouldn't have quite the same effect as live music, but still, it would be better than awkward silence. Then he registered what Ash had said.

"Oh, no," he told her quickly. "He's completely *not* a prick, it's for really good reasons. I promise. I don't blame him. I just, well it put me in a load of trouble again, or so I though. But, you're right." He smiled at her. "We can fix it with Spotify."

She regarded him with a shrewd eye until he fidgeted on his feet. "Would this guitarist," she said slowly, "happen to be that guy Fynn from the club?"

Nicholas's jaw dropped, giving the game away before he could even consider thinking up a decent lie. "How did you…?"

Ash shrugged, then pulled him into a hug. "I can spot a crush a mile off," she said, rubbing his back. "Is that why he bailed? Is he straight?"

Nicholas's cheeks burned as Ash stepped back to look at him. "Um, no," he mumbled. "Very gay actually."

"Ahh," said Ash with understanding.

Nicholas coughed and rubbed at his scars. "No, he got a chance to see a big music producer today. I told him to take it. Yeah, it kind of sucks for the wedding, but getting a record contract is way more important."

"Uh huh," said Ash. "So, why'd you have to break up? You that pissed at him for bailing?"

Nicholas scoffed. "We weren't really together. He was only going to be around for the wedding anyway, so, it's best just to part ways now." He ran his hand through his hair. "I'll, um, buy his CD someday, maybe." Ash just stared at him, her eyes narrowing. "What?"

"He said he didn't want to see you anymore?"

"Actually," admitted Nicholas, scuffing his feet on the patio. "He said he'd call me. But, he won't," he said with conviction. "He can barely text. It's fine, you've fixed the music problem, so, what's there left to talk about?" She plonked her hands on her hips, and raised her eyebrows at him. "What?" whined Nicholas in exasperation.

She sighed, softening her posture and wrapping her arms around him again. "I don't know him like you do," she said into his neck. "But, maybe don't give up just yet, yeah? Sometimes things have a way of working themselves out."

Nicholas thought that was very nice of her to say. He didn't believe her, especially not after this week, where he'd never in his life been witness to so many things *not* working out, but still, he appreciated the sentiment. "Thank you."

"You're welcome."

They stayed like that for a minute more, but there was no hiding on a day like today. So with a shared sigh and shrug, they both headed back towards the kitchen door.

As they re-entered the house, it was clear from the babble of chatter and childish shrieks coming from the hallway that Lauren and company had arrived from the hotel. Ash stopped in her tracks, looking to Nicholas for guidance. He chuckled.

"They're not that scary," he assured her. "Do you want to come meet them?"

Ash hadn't yet had the opportunity to get to know her future sister-in-law much beyond Facebook. But before they could make it through the kitchen, they were accosted by a small creature known as the 'Milly Monster'.

"Uncle Nicky, Uncle Nicky!" she screeched as he automatically bent down to let her throw her arms around his neck.

"Monster!" he cried back, picking her up and spinning her around. He was vaguely aware of the stealthy photographer snapping away in the background. "Wow, you got big!" She really had. He tried to Skype semi-regularly with his sister, but the last he'd seen his niece on screen, he hadn't realised what a growth spurt she'd been through. Her dark brown hair had grown too, almost reaching her waist. The hairdresser was going to have fun with that. "Look who's here," he said. He stopped spinning so they were facing Ash, who was smiling at the both of them. "This is Auntie Ash. Can you say 'hello'?"

Milly frowned and leaned over, reaching her little hand to pat at Ash's short hair with the sparkly flowers in it. "Auntie Ash," she said experimentally. She touched the hair again, and Ash leant into the touch. Milly turned back to Nicholas, still frowning.

"What's up, Doc?" he asked.

Milly looked at Ash again. "Is Auntie Ash a boy or a guwl?" she asked. She chewed on her lip and pulled at her own long hair.

Ash laughed, clearly delighted. "This one's a keeper," she announced. She held out her hand, and after a moment's consideration, Milly stuck hers out to so they could shake. "Well Milly – that's your name, right?" Milly nodded, using her whole body so Nicholas had to hoist her up again and re-establish his grip under her bum. "Sometimes girls can have short hair too. Is that okay?"

Milly hummed as she thought about it. "Yes," she decided, and patted Ash again.

"Good, thank you," Ash told her.

Nicholas let her down again, and she ran back to where everyone else was congregated. Lauren's boyfriend Franko was a typical tall, dark and handsome Italian, and he greeted them all with three kisses on the cheeks that lead to numerous nose bumps, almost snogs, and several cries of 'Oops, sorry!'

Lauren had met him when she'd been travelling. He knew their parents had thought it was going to be a holiday fling at the time, but Lauren was never one to do what was expected. She cancelled the rest of her planned trip, got a job in Rome with a human rights charity, and not long later Milly had come along. It had all been very romantic.

With a pang, he thought about Fynn. They'd only had one date, but it had been pretty romantic for his first ever date, and he hadn't been able to stop himself hoping there would be more. He wished there could have been more.

He made himself smile and shake away his melancholy. Today wasn't about him.

The morning slipped away at an astonishing rate. One by one, the bridesmaids began transforming as they got their hair done and started applying their makeup. Nicholas's mum faffed around with her hat for a solid half an hour, and Nicholas dithered about when to go and put his suit on.

The first hiccup came when Lauren emerged from where she and Milly had set up camp in

Nicholas's parents' room. Nicholas happened to be in the corridor, making his way downstairs again with Kinny, when they both stopped in their tracks when they saw her fully intact bridesmaid's dress.

"Holy crap," cried Nicholas, tugging at his hair. "I totally forgot!"

Lauren looked down at her floor-length dress. "Forgot what?" she asked. "What's wrong?"

"We had to change our dresses," explained Kinny weakly. "Um, come and see."

Danielle had naturally been the first to get her hair done, and when they entered the den, she was unsurprisingly completely ready to go, even though the cars weren't due for another two hours. Hair, makeup, jewellery, clutch bag, shawl, and most importantly, recently altered dress.

She and Lauren regarded each other with wide eyes. "Oh," said Lauren, taking in the new dip-hem line. "I see."

"So, you know Archibald, right? The cat?" Kinny gibbered. "Well, he didn't like the dresses much, so suddenly there was a whole lot less of them, and we had to think fast. But, um, we all sort of forgot you had a dress too."

Nicholas rubbed his forehead and looked between the two different styles. "Do we need to change it?" he asked.

Danielle shook her head. "There's no time," she said. She took a deep breath, and let it out slowly. "If we'd have maybe let Lauren know at the start of the week, she could have organised an alteration to match…"

Nicholas felt guilty again about keeping the accident a secret. But Lauren shook her hands at them all. "Hey, it doesn't really matter, does it? I mean, yours is different too." She pointed at Danielle's waist. "It's got extra blingy bits in the middle." She smiled at looked to Nicholas and Kinny for support.

"I feel bad we didn't tell you," said Kinny.

"Yeah, it's not been the best week," mumbled Nicholas.

Lauren shook her head. "Milly and I are going down the aisle first anyway. So, we'll just be different; Milly's design has always been different anyway, just the same colour as ours. We'll be... Mummy Maid, and Mini Maid."

Nicholas laughed. "That's cute," he agreed. "If you're sure?"

Danielle flicked an eyebrow, as if to ask what they could do anyway. But Lauren laughed. "Yeah, it's fine. As long as Clara looks the most gorgeous. We're just here to prop her up, aren't we?"

Gosh he had missed his sister's easy going nature. She always knew how to put out the fires before they really began. Which was a good job, because the next one was already on its way.

Over the commotion of the flower delivery arriving in the hall, a holler came floating down the stairs in agitated Italian. Lauren frowned, and leant out the door from the den to shout back at her boyfriend.

"Everything okay?" he asked nervously. He'd always meant to learn a bit of Italian, but when they both could speak English, it had never really seemed all that pertinent.

Lauren waited until Franko replied to whatever it was that she'd asked, and raised her eyebrows. "Um," she said, starting out the door. "Minor hiccup."

Nicholas followed with a sense of trepidation. *Please don't be too bad*, he begged the universe silently. *Please just be a little crisis*. He'd got quite good at fixing little crises.

Milly was running around Nicholas's parents room with her arms out like an airplane, making her pink bridesmaid dress fan out behind her. She looked perfectly happy. But Franko was stood in front of Lauren by the time Nicholas got there with Danielle and Kinny, holding out a small pair of very pretty white shoes with glitter along the straps that complemented the grown-up bridesmaids' footwear perfectly.

"What's the matter?" Lauren asked, taking one of them to inspect it in her hand. "Won't she put them on?"

Franko sighed. "No, she was actually happy to wear them, because they are sparkly, see." He pointed at the glitter. That was obviously a prerequisite for Milly's shoes at present, Nicholas assumed. "The problem is they are being too small."

Lauren tilted her head and eyed him with disbelief. "I only bought them last month," she said.

Franko put his hands up and shook his head. '*Lo so*,' he said. "I know, I know, but they are pinching her. She cried."

"Oh no," said Kinny sympathetically.

Lauren clicked her fingers, and called Milly over in Italian. "Hey Baba," she said as her daughter approached. "Did the shoes hurt you?" Milly stuck her bottom lip out and nodded. But Lauren didn't seem convinced, and glanced at Franko. "Could be just a ploy," she said, then turned back. "Can Mummy try?"

"*No!*" Milly howled and bolted.

The next few minutes were spent seeing how many fully-grown adults could chase a single toddler around one room. But eventually, Kinny, who was not yet in heels and had years of teaching experience, managed to grab her by the waist and swing her into her lap as she sat on the bed.

"Look Milly," she cooed, pointing at the child's parents as they each descended on her with a shoe. "Aren't they pretty. They're just like Mummy's, and Cousin Danny's. Don't you want to look like them?"

"Too tight, too tight!" Milly kept protesting. Big tears rolled down her cheeks as she kicked her legs, and Nicholas felt mean. But Lauren and Franko persisted in trying to ease them on, until seemingly as one, they both knelt back and admitted defeat.

"Well...*fiddlesticks,*" grumbled Lauren.

Milly scrambled off of Kinny's lap, and allowed herself to be scooped up into Nicholas's arms.

"It's fine," he told them all as she shivered against him. He stroked his niece's dark hair and kissed her wet cheek. This was *surely* a mini crisis compared to some of the other things they'd faced. "Honestly, it's not a problem. Can't she just wear another pair of shoes?"

Lauren and Franko shared a look, and sighed. "She hasn't *got* another pair of shoes," said Lauren. "Not ones suitable for a wedding, anyway."

"What do you mean?" asked Danielle.

Franko went to the suitcase they'd brought with them from the hotel, and retrieved a very small, hot pink, and sparkly pair of wellington boots. "She has refused to wear anything else since Christmas."

Nicholas was tempted to laugh, but he could tell this had been a battle they'd been having for months. "Well, how come they fit, and the wedding shoes don't?" he asked.

"They were always too big for her," Lauren explained as Milly leant out as far as she could from Nicholas, her hands grabbing for the boots.

"There was only one size on display, but she screamed until we bought them. She's been wearing them with two or three pairs of socks."

Nicholas sighed, and released Milly so she could scamper over to her dad and jam her feet eagerly into the wellies. It seemed now that they fit fine with just one pair of socks.

"Honestly," said Kinny, regarding the child as she spun happily around. Her tears had dried on her face, completely forgotten. "I think that sort of looks cute."

Nicholas tried to look at the outfit objectively. It didn't look all that wedding-y, but, Kinny was right. "It kind of fits with the spring theme," he offered, watching as she began jumping up and down like a little kangaroo. "It makes me think of gardening and April showers."

Danielle looked at the clock on the wall. "I mean," she said. "Uncle Robert probably has time to run her into town and buy her something new, but do you think she'll have a tantrum if we try that?"

Lauren and Franko looked at each other. "Yes," they said as one.

Danielle sighed, and rubbed the back of her neck. "Okay," she said, then held out her hand for Milly to take. "Hey sweetie! Shall we go show Auntie Clara your pretty boots, see if she likes them?"

"Yes, yes, yes!" yelled Milly. She punctuated each word with a jump as she bounced over to take the proffered hand.

Clara was in the living room with their mum, getting her hair done up in an intricate knot. She was drinking tea and chatting with the photographer hovering by her side when the gang of them entered, and several emotions flitted across her face as she took in Lauren in her original dress and Milly in her boots. "We've had a bit of a shoe emergency," said Danielle with a big, slightly forced smile.

"Auntie Clawa!" Milly squealed. "My boots are spawkly," she announced. She ran up in front of where Clara was sitting and pointed them this way and that so she could see them from every angle.

"Yes, they are," she said to her. Then she looked over at Lauren, careful not to move her head too much where the hairdresser was working. "I thought you got her white shoes?"

Lauren explained about them no longer fitting and the fruitlessness of trying to run around and buy a new pair now. But Kinny shook her head. "We think they sort of work anyway," she said, repeating Nicholas's point. "It fits in with the spring theme." She then sneezed loudly, and blinked at it having taken her by surprise. "Sorry, excuse me."

Clara stared at her niece running around happily for a minute, until she sighed and her shoulders relaxed. "They are *very* pretty," she told her. "Would you like to wear them for the wedding?"

Milly bunched up her hands and stamped her sparkly feet. "Oh yes please, yes please!"

"Then that's decided."

Nicholas's mum made a few protest noises about how the photos would look, but she was outnumbered. Nobody else had the strength to try and get Milly into a new pair of shoes.

"Hey," said Nicholas jovially. "At least she's all in pink. They could have been yellow or orange."

Everyone agreed this was a very good point indeed.

It was gone midday, so Nicholas felt it was time to start getting ready himself, seeing as the cars would be arriving at one-thirty. But when he was alone in his room again, it was hard to keep a hold of his good mood.

He'd been so excited about Fynn seeing him in his suit. He'd pictured his face again and again as he'd thought about walking into the venue, Fynn on his guitar, wowing everyone, and Nicholas all dressed up. For once, he had imagined he might look good enough to stand next to him for everyone to see. And now, he'd never know if he thought the bowtie was cute, or if he liked the spats shoes.

He sat on his bed and stared at his shirt in his hands for longer than he should have. He wondered how Fynn's day was going. Was he already on the train into London? Or had he arrived early in anticipation of the meeting?

Despite everything, Nicholas wished him the best of luck, with his whole heart. Fynn was too big for Nicholas's little world. He wanted him to succeed and fly up to the stars. Even if that meant doing it without him.

With a sigh, Nicholas made himself stand up, and carry on getting dressed. He looked at the hickey on his clavicle for a while in the mirror, touching it with his finger tip. It gave him a strange sense of comfort to know that in some very small way, Fynn was still with him today.

This was just the beginning, he told himself as he pulled his trousers on. Now he knew he was gay, he could join the LGBT society back at uni. Maybe he could even seek out that cute Politics student again. He'd be much better off with someone more in his own league, perhaps someone who was sweet and funny and actually *replied* to texts.

He could think about that later. Because just then, the idea of comparing anyone else to Fynn wasn't going to work. His heart contracted in his chest, and he placed his hand over it, willing the pain to stop.

Not for the first time, he wondered if he'd been in love.

Not *actually* in love – that was impossible in such a short amount of time, he was certain. But maybe he'd been on his way. Maybe it would have been love in a little while. He guessed he'd never know.

The point was, this wasn't the end of the world. He was bound to meet someone new; he was only twenty. Just because Clara had met her soulmate on the first try didn't mean he had to as well. Lauren had dated a bunch of guys and had loads of hook-ups before she met Franko. There were plenty more fish in the sea.

He kept telling himself that until he had slipped both his contact lenses into his eyes, straightened his jacket, and stepped back out of the door. Then there was too much to distract him to think too long about the heart he'd assured himself wouldn't get broken.

The last hour slipped away in the blink of an eye. The house was a whirlwind of people running around, getting dressed, finding cufflinks and necklaces, yelling about how little time they had left, all while trying not to knock over the flowers that had now filled the hallway. Nicholas envied Peter, getting ready in the quietness of his hotel room.

Each bridesmaid had a flower bouquet as well as a crown for her head. Even little Milly, who Nicholas thought was very good as Lauren and their mum used bobby pins to secure it to her hair. Then Nicholas and his dad had button holes that matched the ones that had been sent over to Peter and his ushers, and finally, there was Clara's magnificent teardrop bouquet. The main flower to make up the arrangements was a delicate little once called Baby's Breath. It looked like something you'd find in a meadow. There was bunches and bunches of it, only interspersed with pale pink roses in Clara's bouquet.

And it turned out, Kinny was allergic to it.

"I'm so sorry," she said, blowing her nose and dabbing at her eyes, trying not to ruin any of her makeup. "I had no idea!" She'd been trying to ignore the increasing sneezes for the past hour, but after she'd had her crown secured to her head, there was no getting away from it.

Luckily, Nicholas's mum suffered quite badly from hay fever, so was already well stocked up on antihistamines, eye drops, and even a nasal spray. But the cars had arrived, and although most people were dressed and ready to go, Clara was still upstairs fussing with their dad, and Kinny couldn't leave until her face had calmed down a bit.

"Let's go into the garden for a bit," suggested Ash, leading her by her arm. "Some fresh air might blow the most of it away while the tablets get to work." Kinny nodded, evidently miserable and guilty, but willing to try anything to ease her symptoms.

"You just have to keep it on until the photos are done," Nicholas assured her as he followed them through to the kitchen. "After that, bugger it. You can chuck it in the bin."

Kinny laughed, and Ash gave him an appreciative smile as she took her outside. She was in her bridesmaid's dress, and although Nicholas could tell she was still not friends with it, she was putting on a good show of being fine.

By the time that Nicholas's dad announced that Clara was ready to slowly start making her way down the stairs in her dress, they were running late. They had to make sure they were at the venue by two o'clock, as the ceremony was at two-thirty, but the registrar had to do the final, separate interviews with Clara and Peter to double check they still wanted to get married, or were in their right minds, or something. Nicholas wasn't sure. He felt sorry for anyone who made it to this point and then decided that no, actually, they didn't want to get married. He wondered how often that happened, and had to reassure himself that that was definitely not going to be the case today. Peter and Clara were so in love, and now they were going to make it official.

Having had a freak out about it on Thursday night, Nicholas had to admit he was a tiny bit worried about seeing his big sis in her dress. If she really hated it on herself, there wouldn't be much he could do about it. But as soon as she came around the corner at the top of the stairs, everyone gasped, and he knew it was all going to be okay.

Their dad was actually misty-eyed as he helped her take one step at a time, and the photographer walked backwards down the stairs, capturing every moment. Nicholas could understand why. Her strawberry blonde hair was piled up into a complex knot around a tiara and veil, and her beaming face was framed with pretty little ringlets. Her skin was glowing from the expertly-applied makeup, and delicate crystals sparkled around her throat on the necklace that their parents had bought her especially.

The dress itself was gathered around her waist and fell to the floor like a waterfall, flowing with every step she took. There were thick straps over her shoulders, wrapped with silver hoops at regular intervals that gave it a sort of Greek feel. The material wrapped over her chest in a sweetheart cut that didn't show off too much of her boobs, but still managed to make her figure look cracking.

Nicholas wiped his eyes with his thumb. "Ahh Geri," he said, affectionately using her Spice Girls name. "If he doesn't cry, I'm going to deck him."

Clara bubbled with laughter that threatened to turn into a sob, and she swatted him with her hand. "Shut up," she said good-naturedly.

Nicholas was overcome with happiness. No matter his own upsets and woes, he knew this was going to be one of the best days of Clara's life.

They had twenty minutes to make it to the town hall in order to be on time for Clara's interview, which they could do if the traffic wasn't abysmal. But it was a Saturday, and the sun was back out, so Nicholas was more than a little nervous as they all bundled into the sleek black cars, each adorned with pink ribbons stretched over the bonnets.

The first part of the route was okay, but predictably, the closer they got to town, the heavier the traffic got. Nicholas chewed his thumbnail until Ash pulled it away from his mouth.

"We'll get there when we get there," she said kindly, but firmly.

The steps up to the town hall were just off the road. So the cars all pulled over in the designated area, and the party had to walk across the square with locals, tourists, stall owners and pigeons all looking on. Nicholas knew that Danielle would have seen this as a fabulous added bonus when they booked the venue. The idea of preening and showing off would have appealed to her. But seeing as they were now ten minutes past two o'clock, and had had to deal with a host of unexpected dilemmas that morning, let alone the rest of the week, he couldn't help but wish they had a little more privacy.

Still, on the whole, the people around them were looking on with excitement and warmth. Some took photos, others waved and offered thumbs up. Nicholas appreciated that.

He didn't want to leave, but as they reached the foyer, his job was done. He and his mum needed to go sit down with Franko and leave Clara with their dad to do the interview before returning to the bridesmaids. Just as he was about to leave, he turned around and grabbed his sister tight, hugging her with everything he had.

"I love you," he said, trying not to sniffle. "You look *stunning*. Please enjoy this. You deserve it."

"Oh bugger off before you make me howl," she chuckled, lightly bashing him with her bouquet.

Kinny sneezed, then hastily blew her nose. "I'm fine, I'm fine," she squeaked, tucking the tissue into her bra.

Nicholas gave all the bridesmaids one last hug, accepted an enthusiastic high five from Milly, then took his mum's arm to walk her inside the hall.

"Isn't this exciting?" she said thickly.

Nicholas still hadn't quite forgiven her for blaming him for the destruction of the wedding cake yesterday. But she was giddy and emotional with delight over her eldest daughter's wedding, the first wedding of any of her children. So he decided to just forget about it, and hugged her close as they drew near the bustling ceremony room.

Compared to when he'd come with Fynn the other day – and he was not going to think about what had happened immediately after that – the hall was overflowing with activity now. There were seventy or eighty chairs, all arranged in semi-circular rows, facing the table that had been set up for the registrar. They were adorned with tightly fitted white covers and pale pink sashes, and most of them were already occupied with excited friends and family, waiting for the ceremony to begin.

Nicholas didn't know a lot of the smiling faces, assuming them to be friends of Clara's and Peter's from school, uni, and their online community. There was also Peter's extended family, who, outside of Ash and their parents, Nicholas didn't know at all. But there were members of his own family who he hadn't seen for years that he happily waved at as he and his mum walked to their places at the front on the rows.

He was very pleased to see his Aunt Sally had made it in one piece. She was pale and slightly clammy-looking under her big hat, but she was still talking with one of Peter's uncles in the row behind her, angling her ample bosom his way and having a good go at a flirt. Her four boys were sat in a line next to her; Noah had put on a bit of weight, Mason was obviously going through a goth stage, Ethan was bouncing on his seat in excitement, and Oliver was ignoring everyone and everything around him in favour of the game he was playing on his mum's phone. When Ethan spotted Nicholas though, he poked his brothers and his mum until they were all waving at him. He grinned and waved back, mouthing *"Speak to you later"* with a thumbs up.

Nicholas's mum spotted her sister, Danielle's mum, Louise. It was painfully clear she wasn't speaking to her husband from the way she had her whole body turned away from him, engaging with her ghastly friend Michelle. Thin to the point of anorexia, she was wearing bright yellow and smirking at anyone who happened to look her way.

Nicholas tried not to give her the satisfaction of scowling in her direction. But it was difficult when thought about what unkind observations she was undoubtedly going to come up with once she saw Clara in her dress.

His mum attempted to drag him over to say hello, but Nicholas implied he had someone else he needed to talk to. In reality, he just wanted to go and sit in his seat. He'd work his way up to small talk later, once the 'I dos' had been all said and done.

He found his reservation card next to his grandma on his dad's side. She was a robust woman still, despite being in her seventies, with a cloud of flyaway hair that had, for once, been tamed in some sort of bun at the back of her neck. She wore a large, blue-feathered fascinator on the side of her head and a blue pantsuit with sensible black shoes. She grabbed Nicholas's hand as soon as he sat down.

"Oh Robert," she said. He'd long ago stopped bothering to try and correct her when she called him by his dad's name. "Isn't this *marvellous*. Who would have thought it would be Clara getting married first?"

"Well," he said uncomfortably. "I guess she is the oldest."

"Yes," his grandma conceded, wobbling her head from side to side. "But, you know..."

He knew all too well. "Lauren had the first baby," he said, patting her hand. "So isn't only fair Clara got to have the first wedding?"

"Hmm," said his grandma. Lauren had always been her favourite. "What about you? You have a girlfriend yet?"

Nicholas licked his lips and really hoped Clara wouldn't be much longer. He caught eyes with Peter, standing at the front with his best man George, and gave him a small salute. Peter nodded back, then carried on looking anxiously over his shoulder at the door.

"No, not yet Grandma."

"Well," she said. "Don't be leaving it too late now, otherwise all the good ones will be gone!"

Nicholas had a horrible feeling he'd just let a good one go.

Thankfully, that was the moment the music playing in the background faded to nothing, and the registrar came and stood before them as they all shuffled into their seats, becoming silent.

"Thank you," she said in a strong Scottish brogue. She was the picture of efficiency, with a dark, pinstripe suit and her short hair cut into a tidy bob. "Ladies and gentlemen. Would you please be upstanding for the bride?"

Danielle had picked out 'Pachelbel's Canon in D' for them all to walk down the aisle to. Nicholas's suggestion of 'Single Ladies' had, quite rudely, not even been considered.

The first to come through the doors was Lauren, hand in hand with a very excitable Milly. Nicholas heard a few chuckles at the sight of her welly boots, but Clara's uni friends gave out a few cries of "brilliant" and "look at her" as they snapped up photos, which made him happy.

They were closely followed by Ash and then Kinny. Ash walked with her head held high, focusing on every step with determination. Apart from having a slightly red nose, Kinny looked perfectly at ease as she glided down the aisle, holding her bouquet as far away from her as she could without appearing strange. The both of them came and sat in the space next to Nicholas. He gave them a thumbs up each.

There was a longer pause before Danielle came sashaying through the doors, beaming at everyone on both sides like she'd just won Miss Universe.

She made eye contact with everyone she passed, bequeathing winks and mouthed 'hello's and the odd 'you look gorgeous'. She certainly knew how to work a crowd.

A nervous tension was building in Nicholas's stomach. He wasn't really sure why, it was ridiculous when you thought about it. All his sister had to do was walk a few steps and then repeat a few words. But still, he found himself holding his breath, until finally, Clara and their dad came into view.

The chorus of sighs and gasps was enough to melt any heart. Clara clung to their dad as she slowly made her way past all the rows, smiling and shaking ever so slightly as she travelled down. Cameras and phones clicked and flashed, and more than one person was already dabbing their eyes on a tissue. Nicholas won the bet. Peter rubbed at his wet eyes with his thumb.

"You owe me a tenner," he whispered with a wink as she passed him.

And then, Nicholas sighed with relief. It may not have been the perfect week, and he may well still have been facing a broken heart; but as far as Clara was concerned, they had bloody well made it.

He watched as Peter grabbed Clara's hands as soon as she'd passed her bouquet over to Danielle, chuckling to himself as his very-almost brother-in-law practically skipped on his feet. "*You look incredible,*" Nicholas saw him say to her.

They all took their seats as the music died down, and Nicholas found he couldn't stop grinning as the ceremony officially began. The happy couple were totally lost in one another, nodding at the registrar's words every now and again, and repeating when they needed to, but they never took their eyes off one another.

Of course, there had to be one last little hiccup.

"If any person present," the registrar intoned, looking around at the congregation, "knows of any lawful impediment to this marriage, he or she should declare it now."

Kinny sneezed so hard, her flower crown flew off her head and went skittering several feet until it stopped in front of the bride and groom.

She froze in horror, but the rest of the room erupted with a good, hearty laugh at the misfortunate timing, with several of the younger guests whistling and cheering. Nicholas couldn't help but laugh as Kinny covered her face in mortification. His Aunt Louise was pretty much the only stony face in the room, but that just made it funnier as far as he was concerned.

Peter and Clara certainly didn't mind, from the amused looks on their faces. Before anyone else could do anything, little Milly scampered to her feet, racing over to fetch the headdress and return it to Kinny's lap.

"Thank you," she whispered as the crowd calmed down again.

Once Kinny had hastily blown her nose, the registrar raised her hand.

"I take it that's a 'no'?" she asked playfully.

The rest of the ceremony transpired with little more than the occasional sniffle, until the moment came to finally announce the couple as husband and wife. "Mr and Mrs Cove!" the registrar cried to rapturous applause as the couple kissed. Nicholas stood and bellowed louder than anyone, clapping his hands and wiping the tears from his cheeks with the back of his hand.

No matter whatever else happened now, Clara and Peter were married. Curse be damned.

There were fifteen minutes or so where they and the witnesses had to sign the official documentation, and then people were invited to come up and take photos. Nicholas got a prod from his grandma.

"Well come on then," she said, waving her smartphone at him. "Help me up. I need to get a good angle!"

Nicholas smiled to himself and offered his arm so she could use it to help her shuffle over and snap several shots of the couple posing with their pens over the marriage certificate. Rather than make her move and sit again, Nicholas maneuverered them into a corner, and together they waited.

"Once again, ladies and gentlemen," cried the registrar. "Mr and Mrs Cove!"

The classic wedding march blasted over the sound system, and Peter and Clara happily waved their way back down the aisle as their loved ones cheered them on. "Come on Grandma," said Nicholas once the throng began to slowly shift and follow them out. "Let's make sure we get a good spot behind the photographer.

The staff from the town hall were keen to usher them all outside, as they had to hurriedly transform the room so it was suitable for the wedding breakfast in less than an hour. They were already rolling in the tables by the time Nicholas and his grandma headed towards the doors, and a dozen or so wait staff were already rallying around with table cloths, stacks of plates and trays laden down with cutlery.

Nicholas had almost forgotten that it was sunny outside after all the rain they'd had the past week. There was a cool breeze in the air, but the sky was bright blue with only a few white and fluffy clouds trundling on their way overhead. The photographer was lining everyone up on two sides down the steps in anticipation of throwing the confetti, and Nicholas allowed his grandma to steer them near the front.

"Here," she said, thrusting a box of paper confetti into his hands from her handbag. "You make sure you get 'em good and proper. I'm going to use one of those slo-mo filters."

The town hall's imposing white columns made for an impressive backdrop to the official photos. After the guests had doused Clara and Peter thoroughly with the confetti, the photographer then began organising people into groups to best capture everyone in attendance. There were still ordinary passers-by who stood around gawking, but now the ceremony was complete, Nicholas felt like he didn't mind them as much. Neither did Clara, from the happy expression she was able to maintain throughout.

Nicholas was required for a few of the family photos, as was his grandma, so he daren't venture too far to get himself a glass of bubbly. But he appreciated it when one of the waiters came by with a tray. It was just what he needed to calm the rest of his nerves.

His thoughts were still tinged with melancholy, but he was determined to just enjoy the rest of the day now. Peter and Clara were only going to get married once, and unless the congregation all got food poisoning, or the best man speech was a disaster, he was pretty sure they were in the home stretch.

He *immediately* wished he hadn't jinxed either of those eventualities. But if he was lucky, the universe was actually done with them now.

"Hey Nicholas," said Kinny as she walked out of the entranceway and down the steps. She'd divested herself of both her crown and her bouquet, and was already looking much less puffy than before. He turned and smiled at her before sipping his drink. His grandma was still on his arm, and Ash had gravitated towards them both as the photos wore on.

"You're looking better," he said with a grin.

"Thanks," she replied with a laugh. "So, I thought you said you'd organised a harp for the dinner?"

Nicholas groaned. After his conversation with Ash, he'd forgot to actually tell anyone about his fuck up. Hopefully there was time now to run in and hook up her Spotify playlist. "I know, there was a mix up."

But Kinny raised her palms to him and shook her head. "Oh don't worry, I just wasn't sure. This guy seems wonderful."

Nicholas blinked.

"What?" he stammered.

Kinny jerked her thumb over her shoulder. "Mr Handsome on the guitar. He's playing a really cool cover of Katy Perry."

Before he'd even registered what was happening, Ash was slipping her arm between his and his grandma's, and plucking the champagne flute from his hand. Stunned, he turned to face her.

"Go," she hissed, breaking into a smile.

He tried not to run.

Many of the guests were already making their way inside again, hugging everyone in the receiving line before they re-entered the room for the meal. Nicholas's grandma had wanted to let the crush disperse before she attempted to get to her seat, so a lot of people were already milling around the room.

That meant Nicholas had to dart around numerous guests as he crossed the threshold back into the hall. The music he was hearing already confirmed what was happening, but he wanted to

see it with his own eyes before he really believed
it.

Because yes, standing there in the corner of the
room with his beloved guitar, was Fynn.

Chapter Fourteen

Nicholas was going out of his mind.

There hadn't been any way he could talk to Fynn while everyone was taking their seats, and then he was stuck for three whole courses while the people around him laughed and drank and ate, and he had to restrain himself from not looking over into the corner every five seconds.

Luckily, the direction he was sat meant he was facing Fynn. He wasn't on the top table, but on one of the family tables to the right of the room. The result was he had almost all the guests between himself and Fynn, but he was still naturally in his line of sight. So while he doubted he was being *entirely* subtle in the attention he was giving him, at least he wasn't craning his neck to look behind him.

What was he doing here? *How* was he here? What had happened to his audition? Nicholas kept swaying abruptly between twisting up with guilt that he might have squandered his big chance to come and be at the wedding, and overcome with joy that he had got at least one more opportunity to see him again, when he thought he might never have.

It was inevitable that they would catch each other's eye, as it felt like Nicholas spent the whole meal staring at him. But every time their gaze met,

Fynn would flash him the smallest smile, then carry on looking about the room as he played.

"He's good, isn't he?" Aunt Sally gushed from his side, elbowing him in the ribs as she caught him gawping. "And pretty easy on the eyes."

"Eww," wailed at least two of her sons.

Nicholas didn't reply, but he certainly didn't disagree.

He recognised most of the songs Fynn played. He could barely focus on eating more than a few bites of each course, as each track brought back different memories for him. No more so though, than Rick Astley.

Nicholas's cheeks flamed as he finally caved and dug out his phone from inside his jacket. He felt certain everyone could read his mind replaying their first kiss, then their first time in bed as he hastily tapped out a text.

'I told you not to Rick-Roll my sister's wedding' he wrote, adding a crying-with-laughter face. *'I'm so happy you're here. Thank you x'*

He forced himself to put his phone back in his pocket after that. Fynn wouldn't be able to read any messages until after he was done playing, and Nicholas was determined not to over-do it and scare him off. He did his best to eat, but mostly fiddled with the newly-made name cards. Nicholas had made his own one first as a test because he knew he'd bodge it up. But he had to say the simple little card hadn't turned out that badly, even if the lace was a bit wonky and the writing smudged.

As people slowly made their way through dessert, he glanced at Fynn again, and then resorted to sitting on his hands.

Finally, things started wrapping up, and the event liaison approached Nicholas's dad at the top table. She was a short and very round woman with a bob haircut. Nicholas might have mistaken her for a mild-mannered aunt, but there was steely glint to her and a purpose to her stride that told him that she was in charge of making the day run as smoothly as possible.

She leant over his dad's shoulder and showed him the microphone she was holding in her hands. Presumably, that meant it was almost time for the speeches. They exchanged a few more words, then nodded to each other, before she looked over and gave the mic a subtle shake towards Fynn. He didn't pause in his singing, but he did nod once to show he'd understood; he needed to wrap things up.

A surge of panic flared through Nicholas. As much as he'd been eager for the meal to end, he'd not quite appreciated that that would mean Fynn leaving before he could go and speak to him. Perhaps he could signal him somehow, but he wasn't sure there was a subtle way to say, '*I know I probably don't deserve one but please could I have an explanation as to why you're here?*'

However, as Fynn drew the Take That song to a close, it seemed he wasn't ready to leave just yet. He sought out the liaison's gaze and gave her a nod. Nicholas guessed he was asking to play one more song. Brilliant, that gave him at least three more minutes to work out what he was going to do from the confines of his table.

The first few bars of music were unfamiliar to him as they drifted across the chatter in the room. But as soon as Fynn began the lyrics, Nicholas's mouth dropped open in disbelief. He couldn't even remember if he'd told him about Clara and Peter's slightly embarrassing favourite song, but apparently, he must have.

"*I'm giving you everything, all that joy can bring, this I swear,*" he began. Most people carried on as they had been, but Nicholas didn't miss the way Clara's face lit up in astonished recognition. She tugged Peter's sleeve, and pointed at Fynn. *"And, all that I want from you, is a promise you, will be there – Say you will be there."*

Clara searched the room until she found Nicholas, then pointed at Fynn again. "Spice Girls!" she mouthed over at him. He nodded and gave her two thumbs up. She pointed at him, and raised an eyebrow. *'Did you do this?'* he guessed she was asking. He nodded, and she blew him a kiss.

"But any fool can see they're falling, I gotta make you understand."

Clara had started singing along, with Peter murmuring some of the words too. So that got some of her school friends paying attention, and they started singing as well. Fynn winked at the bride and groom and made his performance louder, nodding at the other guests to encourage them to join in too.

"I'll give you everything on this I swear! Just promise you'll always be there!"

Nicholas laughed as more people started signing. Even his old gran joined in across the table from him, clapping her hands as she enthusiastically got almost all the words wrong.

"I'm giving you everything, all that joy can bring, this I swear. And, all that I want from you, is a promise you, will be there."

Nicholas applauded with the rest of the room as Fynn removed his guitar from over his head, and took a bow. He propped the instrument against his leg, then turned the applause to the bride and groom.

"Wasn't that wonderful?" the event liaison said into the microphone, getting everyone's attention as the room calmed down once more. "Now, I hope you all enjoyed your meal as much as you did getting serenaded by the very talented Mr Dumashie. How about another round of applause for him and our lovely catering staff?"

The party cheered eagerly, and one of the tables filled with Peter's uni friends rang their cutlery against their glasses. Nicholas smiled, so proud of how well Fynn had done. It was hardly a concert, but he'd entertained the group effortlessly, and from their enthusiasm he'd say they were definitely wanting more.

But the liaison was soon drawing them back in to face the front once more. "It is my great pleasure to hand you over to the father of the bride. I'm sure he's got some wonderful stories for you all." She extended her hand as Nicholas's dad got to his feet. "Everybody, Robert Herald!"

Nicholas had forgotten his anxiety in the excitement of the last song, but now he turned his attention back to Fynn, only giving his dad a couple of half-hearted claps. Fynn was already snapping the clasps shut on his guitar case, obviously keen to slip out unnoticed. But Nicholas could never not notice him. When he looked back up, Nicholas gave him a hopeful smile, which he was pleased to see reciprocated. But then he inclined his head, and headed soundlessly to the door. Nicholas tried not to make it totally obvious as he watched him until he disappeared from sight.

As his dad started his speech, Nicholas snatched his phone from out his pocket again. '*Please don't go x*'

He had so much he wanted to say, but it didn't feel right to do it over text. Whatever had happened, Fynn had made Nicholas feel so achingly important by showing up to play. He was desperate to know what had happened with his audition; it would be awful if he'd cancelled it out of a sense of obligation.

He had to physically grip the chair to stop himself going running off to see if he could catch Fynn before he disappeared out of Nicholas's life again. There was absolutely no way he could bail on the wedding speeches though, so for the time being, he was trapped.

He couldn't leave and he wouldn't let himself text again. So it was all he could do to hold the phone in his lap and surreptitiously check as often as possible whether or not Fynn had seen his message. He knew it was rude, but not as rude as absconding, so if any of his relatives disapproved, they'd just have to lump it. As the minutes trickled by, he willed Fynn to look at his phone before he went home. But no matter how much he glared at them, the ticks remained grey.

Unable to do much else, he knocked back his champagne and allowed the buzz to help him drift off a bit.

At least his dad's speech was really good. It was filled with anecdotes of Clara from when she was small that made the room laugh, but also so much sincerity it was hard for even Nicholas in his distracted state not to be moved. Then Peter fumbled through his short, but sweet, ode to his new wife. His timing was a bit off, and he didn't always manage to speak into the microphone properly, but it was obvious how much he adored Clara. By the end of his five minutes, his cheeks were pink, and his eyes were damp behind his wire-rimmed glasses, but everyone was smiling at him.

"To the bride," he called out.

"*To the bride!*" the room chorused back.

And then came Danielle.

Nicholas knew that she had been working on her speech for weeks. He'd heard her muttering it to herself as he passed the den, or in the kitchen when she'd been making her smoothies, even once or twice through the closed door when she'd been on the loo. She'd obviously put a great deal of effort into it, so it wasn't really a surprise that when she took the mic, she signalled to the event liaison for a projector and laptop to be wheeled out. Nicholas used all his willpower not to groan, knowing that more than likely meant they were going to be here for a while.

He had never wanted to be somewhere else more in his life, so of course, there was no escaping any time soon. Instead, he gave in and checked his text messages again. No joy.

Danielle waited until the projector was all hooked up and beaming onto the darkened wall, then opened the first slide. *'Clara and Danielle: A Friendship Through the Ages'* read the title. Nicholas felt a cold sweat prick on his skin.

"I first met Clara when I was just two years old," Danielle began. The next slide showed a blurry photo of the two of them together as babies, the slightly bigger Danielle with her arms wrapped around a squidgy Clara. That got an 'aww', and for a second Nicholas thought they might have been okay. "We've been best friends ever since," she continued with relish. "Which was a good job, because I'm pretty sure she would have been totally lost without me."

The next photo showed the two girls standing side by side at about five and seven years of age. They were both in ballet gear; however, where Danielle was stood pretty and proud with her toes pointed and her arms held perfectly in front of her, Clara had hers folded and looked to be on the verge of tears. Danielle laughed into the microphone, but aside from Aunt Louise and her friend Michelle, there were only a few, awkward chuckles from the rest of the room. Clara was looking at the photo with wide eyes as she bit her lip. Nicholas sunk down in his chair and peaked between his fingers.

By the time they'd been treated to the tale of how Danielle had saved Clara and her friends from crashing and burning at the school talent show, and the unforgettable incident when she'd visited at uni and rescued Clara's other mates from the horrors of their favourite kebab shop by getting it closed down due to health and safety regulations, the staff decided to be absolute heroes and top up everyone's wine glasses, even though they weren't supposed to, now the speeches were underway. They could probably see the growing horror on the group's faces and figured that a little extra on the bar bill for Nicholas's dad was probably better than a riot.

They heard about how Danielle had found Clara a new flat after the estate agent had screwed her over when she'd signed the contract without reading it properly. And how she'd fixed Clara's hair after a particularly disastrous fringe and highlights cock up; Nicholas felt that particular story could really have done without the accompanying photo. In fact, why was there even a photo of that tragedy in the first place? Clara looked stunned in it, like she had been taken by surprise. Had Danielle snapped it at the time hoping to use it in this very speech some day?

"But despite the many catastrophes," Danielle said, and Nicholas prayed to the heavens above that this might signal they were coming to the end. "Clara beat the odds and found someone to fall madly in love with her." At least that was sweet. Sort of.

Nicholas checked his phone for what felt like the thousandth time. Fynn still hadn't read his message. He resisted the urge to growl in frustration. As strong as his feelings were for him, this complete inability to use a bloody phone was utterly infuriating.

He was fidgeting so badly by the twentieth photo of Clara and Peter together, his Aunt Sally leant over and told him if he needed to pee, he should pee, because it was starting to look scarily like there was no end in sight. But Nicholas felt they had to be getting there soon, they just had to be. In any case, even if he was bursting, he knew that if he popped out now, he wouldn't stop until he got a hold of Fynn. Even if that meant going over to his damn house. So he felt it best to stay put.

Danielle, who was growing hoarse, finally took mercy on them, and clicked on the closing slide of a genuinely charming photo of her and Clara hugging a few years ago. "So I'd like to make a toast," she said lifting her full glass. Most of the other guests had a mouthful or so still left to raise at least. "To my best friend, the beautiful bride – *Clara!*"

"*To Clara!*"

She handed the microphone over the best man George as people cheered. Although Nicholas suspected they were clapping for the fact that the ordeal was over as much as they were being polite.

He was sorely tempted to pretend he couldn't hold his bladder any longer and do a runner. But what kind of tool skipped out on the best man's speech? Besides, George was a nice guy, and he was looking extremely wary at the prospect of holding people's attention after Danielle's epic saga.

"Um, hello," he said. The feedback squeal made him jump as much as the rest of the room, and he winced. "I think this thing wants to get to the bar as much as the rest of us," he joked. But the laugh he received was bigger than anything Danielle had had in her whole forty-five minutes, and he visibly relaxed in front of the crowd. "I'll do my best to keep this short."

Nicholas seriously considered giving him a kiss if he could live up to that promise.

There was no way that Fynn had stuck around for this long, so now Nicholas was thinking his best plan would be to call him. The worst he could do would be to not pick up, but hopefully he would. That way they could maybe talk, and Nicholas wouldn't have to abandon the wedding. He was *burning* to get answers to his questions, and knew he would be distracted until he did.

Thankfully, George was talking for less than ten minutes. He managed a few more laughs, but mostly he just talked about how brilliant his best friend was, and how much cooler than George he was, and how much better his World of Warcraft scores were. It wasn't going to go down in history as the best speech ever, but it was sweet and heartfelt, and Nicholas felt that was worth more than all the jokes in the world.

He felt like weeping when the final toast came. "To the happy couple," George cried.

"*The happy couple!*"

And then that was it. They were free to leave.

Nicholas bolted.

He really did nip to the loo first, as he didn't want to have any distractions while he was on the phone. He also took a moment to splash cold water on his face and neck, then looked at his reflection in the mirror. He took a deep breath, then let it out again.

"You can do this," he urged himself.

He needed to find himself a quiet spot where he could talk and not be interrupted. Despite his earlier, rash, thoughts, he was adamant that he wasn't going to ditch the wedding reception entirely. However, he figured it was probably okay to pop outside for a bit and maybe wander down the road. *If* he got Fynn on the phone. Otherwise, he needed to prepare what he was going to say to the voicemail.

He made his way back into the foyer, where people were mingling as the staff worked their magic again, disappearing the tables as fast as they had arrived. A bunch of the uni lot were at the bar ordering a startling amount of shots while the DJ got warmed up, and the new evening guests began mingling with those that had been there all day.

If he was going to be talking to Fynn (or leaving a half coherent voicemail) he thought it would probably be best to have a drink to refresh himself. So he eased his way up to the bar, declined the shot he was offered, and got himself a pint of water.

As much as Nicholas couldn't seem to shut up when talking in person, and had almost zero impulse control when it came to texting, he really had a thing against speaking over the phone. The lack of body language to read people made him panic, and for most of his life, he'd hardly ever been able to get through a conversation without picturing the other person rolling their eyes at him. He almost never called people.

But this was an emergency, he reasoned. as he downed half his water in one gulp.

He turned so his back was to the bar and propped his elbows on it. He carried on drinking, determined to finish it all, and unlocked his phone with a flick of his thumb. It didn't take him long to get Fynn's contact details up, but he just stared at them with a growing sense of dread as he downed the last mouthful and put the glass down.

"You can do this," he mumbled again. He needed to remember what was at stake. As nervous as he was to tap the call icon, the alternative was not speaking to Fynn, not finding out why he had changed his mind, or what he'd done about the audition. He steeled himself, and placed the call.

It was a good job he looked up as he put the phone to his ear. Otherwise, he might not have realised that Fynn was standing five feet away, waiting for Nicholas to notice him.

Nicholas's brain short-circuited. As he tried to mash out an expletive, the phone slipped from his grasp. He fumbled with both hands to catch it and stop it hitting the floor. He and Fynn looked at each other as he quickly pressed the disconnect button and slipped the phone back in his pocket.

Christ, he was gorgeous. He was dressed simply in a black pair of trousers and shoes, and an extremely well cut white shirt with the top couple of buttons undone. Because Nicholas knew it was there, he could just about see the hickey he had given him by the collar. A pair of metallic grey suspender braces added to touch of flare to the outfit and also did something fizzy to Nicholas's insides. His dreads were at their usual odd angles, but when juxtaposed with the clean, crispness of the suit, their unruliness had added appeal. Nicholas even wondered for a fleeting second if he'd put eyeliner on, but he couldn't definitely tell, and it really wasn't his prime concern in that moment.

"You're here," he said stupidly.

"Yeah," said Fynn. He rubbed his lower lip with his thumb, and they just sort of stared at each other. There were people jostling around them, but

Nicholas didn't really notice. His whole world had reduced to Fynn, standing there before him.

Nicholas wasn't sure of what to say. He had a thousand things he wanted to know, but none of the questions were apparently willing to come out of his mouth. "You were great," he blurted instead, nodding towards the corner in the now-darkened room where he'd played his set.

"Yeah!" one of the passing uni lads agreed. He threw his arm around Fynn's shoulders, sloshing his pint a little as he gave him a squeeze. "You should go on *X-Factor* or something dude. You've got serious talent!"

Fynn only winced a little and gave him a half-smile. "Thanks man."

Luckily, the guy let go to follow his friends to the dance floor, leaving Fynn with Nicholas once more. He stepped closer to him, still not sure what he wanted to say, but knowing he needed more of Fynn in whatever capacity he could get. He was *right there*, and Nicholas couldn't stop himself from grinning.

"I thought you'd left," he said.

Fynn shook his head, his expression hard to read. "I couldn't," he said. Nicholas's heart swelled with hope. "Um…" He stepped forward, and hooked his little finger around Nicholas's. "Could we maybe talk? Somewhere a bit quieter?"

Nicholas was glad the lights had dimmed for the evening disco, as he could feel heat rising on his cheeks. He couldn't fight the impulse to rub at his scars with his free hand, but then he inched closer to Fynn again, and laced their fingers together. "Talking sounds good," he admitted.

Please be a good talk, Nicholas begged silently as Fynn steered him through the crowd. He was in such a blurred state he wasn't sure if anyone saw them holding hands. In that moment however, he couldn't say he cared all that much, although it would be a terrible time to discover that Peter's family were secretly a bunch of raging homophobes.

They made it back out into the foyer though without incident. Nicholas assumed they would go outside, as that's where he had intended to call Fynn. But instead they went back past the loos and through a different door.

It was the cloakroom, which surprised Nicholas so much he stopped walking. It was populated with a number of the guests' coats and bigger bags, and in the corner, he spotted a familiar guitar case nestled under a faux fur wrap and a combat jacket. He turned and faced Fynn and he closed the door behind them. There was enough room for them to stand comfortably and not be squashed, but there was no contesting that the setting was intimate.

Nicholas's apprehension must have shown on his face, because Fynn gave him a warm smile and took booth of his hands in his own. "I thought some privacy might be a good idea."

"Right, sure," Nicholas agreed, a little breathlessly. "So, um, what did you want to talk about?" He was so nervous he could barely hear his own voice over the thud of his pulse in his ears. "You didn't text." Not that that was very shocking. "To say you'd be here. It was a surprise – a *good surprise*, but, um, yeah…"

Fynn shook his head and exhaled. "I didn't know what to say. If you were still mad at me." he said. "But now…I thought I'd start by apologising."

Nicholas was stunned. "What?" he cried. He pulled their hands up so they were resting on his chest, by his heart. "Why would *you* apologise? I'm the one who blew it all out of proportion! I was selfish, and now you've ruined your big chance with Storm-Pilot-Whatshisface." He sighed and rubbed his thumbs against Fynn's skin. "Seeing you here was the best thing ever, but was it really worth it?"

He searched Fynn's expression for the resentment he thought he would inevitably see creep in. But instead, he was graced with a full smile, the one Nicholas liked to think was reserved just for when Fynn was truly happy. When he was with him.

"I need to apologise, because I should have tried harder for you."

"You just totally knocked everyone's socks off," Nicholas reminded him, jerking his head back in the direction of the wedding reception.

Fynn shook his head again. "But I should have been more considerate of you."

His words were making Nicholas feel all tingly, but he wasn't entirely comfortable with him taking all the blame. "Well I should have been more respectful of your chance with the music producer. You threw that all away, for me?"

Fynn kissed the top of Nicholas's knuckles. It was simple and chaste, but it managed to make Nicholas's knees go weak all the same. "As much a you're worth doing that for," he said, kissing the knuckles on his other hand, "who says I threw anything away?"

"Huh?" said Nicholas. "But – you're here. You're not in London."

Fynn grinned. "Someone much cleverer than I am suggested I just *ask* to audition at a different time."

Nicholas looked at him, reading the happiness behind his eyes. This, *this* was why he hadn't wanted to talk over the phone. "And?" he rasped.

"And," said Fynn with a sigh, "I saw him nine o'clock this morning. He loved me."

Nicholas didn't even try to hold back the scream. He flung his armed around Fynn's neck, which meant standing on his tiptoes, but he didn't care. "Really?" he squeaked.

"Well," said Fynn, easing him back so they could look at each other. But he kept his hands on Nicholas's waist, which felt comforting and delicious provocative at the same time. "He liked my demo, but he asked if I could play him something there and then. I think he wanted to see what I'd be like live, feel the energy, you know?" Nicholas wasn't sure he did, but he nodded anyway.

"And you dazzled him."

"Actually," said Fynn. He ran his hand over his hair, then cupped the side of Nicholas's jaw. "As soon as I started the first song, I could feel I wasn't really 'dazzling' him. I guess he wanted something he hadn't heard on the CD." He brushed his thumb against the same scar that Nicholas had a particular habit of worrying. From Fynn though, the action was caring, not self-deprecating.

"I thought he liked the CD?" Nicholas asked, not quite following.

"He did," Fynn said quickly. "But he probably gets a lot of great demos through his door. I think he was looking for something special."

"The X-Factor," Nicholas quipped, thinking of Peter's friend earlier. Fynn grinned and nodded. His warm palm felt so perfect against Nicholas's cheek. He could get used to that. "So, what did you give him?"

Fynn bit his lip, and looked down at Nicholas's mouth. It sent a shiver straight down his spine. "I gave him you."

Nicholas went from feeling turned on to completely confused. "Me?" he questioned. "What can I do?"

Fynn's grey eyes were sparkling, and even though he was thrown, Nicholas felt encouraged.

"You inspire me. Remember?" He rested their foreheads together. "*Take your troubles out to fly, give me a wink as I pass by. And never let the sun stop shining on you.*"

Nicholas went a little slack with shock. "You – you played him *that?*"

Fynn nodded, but only fractionally as they were still resting against each other. "He loved it. He started waving his hands around and making notes, right there and then."

Nicholas felt tears prick behind his eyes. "Oh my god," he whispered. "Fynn, I'm so happy for you. You deserve this. I'm so glad you could make it work, to get your audition and still find time to come back for the wedding."

Fynn's expression became serious. "I *want* to make time for you Nicholas," he insisted. Nicholas remembered when he'd said his name at the doughnut store had felt claustrophobic. Hearing him use it now though made him feel freed. "God, I'm *so* sorry. I should have just tried to do that in the first place. You were right. I never meant to make you feel unimportant."

He reached up and ran his fingertips through Nicholas's hair, and made his whole body shiver. *Get a grip*, Nicholas hissed silently. He had to keep his head right now.

"I'm sorry too," he said, maintaining his composure. "I wanted you to take this opportunity, I really did. I just – it felt too easy to just think you'd want to leave. But," he added hastily, trying to put his point across coherently. He placed the palms of his hands on Fynn's chest. "I don't want you to leave. I know I'm supposed to play it cool or hard to get or whatever. But, I like you. I *really* like you, and I don't want to stand in your way, but, well, liking you kind of means I want you around. A lot. So, um…"

Blissfully, Fynn leant down and placed a soft kiss on his lips. Nicholas thought that morning he'd never get to kiss him again. It was over too soon, but the tingle stayed with him after they parted.

"You're not standing in my way," Fynn said, with a tinge of exasperation. "You're lifting me up. Didn't you listen to the damn lyrics?"

Nicholas laughed. "Sort of," he mumbled. "I'm still sorry though. For fighting when we didn't really need to."

Fynn kissed him again, just a sweet pressing of lips together. "That's alright," he said. "All couples have fights, don't they?"

Nicholas felt the world shift underneath him. A few hours ago, he'd been convinced he was never going to see Fynn again. And now…

"Couple?" he squeaked.

Fynn bit his bee-stung lip. "If that's what you want?"

Nicholas crashed into him so hard he smashed his back into the wall and dislodged several coats. He hoped the fierceness of his kisses conveyed how he felt about that.

They couldn't spend forever hiding in a cupboard, even though Nicholas was sorely tempted. So before he got too dishevelled, he pulled back and straightened Fynn's collar. "I'd want that very much," he mumbled, in case he hadn't been clear enough. He ran his fingers down the suspender belts and resisted the urge to snap them against his chest.

He didn't understand why Fynn was rubbing his fingers gently over his cheeks, until he realised he'd started crying. Nicholas hastily stepped back, wiping his own face and choking out a laugh.

"Fuck, that's embarrassing," he coughed out. "Sorry."

"Stop apologising," Fynn retorted automatically. He pulled Nicholas back to him. "Although maybe I should try apologising again, if I really hurt you that much?"

Nicholas shook his head though. "No, these aren't from that." He was not going to admit how much he'd cried into his pillow last night. "I'm just so happy you're still here. I assumed you'd have left when the speeches started," he explained.

Fynn looked stunned. "Why on Earth would I leave?"

"You didn't read my messages," said Nicholas.

Fynn frowned. "You messaged me?"

Nicholas swatted his firm chest. "Hello, have you met me?" he cried. But it lacked rancour. "Of course I did, you're lucky there weren't ten times as many." He inhaled and got a bit of composure. "I asked you to stay. I hoped we could talk. But the ticks showed you hadn't looked at it."

Fynn frowned and pulled his phone out of his pocket. "What ticks?" he asked.

Nicholas might not have believed he didn't know what the grey and blue ticks meant, if he hadn't spent the last week with him. He let out an exasperated sigh, and watched on fondly as Fynn read his correspondence.

"Oh darling," he said, looking up. "I'm sorry." He kissed him. "Of course I couldn't leave without clearing things up with you," he murmured against his lips.

Nicholas felt flush with happiness. "You don't have to leave at all, you know?" he offered, a ball of butterflies in his stomach. He still couldn't believe that someone like Fynn would want to hang around with him. But the evidence was mounting up, and unless he wanted to get annoying, he needed to start accepting it. "You could stay? Um, maybe be my date?"

A smile slowly spread all the way over Fynn's face, and he hugged him close. "I'd be honoured." He reciprocated Nicholas's ministrations by running his hands over his shirt and jacket, and tweaked the bow tie a little. "You look seriously hot, by the way," he told him, a glint in his eye.

Nicholas tried not to preen too much, but then he figured, *what the hell?* "Thank you," whispered, then tugged at Fynn's hand. "So do you."

Well, it would have been rude not to have a *bit* more kissing after that.

"Okay," he said, once they'd calmed down again. "Are you ready to come face my crazy family?"

Fynn chuckled and let himself be pulled out the door. "I've already seen them," he protested as they emerged into the hallway. Thankfully, no one was there. Nicholas was feeling brave, but not *quite* ready to face his grandma directly after a snogging session.

"Yeah," he scoffed. "Seeing them and *meeting* them are two quite different things, I can assure you."

The corridor remained empty as they made their way back to the hall. Nicholas realised why as they approached the doors into the main room; Clara and Peter had just started their first dance.

"Oh," he said, and hurriedly tugged Fynn inside. He would have felt bad to have missed that.

They'd chosen an obscure song that Nicholas still couldn't remember the name of. He did know it was from a film they both liked, and Nicholas edged around the guests clumped in a circle watching on until he could see.

Maybe it was because he, himself, was happy now, but he thought his sister looked especially radiant with joy as she gazed up at her new husband's face. They swayed back and forth, talking to each other in words swallowed up by the music, and traded sweet kisses. Nicholas sighed and felt a lump rise in his throat. Danielle had been right about one thing: despite all the catastrophes, they'd made it in the end.

He felt Fynn standing behind him and shivered when he laid a hand on his hip. It was barely a touch at all, but to Nicholas it felt like a neon sign pointing above their heads: *This one's with me*. He leant back into Fynn to show he felt the same way.

With a thrill, he thought how anyone looking their way would be able to see them and deduce they were together.

A couple. He couldn't believe it.

He didn't want to hide it. He remembered how scary it had been to come out to Ash, but then how relieved he'd felt afterwards. If Fynn was going to stay with him for the evening, he wasn't going to shy away from showing what he meant to him in front of everyone. So as Clara nodded to Lauren for her and Franko to lead the couples in joining in the slow dance, he turned and looked at Fynn.

"Do you want to?" he asked.

Fynn raised his eyebrows. "Dance?" Nicholas nodded. "Well, yeah, I'd love to. But, are you sure? I thought you hadn't come out yet."

Nicholas shrugged. "I told Ash – after that night at the club actually." He smiled at the memory. "But I don't really feel like making a big deal of it, you know? Why have twenty conversations when nothing's really changed? I'm still me. I just have you now, too." He felt a warmth in his chest at the smile that put on Fynn's face. "So, what do you say? Fancy a spin?"

Fynn held out his hand and Nicholas took it.

For all his confident words, even that simple act turned him into a bundle of nerves. As much as he wanted to believe that no one would have a problem, he couldn't say for absolute sure how this was going to go down. He and Fynn didn't move far into the throng; they stayed on the fringe as they turned to face each other. Nicholas thought he'd be hyper-aware of who was around them. But as soon as Fynn slipped his hands around his waist, Nicholas did likewise, and the rest of the room melted away.

There wasn't much of the song left, but Nicholas was determined to make the most of his and Fynn's official first dance together. He'd never really danced with any girls at school – he and his friends had always been too shy and awkward for that. But it felt so natural to rest his head on Fynn's shoulder, their chests pressing together. He was immediately calmed, and if anyone was dropping their wine glasses in shock over the fact that Clara's little brother was in fact homosexual, he had absolutely no idea.

The song changed to something a bit more up tempo, but a quick glance around showed other couples were still dancing together, so Nicholas pulled Fynn closer to him.

Fynn laughed. "I'm not going anywhere," he promised.

"Just making sure," Nicholas mumbled back sheepishly. Fynn laughed again, and pecked a swift kiss on his temple.

People were definitely looking at them. It was hard not to notice. But from what he could see out of the corner of his eye, they didn't seem hostile or disgusted. Mostly they just seemed curious, or surprised. It had come a bit out of blue, Nicholas had to concede. He hadn't even known he was gay this time last week. So he tried not to feel like a specimen at the zoo and instead just focused on Fynn.

They weren't doing anything complicated, just swaying back and forth, but Fynn was still guiding them. He had superior rhythm after all. Nicholas let himself be moved, not paying attention to anyone else until the song ended and they naturally stepped apart. Not too far though; Nicholas still kept hold of his hand.

When he turned, he was met by both his sisters.

By the looks of it, Clara had grabbed Lauren's arm and dragged her across the dance floor. Now they were both standing in front of Nicholas and Fynn, barely-concealed glee on their faces.

"Hi," said Nicholas tentatively.

"Hi," they chirped back, and Clara dropped Lauren's arm so she could offer her hand to Fynn.

"I'm Clara," she said as Fynn accepted the shake.

He gave her a lopsided smile. "I know," he said gently, letting her go. "You're the bride."

She frowned, as if that hadn't occurred to her. "Oh, yeah. Well, you're the guitarist, aren't you?"

"I'm Lauren," his other sister butted in. She grabbed his hand for her own shake. "I'm the one who lives in Italy. I guess you guys know each other, huh?"

Her fishing for information was painfully obvious, but Nicholas didn't really mind, as they both seemed buzzing with excitement. It bolstered his confidence. "Um, yeah. Fynn is…"

He looked up at him, not sure what to say. Fynn raised his eyebrows. "…his boyfriend?" he offered.

Nicholas's heart skipped a beat. Hearing it out loud was strange and exhilarating. "My boyfriend," he confirmed, taking his hand again.

Clara squealed and threw her arms around a very startled Fynn. "It's so nice to meet you."

Lauren punched Nicholas on the arm. "You kept that very quiet," she accused. But she wasn't really bothered, he could tell. That was her way of asking how long – how long he'd known about his sexuality, how long they'd been together.

"It's all very new," he said, answering both queries in one. "I hope you don't mind I invited him to stay for the evening."

"Oh don't be silly," said Clara with a wave of her hand.

"Or that I'm not a harpist," Fynn added with a wink towards Nicholas. He swatted his arm playfully.

"That's how we met," he explained. "Fynn saved the day."

Clara was frowning again. "Oh yeah," she said to Lauren. "It was supposed to be a harp for the dinner." She shrugged. "I'd forgotten anyway. Thanks for playing Spice Girls I think my aunt was pretty horrified, but everyone else thought it was a riot."

Sure enough, Nicholas looked over to the table Clara had nodded towards. Aunt Louise and Michelle were sat with their backs straight and shoulders tense and they sipped white wine and quite obviously regarded Nicholas and Fynn with unpleasant curves to their mouths. They were almost certainly discussing them. If he knew them like he thought he did, they were probably admonishing their vulgar public display of affection. No doubt he'd hear later on about how that sort of thing should be kept behind closed doors. Not if you were heterosexual of course, but nobody needed to see the gays hugging each other.

Nicholas smiled. He didn't give two figs what they thought. Lauren and Clara were chatting excitedly with Fynn, telling him he needed to come meet their other halves, and their parents, and Grandma. Nicholas had hoped to not overwhelm him right away, but it seemed they didn't have much of a choice. But just as they were pulling them away to go make some introductions, Nicholas spotted someone by the door and his jaw dropped.

"Can you hang on actually? I'll, um, just be a sec," he said, then glared at Lauren. "Look after him."

Lauren crossed her heart, but Clara was already asking Fynn about his music, so he knew they'd have plenty to talk about for the moment. So he squeezed Fynn's hand, then went over to the figure hovering nervously by the door.

Ash had gotten changed.

Gone was the delicate, sparkly pink dress. Instead, she'd completely transformed with a well-fitted suit. As he approached, he could see it was a chocolate brown with a fine pink pinstripe. The trousers had a slight flare over the heeled boots she was wearing, and the jacket and waistcoat were synched at the waist, making her boobs look more prominent even though they were completely hidden by the white shirt and pink cravat. She fiddled anxiously with a pocket watch on a chain, regarding him as he approached.

"I couldn't be a girl any more today," she blurted as soon as he was close enough. "I was crawling out of my skin. Did you think Clara will mind?"

He smiled at her and drew her into a hug. "I can guarantee she won't be bothered at all," he assured her. He pulled back and looked her up and down. "You look stunning."

Ash beamed at him. "Really?"

He nodded. He still couldn't say he fancied her, but objectively speaking, she really suited this gender-ambiguous look a lot more than the very feminine dress.

"So," he said. "Do you want me to call you 'he' now? How does it work?" He thought it was best to ask, before he inevitably put his foot in it.

She smiled fondly at him. "No, don't worry about that. Maybe 'they' if you want? I don't mind."

"I can cope with 'they'," he assured them, squeezing their waist. "Hey, did you know I have a boyfriend now?" He pointed at Fynn, still being playfully grilled by Clara and Lauren.

"I did." Ash laughed. "I caught the end of you two dancing. Bold move."

Nicholas shrugged. "Nah, not really. I just said, 'Do you want to dance', and that was the end of that."

Ash bit their lip, and glanced out over the room. "Is that so?" they asked.

Nicholas followed their gaze and saw the object of their attention. Kinny was standing with a group of her and Clara's friends, but she was looking back at them. At Ash in particular, her eyes travelling over her new look with a slightly slack jaw. Nicholas frowned, then snapped his head back and forth between the two of them. "Hang on," he spluttered. "Are you two—?"

"No," said Ash hastily. "I mean, um. Do you think, if I asked her to dance…she might say yes?"

Nicholas felt like he'd missed several steps. But then, that's what people could easily say about him and Fynn. So rather than try and unravel what had passed him by, he just nodded. "Yeah, yeah, go ask her to dance!" he enthused. "By the looks of it, I think Boy Ash is ticking her boxes too."

Ash rolled their eyes at him, but then gave him a hopeful smile, before waving shyly at Kinny. Kinny waved back. "Okay," they said. "Thank you."

"Go get 'em, tiger," said Nicholas with a wink.

He didn't want to intrude, but he couldn't help but watch as Ash steeled themselves with a deep breath, then walked over to talk to Kinny. When he saw her smiling and nodding, he thought he should probably leave them to it. Besides, he had his own boyfriend to get back to.

The evening passed in somewhat a blur. His parents were pretty astonished to see their son with a boyfriend, and Nicholas could tell they probably had several more conversations ahead of them on that front. But they reacted positively enough, and his sisters were soon whisking them both away to formally meet Peter and Franko. Nicholas's grandma had a rather pinched expression upon finding out that her grandson not only a had a boyfriend, but a black boyfriend. She didn't say anything of course, but Nicholas had gotten pretty good at reading the particular way her eyes squinted when she was displeased, and pulled Fynn away from her before she could say anything catty or passive aggressive.

There was a group of lads who Nicholas thought might have been uni friends of Peter's. They had openly hostile looks on their faces as Nicholas and Fynn passed, but they didn't come over, and Nicholas hoped they would keep their judgements to themselves. His heart beat faster at the idea they were offended by his happiness. Trusting they wouldn't start anything in the middle of a wedding, he determinedly turned his back on them. He wasn't going to let a bunch of closed minded strangers spoil his joy. No way.

The only other person Nicholas cared about introducing Fynn to was his Aunt Sally, who was sat on one of the tables with a plate of food from the buffet. So Nicholas suggested the two of them get something to eat too – he'd hardly had any of the lunch after all – and went to join her. She hooted with laughter when Nicholas introduced Fynn as his boyfriend.

"I said he was gorgeous, didn't I? No wonder you couldn't take your eyes off him." Nicholas blushed and tried to tell Fynn it wasn't that bad, but he shook his head.

"Every time I looked over, you were ogling me," he teased. Nicholas didn't really mind, because it was basically true.

He didn't really want to leave Fynn by himself, but he got up to do the 'Macarena' with little Milly. By the end of the track, she knew it better than he did. He also danced with Clara for a while. She was adorably drunk and chatted his ear off about how happy she was, and what a perfect day she'd had, but how much her feet were hurting, although she *couldn't* take her shoes off yet. Because they were special bride shoes and she was going to get the most out of them that she could. Because everything was perfect. Nicholas thought it best not to remind her of all the near misses they'd had, and just agreed. Because she was right; for all the ups and downs, it really had turned into the most incredible day.

On his way back to Fynn, who had made great friends with Aunt Sally, he was surprised to see Mrs Sadik along with Kinny's Bas and Enver. All three of them were dressed up for the occasion, and Kinny was stood talking to her mum. He was warmed not only by the fact that Ash was by her side – that dance must have gone quite well then – but also that Mrs Sadik was nodding, and Kinny tentatively smiling. As he watched, Kinny threw her arms around her.

"I didn't realise they'd had a fight."

He turned around to see Danielle also watching on. She had a glass of bubbly in her hand and her other arm wrapped around her waist. "Uh yeah," said Nicholas, turning back to watch the reconciliation. "She still asked her to mend the dresses though. It took a lot of guts."

Danielle nodded. "I know. That's why I invited her tonight. I also insisted she be properly paid for the work she did." She took a sip of her drink.

Nicholas felt himself relax his shoulders a little. "You really did do a great job with this wedding Danielle," he said. "I hope you know that."

She turned her head to him, and after a moment's staring, her lip wobbled. "Oh," she said thickly. "*Really?*"

"Um," he said. He'd not expected this. "Yeah, of course. It's been fantastic."

"I was worried everyone thought I was a massive *bitch*," she said tearfully.

Nicholas schooled his face extremely carefully. "Oh, no – what?" he said. He rubbed her arm. "No, you did great, honestly." Danielle continued to sniffle, so he steered her into a nearby chair and sat down next to her. "You just care a lot, that's all." To a certain extent, he did believe that was true.

"I am a *bit* of a bitch though," she said. She wiped her eyes with the pads of her fingers, careful not to smudge any makeup. "I always thought..." She bit her lip, and sighed. "I always thought I'd get married first," she said in a rush. She pulled at the tablecloth. "I'm the oldest, I did everything first. But..." Her lip trembled again. "I can't even keep a boyfriend. Even you've got a boyfriend, why can't I get one?"

Nicholas didn't miss the way she scoffed about Fynn, and didn't congratulate him on coming out, but he decided to give her a pass on that one. Because he did have a boyfriend. An awesome one. So he was willing to let his cousin be a little bitter.

"I'm sure there's someone great out there for you," Nicholas assured her. "I mean, come on. You're gorgeous, and you have a killer job. You're a catch."

She huffed, and gave him a nod. "You're right," she said with determination. "Besides, a career is more important than a man. Boyfriends are overrated." Nicholas felt she'd probably change her tune once she managed to tie down a man, but he let that barb slide too. He'd rather she was amicable. He watched her down her drink. "I'm heading to the bar. Do you want anything?"

Nicholas shook his head. He hadn't had anything alcoholic to drink since the wedding breakfast. The lack of sleep was catching up with him, and the thought of it had made him feel a bit queasy.

Instead, he finally made his way back to Fynn, who was happily sitting by himself, watching the dancers. It seemed Aunt Sally had managed to corner that uncle of Peter's that she'd been speaking to before the ceremony, and was using her large frame to dance him into a corner, presumably in hopes of a snog. Nicholas laughed and sat down.

"You look shattered," said Fynn, taking his hand.

Nicholas sighed. "Well thanks," he complained, but he didn't mean it. "You look gorgeous, as usual."

Fynn bumped their shoulders. "You can still be gorgeous and tired," he said smoothly. "Hey, I got us some wedding cake." He pushed a napkin over to Nicholas. He'd nabbed them two of the heart shaped Krispy Kremes, which in Nicholas's opinion were the best. They had sugary white glazing, pink chocolate shavings, *and* cream in the middle. "To make up for the one you got me yesterday."

Nicholas regarded him fondly. "These are better," he assured him. He didn't want to think about their falling out. It was over, and he squeezed his boyfriend's hand to remind him of that.

The longer he sat, the more he could feel his eyelids dropping. Even with the sugar rush thrumming through his system, he wasn't sure how much longer he could take.

"Do you have to stay until the end?" Fynn asked, reading his mind.

Nicholas shrugged. "I feel like I should, I want to. But I only got a couple of hours' sleep, and it's been, well, emotional." He didn't want to make Fynn feel bad, so he shrugged it off. "I mean, with all the mishaps and such." He watched as people started doing the conga around the room, led by a very enthusiastic Clara and Peter. "I suppose if I slipped out early, no one would really notice."

It was only ten o'clock, but Nicholas was pretty sure he wouldn't be able to make it until midnight. As he looked around the room, he saw Lauren had pushed two chairs together and little Milly was lying across them, fast asleep. Still with her welly boots on, of course. Right then, that didn't look like a bad plan. He felt he could fall asleep anywhere.

Fynn rubbed his back. "I think that might be a good idea," he said. "Shall we see about getting you a taxi?"

"Oh, no," said Nicholas, shaking his head. "We've all got rooms at the Clarion, down the road. Dad treated us, so I just need to grab my bag.

I guess he put it in the cloakroom." He hadn't checked, but that seemed logical.

"Great," said Fynn. "Do you want to go now, or hang on a little longer?"

Nicholas opened his mouth to say he might as well go now, but his brain got caught on Fynn's words. It sort of sounded like he would leave too if Nicholas did. That they'd leave *together.*

Why couldn't they?

They were both adults, and more importantly, they were *boyfriends.* They obviously hadn't had a chance to discuss how things were going to work when Nicholas went back to uni in a few weeks, but he knew he wanted to make the most of the time they could have together until then.

"Um," he said, feeling tongue tied. "I mean, you could, uh, stay too. If you wanted."

Fynn's face lit up. "At the hotel?"

Nicholas didn't know if he was being too forward. "I mean, because we're both living at home, it might be nice to take advantage of having some space of our own. Not that, um," he could feel the heat rising up his neck. "We don't have to, you know, *do* anything. But I thought I could be cool to spend the night together. If you fancy?" He cleared his throat and tried not to fidget. But he wasn't an idiot. He was asking Fynn to sleep with him, and that might involve more things than just sleeping.

Fynn rubbed his thumb over the back of Nicholas's hand. "I'd absolutely love to," he told him.

Suddenly, Nicholas wasn't quite so tired any more. "Then, I suggest we leave now," he said excitedly. Fynn laughed, and leant over to kiss him.

Chapter Fifteen

Nicholas had enough butterflies in his stomach to fill up Kew Gardens.

They hadn't made big deal out of leaving. They just managed to grab Clara and give her a hug goodbye, then Nicholas had dropped his parents a matching text each to let them know he'd crashed and was going to the hotel. He left out that he was going with Fynn.

Once they'd retrieved their belongings from the cloakroom – including Nicholas's overnight bag, which had indeed been stashed there – they started the short walk to the hotel. Unusually, Nicholas couldn't think of a single thing to say.

He knew he'd told Fynn they didn't have to do anything; they could just sleep next to one another if that was what he wanted. It wasn't the sex that was troubling him, funnily enough. He was about to spend the night with someone, share a bed with another body in it. What if he did something embarrassing, like kicked Fynn? Or talked in his sleep? Or *farted?* Would Fynn still think he was cute when he saw how much bio-oil he had to put on his scars, or when he had morning breath?

He had no idea what the social etiquette was for getting changed. Was he supposed to be okay now with getting casually naked in front of Fynn? Because even though he was quickly becoming used to the sexy side of things, he didn't think he'd be comfortable walking around starkers just yet.

He was pulled from his thoughts when Fynn stopped walking. "Huh?" he said stupidly.

Fynn smiled at him. "I thought I'd stop and get a toothbrush," he said. He pointed to their right, where there was a small Sainsbury's convenience store. "Do you want to wait here?"

"Um, sure," said Nicholas.

The street was still relatively busy seeing as it was a Saturday night in the centre of town. Nicholas leant against the wall and watched the people pass by. He wondered what had happened to them this week – had any of their lives changed as much as his? Had any of them started new relationships, or maybe had a breakup? How many other weddings had there been, or births, or deaths? He hoped at least some of them were as happy as he was.

And that was what he needed to remember. He didn't know what was going to happen tonight, but he was there with Fynn. Despite spending most of the night before feeling wretched and empty, here he was now part of an official couple. Deep down, he was starting to trust that Fynn wouldn't suddenly realise he was an embarrassment to be with and leg it. So really, what was there to be nervous about spending the night together?

He still didn't want to embarrass himself by being weird or gross, but when he thought about it, Fynn had already seen his scrawny, scarred body, and he'd seemed more than a little into it over that past few days. He knew what he was signing up for, so Nicholas needed to stop fretting.

Fynn joined him presently and Nicholas felt a bit lighter the rest of the walk down to the hotel. It was a big, square shaped building made of red bricks, cream archways and Tudor style windows.

Nicholas walked into the lobby and crossed the black and white chequered floor with as much confidence he could muster. "Hi there," he said to the guy behind reception. "I'd like to check in. Nicholas Herald, but my dad Robert made the booking."

He felt Fynn beside him, but Nicholas wouldn't let himself fidget. So what they were two blokes checking in together? There was nothing wrong with that. His heart might have been beating a little faster than usual, but he refused to act any differently than he would have if he'd been checking in alone.

The receptionist didn't even flinch. He just clicked a few things on his computer with the mouse and asked to swipe a credit or debit card of Nicholas's as insurance for the room. He then fished out a couple of key cards to place in a little cardboard wallet with the hotel's logo on.

"There we are Mr Herald," he said, handing them over. "Your room is on the second floor. Should you need any assistance, dial zero for reception."

Nicholas couldn't help the relieved smirk that crept onto his face. He'd acted normal, and it had been normal.

"Thank you," he said genuinely. "Have a great evening." The guy was obviously going to be stuck behind a desk for most of the night, but he had the graciousness to nod in response to his well wishes.

They didn't speak on the elevator ride up, but Nicholas felt like there was electricity crackling between them. He was aware of every move Fynn made, and every time he looked over and caught his eye, he gave him a small smile and heated look from under his dark eyelashes.

Nicholas fumbled getting the key card to work on the door. But eventually the damn thing worked the way it was supposed to, and they stepped inside. As far as hotel rooms went, this one was pretty standard. By slipping the room card into the slot by the door, it turned the bedside lamps on, illuminating the space with a dim glow. It was cosy.

There was a large, squishy looking double bed strewn with several throw cushions and pillows, a big flat screen TV hanging from the cream wall, and a reasonable-sized bathroom through the door to their right. Nothing particularly revolutionary, but still nice.

To Nicholas though, it seemed very special indeed.

He dropped his bag on the armchair in the corner and removed his jacket. Fynn carefully laid down his guitar on the far side of the bed, and dropped his carrier bag from Sainsbury's beside it. Then they looked at each other.

Nicholas wasn't sure who moved first, but in a heartbeat, they had collided at the foot of the bed. Nicholas grabbed a hold of Fynn's suspenders and Fynn threaded his fingers through Nicholas's hair with one hand, pressing the palm of the other against his back. The kiss was fervent and a little sloppy and had too many teeth in the way, but in terms of passion it was one of the hottest things that Nicholas had ever experienced.

Fynn's fingers moved to Nicholas's throat, where they began slipping through the knot of the bow tie. "Did I mention this was really cute?" he mumbled between kisses.

"Were you just imagining undoing it all afternoon?" Nicholas asked.

"Maybe," said Fynn, grinning against his mouth.

Nicholas hooked his fingers under the suspender belts, and pinged them so they slapped lightly against Fynn's chest. It made him jump and pause with the tie. "I might have been imagining *that* all afternoon," he said. He knew he was flushed, but he didn't care. The way Fynn's face darkened made his stomach flip.

"Oh really?" Fynn attacked his bow tie again.

As much as they both found the other attractive in their formal wear, it was nothing compared to the giddy excitement of pulling it all off. Nicholas felt a bit dizzy as Fynn yanked him onto the bed once they'd got down to their underwear, and was glad to dive under the covers and snuggle into the pile of pillows before his knees gave way on him.

For a while, they just kissed, legs tangled together, hands exploring bodies reverently. Fynn seemed to like laying on top of Nicholas to a certain extent, which worked well because Nicholas loved the sensation of being pressed under him. Fynn's skin was hot and his muscles firm, and feeling all of him against all of Nicholas was overwhelming and somewhat divine.

Nicholas found himself reaching upwards, chasing kisses as Fynn pulled backwards. Judging by the grin on Fynn's face, he enjoyed that very much.

"I thought you said you just wanted to go to sleep tonight?" he said.

"Shut up and kiss me," said Nicholas.

Fynn rolled on his side and slid his hand under Nicholas's hip so he could grab his arse with both hands and haul him up against him. Nicholas yelped, but the thrill at being manhandled was a definite turn on. They continued to kiss, but now their groins were rubbing together through the material of their briefs, and Nicholas couldn't help but moan.

He was quite happy to what they did before – 'frottage,' he'd learned was the proper word. But he couldn't help but think back to the videos he'd watched, and even though he was apprehensive, he was also a writhing ball of lust. The idea of Fynn and him maybe doing more had seized him, and wasn't going away.

He didn't have the first clue how to go about any of it though. What did guys do? What did men and women do? Was it a massive buzz kill to talk about what you wanted to do during the pre-shagging build up? Was someone supposed to just take charge? If that was the case, he'd naturally assume Fynn to be the one calling the shots. But then how was Nicholas supposed to ask for what he wanted?

"Hey," Fynn whispered, brushing their noses together. "Are you okay with this?"

Nicholas nodded quickly, causing their noses to bash. Luckily Fynn laughed. He was probably going to have to get used to Nicholas being clumsy in bed, because even if he got more experienced, he couldn't see himself transforming into any sort of smooth Casanova type any time soon. "Yeah, I just – sorry, I don't know what I'm doing."

"You're doing great," Fynn promised. He squeezed Nicholas's backside, encouraging him to grind into his erection, and Nicholas shuddered and groaned.

"Okay, good," he stuttered once he could think clearly again. "I just, uh…"

Fynn stopped undulating against him and brushed his hair back. "What, darling?"

Nicholas squirmed, but he was determined to ask. "What do you, um, like doing? We can do other things. I – I want to try."

Fynn kissed his cheek, right on the horrid scars. "We don't have to rush anything," he said. He kissed his earlobe, then gave it a little suck. It made Nicholas's toes curl. "This is great."

Nicholas huffed. "I'm a twenty-year-old virgin," he griped. "I wouldn't mind putting a bit of a rush on certain things."

To his surprise, Fynn chuckled. "You're not a virgin," he said. He kissed Nicholas's shoulder, over the hickey he'd given him the other day. His breath hot and wet on his skin. "I was there."

"Does, um, that count then?" Nicholas felt stupid for asking, but who else was he going to talk to? His friends counted losing their virginity as the moment they stuck their cock in a girl and had an orgasm. The orgasm part had always seemed optional for the girls, which Nicholas thought was most unfair. Fynn had made him come twice, so even though no one had stuck anything inside anyone, maybe it did count?

"I say so," Fynn told him. "But, we can try more. If that's what you want?"

Nicholas chewed his lip and played with one of Fynn's dreadlocks. "Well, that's why I was asking. What do you like doing? What did, um, you and your ex do?"

Fynn pressed his finger to Nicholas lips, and raised an eyebrow. "No talking about other people during sex," he said. The commanding tone could have come across as patronising, but Nicholas's whole body shivered. "It's just me and you here. No one else matters, okay?"

Nicholas's lips curled into an involuntary smile, and he kissed the fingertip. "Okay," he whispered back.

Fynn traced his fingers along the side of Nicholas's jaw. "Whatever I do with you will be different anyway. Special. Because it's you." Nicholas found that a bit much, and had to look away. Fynn took that as a good opportunity to kiss his neck some more. "I like doing lots of things though. Did you have something in mind?"

Nicholas ran his hands along Fynn's back, feeling the muscles shift. "Well," he said, then cleared his throat. *You can do this,* he told himself. "Did you, uh, want to have sex, like, the whole way? Did you want to shag me?"

He was utterly amazed he got the words out. His skin was burning with embarrassment; not just on his face, it felt like his whole body was on fire. But he couldn't get the image of those two porn stars out of his head, the way they'd moved in and out of one another. He was sure it would be uncomfortable, and he wasn't wholly convinced he really wanted to be the one getting fucked. But the idea of being confident enough to do that to Fynn was out of the question, so he was willing to give it a try.

Fynn pulled away and forced him to meet his gaze. "We really don't have to do that to have a good time here," he said.

Nicholas deflated and a lump rose in his throat. "It's fine if you don't want to," he mumbled.

Fynn captured his chin between his finger and thumb, and wouldn't let him wriggle away. "I didn't say that," he told him. "It's a big deal, and I don't want you thinking you have to offer it. Or that you have to bottom." He grinned and rolled his hips against Nicholas's, reminding him of what was down there. "I like doing it both ways."

Nicholas shook his head. "Christ no, I wouldn't be able – I mean – not yet." He was babbling. It didn't help that his cock was far more interested in finding Fynn's to play with again than anything his mouth had to say. "I've got no clue what I'm doing. If you show me what you like, I can learn what I like."

That seemed to get through to him, and he cradled the back of Nicholas's head, their eyes locked. "That sounds like a really good plan to me."

Nicholas smiled with relief. "I, um, I know you're supposed to use lube, but I didn't know if we could still try?"

Fynn arched an eyebrow. "Oh baby, no," he admonished like an exasperated teacher, which Nicholas supposed he was. "You need lube. *Lots* of lube. And a *condom*."

Nicholas felt stupid, but Fynn was stroking his hair to lessen the blow from his harsh words. "Oh," he said. "I guess we'll just have to try that another day then." He was disappointed, which told him how much he'd wanted to actually try shagging rather than not. But Fynn was right. There was still plenty they could do still.

Fynn gave him a wicked grin, and rolled him onto his back, hovering over him. "I might not just have bought a toothbrush earlier."

Nicholas felt his eyebrows lift. "You were *totally* planning on shagging me!" he crowed.

Fynn rolled his eyes. "I figured we'd need them at some point, so why not be prepared tonight? But no, I did not have a grand plan to fuck you." He kissed him softly, then held his gaze. "But if you want to, then I'd love to."

Nicholas nodded, his heart in his throat. "I'd definitely love to."

Fynn's smile was dazzling. "Okay, but we'll take it really slow, and if you want to stop you have to promise to tell me. I won't be pissed off, I swear."

Nicholas regarded him, apprehension creeping into his guts. "Um, is it really that bad on the bottom?"

Fynn considered him, and played a bit with his hair. "It can be painful if you don't do it right. But I know how to do it right," he added hastily. "It's more that it's kind of weird having someone else inside your body, and I just want to make sure you're happy. If you freak out, that's totally normal."

Nicholas really didn't want to freak out, and the tension in his chest did lessen a tad knowing that Fynn's priority was for his wellbeing. He was anxious not to be a killjoy. "I want you to be happy, too," he said in a small voice.

"Whatever we do here, I'll be happy so long as you are." He cupped his face, which was sweet, but then he waggled his eyebrows, making Nicholas laugh. "I'm *pretty* certain I'm getting laid tonight by my hot boyfriend. I don't really care how it happens."

Nicholas gave him a playful shove. "Alright then, Romeo. Let's give it a go."

"Oh how romantic," Fynn said, giving him a kiss. He moved away, letting a draft of air in under the covers that made Nicholas suck in a breath through his teeth. But it also cooled his over-heated skin down, which was probably a good thing.

Fynn fetched out a box of three condoms and some KY jelly. Nicholas had no idea you could buy those sorts of things at Sainsbury's, but he was extremely relieved that was the case.

"Um," he said shyly as Fynn placed his purchases on the bedside table. "So, where do you want me?" There had been all kinds of positions in the videos, and he had no idea of the pros or cons of any of them. But he vowed to try Fynn's favourite.

Leaving the lube and condoms on the side, Fynn scooted back over to him and rubbed his back. "It's easiest and most comfortable if you lie on your stomach, and we put a pillow under your hips."

Nicholas frowned at him. "Doggy style?" That didn't seem all that dignified, but he'd told himself he'd do what Fynn wanted.

Fynn pulled a face. "Not really, unless you want to kneel for ages. This way you're lying down. Trust me, just while you get used to it, this way is the least painful. It was for me anyway."

Nicholas wasn't sure. That didn't really feel like they'd be connected in the same way they were the last time. "Can I, um, still kiss you like that?"

If he'd had any doubt before about his feelings for Fynn, the tender way he responded to his quite frankly ridiculous and pathetic question confirmed them tenfold. "Yes darling," he said, kissing him hard as if to prove the point.

He might have thought that being called 'darling' would make him feel wussy. But Fynn said it without the 'g' – 'dar-lin', and that somehow made it seem less delicate. No one else had ever called him that, that was for certain, and the uniqueness of the pet name added to its appeal. He liked being Fynn's darlin'.

His arousal had flagged somewhat while they'd been talking, but Fynn soon had him breathless again with his searing kisses and wandering hands. He grabbed one of the flatter, softer pillows from the pile and helped Nicholas slip it under his hips. They were still beneath the covers, so Nicholas didn't feel that nervous pulling off his underwear. And then he lay down over the pillow, rested the side of his head on his crossed arms, and waited for Fynn to come to him.

Fynn discarded his own briefs out the side of the bed and plucked the tube of lubricant to bring back over with him as he spooned up to Nicholas's side. His cock was heavy and warm against his leg, and Nicholas tried not to think about what they were going to attempt. It had felt so good rubbed up against his own last time, so he told himself it would feel good again this time, just different.

True to his word, as Fynn caressed his right hand down Nicholas's back, he bestowed sweet, slow kisses on Nicholas's lips. So far, everything was feeling pretty great. He stroked the curve of his bottom, letting his fingers tickle the inside of Nicholas's thighs, making him squirm.

"You like that?" Fynn asked.

Nicholas couldn't bring himself to do more than utter a closed-mouth "Um hum."

Fynn wriggled a bit to get the lube, and Nicholas closed his eyes so he could focus on keeping his breathing even. "Just relax darling," Fynn mumbled in his ear. The cap snapped shut on the tube, and the next thing Nicholas felt was Fynn shifting the covers over his back, and then...

He gasped as his eyes flew open and he jumped forward and inch or two. "Sorry," he giggled. "It's cold."

It was, but it was super slippery as well, and Fynn traced his fingers down the crease between his cheeks. He stroked the sensitive ring of puckered flesh, and Nicholas's eyes fluttered shut again.

Fynn was right; if he thought too much about what was going on, he was going to psych himself out. Sure, that was pretty much the most intimate and private part of his whole body, but if he stopped thinking of it as a 'thing', and instead just enjoyed how nice it felt to be touched there, it was fine. It was great actually.

Fynn pushed one of his fingers against his hole, breaching just inside him. "Oh, oh," Nicholas panted, his fingers clenching over the bedsheets.

"Okay?" Fynn asked.

He pulsed the digit slowly, and after he'd caught his breath, Nicholas had to admit the sensation was actually quite pleasant. He hummed, and willed himself to relax, getting accustomed to the feeling.

Fynn was cuddled up next to him, and he was slowly shifting, rubbing his body and his cock against Nicholas's side as he gradually worked his finger in deeper, easing it back and forth until he reached the knuckle. Nicholas was enjoying himself now, pushing back, asking for more. And all throughout, Fynn didn't stop kissing him.

Not just on his lips. He traced his mouth down Nicholas's neck and across his shoulder blades, and as he licked and nipped his way down his spine, he pushed another finger inside.

That one took some more getting used to. If he was honest, it sort of burned. It didn't feel right. But Nicholas focused of his breathing, on his hard cock rubbing against the pillows, and the way the rest of Fynn was feeling so exquisite pressed up against him.

"You're doing great," Fynn murmured to him.

Nicholas peeked an eye open to see Fynn grinning down at him. He had a sheen of sweat over his skin, so Nicholas's brief worry that he was bored subsided. He wasn't quite sure why, but he was getting off on this too.

Nicholas dug his fingers into the mattress. "It feels good," he gasped. It did, once the burning sensation subsided.

Fynn licked his lips, then captured his mouth with his own for a kiss, before he tugged the bottom lip between his teeth like Nicholas had done to him. "I'm really, really happy to hear that."

He removed his fingers, but before Nicholas could protest, he squeezed another thick dollop of lube on them, then pushed them back in. He was being a bit more forceful now, and, yes, the realisation that something was intruding inside his body was sort of disturbing. But it was Fynn doing this to him; gorgeous, talented, occasionally infuriating but actually really lovely Fynn. And Nicholas liked it.

He wasn't sure how long they kept that up for. At least until Nicholas was a whimpering mess. He was having to force himself not to hump against the pillow too much; blowing his load early would definitely count as one of those Humiliating Things He Didn't Want to Do. Fynn felt like he was pulling his fingers apart as he moved them inside of him, like a scissoring motion, and he could feel himself gradually stretching with it.

He was saying all sorts of stupid, incoherent things when his lips were unoccupied by Fynn's. He wasn't aware of half the words coming out of his mouth, but there were a lot of 'yeses' and 'don't stops' and 'like thats'. And 'Fynns'.

"Fynn, oh Fynn," he breathed, feeling himself starting to build to something quite spectacular.

That was when he stopped though, pulling his fingers out and shuffling around. Nicholas peeled his blurry eyes open, blinking to see what was going on.

Fynn was sat up, carefully ripping the top of the condom packet open.

"Oh," uttered Nicholas. He really was articulate under pressure.

Fynn leant back over, holding the packet between his sticky fingers on one hand, and holding the side of Nicholas's jaw gently with the other. "Are you still sure?" he asked.

The asking made it better. If he'd just ploughed ahead, Nicholas was certain he might have panicked. But speaking to him, looking into those bright, grey eyes, reminded him that he was safe, and he was having a good time, but he could still stop at any moment if he wanted. He didn't though. Having Fynn's fingers working him had been like nothing he'd ever experience before, but this way, Fynn would be enjoying it too, getting his own satisfaction. Nicholas wanted that more than the physical pleasure he was experiencing.

He had felt so off their first time, when Fynn hadn't come. It had been unbalanced, wrong. Nicholas wanted them to join, like they had the second time. This would be like that, just, more. At least, he hoped.

"Yes," he rasped. He was embarrassed his throat was a bit dry from the moaning and gasping he'd been doing. "Yes, I'm sure."

He looked down between them. It was pretty dark under the covers, but he could see enough to tell Fynn had gone soft while he'd been tending to Nicholas. He bit his lip and looked at his cock. It still seemed intimidating, but slightly less so after Fynn had had his fingers in him.

"Can I—?" he asked, his voice timid. He reached downwards, then looked at Fynn.

His grey eyes widened. "Yeah, of course," he said. He put the condom, still in its wrapper, beside them on one of the pillows, and moved so he and Nicholas were side by side. As he shifted, Nicholas appreciated what Fynn had been doing with his arse; it was sensitive in a good way. He didn't want to focus on that for the moment though, he wanted to concentrate on finally giving Fynn something back.

Fynn cupped the side of his face with one hand and the edge of his hip with another, angling his pelvis between them, inviting Nicholas's touch. He felt horribly clumsy, but Nicholas decided to just go for it, and wrapped his fingers around the length of Fynn's shaft.

He immediately sucked in a breath and closed his eyes, which Nicholas took as a good sign. "Is that okay?" he asked. Fynn nodded, so he carried on stroking, bringing it to life. The skin was hot and almost felt velvety, and he was delighted as it began to grow and harden under his touch. He leant over and kissed Fynn, shifting so his own cock came closer, and he could attempt to rub them together, just like Fynn had done for them back in his bedroom.

He moaned, and it was one of the most pornographic sounds Nicholas had ever heard. "Yeah?" he asked.

"Yeah," Fynn stuttered. "Do you want to roll over?"

Nicholas was almost tempted to carry on as they were. He knew this was good from the last time, despite his reservations it wasn't 'real sex'. But he wanted to try this with Fynn so badly, he wanted to go further. "Yes," he uttered, and let him go.

As he turned back on his belly, Fynn crawled back up to retrieve the condom, then sat up so he could apply it. It smelt kind of funny, a mix of plastic and bitter chemicals, but Nicholas wasn't put off. He was more preoccupied with what Fynn was about to attempt, so he went back to his eyes-closed, sheet-gripping, *not*-freaking out position. *Breathe in. Breathe out.*

Fynn crawled over him, pressing his chest to his back and trailing open-mouthed kisses along hi neck and his jawline. "Hey darling," he whispered. Nicholas cracked an eyelid open and glanced over his shoulder.

"Hey," he said.

Fynn gave him a peck on the cheek. "Give me your hand."

He waved his left hand, and Nicholas obediently released the bedsheets with his own and held it out. Fynn put his over the top – it was notably larger – and laced their fingers together, curling them into a ball, and pressing them back into the bed.

"I've got you, okay," he said, his warm breath tickling behind Nicholas's ear. He nodded.

"I trust you."

There was even more lube – Fynn had been right, he wasn't skimping. He coated Nicholas inside and around his hole, then he smeared it over the already glistening condom. Nicholas found he couldn't look at that directly though, it was a bit too much. Maybe next time he'd feel braver.

The KY tube discarded, Fynn angled himself, and then he was pressing against Nicholas's entrance. Both of them cried out, despite him only breaching with just the tip, and Nicholas gritted his teeth. This was already much more than the fingers, and the burning sensation was back. He realised he was breathing a little too loudly, and reeled it back in. He'd get used to it he knew he would.

Plus, his hard-on was just about killing him, and if he didn't get some release soon, he was going to combust. "I'm okay," he managed to utter. He wriggled backwards. "You can move."

"Yeah?" Fynn sounded pained.

"Yes," Nicholas insisted.

Fynn pushed into him, slowly, and Nicholas did his best to relax and remember that he wasn't trying to hurt him. Under Fynn's instruction, each time before he pushed the next inch or so, Nicholas clenched, and then relaxed as he eased further in. Slowly, they made progress.

It was uncomfortable, and the burn as he stretched to accommodate him wasn't exactly nice.

But Fynn was gripping his hand, rocking his body over Nicholas's and murmuring his name tenderly. He breathed, and he curled his toes so much they ached, but it meant he could relax his arse enough to start easing the burn.

Fynn bottomed out, going as far as he could, and both of them panted like they'd sprinted a hundred metres. Nicholas fidgeted, trying to get used to the sensation of a cock up his arse.

He couldn't help it. He giggled.

Thankfully, Fynn joined in. "Something funny?" he growled, and captured Nicholas's earlobe between his teeth.

"I don't know," he admitted truthfully. He was mildly hysterical. "This is brilliant, but it's sort of awful, and I just want more, and you're awesome – did I mention that before? Thank you. Oh! Your eyes are pretty. I thought that the first time I ever saw you, and now we're here, and it's been a really strange week."

Fynn hummed and sucked on his ear some more, making him squirm. They both shifted, and that made Fynn's dick touch something electric inside of him.

"Whoa," he spluttered. He stopped laughing and froze in shock. "What the fuck was that?"

Fynn let his earlobe go with a pop. "What?" he asked innocently. Then he rolled his hips. Nicholas yelped and jerked, feeling like he'd touched a live wire. But in a good way. "That?"

"Yeah," said Nicholas. He nodded and pushed shamelessly back into him, chasing the feeling again. The too-full, aching sensation was easing considerably in the wake of that magic moment. "Um, I liked that, that felt good."

"Really?" Fynn checked. Nicholas nodded again. "Brilliant."

Nicholas understood the term 'pillow-biter' as Fynn slid part of the way out of him, then back in again. He was assaulted by the okay-ish way Fynn's cock rubbed in the inside of his rim, forcing its way out and in. But when it nudged against that sweet spot, he let out a kind of howl. It was like his whole body was flooded with light.

Gradually, he became more accustomed to Fynn moving in him, aided by the hot jolt of pleasure he got every time he hit the right spot inside him. This was why those guys on the internet had looked so bliss-filled. Nicholas was going out of his mind.

He could feel himself building, and he was unashamedly rutting against the pillow now, his cock desperate for friction. After a few more thrusts though, Fynn paused to haul his arse upwards. Suddenly, he was pounding into him from a better angle, and he wrapped his hand around his shaft, speeding up his impending climax dramatically.

"I'm going to—!" Nicholas croaked out.

That was all the warning he was able to give before he felt like his whole body shattered apart, and he wailed.

Fynn rammed into him a couple more times, but then he was grunting through his teeth, gripping his hips so tightly with his hands he would surely leave bruises, and he suddenly stilled.

After what felt like an age, they fell together into a boneless heap on top of the mattress. Nicholas could have sworn he saw stars. He was also lying in a pool of his own, cold mess, which didn't feel great. But the rest of his body was thrumming with aftershocks, and his brain felt like it was bathed in warm bubbles.

"Oh my god," he breathed out.

Fynn kissed his shoulder blade, then eased out of him. He did it carefully, but Nicholas still hissed in pain. He was suddenly very tender down there. "I'm sorry," said Fynn. "Are you alright?"

"Great," Nicholas assured him quickly. Blimey he was sleepy. "Just…sore. But it was good, I liked it."

He looked up, making sure Fynn believed him. By the smile on his face, everything was alright. "Stay there," he said with a kiss to Nicholas's cheek.

Fynn slipped out of the bed and darted into the bathroom. There was a flush and the swing of the bin lid, and after a moment or two he walked back in with a roll of toilet paper. Nicholas was bold and allowed himself to look directly at Fynn's cock hanging between his legs, seeing as it had just been inside him. It was only slightly darker than the rest of his skin, and about the same length as his own, but thicker. He felt irrationally proud that he'd managed to cope with it. He was also pleased he hadn't looked too closely before, otherwise he wasn't sure he would have attempted getting it inside him.

He couldn't say he'd wholly loved the experience; after all the fuss he'd put himself through over having 'real sex', he preferred the simpler frottage the other day if he was honest. But there was something so deeply intimate about what they'd just done that he knew he'd absolutely treasure once his backside had stopped throbbing. And from the sounds of it, it got easier the more you did it. Plus, Fynn said he'd be up for trying it the other way around, which, now he'd gotten over the first hurdle, Nicholas felt he could work his way up to tying one day.

He realised as Fynn approached, that he was preoccupied thinking about the future. Their future. They would, he hoped, be doing this a lot more in time to come. That, along with his post-orgasmic high, made him grin to himself like a nutter.

"I'll stop asking if you feel alright with that look on your face," Fynn teased as he got back into bed.

He offered Nicholas a wad of tissue so he could clean himself up, while he chucked the wet pillow away on the floor. Nicholas felt a brief moment's humiliation when he thought of housekeeping having to deal with that in the morning, but then he reasoned that a) they had probably seen much worse, and b) he honestly didn't care. He was so happy and content he could deal with some anonymous maid disproving of him. Or maybe they'd congratulate him? Who knew?

The pillow had obviously been placed to get his hips at a better angle, but it also had the added bonus of absorbing most of Nicholas's orgasm. Between getting rid of that, and the tissues to mop up the excess lube, the bed was much more comfortable when they settled down again.

Fynn pulled Nicholas into his side, encouraging him to lay his head in the dip below his shoulder. Nicholas fought to keep his eyes open as he traced his fingers over the hickey mark he'd branded Fynn with back at his house.

"You liked that, yeah?" Nicholas asked. He was slightly nervous at hearing the answer, but he had to know it was okay. Fynn had done all the work, what if he hadn't enjoyed it?

But he stroked the side of Nicholas's face, and they looked at each other. "It was perfect," he said. "I—" He bit his lip, and smiled. "I'm so glad you forgot to book that harp. I'm so glad we met."

"Me too," Nicholas said. His heart was thumping in his chest, and not just from the residual sex-fuelled adrenaline. He still couldn't quite believe someone like Fynn wanted to be with someone like him, but, he was maybe beginning to understand. "We fit well," he said. "Like...jigsaw pieces."

A sleepy grin spread across Fynn's face at the metaphor. "Different shapes," he agreed. "But they slot together."

Nicholas wrapped his arms and legs around Fynn's naked body like a monkey. "My puzzle piece," he said, his head resting on his chest, listening to his heartbeat as he lost the battle with his eyelids. "Can we sleep now?"

Fynn pressed his lips to the top of his head. "Yes darling, we can sleep now."

Chapter Sixteen

(2 weeks later)

It was windy standing on the train station platform, but the sun was shining and the rain that was forecast hadn't started yet. Nicholas gripped onto the extended handle of his suitcase, and looked anxiously down the track. They still had a few minutes before the train into London was due.

"You're sure you're okay to Skype tonight?" He was trying not to freak out, but now the moment had come to say goodbye, he'd be lying if he said he wasn't just a little bit nervous.

Fynn smiled at him and squeezed his shoulder. "Yes darling," he said warmly. "Just let me know when you're back in your room, and we can test it out." As much as Nicholas wasn't keen on phone calls, he was even less keen on the idea of not seeing Fynn every day after they'd been inseparable since the wedding. Video calling seemed like a good way to get around his phobia of talking over the phone.

He was on his way back to Bristol, to complete the final term of his first year. They'd already made plans for Fynn to come and visit him for the weekend next month, but it looked like they'd probably be doing the long-distance thing for a while, and Nicholas was eager to train Fynn out of his bad communication habits as soon as possible.

He bit his lip. He didn't want to make a fool of himself, but he was going to miss Fynn a lot. He'd fallen into the routine of being in a couple like a duck taking to water. It wasn't just the sex (oh dear *lord*, the sex) but the comfort and fun of having Fynn by his side almost every day. He liked who he was when he was around him, and he needed to take that and learn how to be that version of Nicholas by himself.

He had a bit of extra confidence now, and he was getting used to the idea of being gay more and more every day. He was slightly dreading coming out to his uni friends, but once he did, he'd promised himself he could change his relationship status on Facebook, and that was a very enticing bribe. He couldn't wait to tell the world that Fynn was his; that out of everyone he could have picked to be with, he'd chosen Nicholas. The thought made him giddy.

Fynn sighed and hugged him to his side. "It's going to be okay," he said.

Nicholas nodded. "I know," he said. And he meant it. "I'm just going to miss you."

"No, you're not," said Fynn. He grinned and rocked them back and forth. There were a few people on the platform with them, but Nicholas didn't care if they judged them. He just cared about his last few moments with his boyfriend. "You're going to be crazy busy, and we'll talk all the time. I'll be down to visit before you know it."

Nicholas pinched his arm playfully. "Alright," he grumbled. "But you better miss me. And no slacking on the texting while you're in Stockholm. I want to hear all about how the recording goes, okay?"

Fynn crossed his heart. "I promise," he said solemnly.

The announcement over the tannoy informed them that his train was approaching. Nicholas cleared his throat, and resolutely promised himself he wouldn't cry. He was not *that* much of a wuss.

In fact, if his sister's wedding had taught him anything at all, it was that he was capable of a lot more than he'd previously given himself credit for. He was resourceful and could keep his head in a crisis, and despite the voice that occasionally niggled at the back of his mind, he was really starting to believe he was good enough to be with Fynn. So there really wasn't any reason to fret.

They'd said their proper, steamier goodbye back in Nicholas's room. He'd learned it was safer all around to not go over the top with public displays of affection, just in case there was someone around who would get nasty. That did upset Nicholas – that they had to be more careful than a straight couple – but he knew they wouldn't change anything by snogging on a train platform. So he contented himself with a simple peck on the lips, then stepped away to go towards the yellow line.

He let a couple of people off the train first, then lugged his bag up into the compartment. He turned to wave at Fynn, but he'd already hopped up beside him, and in the slightly improved privacy of the doorway, he let himself be kissed properly.

"Have a good journey," Fynn whispered, then jumped back down again.

Nicholas smiled as the doors slid shut on him, and they waved through the glass window as the train began to move. When Fynn slipped out of sight, Nicholas did allow himself a little tear, then laughed at his own sappiness.

It only took twenty-five minutes to get into St Pancras, but then he had to navigate the Tube with his suitcase and rucksack. The train from Paddington to Bristol took just under two hours, so he'd wait to get his laptop out until then. It was a good job Fynn worked most evenings at the Italian place still, otherwise Nicholas would never have got any of his course work or revision done. But despite that, he still had part of one of his essays to finish, and doing so on the train would distract him from leaving Fynn behind.

He sighed, and once he'd stowed his luggage in the rack, he went and found himself a seat. He was feeling better already. He trusted Fynn to stay in touch, and a bit of time apart would do them some good. Although it had been amazing the past couple of weeks, it would be great to spend time with his other friends again and catch up on some of his favourite TV shows.

When he hadn't been with Fynn, he'd made time to sit down with his parents and make sure they were okay with him now he'd come out of the closet. His mum had had all sorts of anxious questions and seemed more concerned what other people would think of him rather than having much of an opinion herself. As long as he kept himself safe (in every interpretation of the word) she didn't appear to mind that he was gay.

His dad had been a bit sceptical, but he just said if Nicholas was happy, then that was okay. He'd balked at any hint of hearing further details about him and Fynn's relationship in the intimate sense and didn't seem very comfortable when they held hands, but he'd not said a word against it. Nicholas hoped in time he'd come to treat them as easily as he did Clara and Lauren with their partners.

He'd also spent more time with Trev, who hadn't cared one bit that Nicholas was gay. They'd mostly just played video games and talked about the developments with Trev's comic book.

Nicholas promised that he and Fynn would come visit him at the MCM convention, so the two of them could get to know each other a little better.

It had been a relief when Danielle had finally moved out of the family home back to her flat in London. Unsurprisingly, she suffered the worst from the post-wedding comedown, spending a couple of days in her pyjamas eating nothing but Chinese food and watching old reruns of *Friends*. But then she'd downloaded a couple of dating apps and decided that her love-life was going to be her next project, setting up several dates within the first day. Nicholas wished her all the luck in the world, although he did feel a tiny bit sorry for the guys she was going to be meeting. But, who knew? Maybe there was someone perfect out there for her?

Clara was still on honeymoon and Lauren had gone back to Italy, which meant their parents got their house all to themselves again. Well, almost. Nicholas suspected Archibald was going to very much enjoy ruling the roost once more.

Much as him forgetting to book the harpist had brought him and Fynn together, Archibald trashing the dresses had made it so that Kinny and her mum could bury their old feud and make friends again. Nicholas was thrilled to hear they'd been spending more time together, and according to Ash, they were hoping to tell Kinny's family about their relationship over dinner next week. That made him smile. Kinny had seemed completely shocked to find that, quite without her noticing, she'd fallen head over heels for Ash. They made the cutest couple, and he wished them all the best.

He twitched in surprise as his phone pinged. No one in his carriage seemed annoyed, but he'd still put it onto silent after he'd read the message. He fished it out of his pocket, and heart leapt as the display showed it was from Fynn.

He'd not been expecting anything yet. Although Fynn was getting better at communicating, they'd left it that he'd wait for Nicholas to contact him once he was settled back in halls. Maybe Nicholas had forgotten something? He opened the message with a hint of apprehension.

That very quickly turned to stunned disbelief as he took the three little words in.

'*I love you x*'

Nicholas couldn't believe what he was seeing. They hadn't said anything of the sort to each other. He was still staring when a follow-up message appeared.

'*See, I told you I'd text ;)*'

Nicholas laughed, feeling light headed. '*You git!*' he shot back. '*You can't tell me you love me for the first time over a bloody text!*'

'*I just did*' He tagged the crying-with-laughter emoji onto the end of that one.

Nicholas felt warm and fuzzy all over, and a lump had risen in his throat. He loved him. Fynn loved him.

Despite his fears how their relationship would work over such a distance, Nicholas had to have faith. Disaster may have brought them together, but he knew that just meant it would take one hell of a catastrophe to ever pull them apart.

'*I love you too x*'

SOUNDTRACK

This is a list of every single song that gets
mentioned throughout the book. I urge you to listen
to them by legitimate means, and support the artists.

Katy Perry – E.T.
The Knife/Jose Gonzalez – Heartbeats
Lady Gaga – Telephone
Taylor Swift – You Belong with Me
Taylor Swift – Style
John Legend – All of You
Ruelle – War of Hearts
Spice Girls – Say You'll Be There
Beyoncé – Halo
Christine and the Queens – Tilted
Ella Henderson – Glow
Hanson – MMMBop
Ricky Martin – Livin' la Vida Loca
Spandau Ballet – True
Dinah Nah – Make Me (La La La) (Acoustic and
original Melodifestivalen versions)
Suzanne Vega – Tom's Diner
Fall Out Boy – Centuries
Don Henley – The Boys of Summer
Taylor Swift – Bad Blood
The Rolling Stones/Charlotte Martine – Wild
Horses
The Killers – Mr Brightside
Jimi Jamison – I'm Always Here (Theme from
Baywatch)
Rick Astley/Hannah Trigwell – Never Gonna
Give You Up
Katrina and the Waves – Walking on Sunshine
Johann Pachelbel – Canon and Gigue for 3
violins and basso continuo
Beyoncé – Single Ladies
Los Del Río – Macarena

ABOUT THE AUTHOR

Helen Juliet is an M/M author currently living and working in London. She's been writing stories since she was young, and got her start publishing fanfiction of sites like Wattpad. Fifteen years and over a million words later, she discovered the world of M/M fiction and found it was just as good as the fanfiction she was reading. She fell head over heels in love with the genre and became determined to try her hand at a book herself. On December 31st, 2016, she rang in the new year by publishing her first original novel, and hasn't looked back since.

CONTACT THE AUTHOR

You can contact Helen via the following social media:

Website: www.helenjuliet.com

Email: hello@helenjuliet.com

Facebook: @helenjulietauthor

Facebook Group: Helen Juliet Books

Twitter: @helenjwrites

Instagram: @helenjwrites

Tumblr: helenjwrites

ALSO BY HELEN JULIET

Glitter on the Garland

Matt Bartlett and his family have been pulled apart in the last year by his dad's affair and the subsequent divorce. Now Christmas is looming, and Matt and his sister are expected to play nice and share the holidays with his dad's new family.

Lucky for Matt, his best friend Aedan Gallagher arrives on his doorstep on Christmas morning, bringing with him a much-needed blast of festive cheer and plenty of sparkle.

As they navigate Matt's vindictive step-mother and Aedan's own family trouble, Matt starts to realise that Aedan might be more than just a friend to him. But with everything else threatening to fall apart around them, he's not sure if he should dare risk taking the next step. If he doesn't though, he could lose Aedan forever.

A stand alone, New Adult romance with a happy ending.

49,000 words approx.

COMING SOON

Without a Compass

Riley's idea of a good time involves things like bubble baths. Cold white wine. Dancing with a sexy boy. From the moment he earned his own paycheque, his holidays have always revolved around room service, infinity pools and exotic sunsets.

For years, there not been a single tent pole in sight.

Until now.

This summer, his family has decided to go on a scouting retreat for his father's fiftieth birthday. Seven days of campfire cooking and communal showers. It's his family's element, but Riley feels like a duck out of the water they're going to be canoeing in.

There's no getting out of it, though. And to compound the misery of a week spent sleeping on the ground with no WiFi and far too many insects that want to snack on his sensitive skin, his older brother has also invited his best friend. Kai is big and tough, loves hiking and anything else outdoorsy, and most importantly, is very straight. So Riley's age-old unrequited crush on him is most inconvenient.

After an unexpected twist of fate leaves the two of them spending more time together than ever before, they discover they might have more in common than they thought. Perhaps this trip won't be as hideous as Riley first assumed.

Lightning Source UK Ltd.
Milton Keynes UK
UKOW05f1042150617
303281UK00007B/13/P